TEESSIDE SHADOWS

TEESSIDE SHADOWS

JOHN NICHOLSON

Nick Guymer Series
No.9

http://www.johnnicholsonwriter.com

Thanks to everyone who helped make this happen, especially Dawn for the Elvis impersonator idea, from which the whole story grew. Also to Robert for his editorial wisdom and Janet for her eagle eyes.

The book is dedicated to anyone who lives or has lived under a shadow. Believe me, the light will shine on you someday soon.

"So I come to you with open arms,
Nothing to hide, believe what I say,
So here I am, with open arms,
Hoping you'll see, what your love means to me.
Open arms"

CHAPTER 1

'I have huge news,' said Jeff.

'News about something that is huge, such as the planet Jupiter?' said Nick.

'Don't be a smart bottom. I mean news that is huge.'

'Ah, but is it really huge? I mean huge is several notches up from common or garden big...you do know that, don't you?' said Nick, taking out a bag of potting compost from the boot of his car and unlocking the allotment gates. 'I mean, no pressure, but you might want to amend your definition. I don't want to be led up the garden path with tiny news masquerading as huge news.'

'I am confident in the hugeness of this news to call it huge and to lead you down your allotment path with it. If anything, I'm underselling it with the word *huge*.'

'For a man who is in possession of huge news you seem very calm, though,' said Nick, as Jeff held open the gate. He carried the 50-litre bag on his shoulder down to his allotment, dumping it by the potting shed. 'Huge news would normally require a more excited response, or beads of perspiration, or the need for a toilet.'

'What can I say? I'm just a very cool man. Hey, this is looking very tidy now,' said Jeff, following behind.

'You like it?'

Jeff tugged at his beard and looked at the two strips of earth which Nick and Julie had hoed into a fine tilth. 'It's smart. Some things are actually growing.' He pointed at two green rows.

'Early broad beans. I bought some plants from the garden centre just to get a head start. Did the same thing with the peas, as well. So what's this huge news? You didn't get a copy of that first Jethro Tull single which was misprinted as Jethro Toe, did you? Now that would be huge news. £1,000 worth of huge news.'

'That *would* be suitably massive but this is even bigger and it concerns the Argmeister.'

Nick moved the bag into the shed and wiped a smear of sweat from his forehead.

'Argie? He's alright, isn't he?'

'Aye, he's on top form, or he was when I left him with mam earlier. Bloating up at top speed, apparently. His head doesn't look so big now that the rest of him is giving it the full chubbage.'

'So how's it about him?'

'I've just come from Brian's.'

'Brian Salmon? Your actual dad, as opposed to the man who raised you? I didn't realise he was back from the Bahamas.'

'Yeah, just back last week. He invited me over there this morning. Mind, that house is still in a right mess after the explosion last year. Half of it is still under plastic sheeting.'

'I thought they were rebuilding it.'

'They've made a good start but it's a really big job. Anyway, he'd been mulling over a few things while away.'

'Mulling? Who mulls?'

Jeff raised his bushy eyebrows and pointed at Nick. 'You do, for one. I don't mull, myself, but you're an expert muller of all things. None more qualityful muller of mulling than you.'

Nick shrugged. 'Aye, I suppose I do like a mull. If you lived on the west coast of Scotland and were prone to think about the process of thinking, you'd be a Mull muller who mulled about mulling, wouldn't you?'

Jeff applauded him a little. 'All those years of state education clearly didn't go to waste on you.'

'Go on, then...what has he mulled over?'

'His money and estate.'

'I wish I had some money and estate to mull over. It wouldn't be a long mull, right now. I'm up to five grand overdrawn again.'

'I feel your pain. As you know, Brian is richer than God, but seems to be taxed as though he's a poor man. Not sure how he works that out. He's actually far too rich. He's one of the elite. It's like he can't stop earning huge money all the time. The interest on it all is probably tens of thousands a day.'

'The richer you are, the less you pay. That's capitalism's number-one mantra, along with "it's the fault of the poor" and "my house is bigger than your house".'

'This is true. He's a funny old lad, is Bri. Very easygoing, gentle soul but also, from what little I know, utterly dedicated to squirrelling money away in various tax avoidance schemes, even though he doesn't even need it. But crucially, Argie is his only grandchild and he's decided he wants to give him an inheritance, especially as Big Fish, his son and heir, hasn't produced any kids and any that he might produce are likely to be devil children with the swivelling, vomitty heads, shouting "talk to the beard" from the age of three months. Those were not his exact words, but you get my drift.'

'Wow. Has he? That sounds good,' said Nick, squatting down and plucking out a couple of blades of couch grass. Bloody stuff got everywhere. Sprouted from even the tiniest bit of root. He went to fill a watering can from a stand pipe, returning to water the broad beans and peas. 'So he's going to gift Argie some cash, is he?'

'Yeah. Well, he's one super-rich dude. So he's offered young Paul Simon Argent what I think financial analysts might call a fuck-ton of money.'

Nick stopped watering and looked at Jeff, his long, greying hair streaming down his back over a baggy red and blue plaid shirt.

'Really? How much - if that's not a vulgar question.'

'You don't want to know.' Jeff spoke a bit awkwardly.

'No. I really *do* want to know.'

Jeff looked almost embarrassed to tell him, stuffing his hands in his army pants pockets and kicking at a dandelion with his size 12 boot.

'It's a million-quid trust fund. Pays out every year once he's 21.'

'Bloody hell...that'd be...what...about £20k a year?'

'More like 30 with compound interest. And for pretty much his whole life. He'd not have to work really...or not much...and there something else...'

'...there's more?'

Jeff nodded and sucked his bottom lip. 'Shares in the Blakeston Estate. A 20 per cent stake worth about five million today but shit knows how much it'll be worth in 20 years. Land prices go up and up. So if it was ever to be sold, he'd be minted beyond all imagination. There's stipulations and such, but even so...'

Nick was stunned into silence. That *was* huge news. Bloody huge. A million times huge.

'Well, it's brilliant news, isn't it?' he said, finally. But Jeff didn't seem especially elated.

'Well, yeah. In a way.'

'Didn't you grab his hand off?'

'No, I did not.' He said it with a degree of indignation.

Nick pulled out a sprouting thistle. And thought about it for a bit.

'Is it because *you* want to provide for Argie and not a sugar daddy?' he said, tapping the big man on the chest with the thistle.

'Got it in one, my supposedly non-perceptive loony friend. I mean, it's mega-generous, but he's my boy and I'll look after him and he'll have everything he needs courtesy of the income from the retailing of second-hand vinyl records.'

'Well, that's very noble of you - but don't jump into any decisions yet. You've not, have you?'

Jeff shook his head. 'No, if for no other reason than it'd be rude. I was clear from day one that I didn't want to get in between him and Big Fish. I don't want Brian's money. I told him that in the first weeks after I found out he was my dad. I'm not having him or anyone else think I'm creaming it up off him. Anyway, I don't need anything and you know what - that money he's offering Argie, it's too much money. You can only wear one shirt at a time. Only eat one meal. It's wrong. I like Brian a lot, he's a peaceful old dude, but, like I say, he's too rich and I want Arg to work for his living, not be some dossing rich kid.'

'I totally see what you mean, but he might use it for the greater good. Spread it around more than Brian will if you let him keep it. I mean, I do agree. It's obscene how rich some people are. Half the world's wealth is owned by 85 people. That is disgusting, but you've got to think of the long game. By the time he's 21 he'll be a young man and, if I know you, he'll be a decent bloke who won't want a fuck-ton of money, but he could put it to work for other people. You've got to think of that. It's not inevitable that he'll turn into a spoiled rich kid.'

'It's not, but it's much more likely if you've got a trust fund than if you're running a record shop.'

Nick pulled up a few more weeds and took them down to their small compost bin. Jeff followed him. 'Well, I said I'd have a good think about it. It's hard to turn something like that down without making it seem like you're really saying "I wouldn't take money off an evil rich bastard like you", which isn't how I feel really...but you know...it is awkward.'

'Hmm, tricky. You're a good diplomat, though.'

'Don't mention any of this in front of Big Fish, if you ever have the misfortune to be in his company, that is. I suspect he'll get a major cob on. He's a greedy bastard and won't want his inheritance being diluted.'

'If I never have to speak to the BF again, it will be too soon.' Nick locked the shed door and brushed soil off his hands. 'We'll get off, then.'

Jeff stood looking across several plots.

'What is a man dressed as Elvis in a white jumpsuit doing in your allotments, near that herb bed? Don't tell me, he's Elvis Parsley, isn't he?' said Jeff, putting one foot forward, arms out wide to declare the joke.

'That's a good herb-based pun. I think I've seen him around...or I've seen his posters in pubs,' said Nick.

'Yeah, I have, too. He's worked with Big Fish or played at his clubs. He looks weird.'

They stood and watched the man with dyed black hair and dyed black sideburns as he put on a mesh-covered hat.

'He's obviously a beekeeper,' said Jeff, watching him approach three white hives.

'He's an apiary Elvis?' laughed Nick.

'Yeah, he's an apiary Elvis. Ha ha.'

They stood and watched as he puffed smoke into the hive to subdue the bees.

'I mean, maybe I'm just narrow minded, but is it strictly necessary to be dressed as Elvis to tend your bees, though?' said Nick, arms folded.

'Not traditionally.'

'The sun is flashing off his rhinestones. It's like watching the King in Vegas...or it would be if we were in Vegas and yer man there was actually Elvis and not a short, fat auld Teessider,' said Nick.

The King began inspecting the honeycombs one by one, pulling them out individually but as he did so, a small dark cloud of bees rose out of the hive and began circling around him, quickly followed by another group from another hive.

'The bees aren't so keen on Elvis,' said Jeff.

'Maybe they're Jerry Lee Lewis fans or think rock 'n' roll is the lewd work of the devil.'

'Nah, he's not even swivelling his hips.'

He puffed at the bees with his smoker to try and subdue them, but it didn't seem to work. Soon bees were all over the place, buzzing around him. He panicked and began wafting at them with his hands, fighting them off with flapping, vigorous chopping movements of his hands and kicking out at ones which were circling around his 26-inch polyester flares.

Nick and Jeff couldn't stop laughing. It looked for all the world like Elvis was doing some of his trademark Vegas-style karate chops and kicks to defend himself against the bee attack.

'Bloody hell, he's putting on a show for them. He's doing "Guitar Man" or "Burning Love", isn't he? All his best moves. Look at him go! Ha ha!'

Unable to shake them off and now very scared by the bees, Elvis made a run for it across his allotment, weaving in and out of paths and finally heading towards the gates, his mesh hat still on.

'Exit stage left, pursued by bees. Elvis has left the allotment,' said Nick, in a stage announcer's American voice, between gasps of laughter, wiping a tear from his eye.

'That was the funniest thing I've seen, possibly ever,' said Jeff, holding his sides and gasping for breath. 'Shall we see if he needs a hand? As we're the only ones here, like. He can't leave all those wooden frame thingies just lying there, can he?'

'I'm scared of bees, man,' said Nick, reluctantly. 'Bees, wasps and especially hornets. You get them around here, remember?'

Jeff made a fearful face and flapped his long hair up and down like it was a pair of dog's ears. 'The evil summer of 76 hornet attack, how could I forget? They were so huge we could have saddled them up and flown off on them.' He tapped him on the arm. 'Owee, it'll be alright. Those bees have left him alone now.'

They walked up to Elvis, who had pulled off his mesh hat. He was about five foot six and 15 stone. He had grease stains down the front of the jumpsuit and flaky pastry from a pasty stuck to its oversized collar. His skin was tight and smooth and reflected the sun a little, as though it had been polished.

'Do you need some help, pal?' said Jeff. 'We saw the bees were after you.'

'Bloody evil little sods...I dunno what got into them,' he said, looking around him a little nervously.

'I think it might have been the rhinestones dazzling them. They thought they were under attack,' said Nick, laughing a little. The bloke looked odd. With fleshy lips and the smooth tight skin, Nick wondered if he'd had some sort of skin peel or had a bad allergy.

'I think youse might be right, like,' he said in an accent surely carved by a life in Billingham in the shadow of the prilling tower. 'I'm just on my way to a show.'

'Ah, you're an Elvis impersonator,' said Nick, nodding.

The man looked at him like he was possibly the most stupid man on the planet. 'Of course I am. What did you think I was, like? This isn't me beekeeping outfit, is it?' he said, arms wide, looking himself up and down. 'I think they've settled down now. They're normally a bit sleepy early mornings in May. Bit like lazy Teessiders on the dole.' He turned to Jeff. 'Hey, I know you, don't I?'

'Possibly. I'm Jeff Evans. I run Jeff's Records in town...probably from there.' Everyone knew Jeff around town, these days. As he walked down the High Street, he was always waving and saying hello to people. It helped that he was six three and had long greying hair half way down his

6

back, of course.

'Oh, aye. You're Big Fish's brother, aren't you?'

'Yeah, though I don't like to admit it, unless I'm under oath or being paid handsomely.'

'I think I've seen you around at the Blakeston Estate house.' He smiled at Jeff and for a moment it appeared that his mouth might tear open at the side, as the skin stretched taut. He had to have some sort of allergy. But then, in some ways, this Elvis was quite a pretty man underneath the extra 70lbs of weight, with long eyelashes and quite delicate features.

'Probably, aye. I drop in and see Brian occasionally. He's been away, though.'

'I play in Big Fish's club in the Boro. The GC? You know it? It's a topless bar.'

Jeff nodded. 'I am familiar with that particular den of iniquity, aye.'

'Eh?' said Elvis, his lip curled up in puzzlement. Even the way he stood, legs apart, knees slightly bent, appeared to be in imitation of the Great Man. He made a good Fat Elvis.

'I know it. Yes,' said Jeff, by way of clarity.

'Mind, most of the women who work there are nowt to look at,' said Elvis.

Nick looked away. Blokes like this...bloody hell...it was like it was still 1972 to them. Topless bars, indeed. But he also knew that if he said such an attitude was outdated, vulgar and sexist in the extreme, he'd get a look of total bewilderment. It was pointless. Even though he couldn't have been any older than Nick, it was useless to challenge men like him because he would never change.

'Are you voting for him, then?' said Elvis to Jeff, ignoring Nick like he wasn't even there, maybe sensing disapproval emanating out of him.

'What do you mean?' said Jeff.

'Are you voting in Big Fish's election thing?'

Jeff looked at Nick, his face set in a frown. 'Come again?'

'Are you voting for...'

Jeff cut him short. 'I heard you, I just don't know what you're talking about.'

'Has he not told you?'

They'd be here all day if it went on like this and standing in an allotment in Oxbridge talking to a man dressed as Elvis in 1972 was, to say the very least, surreal. He looked at his watch. It was nearly 11am. Jules would be down soon to look at his knackered car. The old BMW couldn't go on forever and it had been making odd noises.

'Just tell us what you're referring to,' said Nick, eager to end the conversation.

Elvis looked from one to the other. 'He's got his own manifesto you can vote for.'

'Get outta here. He hasn't,' said Jeff, waving away the statement like it was an errant bee.

'Aye. He has,' insisted Elvis.

'How has he got a political party?' said Nick.

Elvis shrugged. 'It's not political. It's just a daft laugh, isn't it? He's taking the piss out of people. Quality humourist is yer Fish.'

Jeff looked over Elvis's shoulder down to Oxbridge and then it dawned on him.

'I know what this is all about. He's got his big comeback tour starting in the late summer and he's working up a new catchphrase...'

'...what, to replace "talk to the beard"?' said Nick. 'That was his big hit.'

'Aye, well after what happened to him at the Teesside Blues Festival, he wants to draw a line under all of that, so he's shaving off the beard and launching his new one: "Don't cross the Tees".'

Nick repeated it once and then a second time. 'I don't get it.'

'What? Like you got "talk to the beard"? That made no sense either. It doesn't have to make sense. Paul Daniels pulled off "not a lot" for 30 years...and that's literally, not a lot. He's using "don't cross the Tees" in the sense of "don't mess with Teessiders"...I think that's it. He's offering himself up as the embodiment of the Tees. And not just in that he's dirty and wet.' Jeff shook his head at his own words. 'He'd bloody use that joke, an' all.'

'One of his policies is, fat birds have to bring their own water to swimming pools, 'cos so much splashes out when they jump in, like,' said `Elvis and he laughed heartily as though it had been invented by Lenny Bruce. 'Another is a tax on salad bars. The thinner you are, the more you pay. Class.'

Jeff looked at Nick and raised his owlish eyebrows.

'Yeah, same old shit jokes, just with a new tag line. He'll be doing some mock political party event just to promo the tour. It's huge, man. I saw the posters the other day...'

'Is it? I hadn't heard.'

'He's not announced it yet, but he's playing the biggest-capacity venues in the country, so he's got to start pushing it hard to sell the tickets when they go on sale. That's what this is all about...bound to be. He never does anything without an eye to his career.'

'He's the only comedian who tells it like it is and doesn't kowtow to all the PC brigade.' Elvis paused and looked around him, as if checking to see whether anyone could overhear him. 'And he doesn't employ any Russians in his team. Bloody Ivans get everywhere these days.'

Nick looked away in weary disdain. Russians? Why Russians? What had the Russians ever done to this Billingham bloke? You heard this sort of stuff about East Europeans all the time now, just like you heard it in the 1970s about people from the Asian subcontinent, or Kenya, or wherever. For some people, it was always the foreigners that were to blame for whatever it was they particularly disliked about society. It was as predictable and tedious as the regard that Stevie Salmon was held in by his fans. Anyone would think he was a man of the working class and not the privileged son of a multi-millionaire landowner.

Elvis went back to his bees. They watched him go. He had a slight limp in his left leg and had got muddy splashes all up the back of the white jumpsuit legs.

'That is one weird dude. Why didn't he come out in his normal clothes and get changed before he does his show?' said Nick.

'Show? He's singing to a backing track in a working men's club. That's not a show. He thinks he's *it*, doesn't he? Weird shiny face on him, too.'

Nick looked on for a moment and twirled a strand of hair around a finger, a habit he'd started to pick up from Julie. 'But he looks so ridiculous.'

'One man's ridiculous is another's sex god,' said Jeff, with an eyebrow raised.

'True. And if he was five stone lighter, had a good wash, and a change of clothes and personality, he might actually be quite good looking. Does he do the Elvis thing for a living?'

'I don't know, probably. We live in strange times, brother.'

Nick unlocked the allotment gates just as he heard the deep rumble of Julie's Porsche approaching down Grangefield Road. She parked up alongside Nick's old BMW and Jeff's white Transit van.

'Hey, Jules,' said Jeff, waving. 'Good to see you.' He put a quick arm around her shoulder as she got out of the car.

'Now then, boys,' she said, dressed in navy blue overalls and white Adidas trainers, her hair tied up in a psychedelic silk scarf. She patted the BMW on the bonnet. 'I just picked up your message. So is she shagged out, then? I have to say, it's been on the cards for a while.'

'There's a lot of spluttering and coughing and weird noises. I think one of the cylinders has gone,' said Nick.

She laughed and got her toolbox out of the Porsche, tapping him on the belly with a small spanner. 'Like you even know what a cylinder is, you. Don't forget, you're not a *proper* man, ladyboy.'

'Oh, yeah. I forgot. I'm a proper woman.'

'Well, you are wearing those new, tight jeans,' said Jeff. 'They do make your arse look 100 per cent more female.'

'Eee, are you saying he's got a nice arse, Jeff?' said Julie, with faux shock.

'Aye, I seem to have accidentally revealed my secret gay crush on him,' said Jeff, blowing Nick a kiss.

Julie yelped out a laugh. 'Well, he has got a nice arse in those, at least until you see the spots on it. We got them at a car boot last weekend.'

'You got the spots on his arse at a car boot? That's one weird car boot you've gone to, there,' said Jeff. 'Will you pick me up a bag of warts at the next one?'

'Can we all stop talking about my arse, please?' said Nick. 'It's strictly for talking out of and not talking about.'

'Boom and indeed boom,' said Jeff, clapping.

She opened the bonnet, propped it up and peered inside, then pulled on some latex gloves and began tugging wires and taking out oily-looking bits of metal.

Jeff looked over her shoulder, nodding in an exaggerated manner. 'Ah yeah, y'see, your big end has gone, Jules, and you've got a huge gap between your injection flaps.'

She looked up at him.

'Aye, the F hole is all clogged up with shaft fluid, so I need to grease the hard nipple and insert the vibrator in order to make the friction slit slippery.'

She grinned at him. He laughed and patted her on the back, a little tentatively. 'I'm going to stand back now as I have been completely out innuendoed. I bow to the master.'

'...to the mistress, please.'

'You're looking good, Jules,' said Jeff, leaning forward and patting her on the back again, instinctively. It looked odd. He wasn't a tactile person at all. Not normally.

'Yeah, right. It's the glamorous clothes, isn't it?' she said. 'These are Dolce and Gabbana overalls, y'know?'

'They're not, are they?' said Jeff, looking her up and down.

She hooted a laugh. 'No. Of course not! They're from that car boot and they're about three sizes too big. They fit where they touch.' She let out a big, tense sigh. 'I just can't keep any weight on us. I seem to burn up everything I put in my meat hole...'

'That's your problem y'see - you're putting it all in your meat hole, you should be putting it in your cake hole,' said Nick. They all laughed, but he was worried about her. She was trying hard to be herself, but she wasn't succeeding, not really.

'I feel like I should make an off-colour joke about Marianne Faithful and a Mars Bar at this point, but being a sophisticated dude, I wouldn't dream of it,' Jeff said. 'I'm so innocent and pure that I don't even know to what I was referring in my previous sentence. Who said that?' He looked around himself with a puzzled expression.

'She was drinking Guinness last night, weren't you?' said Nick. 'Trying to get more calories on board.'

'I can't drink more than two pints of Guinness. It just feels like I'm bloody drowning after that and it sits in your guts like lead.'

'Where did you go, like?' said Jeff.

'The Parkwood,' said Nick.

'The Parkwood! Did you wear your cardigan and smoke a pipe? I can't see youse two in there. It's a bit too middle aged.'

'We are middle aged, man. We don't want to sit with a jukebox blaring out drum 'n' bass, do we?' said Nick. 'And it was so warm in the sun that we sat outside. We like it in there, don't we?'

'Aye, it was nice. Not exactly living high on the hog, but at least there's no fizzin' chance of being glassed, not unless some old fella has a stroke and drops his pint on your head,' said Julie.

'I thought you'd have been down Big Meat for some scran,' said Jeff.

'We're too skint, man. Really running on empty,' said Nick.

'I can sub you some if you're short,' said Jeff, immediately.

Nick held up his hand. 'Thanks man, I didn't say it for that reason...'

'I know...but you just have to say if you need a couple of hundred.'

'We'll get by,' said Julie, head in the engine. 'We're eating all the cheap meats. I was a bit anaemic, so I've been eating liver, heart and kidneys.'

'That's an offal diet, that Jules. Offal diet!! Boom boom! C'mon, that's worth some love...see, comedy runs in the family. Alright - no, it doesn't, I'm the only funny one...'

She laughed. 'Go and turn it over for us, will you, you hipster dufus?'

Jeff sat in the cab and turned the ignition. It spluttered into life but couldn't tick over and died out.

'Do it again,' she said and wiggled a pipe or something. She winked up at Nick. 'Don't worry, kidda. I'll get her going.'

'I think it's a he, actually. I've always thought of this car as male.'

'Hmm, you might be right, he does have a nice long, thick exhaust pipe.' She winked at him again.

It coughed again but kept going this time. She leaned inside and played with it some more. 'Gotcha.' She made a throat cutting sign to Jeff to turn off the engine and went to her tool bag and pulled out a pressurized can of air, a fine plastic tube, some WD40 and an old toothbrush.

'Do its teeth need cleaning?' said Jeff.

'Sort of. I reckon a fuel injector is filthy. I think that's why it's misfiring. Don't think it's the cylinder. Not sure if this will fix it, but it'll have to do.' She set about cleaning up the injectors and squirting air into them to knock out any muck.

'So how are you then, Jeffrey? I've hardly seen you for the last few weeks, what with one thing and another, you moving house and setting up the shop cafe. Nick's said you're getting that rock club sorted. It's all go for you, eh?'

'Yeah, the wheels are in motion. Still living out of boxes, but Argie seems to like the new place in Hartburn Village. Well, he sits there and eats his mush, looks pleased, does a massive shit and then falls asleep, so I take that as approval, as I would from any human.' He stood with his arms crossed, a smile under his beard. 'I've gotta say though, Jules, there's a proper rosy glow to you.'

He was being overly, and a little awkwardly, concerned about her.

'Having last week in bed did you the world of good, didn't it?' said Nick, taking her around the waist as she bent over the engine and squeezing her tightly on her bony hips.

'Totally, aye. I'd recommend it to anyone. Just getting some proper rest is a great treat. You don't realise how knackered you get. If you ask me, doctors should prescribe it. We all work too hard and push ourselves too much. Nowt wrong with a good doss for a few days. That's why the upper class live so long. They do sod all.'

'Do you mind, Mr Guymer? We'll have no back door lovin', al fresco, thank you very much,' said Jeff, pulling Nick away from Julie.

Julie laughed again, maybe a little too loudly. 'Thank you, Jeff. That *was* a little distracting. There's nowt wrong with *his* fuel injector, even if it could use being cleaned with a toothbrush.' She waggled the old oily brush at him.

Jeff put his thumbs in his ears and scrunched his face up, 'As the great Graham Taylor once rhetorically asked, "do I not like that?" '

'Right, give that a go,' she said. Nick got in and started the car. It went first time and purred over very evenly.

Julie held her arms aloft and punched the air. 'Get in! One-nil!'

Jeff applauded. 'Is there no end to your talents?'

She pulled off the latex gloves and let out a tense sigh, a sigh which hinted at the dark shadow that was cast over her these days. 'Well, I'm rubbish at staying pregnant, but apart from that, I'm not without skills.' She spoke the words in a contemplative half-whisper. She looked at her watch. 'Just time to get home, get changed and get to work. Are you coming home, fella?'

Nick saluted. 'What time are you looking at the potential new club premises, big man?'

'Three pm. Come into the shop later and we'll go down together.'

The allotment gates opened and Elvis came out, clutching a black attaché case and his netted hat. Julie turned and did a double take at the extraordinary sight.

'See you, mate,' said Jeff, with a wave. Elvis nodded and got into a mid 80s Mini Metro, surely one of the few still left on the road. As he did so a black Range Rover that was coming down Oxbridge Road, slowed. The side windows were blacked out. It quickly accelerated away.

'Hard to believe so many people really loved a Mini Metro, isn't it?' said Julie, as Elvis drove off down the road.

'Looks like a cheap shed crossed with a small chest freezer on wheels,' said Jeff. 'About right for a cheap Elvis.'

'Is he a bit mad, or what?' said Julie, with a laugh in her voice. 'He looks really odd.'

'He's an impersonator,' said Nick.

'Gettaway, I thought he was the real Elvis. Remember that great Living Colour track, "Elvis Is Dead"?'

'Ah, late 80s, brightly-coloured, wonky headstock rock at its best,' said Jeff, nodding and playing air guitar.

'I saw them in London along with Extreme. They were both ace. I could've eaten both Vernon Reid and Nuno Bettencourt with a spoon and come back for seconds,' said Julie, pulling a lustful face. 'Right, I'm getting off, come on you cute-ass lovely, get in your newly purring BMW.' She slapped him on the backside and had just pulled open the door of the Porsche when there was a massive screech of tyres at the roundabout further down the road, followed by the unmistakable crunch and scraping metal sound of a big collision between two cars, followed a few seconds later by a shattering glass noise, then, a few seconds later still, another screech of tyres.

They all looked at each other as the noises echoed out. Julie pulled a face and got out of the Porsche. 'Ouch, that sounded like a bad one.' They wondered what to do.

'Should I call 999?' said Nick, taking out his phone.

'Nah. let's just take a look first, sometimes these things sound worse than they are. A bit like cats fighting,' said Jeff.

So the three of them walked down the road until the roundabout was visible. In the distance, Elvis's Metro was at right angles to the road sitting on the grass verge, the driver's side window shattered. There was no-one around and the slumped shape of the driver suggested things were not looking too good for the King.

'Bloody hell, you *had* better call 999, Jules, I'll see if he's alright,' said Nick, sprinting off down the hill, Jeff some way behind. As he ran people were coming out of the little bungalows on the opposite side of the road to see what had happened. As Nick bore down on the crash scene, he tried to make sense of it, but it didn't really make sense. The car looked like it had been smashed hard on the driver's side, but no other car was around.

Maybe he had lost control coming down the gentle slope of Oxbridge Road. He had braked to go into the roundabout and they had failed on him. It was an old knackered car. Nah, that wouldn't explain the skid marks on the road. There were two sets, one clearly the Metro and another, much wider, set. As he reached the scene, he already had it sussed. The rubber on the road gave it away. A much bigger car had come clockwise around the roundabout and slammed into the Metro, knocking it off the road, putting a big crunch in the side and breaking the window. Then it must have just driven off.

Nick reached the vehicle, sucking air in big gulps. Elvis was slumped to the left, hanging over the steering wheel.

'Are you OK, mate?' he, shouted and leaned in across the broken glass, touching Elvis on the arm of his white jumpsuit. He gripped him, shook him, then tapped him on the back. No response at all. Laying his hand on the back of the white jumpsuit, he couldn't even feel him taking small breaths.

Jeff came up behind him, panting, 'Is...is he alright?'

On the passenger seat was the slim black leather attaché case. Its zip was wide open and a beekeeping magazine and some glossy brochures with the name 'Bacto' on them were scattered on the seat along with his beekeeping hat.

Elvis wasn't alright at all. Nick knew right away that he was dead. His body was totally unresponsive. He was heavy and lifeless. The stillness told Nick that this was a fatal crash. Also his head was at peculiar angle...or maybe not peculiar, but oddly stiff and turned in a way that no-one would ever hold their head - tipped down and to one side, as though it had been pulled or knocked off its axis.

Nick turned to Jeff. 'He's dead. Probably broke his neck. There's no blood, though.'

Jeff looked at him in bewilderment. 'Dead?! What? Just like that? Are you sure?'

'Yeah...the show's over.'

Jeff leaned in over the shattered remains of the glass and inspected the body and then turned back to Nick. 'Bloody hell, you're right. Elvis really has left the building.'

A police car came quickly, followed by the fire brigade and an ambulance. The accident teams swung into their daily dance with the results of destruction. It had to be the hardest job. All you saw every day were dead bodies and broken lives. But someone had to sweep up the remains of a life and a car and get the road clear for the still living. Death on the roads was a brutal business, often seen by people as little more than an inconvenience that is slowing them down and making them late for an appointment at the hairdresser's. Death on the roads is so common that it is a devalued demise. Meet your maker in almost any other circumstances and it warrants more time and attention, but get hit by a car or crash into something and you're just a nuisance to the smooth functioning of the road system. Nick and Julie and Jeff explained what they'd seen to the officers, which wasn't much. One of them took Nick to one side whilst the body was cut out of the car.

'So you didn't see what hit the Metro?' said the copper, a young bloke in his early 20s with a ham-coloured face, who had yet to start shaving. Policemen really did get younger every year.

'No. We were by our cars, parked next to the allotment gates, so it was all out of view.'

'How long was there between hearing the collision and you running to the car?'

Nick thought for a moment. 'We stood around for a few seconds...we thought maybe it wasn't that serious...it was maybe a minute or two in total before I actually got down here and looked in the car.'

'Did you see any other vehicle driving away from the scene?'

'No. But then, I wasn't really looking for one. I was just focused on the crashed car as I ran. There was the noise of the impact, then a scraping sound, then breaking glass and tyres screeching. But that had all happened before I ran to the car.'

The copper turned and looked at the junction. Oxbridge Road was a two-lane road which led into a roundabout at 6 o'clock from their perspective, with exits at 9, 12 and 3 on the clock. Whatever had pushed the Metro off the road had to have hit it at about 7 o'clock, as the Metro had emerged from the junction.

The policeman made notes as other police turned up to take photos. Nick walked back up to the cars.

'An old lady from the bungalows was just up here. She saw the collision. Or she reckons she did,' said Julie.

'Oh, yeah? What was it? It must have been powerful and big to make that much damage and survive,' said Nick.

'It was a black Range Rover with bull bars on. They're beasts, those cars. The top end of the range is massive,' said Jeff.

'Were they drunk, do you think?' said Nick.

Julie shrugged. 'She says she saw a man lean in the Mini's window and then run back and drive off. Did you two see it driving away? I didn't.'

Jeff shook his head. 'We were all focused on the crashed car, weren't we? Doesn't seem to have been any other cars on the road when it happened. Classic hit and run, if you ask me.'

She looked at her watch.

'Bloody hell, I'm really late for work. I'd better go and make my excuses. I'll see youse later,' said Julie, getting into her Porsche.

'Well, we're done here. Do you still fancy going to look at potential venues for the club? We'll need to get off,' said Jeff.

'Yeah. I'll park at home and then meet you at the shop and we'll walk down.' Nick cast a glance back down the road. 'Poor Elvis, though, eh? I mean. He was odd and a bit of a grumpy get...but even so. God bless him, eh.'

Jeff stopped and followed Nick's gaze. 'You know, there's something really odd about that crash, if you ask me.'

'You've not got a conspiracy theory already, have you?'

Jeff cocked his index finger, head on one side. 'Think about it. There was no traffic around, it was a clear road, it was good weather, so why would a Range Rover slam into a car just like that, if it wasn't deliberate?'

'It was a drunk or stoned driver. You're not telling me that Elvis was assassinated?'

'I'm just saying it was odd. After all, we don't know anything about him. He might have had enemies and he was, even by Teesside's high standards, an odd bloke. You never know. Many a bright light is hid under a bushel.'

'What is a bushel, exactly?'

Jeff shrugged and held his arms out wide. 'I have no idea, nor, before you ask, how you might get a light under it. I'll tell you what, the Gentleman's Club in the Boro is a right den of iniquity. All sorts goes on in there. Maybe it was a drug dealer he owed money to who wanted to scare him, but it just went wrong.'

'Aye. Maybe. It did seem a weird accident. But then, weird shit happens, sometimes, doesn't it?'

'It does indeed, my peachy-arsed friend. But sometimes, just sometimes, weird shit happens for a very good reason.'

CHAPTER 2

'I'll just use your toilet before we get going,' said Nick, walking through Jeff's stock room.

'Hurry up then, we're late as it is,' said Jeff.

Nick unbuttoned his jeans and just stood there. Nothing. He'd immediately feared this would happen. The knowledge that Jeff was waiting for him had frozen up his bladder. He really needed a piss, as well. He stared at himself, pulled at himself, and massaged himself, willing the urine to start coming out and hating himself for it not happening. But it just wouldn't. And the more he wanted it to, the less likelihood there was of it happening. He pressed at his bladder with his finger tips, trying to force it out of him. No good. Why did he bother trying? It never worked. After a minute, as usual, he just gave up, flushed it, washed his hands and went into the shop, pretending he had used the toilet like a normal person and not struggled, as he always did in such circumstances these days, with paruresis. The pressure to do it when someone was waiting on you just locked the whole thing up. He'd had this happen to him, on and off, for the best part of 10 years and it was getting worse and worse now. So much so that he couldn't really ever use the toilet outside of the house. It was mad and it needed sorting.

'So where is this place, then?' said Nick as he and Jeff crossed over the High Street and walked down Dovecot Street, stopping off at a cafe to buy some coffee to go.

'Way back in the mists of time it was the Incognito and it's been loads of different places since,' said Jeff, as they queued up. 'You remember that, don't you?'

Nick nodded. 'Of course I do. I got off with a great lass in there once. It was some sort of end of term thing in 1979. Lots of snogging and general gropage. Sometimes I really miss being innocent, y' know. We all wanted to grow up so quickly but now I know what life can do to you, I wish I could return to being a gauche 17-year-old again.'

'You know what I was thinking the other day? Back when we were all innocent and virginal and didn't know much about sex, a bit of kissing and that...it was brilliant,' Jeff turned to the barista. 'Two black Americanos please, mate.' He continued. 'It's like when you go out for a meal, there is much to be said for dining from a menu with a couple of quality items on it, rather than being presented with every dish that was ever invented. That's what it was like. Know what I mean?'

'Totally.' Nick dropped his voice. 'I especially loved the dry humping on the carpet or sofa. Sometimes I think it never got better than doing that when I was 17. It was all so exciting. Intimate, but also a bit repressed and covered up. It's a quality erotic mixture, that, for me, anyway.'

Jeff chuckled and nodded keenly. The barista put their coffee on the counter and Jeff paid him. Nick wondered if he had time to use their toilet. No. No point, he would just be under pressure again and would again be unable to perform.

They walked back outside and continued down Dovecot Street. A group of blokes stood outside the Pound pub necking pints and smoking. Two were gaunt, two had huge, sticking-out bellies.

'You were mushier than mushy peas about that girl you met in the Incog. I'd never seen you like that about anyone before. You would just never shut up about her. Must have been love,' He grinned at him. 'She was quietly sexy, though. Didn't put all the fruit at the front of the shop.'

'That's well remembered. Never really told her how much I liked her, though. Not enough, anyway. I was thinking about that recently, actually - as a reminder to tell Julie how much I love her. Not take it for granted, like. Back then, I was probably trying to be cool, you know, the way you do when you're a kid. I still feel bad that I got totally distracted away from her by other women when we got to college.'

Jeff sipped at the coffee, rolled his eyes and punctuated his words by slapping at him on the shoulder.

'Oh, for god's sake, man. No. You. Don't. That's so self-indulgent. You do not feel guilty about that, all these years on. You didn't even feel guilty about it at the time. Bloody hell, it's half a life ago and you were a horny 18 year old who, let us not forget, was a popular lad at college.'

Nick sighed. 'Yeah, you're probably right,' he said, running a hand through his hair. He was working with Marc, his therapist, on not defining himself by his failings.

'Can I just remind you that when we went up to Newcastle Poly, you were always at it, right from Freshers Week onwards. I don't know what they saw in you, but you were all but fighting them off with a shitty stick for a while. If you'd had boots, they'd have been well filled.'

'That's an exaggeration, Jeff. And I did have boots - desert boots. We all had desert boots.'

Jeff pinched his nose. 'Oh, god yeah. Mine were a new life form by the end of the summer. You know your trouble, you rewrite your past to fit in with your current sense of self.' Jeff made another sudden wild face at him, as he often did when he thought he'd come up with a good point, then putting an index finger on his nose and, pointing at Nick with the other, he said, '100 per cent true, that. I'm on a roll here. Don't stop me now, momma!'

'Ha ha...yeah, well, Jules always says I have a habit - an "annoying" habit - of looking for things that make me look bad, or make me appear to be different or isolated.'

'There you go, then, and she's cleverer than both of us put together. You don't celebrate your triumphs enough - you never have. You're far too wrapped up in the stuff that goes wrong in life. You expect things to go wrong.'

'Well, given what happened last month, that's not surprising, is it?'

'No, but you need reminding of your qualities, you do. More than most blokes. The rest of us exaggerate how good we are, you exaggerate how bad you are. So let me remind you that when you got to college you were out with a different woman most weeks. Let's see now, I can actually remember a lot of them.' He held up his right hand and put one finger in the air at a time. 'There was a lass with blonde crimped hair from Leighton Buzzard, I don't why I remember her...actually I do, it's because I said I thought Leighton Buzzard was a bird of prey and she nearly wet herself laughing. See, I was the one with the charm and pulling power, you just pleasured them with your body. Then there was that nice little woman on your course with dark ginger hair. A Geordie.'

'Jenny. She had bright ginger pubic hair. It was like a rusty Brillo pad. Very exotic, I thought. She was a panter, her.'

'A panter?'

'Panted like a hot dog all the way through sex. Was a bit off-putting. Wasn't as good as the dry humping earlier in the year with the Incog lass, if I'm being honest.'

'And you hooked up with that half-German woman who looked about 35 but who swore she was 21.'

'Dagmar. God, I've not thought about her for 30 years. No way was she 21. Totally bossed me around, her. I quite liked that.' He laughed to himself at a particularly vulgar, disgusting thing that had happened to him with Dagmar, but it was something he wanted to keep to himself.

'See, that's German's for you - they've got a ruthlessly efficient, machine-like approach to sex. I speak as a long-time lover of German women, especially Heike Drechler - remember her? The runner. She was mint.'

'Oh, god, aye. I'm with you on that. Have you done recalling my sex life, now?'

'No, I've not finished yet. Remember that lass Marti, who we met in Fresher's Week? She was nice. You actually went out with her for a while, didn't you?'

'No, I didn't go out with her. Not out as such. I'm afraid we actually just had sex in her halls of residence. I don't think we actually ever went out except a couple of times to the student bar. It was a bit weird. I'd go to her room, we'd chat, have some tea, have it off and then I'd leave.'

'Throw in a couple of decent albums and a steak and you've got a perfect lifestyle, there,' interrupted Jeff.

'I remember she had a light perm, was a Yorkshire lass and always wore blue and white stripy underwear. And that's about all I do remember about her.'

'Have you ever considered that maybe she just never changed her knickers? It was always the same pair.'

Nick laughed. 'Ha ha...no, that never occurred to me. I liked her but it was never going anywhere, that. It was just mutual lust.'

'She liked Rush, which was more rare than finding gold in one's foreskin. I was so jealous I could have killed you and worn your skin as a coat just to try and get off with her.'

Nick laughed again, recalling something he hadn't thought about for decades. 'Marti had a really funny thing that she did.'

'Funny as in odd? And, more importantly, thing, as in sexual?'

'Aye. I didn't know it was odd at the time, not being especially *au fait* with how women might typically behave in bed. We'd start, y'know, doing it...and immediately she'd just start thrusting her groin up and down really fast - like really, really fast...' he flapped his hand up and down at great speed, '...and she'd orgasm almost immediately...'

'...Oh, aye, I remember you telling me about this. Ha ha. I never heard of a woman suffering from the female equivalent of premature ejaculation, nor of having a hair-trigger crotch. She is possibly the only woman ever to suffer from the condition. Trust you to get lucky and find her. You must have thought you were the finest lover on earth.'

Nick shook his head, his bladder hurting now. 'She got bored of me and went off with an older lad. Maybe he taught her to stop getting in such a lather so quickly. God knows, I didn't know how to.'

'I like the idea that she's still out there somewhere in her late 40s, still going hell for leather as soon as a stiff breeze blows past...still blissfully unaware that she's the fastest orgasmer in the land.'

Jeff kept bringing up old girlfriends of Nick's, he had such a good memory for these things. Nick had all but forgotten most of them. It made him sound like a proper Lothario, though it had never seemed like that at the time. In fact, all it did was make him remember a lot of awkward and unpleasant break-ups. They stopped at a wooden bench to finish their coffee.

'You know what? Talking about the women I went out with makes me remember what it was like for all those years before I met Julie. For all the stuff that's gone wrong, I'm so lucky to have met her. I hope she realises how I feel. I should tell her more.' He sat down and groaned a little. 'Ah, that's better. I can't talk, walk and drink at the same time,' he said, grateful to ease the desire to piss in doing so. 'Am I alone in this inability?'

'Yes. You're a weirdo. It's basic grown-up human behaviour.'

'I'm the same when it comes to eating and talking. That's why I hate dinner parties.'

'Dinner party. Bah! I hate the very expression. It's trying to make eating food at someone's house into a posher, more middle-class social event. How come it's called a dinner party if you're sitting around a table eating cous bloody cous and drinking chateauneuf-du-pape, but it's not if you're eating pizza, drinking lager and watching TV? It's all pointless snobbery.'

'That's Britain all over, though, isn't it? We're world leaders in trying to give the simplest of acts a class-based definition so we can look down on someone.' They walked on. 'By god, it's a bit grim down here now, isn't it?' said Nick, looking around Prince Regent Street.

Jeff turned his mouth down and pulled on his beard. 'Aye. Since they cancelled the building development that Con was working on, it's all going nowhere fast. Too much of town is like this. Needs a properly planned upgrade. When you think about what it's like here compared to where we lived in Harrogate...' he shook his head. 'I mean, bloody hell, it's like night and day, isn't it?'

'Yeah. I miss Harrogate in some ways. Do you?'

Jeff nodded vigorously. 'Yeah. I do. We had good lives there. Well, on and off. We had a nice little circuit of pubs and bars. I know it was a bit grim for you, at times, especially when Jules moved down, and I was a massive fat bastard on an almost permanent bender, so maybe we weren't always the happiest of people but I'll tell you what I miss most - people being positive.'

'Eh? It was North Yorkshire, remember? Yorkshire folk are *not* positive about anything, unless they're on drugs or clinically insane. They take a moral pleasure in being sour and miserable and resisting human warmth. Apart from that, they're lovely. I speak as a man whose whole extended family are Yorkshire folk. None of them would crack a smile unless they were in pain.'

Jeff scratched his beard. 'Ha, yeah, true. Very true. I just mean people in Harrogate weren't down on the place. Aye, they'd have a moan up about this and that, and there were plenty of rich tossers and right-wing bigots, but you didn't get anyone coming in the shop going, "You know what's shit about this place?" and that happens all the time in Stockton. I get 'em in the shop and all they do is bitch about the place. It's got to be said, it's got its fair share of moaning bastards, has Teesside, people who can never see any good in anything. That really pisses me off, sometimes. We should see the good in things more and bad in things less. There's a lesson for you, an' all, by the way.'

'Aye, I've noticed that since we've been back, especially on some of the online forums. Jules reckons it's because a lot of people are clinically depressed. Undiagnosed, like. I think she's got a point.'

Jeff nodded. 'Maybe. Aye. I never thought of that. All the poverty and workless years must mess with your head. It does seem like it's a clinical condition for some people. I know there's a lot to complain about, but at some point you've got to try and see the good in things. Sometimes it seems like if you gave away a free million quid to everyone, someone here would say, "Aye, but a million isn't a million like it was in the good old days...why isn't it two million?...how come they didn't give it to us years ago?" I know Stockton is a long way from perfect, but it'd be a lot better if everyone just gave themselves a break from the whining - he said, hypocritically whining, just like the very people he despises so much.' He slapped himself on the side of the head.

They put their cups in a bin and walked on to a pair of black doors set into an unprepossessing strip of shop units, built sometime in the late 60s. Jeff pulled at the door. It opened. Lights were on inside as they went up some stairs.

'We're 15 minutes late. The landlord's agent will already be here.'

'Who owns it, then?' asked Nick.

'I don't know. Some company or other. Does this look familiar?'

'Not at all. Then, I was never a regular at the Incog, not being what we used to call a disco dancer. Do disco dancers still exist?'

'I doubt it. No-one has a disco any more. Everything is called a club. A club sounds much more upmarket.'

'So, in a way, the club is the dinner party to disco's pizza in front of the telly.'

Jeff turned and put both thumbs up. 'I like what you did there. You should write that down. Shame to waste such profound insight.' They stood at the top of the stairs and looked around. 'I think it's all been sliced and diced since the late 70s. It's a totally different space.'

The carpet was quite plush but the whole place smelt of a depressing pot pourri of damp, beer and vomit.

'Mister Evans?' said a man in a dark suit and white shirt, stepping out of a side room.

'Yeah. Call me Jeff, though. This is my pal, Nick.'

'Great. I understand you're thinking of opening a rock club.'

'Yeah, I am. First question here though is, can we get the gear up? Is there a lift?'

'There's a service elevator, yes. I'm sure we could get planning permission for a live music venue and a licence is no problem. I'll show you around.'

In essence it was four different spaces, each of which led off a larger dance floor. It didn't look like a rock club and it was too small, the roof too low and the whole vibe wrong. It'd need a major refurb to give it a chance. Nick turned to Jeff and put his thumb down as they walked behind the sales agent.

'Who owns this place now?' asked Jeff after they'd been shown the space.

'It's a property investment group. Beckwith Investment Group.'

'Really? Oh. Right,' said Jeff, an eyebrow raised. 'I'll let you know if I'm interested. I'm seeing loads of places.'

Outside as they walked around the corner onto Yarm Lane and back towards the High Street, he said, as soon as the agent had left, 'B.I.G. is a Cavani company. The notorious B.I.G. you might say, at least you would if you knew enough about rap music to understand the joke.'

'Mike Cavani? Really? How do you know that?'

'Big Fish told me. Cavani's mob are moving into Teesside commercial property in a big way this year, apparently. There are so many cheap places to be had, he's sinking loads of his dirty gangster money into commercial property to clean the money up.'

'He wouldn't touch us. He knows we've still got all that incriminating info and pictures from his phone in the cloud.'

'True. But it wasn't right in there anyway, was it?'

'No. it was horrible. You want a proper building.'

'There's an old Methodist hall just off the bottom of Castle Street. That's available but it'd need a licence application and there'd be planning permission for change of use. Might be a bit bureaucratic.'

'Yeah, but Brian's legal team will sort it for you, won't they?'

Jeff flicked his hair over his shoulders.

'Aye, probably. He does have a lot of clout - largely because he donates so much money to various projects around the area. And anything which looks like it's supporting a small business usually gets the go-ahead. I mean, often it shouldn't. You only need to look around to see how piecemeal and short term the development of this town has been in the last 50 years. If someone proposed a nuclear waste dump on the High Street, the council would give it the go-ahead as long as they could say it had created high-quality jobs for doctors specialising in radiation burns and Strontium 90 poisoning experts.'

Nick thought that was very funny and kept laughing at it as they walked. 'Owee, let's go and have a look at it. Can you get a key?'

Jeff stopped and made a call to the estate agent handling the building. Nick crossed his legs. His bladder was distended now, a small, hard football in his lower abdomen. 'Sorted. We just need to go to Johnson's for the key.' They walked on to the estate agent's on the High Street. 'You know, I keep getting shocked by the thought of dead Elvis.'

'Yeah, me, too. It's really awful. Poor bloke. His life just ending like that. Sometimes life seems so fragile. And being dressed like that somehow made his death tragi-comic.'

'Aye. I want to laugh about it, in a way, but then it feels wrong. Mind, if you're going to go, why not dressed as a low-rent Elvis? It makes no odds to him now.'

'How old was he, do you think?'

'No idea. Probably our age, or a bit older. Hope he didn't leave a wife and kids. I reckon he didn't. He seemed a bit of loner to me. Know what I mean? You get to instantly recognise the type in my line of business.'

'Yeah, I know just what you mean. He was a bit odd, to say the least.'

It was a warm May afternoon. Nick wiped a drop of sweat from his forehead and wafted his v-neck t-shirt a little. Maybe he could sweat the piss out?

'Jules was on good form earlier, eh,' said Jeff as they crossed the road and walked down Silver Street to the small office. 'I thought she might be feeling a bit washed out, but if anything she was more perky than usual and, y'know...giving it the full Jules.' He paused and cleared his throat. 'And she looked pretty damn good, as well. I mean...you'd never know what'd happened to her.' He paused a little, then added, 'Am I allowed to say she looked rather glamorous, even in the overalls? Or is that sexist?'

Nick smiled a little, but didn't say anything for a bit. 'I know what you mean. She went into the Boro and got her hair coloured and had some long curls put into it, bought herself some Calvin Klein perfume, which she's always loved. All just to perk herself up, like. Start anew. But I'm more than a little bit worried about her, though.'

'What? Since she lost the baby? You've not said.'

'Hmm. I know...well...things have been tricky. I'm trying to work it all out.'

Jeff pushed open the door, got the keys from the estate agent while Nick waited outside, and came back out, shaking the bunch at him.

'We have access,' he said. They went back up the High Street and took a right, walking past the impressive 1960s glass cube library. 'So how have things been tricky, then?' said Jeff.

'Well, it's six weeks since she mis...' he swerved around the word '...since it happened and she's given the impression that she got over it, just like that.' He clicked his fingers.

'Well, that's good, isn't it?'

'On the face of it, yeah. But I'm just not sure she's dealt with it properly. At some point, I think all of the emotion and upset she's swallowed down will come out. She's just keeping a lid on it. She keeps letting out these tense little gasps and...I don't know...it's as though she's trying too hard to be her normal self. She's also been distracted sometimes, like she's in a world of her own. All very un-Jules-ish.'

'She's a very practical lass, though. Always has been. She's good at keeping things in perspective.'

Nick went quiet again for a few seconds. 'Yeah, normally, but...this happening wasn't just disappointing...it was the end of a dream...of all our plans...of a future we thought we were going to have. I mean, there aren't any words for that, none that come close to saying how it feels. It was a bloody big thing and since it happened, it's been like she's pretending it wasn't that big a deal for her, which I know isn't true. So when the lid comes off all that bottled emotion, watch out, the shit will really hit the fan. I think she needs some talking therapy.'

'Have you talked to her about it?'

'We've talked it through but there's not much to be said except, shit, I wish that hadn't happened. But I feel like it's something that has come between us. All that talk of old girlfriends makes me remember just how lucky I am to have Julie, y'know, to have someone who understands and loves me for what I am. It scares me, though, especially because it feels like things have changed.'

'I don't get you. How has it changed? She wasn't like that earlier. She was her usual flirty, dirty self.'

'That's just on the surface. She's hiding behind that. Playing the role of Julie, rather than actually being it. I feel like she thinks she's let me down and that maybe I'll want to have a kid with someone else. She feels diminished. I've tried to reassure her...'

'Well, it's still early days, man. Takes time to get over something like that, especially as it was the second time.'

'Yeah. It is. Being a bit distant is to be expected, I suppose. I just want the old Jules back and I'm worried she might be gone for good. That losing two babies might have changed who she is.'

Jeff didn't know what to say, so he said nothing for a bit. 'That's not likely. Not at her age. She's just getting over it.'

'I really hope so.'

'And how about you, then?'

'Me?' Jeff rarely asked after his health so it was a bit of a surprise. It made them both feel awkward.

'Yeah. How are you dealing with it?'

Nick hadn't discussed how he'd been dealing with it with anyone, except Marc, his therapist and he'd only seen him once. It seemed like something Julie had to deal with, mostly. Anything he'd had to endure was insignificant by comparison. 'Well, I'm back on the Phenibut, more as a preventative measure than any great need. I thought it was the best thing to do.'

'Trying to head the depression off before it arrives, you mean?'

'Aye. One of Marc the therapist's big things is knowing yourself and when you might be vulnerable and taking the right measures to make sure you don't fall into the big black hole.'

Jeff nodded, but didn't say anything more for a minute. 'That makes sense - as long as the Phenibut isn't corrupted like last time and sends you loopy.'

'Well, yeah. Obviously, that's a given. I think it's OK, though.'

'You feel good, then? You seem to have been alright since it happened.'

'I feel...y'know...sad about not being a dad...but I'm coping. Horny as a rabbit on Viagra, of course. The pills always do that to me, especially when I first start them.'

'Hardly a troublesome side effect. At least not when you've got an accommodating missus, like Jules.'

Nick paused, not sure how much to say. 'Well, that's another thing. There's been no action on that front since it happened, which, again, is very out of character.'

The urge to urinate had passed all of a sudden. That was odd. Maybe it was leaking out inside of him.

Jeff tried to put a positive spin on it. 'Well, it'll have messed with her body, won't it? Hormones and that.'

'Yeah, that's what I thought. And I'm not exactly tugging at her nightie for it. It'd seem crass or vulgar to do that, wouldn't it? She's apologised for not feeling like it - which is totally not needed and I've said that to her - but it's all part of her upset and another reason she feels she's letting me down.'

'In my limited experience, women don't want men sniffing around them like a horny dog at the best of times, let alone when you've been through something like Jules has.'

Nick paused in recollection.

'Yeah, actually seeing the little thing that would have been your girl - would have been our Joni - was just very upsetting and very weird, too. It's not something either of us can un-see now.'

'I bet it was...a bit horror movie-ish.'

'Totally was. But, for me, at least, it's sort of helped. It made it all real and as Jules says, tragedy is just part of the human gig. God knows, worse shit happens to people than that. I'm just grateful she didn't suffer more than she did, for longer than she did. It was bad enough as it was. And I'm glad I could get her to the hospital quickly because she seemed to lose a hell of a lot of blood and...y'know...stuff. Although it happening at her mother's house wasn't exactly the best place in some ways, at least it's only a couple of minutes from the hospital.'

Jeff winced. 'It was like actually giving birth, you reckoned?'

Nick had only briefly talked about it to Jeff, since. It wasn't a nice thing to have to recollect. 'Well, you'd know more about that, having seen Argie come out. I've nothing to compare it to, but she said it hurt like hell for a while, unlike last time. She was at least 18 weeks this time, though, so they said it was a much bigger deal because of that. It all just came away in a massive rush and honest, Jeff, it was like a sodding slaughterhouse in that hospital room. I insisted on staying with her through it, obviously.'

The big man winced again. 'Rightly so. Can't leave the lass to go through that with only strangers around.'

'Sometimes it can be gradual thing over a few days but this was a massive four-hour expulsion.'

Jeff winced once more. 'I feel for her. When Rita dropped my Argie, it was brutal, man. Like a slasher movie. Even just thinking about it makes my hands sweat in fear. Blood and guts, or whatever it all was, everywhere and out of it all emerges our Arg - this greasy, massive blueish thing. I thought there was something wrong with him - stupidly I'd expected him to emerge all clean and tidy. Man, was I ever wrong.'

'Aye, this was very messy. And you know...you could see the baby...' Nick groaned a little '...in amongst it all. Neither of us was expecting it to be so obvious, but there she was - this little miniature human that we'd created. Bless her. She'd been alive for over 126 days...but she just couldn't make it, poor little thing.'

The last three words of his sentence brought a sob rising into his throat. He had to stop walking, jam his hands into his pockets, stare at the pavement, take a deep breath and swallow it down. Jeff stopped too, turned to him and very unusually, put his arm around Nick's shoulder. They rarely if ever touched, except to hi-five. He didn't say anything more and Nick felt glad about that. It was upsetting, but much more upsetting when you talked about it and much easier to deal with when you didn't. There was some value in good old British stoicism and the art of just suppressing your emotions. They could overwhelm you, otherwise.

'So this place is for sale, not for rent?' said Nick, as Jeff unlocked the heavy wooden door to what looked like a large old Victorian church hall.

'Aye. The church still owns it. Only 100 grand. I say only...but you know what I mean.'

They went into the dusty, warm space. The wooden parquet flooring was scuffed from the thousands of people who, over the years, had used the hall for everything from amateur dramatics to prayer meetings and Sunday school.

'This is a great space, Jeff,' said Nick, standing in the middle of the hall looking around. 'You put the stage at this end and then you have the back wall as the bar. You'll need to put big curtains up at the windows to improve the acoustics, and some plumbing. You'll need some decent bogs put in. There's only one, by the look of it and that'd be no good for...what...how many would you get in here, do you reckon?'

Jeff was over the other side of the room looking at a board onto which lots of fuse boxes and electrical supply units were secured.

'Here? You'd get 250 in, easy. If it was still the 70s, they'd have allowed you 500 in but we'd get smacked wrists if we tried that now. The space is good but the wiring is antiquated. It needs totally overhauling and modernising. Got to be at least 50 grand's worth of work needed in here just to get it up to code. I say "up to code" like I know what that means when, obviously, I've just heard Americans say it in movies.'

Nick wandered out of the room. There was the old single toilet sitting there, invitingly. They were in no hurry. It was still and warm and quiet. Perfect. No pressure.

He stepped inside the small brick room and within a second unleashed a torrent of urine, so powerful that it was a surprise it didn't break the old porcelain. And it went on and on and on. He seemed to void at least three different bladders. Just as it faded to a dribble, he pushed a new surge out.

'Where've you gone?' came Jeff's voice.

'I'm here!' said Nick, still, rather satisfyingly managing to find a few last squirts and drops in the darker recesses of his bladder.

Jeff peered around the wall. 'You've only just had a piss at the shop. You're like a mouse, you - incontinent.'

'Just thought I'd inspect the facilities. You'll deffo need a couple more toilets putting in. Can't just have this one.'

'Not if everyone takes as long as you do, no we can't. Owee, you'll be desiccated if you do that any more.'

Nick flushed it. 'Sounds like you'll need to spend more than a penny - geddit! You've not got that sort of money, have you?' He walked back into the hall with a slightly sore empty feeling where his giant piss ball had been.

'I've got under a hundred grand - that's what's left over from the sale of the Harrogate flat, now that I've bought the Hartburn Village house. Seems mad to sink it all into this, though. I'd have to get a loan to top it up and finish the upgrade.'

'Yeah, but think about it - we get 200 people all paying a tenner. That's £2,000 per gig, plus bar takings. Say you make a pound a pint after costs and you sell an average of three pints to 200 people. That's another £600 profit on drinks.'

'That'd be conservative for Teesside drinkers. Let's say it's £3,000 a gig, door and drink combo. Then I'd have to pay bands and staff. Say I've got a grand left over after that. That's 100 gigs before I get the cost of the property back...but they won't all sell out, so let's say 200 gigs...which, given we'd probably only do them on Wednesday, Friday and Saturday is about 20 months until we break even. Call it 2 years if the modernising costs a lot.'

'Or a year, if you sell a lot more drink and more tickets. That's not too bad, is it? It'd be packed out at Christmas and New Year. Everywhere is. You'd totally coin it.'

'I'm still a bit wary about it. At least if I rent a place, if it all goes tits up, I can walk away. This place is a much bigger investment, but then the pay-off might be much bigger. That's the capitalism gig, I suppose.'

They stood outside and looked around.

'Can you imagine people queuing outside of here to get in to see some new rock band or a blues dude?' Jeff said, after he'd locked the door.

Nick put his hands in his back pockets and looked up and down the street. 'Yeah. Easy. It's also got a nice quirky feel about it. It's a little churchy and it feels like a venue. It feels like somewhere you'd go to for a night out. It really does.'

'Yeah, well, rock is religion, after all, eh. I'll get Brian's accountants onto the job and we'll take a closer look and see exactly what needs spending. They might lower the price if we press them. It's not like the church is poor.'

'Yeah. Why is the church not poor? Why does it own so much land? Jesus didn't own land. Why aren't they being like Jesus?'

'Why don't you ask your new mate, the Reverend Don Preston?'

'Maybe I will. The thing is, Don is such a nice bloke, he'd not even argue. He'd ask you a question instead.'

'Well, that'd annoy me,' said Jeff as they walked away in the late afternoon sunshine.

'Yeah, but then you feel like you're being unreasonable by contrast. So ultimately, it makes arguing with him impossible.'

'No, it doesn't.'

'Yes it does.'

'Nah, I think you'll find it doesn't.'

'It bloody well does.'

'I beg to differ, but I don't want to argue about it,' Jeff raised his large hand into Nick's face.

Nick pushed it away and grabbed him by the throat and pretended to choke him as they walked back to the shop.

'So are you still offering up prayers to the Omniscient Dove from Above, then?' said Jeff as they walked through Stockton Parish churchyard.

'I thought God was the Big Sky Pixie?'

'Ah, I only believe in the Dove from Above these days. I've changed denomination.'

Nick looked at the ground, feeling that this stuff was something he still largely wanted to keep private.

'I've not got religion, if that's what you mean. And God didn't exactly pull through for us with Joni...not in the way you sort of hope he - or she - might. But I still have a word in my head, yeah. I find it sort of comforting. I can't say more than that about it. Take the piss if you want, everyone has to get through life the best way they can.'

Jeff didn't say anything as they walked past the library and up through the path through Stockton Parish Church.

'Yeah, well, you've been through a lot, so anything that does that for you can't be all bad.'

That was quite a concession from Jeff on the subject of religion and one which Nick appreciated. He felt a bit odd about it himself after not being in any obvious way religious in his adult life. But you really do have to get through the shit that life throws at you somehow and a prayer in a quiet moment was really helping in these difficult days. It seemed to centre and calm him.

As they went into Jeff's shop, Emily Davids was sitting at a computer wearing reflective dark glasses, a pile of records to one side, Argie in his pram to the other. She ruffled the top of her hair, took off her glasses and smiled with her bright green eyes.

'Ah, there you are. Your mother dropped the Lord Argington off and then your brother was just in, Jeff.'

'El Huge Haddock? What did he want?'

She shuddered. 'He gives me the creeps. I know he's your brother but...'

Jeff held up his hands. 'But me no buts, lady, I find him morally and physically repugnant as well.'

'...it's like he pretends he knows me, just because I worked at his blues festival last summer. But he doesn't. I hate that degree of overfamiliarity. It's very rude. Anyway, he left four tickets.' She held up a quartet of colourful postcards. Nick picked one up and looked at it. On one side was a portrait of Stevie 'Big Fish' Salmon sporting a buzz cut and now shorn of his trademark exploding beard. He held his arms across himself in an X shape. Underneath it said, 'Don't Cross The Tees'.

'Bloody hell, he's giving it the full suede-head in this, isn't he?' said Nick, taking the card. 'He looks quite intimidating.'

'Yeah, he does. I told you he was thinking of de-bearding,' said Jeff, picking up a card. 'He looks like he's just escaped from some sort of institution by tearing a sink off the wall and throwing it through a window. Look at the big daft git, Arge.' The baby looked at it briefly and then closed his eyes and went to sleep. 'Exactly, son.'

Nick read out what was on the back of the invite. ' "As one of Teesside's V.I.P's you are invited to attend the launch party to end all launch parties. Don't Cross The Tees: the party, the manifesto, the tour. The Big Fish." There are free parmos. Glamorous, eh.' He looked at Jeff. 'What's this all about?'

Jeff shrugged. 'The old whale doesn't tell me much. He fears my acid tongue.'

'Eurgh, you don't kiss, him do you?' said Emily, in mock disgust.

'This is on tomorrow night. It's all a bit short notice, isn't it?' said Nick.

Jeff looked at the card. 'Probably had it organised for a while but failed to tell us. It's all publicity for his new tour and that comedy manifesto thing that dead Elvis was on about.'

Emily picked up Argie, who had started crying, and handed him to Jeff, who began waggling his long beard in front of the baby. It seemed to calm the fractious little lad. 'You mean the Elvis chap that you saw get killed earlier?' she said. 'That was really terrible.'

'We didn't see him get killed, exactly, but yeah, it wasn't nice. Weird really, as there was no blood or anything. He was just lying there, limp,' said Nick.

'He didn't look dead. He looked like he was asleep,' said Jeff.

Emily shuddered and instinctively touched the baby on the head as though to reconnect to the idea of life.

'I think I knew him, you know. Well, not *knew* him. He came in here at least once.'

'In his jumpsuit?' said Nick.

She shook her head as she stroked the baby's little hand. 'No, but he had the sideburns and dyed black quiff thing. He looked odd.'

'Did he look sort of puffy around the eyes and lips?' said Jeff.

She nodded vigorously and pointed at him, 'Yes! Yes he did. You know like when someone has terrible hay fever or an allergy attack. He looked like that. How old was he?'

'About my age,' said Nick.

'Was he really? I thought he was quite a bit younger. He had very smooth skin,' she said. 'Not that I'm saying you look old and wrinkled, Nick, ha ha.'

'I am all too aware that I look every one of my 48, nearly 49 years.'

'When's your birthday, again?' said Emily.

'July 22nd. Four days before Jules.'

'Oh, yeah, you're a Cancer-Leo cusp,' she said, with a smile. 'That explains *a lot* about you!'

'I've been saying he's a massive cusp for years,' said Jeff, dryly.

'So we're all invited to this party?' said Nick, who considered astrology to be patently a load of old bollocks, whilst secretly worrying it wasn't.

'I assume so. He didn't say who was invited, exactly,' said Emily. 'I just said thank you and hoped he'd go away quickly.'

'You fancy going with your Matty?' said Jeff. 'I don't need a ticket - I'm family. There'll be free food and some free, if undrinkable, drink.'

She put her thumbs up immediately. 'That'd be ace, yeah. A free night out is not to be sniffed at. Thanks Jeff.' She blew him a kiss.

'And you and Jules won't turn it down, will you?' said Jeff.

'Right now, I think we need as many nights out as we can get. Anyway, she'd love this, it's at the Middlesbrough Ballroom. That's proper posh in there. Old-school Victorian civic glory.'

'Is it nice?' asked Emily.

'Depends what you like. It's all chandeliers and flock wallpaper, so you'll have to wear a ball gown, Em,' said Nick.

'You don't really think I'd have a ball gown, do you? I haven't. Can I wear my new black leather jumpsuit?'

Jeff looked at the card again. 'It says it's a Best Bib and Tucker event but aye, go on then, give it the full Suzi Quatro, as long as you don't mind Big Fish making off-colour remarks to you...and you know he will...'

'Ah, he's a proper fuckin' gobshite, him, like,' she said, in a very accurate, broad Teesside accent that was totally at odds with her polite, accentless, well-brought up regular voice. It was a habit she'd got into in the last year when she really wanted to make a forceful point. 'And I love Suzi. She is *so* sexy on the cover of that album we've got in the racks.'

'Well, she's part of the pixie race, just like you, isn't she?' said Jeff. 'Tiny wee thing.'

'All the best things come in small packages, Jeff, you know that,' she said pushing her tongue through the gap in her front teeth. 'Well *most* things do anyway. Though, getting an occasional big package is always to be welcomed.' She giggled at her own innuendo.

'You saucy Tiny Dancer. It kicks off at 7pm tomorrow night, so we'll shut up the shop early, get our glad rags on and get a cab over there.'

'I can drive us,' said Nick.

'Nah. That BMW will break down with all of us crammed in it and we're not going in my van.'

'We could try and cram in the Porsche,' said Nick. 'That'd be intimate.'

'So intimate that three of us would actually have to crawl up inside the other two,' said Jeff.

'Well, I'll give anything a go once,' said Emily, eagerly.

'Cool. I'll bring my grease gun,' said Jeff.

'Is that what you're calling it now?' said Nick.

She looked from one to the other and pointed at them and finally at herself. 'Oh, aren't we all so damn witty? Why don't we just eat ourselves and be done with it?' said Emily with a high-pitched laugh and a shake of her head.

CHAPTER 3

'I'm taking Don for a drink in the Rimswell,' said Nick, the next morning, pulling on his brown leather boots and hitching up his jeans. 'What time do you start work?'

Julie looked up from buttoning her white cotton blouse and let out one of her tense breaths.

'I'm just doing a half day. Kick off at 1pm. I'll be home by 5pm to get ready for tonight. Give Don my love...well not my actual love...not unless you get a big gay urge, in which case, make sure you film it for me to watch later.'

He leaned over and kissed her on the top of her head.

'Be assured if I have a big gay urge you'll be the first to know, though I suspect of the two of us, I will remain the only one to have touched Don's holy dongle.'

She squeezed his hand. 'Funny you and Don being matey with each other.'

'Aye. Well, it was the law of averages that I'd be mates with one of your exes at some point. And you're friends with my old schoolboy crush, Shawn, aren't you? Small place, Teesside, y'see. Can be a bit incestuous.'

'I'm actually seeing her later, at a work thing.'

'Well, give her my love...and if *you* get a big gay urge, you know what to do.'

She laughed a little too loudly. 'I'll bear that in mind, if the urge to lez it up becomes irresistible.'

As it was mild and bright, Nick decided to walk the three miles to the vicarage just off Rimswell Road, enjoying the late spring weather as he went. When he was a teenager, walking around Stockton was absolutely second nature. Even getting a bus was something of a luxury and to be done only in bad weather or when you'd had so much to drink you couldn't actually walk. In many ways, the simple act of walking reconnected him to his younger self, even though everything looked different and certainly much smaller than it did in his memory of childhood. It was odd how there was a disconnect between how you recalled something and how it actually was. Proof that life is all perspective and very little objectivity.

Don Preston opened his door dressed in a denim shirt, cream chinos and a black cardigan.

'Hey, Don.' Nick made a wave with his hand.

'Hello, Nick.' He looked up at the blue sky. 'It's a lovely day, isn't it?'

'Cracking, aye. You must have been firing some top-notch prayers up to the Big Man to get weather like this.'

He closed his door. 'Well, they give us a password when we're ordained y'see. It unlocks the communication channel to God. You mere lay folk, you have to put up with the old-school analogue praying but we professionals get full access to the HD, super-fast celestial information superhighway. That's why we get paid the big bucks!'

Nick laughed. Don was pleasingly self-deprecating when it came to his calling. Taking the piss out of religion somehow made it more accessible and, weirdly, more attractive. The last thing you needed was someone giving you the full preacher gig. Don seemed to believe that just being good company was a Christian act in and of itself and Nick was inclined to agree. And anyway, in order to take something seriously, you always have to be able to laugh at it. Those who didn't or couldn't always seemed far more insecure in their faith, whereas Don's seemed unshakeable.

'So how's things at the cutting edge of football journalism?' said Don, as they walked along Bishopton Road West, the bright sun in their eyes.

'I'm phoning it in a bit, really. Have been for a while. I go through phases where football bores me and this is one of them.'

'There seems to be a lack of characters in the game these days. That was always part of the fun when we were growing up - the larger-than-life men.'

'So-called professionalism has ironed all of that out. Nowadays being any good at football isn't enough, you've also got to be a middle-distance athlete or a sprinter. The money is killing the romance of it for me, as well. It's a bit cliché to say it's the people's game, but it always was, and now it seems like it's all part of the elitist culture that seems to be accepted as the way things have to be.'

Don smiled to himself as they walked. A smile was never far from his lips. 'Hmm, if I was a religious man, I'd say that a return to basic Christian values wouldn't be the worst move we could make for society and for football, too. Other religions are available, obviously.'

Don was a pudgy, rather tired-looking middle-aged man, who looked like he'd enjoyed a lot of good dinners. His balding pate gave him a classic monk-like appearance but bright hazel eyes hinted at the attractive young man that Julie had gone out with at university.

'We saw this weird accident yesterday. A man died.' Nick recounted what had happened to Elvis.

'What a strange thing to have happened. God bless him. He must have died quickly.'

37

'Oh, yeah. He can't have suffered. Unlucky really, to die in a side-on shunt. Must just have caught him a certain way and snapped his neck.'

'Upsetting for you to have to see him lying there - expired, as it were.'

'I'm OK with the dead, Don. They don't bother me as much as the living, to tell you the truth.'

Don grinned at him. 'That's a nice line. You should put that in a book.' He tapped him on the arm.

'Hmm, Jeff was just saying something similar yesterday. Maybe I will.'

'Good. And how's Jules doing?'

'As I said in my emails, she took a week off just to stay in bed and get some rest after the...after it had happened. It seems to have done her good - well, physically, anyway.'

'That was a smart idea. I mean, physically, it must have taken a lot out of her.'

'She's fit and strong but yeah, it did. I'm not sure she's really come to terms with it emotionally and...we're still trying to work it out between us. It's been a bit odd, Don.'

Don nodded, hands in pockets and looked at the ground as they walked. 'If I may be a little presumptive, I would imagine she is swallowing it all down and being tough. That was always the way her upbringing taught her to deal with life.'

'That's her all over, yeah. So I have a feeling that at some point she'll let herself feel the emotional upset more strongly, but it's too soon for her at the moment. She's keeping it all at arm's length.'

'Hmm, that is understandable. So how has it been odd?'

'Odd?'

'You said it had been a bit odd between you.'

Nick didn't really want to say. It was embarrassing. 'Oh, I just mean, we're a little...err...distant. Sort of. In terms of...err...being intimate like we were beforehand. That's all. She's a little sort of stand-offish, at least in comparison to how she usually is. Which I totally understand. It's just out of character for her.'

Don nodded but didn't say anything for a few paces as they walked.

'Well she certainly always had a lot of passion for life. Always did at college, at least. She was very popular.' He was clearly using both *passion* and *popular* as euphemisms.

'It's funny to think of you knowing each other back then. What was she like?'

'Julie? She was a high achiever. Straight A's in everything. Was always going to get a first. I think she found her course rather easy to do.'

'I didn't mean academically...'

'Oh, well, I remember she was politically very active against the Tory government. She was what we would today call an enabler or facilitator. She got people involved in protests and fundraising. I used to think she was a natural to go into politics. I vividly remember she led a demo in support of the miner's strike in 1984 and did this rousing speech in the Student's Union about how this wasn't just a fight for the miners, it was about fighting...err...what did she call it now...let me think..."the hegemony of international capitalism", yeah, quite a mouthful. I always remember that. She was cheered to the rafters. I thought she was a *very* exciting person to know. So full of energy and enthusiasm. People orbited around her - or rather, she drew people in. She always seemed very sure of herself and confident, as well. Does she not do public speaking these days?'

'No. She doesn't. Maybe she should. She's very good at organising her thoughts and presenting arguments. I mean, it's impossible to win an argument with her, even when she's in the wrong.'

Don laughed heartily. 'Oh, yes, that I do remember. I also recall that a lot of her contemporaries sort of looked up to her. They'd ask her advice on matters of the heart...'

'..."matters of the heart"?' Nick laughed. 'Where did you pick that up from Don, a romantic novel?'

'I'm getting into the habit of talking like a vicar, I'm afraid.' He put on a droning vicar's voice, 'And lo, I'll be intonating everything soon and verily thee will know God's will. No, I mean they'd ask her about relationships, is what I mean. Made me blush, many a time. Didn't know where to put myself.'

'I'm sure Jules could have helped you with that, as well,' said Nick with an raised eyebrow.

'I'm sure she could. She did try.' He coughed and was plainly embarrassed by the memory. 'And how are *you* doing, Nick?'

They reached the Rimswell pub.

'I'm good, thanks, mate. Yeah, quite strong, by my standards, anyway.' That was twice in two days that he'd been asked that. How odd.

He ordered a pint of lager for Don and a vodka tonic for himself. Don clinked his glass.

'Well, I'm glad to hear that. I was a bit worried about you when you told me about the miscarriage.'

'Were you?' That was nice to hear. No-one, apart from Julie, ever said they were worried about him and it was odd to hear those words spoken in his direction twice in as many days.

'Yes. You'd said about how you'd been praying for the pregnancy to be successful and given what happened, I wouldn't blame you for taking our Lord's name in several colourful shades of vain.'

He had a nice turn of phrase, especially when it came to religious matters.

'Funny thing about that is, I just didn't want to.'

Don raised his eyebrows and nodded his head to one side appreciatively.

'Interesting. So you didn't curse the Almighty for your misfortune.'

Nick sipped at the booze and winced. 'Well, what good would that have done? It's not like anyone promised me that things would go well if I was a good lad and prayed three times a day. No-one let me down. And it just seemed easier to put it down to nature taking its course. Whether that's the same thing as it being God's will or not, is open to debate...maybe it's all one and the same thing.'

'Well, that would be a perfectly respectable pantheistic outlook.'

Nick had no idea what *pantheistic* meant.

'I don't think it's anything to do with panthers, Don,' he said with a grin.

'Of course it is. Panthers rule. Next time around, I'd like to be a panther, if only for the magnificent prehensile tail.'

'Reincarnation? Your lot don't believe in that, do they?'

'No. Technically, I think I'd need an orange robe on to dispense such ideas.'

'You'd look awful in orange, Don. Not right for your skin colour at all.'

'Which is the only reason why I'm not a Buddhist, obviously. Your religious garb must suit your skin hue. Black with a white collar suits everyone and that's why Christianity is so popular. Black goes with anything. It's not the religious texts, it's the colour scheme!'

The both laughed loudly.

In some ways Don reminded Nick of a polite, well-spoken, non-sweary version of Jeff. He had the same off-beat sense of humour and seemed to implicitly understand that only by laughing at things can you ever take them seriously.

'And the wedding is still going ahead at the Riverside in August?'

'Yes, which reminds me, can you officiate for us? Is *officiate* the right word? I mean, can you marry us? Even though it's not in your church or even in any church? Can one rent a vicar for what is basically a secular wedding? Or is that blasphemous, or something?'

Don put his pint down and put a cold hand on his hot arm. 'Of course I can. I'd love to do that. What an honour. Thank you very much for asking.'

'I can't think of anyone better...by which I mean...oh, you know what I mean. It just feels like the right thing to do. Does it cost money to hire you?'

'And lo, there is always a fee to pay in this life,' said Don, hands together, intoning the words like he was delivering a sermon. 'But think of it as an investment in God rather than money in my pocket.'

'Well, we're hoping you can get us in with the Big Man so everything works out nicely.'

'Easy. I can do that.' He smiled at Nick. 'Seriously though, this is a happy moment for me and no, there'll be no charge for you. I feel genuinely privileged that you've asked me. Technically, I can't actually marry you there - but I can act as the celebrant and then the registrar will do the legal shackling of you two together.'

'Excellent. Obviously, Jules will want to make up our own vows.'

'Of course. I'd expect nothing less. Who needs all that 2,000-year-old sexist, patriarchal, religious rubbish?'

They laughed together. Don had something about him that filled Nick's heart. The only word he could conjure to describe it was warmth. Because he was a vicar, it seemed like it must be his religiousness that he found so endearing, but it probably wasn't, it was just the sort of bloke he was, but then, whether that was divisible from his faith seemed unlikely. Coming across a new friend in middle age, a man who you felt was somehow an old friend, was a real blessing.

'You should come around for dinner sometime, Don,' said Nick.

'That'd be nice. Then I can give you my pre-marriage talk about the exciting adventure you are about to embark on and how to keep Jesus in your life and all of that sort of stuff.' He said it in a mockingly reverential tone.

'Ha, we'd both actually rather like that. Any advice is welcome. We've come a long way together since we first met in a bar in Harrogate 10 years ago.'

'Has it been that long?'

'Yeah. We went out for about three years at first. She had just moved back up here and I was in Harrogate. Neither of us was keen to lose our independence, and we had our lives set up with work and such, so we put off moving in together for ages. Then when we did move into my flat in Harrogate, it didn't work at all.'

'Huh. Why not?'

'I wasn't well. I was suffering from depression and drinking heavily...though I really didn't know that was what was actually going on. I understood nothing about depression. And...well, it was awful. So she rightly left after 18 months. Those were dark days and I take a lesson from them to avoid it ever being like that again. I made some big changes to my life.'

'But you found each other again. That's the main thing.' He smiled with his eyes.

'Yeah. Thankfully. I always knew she was the one. It's weird really. She just fills me up and makes me whole, somehow. I'm just scared that changes with what has happened...well, it has changed things. It's not like it was...not really.'

'Everything will be fine,' Don said. Nick felt a bit embarrassed and so moved the conversation on.

'We'll have good party afterwards, probably at Julie's mother's house. There's talk of having a tent in the garden. You and Gail must come along to that.'

'Smashing. Will you try again for a baby?'

'No. That's us done now. I think we've both had enough of that particular emotional and physical rollercoaster.'

Don nodded. 'Well, me and Gail were never blessed with children but there is much joy in other people's kids.'

'Yeah. You just have to accept that things don't always work out how you'd like them to. When I was depressed, something like this would have buried me. I would only have been able to see the bad in it and even though I still have that tendency in me, as Jeff was just saying yesterday, luckily, I don't feel like that now. But I'm worried about Julie. She's cheerful on the surface, but I know she's living in her head about it all, getting wrapped up in it. I want to help her, but I don't know what to do. My sense is that she feels she's let me down. Which is daft but...'

'...she'll reach out to you when she's ready.'

'You think?'

Don patted him on the shoulder reassuringly. 'I'm certain. She's just waiting for the right moment. Waiting until she feels able.'

ꞏ 'I was saying to Jeff, it's made me realise how much I love her for being who she is and how I had taken it for granted a bit recently. She's always so level headed and well adjusted...'

'She'll come back to herself, I'm sure. Life has these ups and downs, from time to time.'

'Is this you doing your Vicarly thing, Don?'

'No, This is me doing my human thing. Same building, same boss, different department.' He winked.

Nick took a drink and nodded. 'She doesn't seem depressed in the conventional sense but I do feel like losing the baby is something that has come between us, in some sort of way.'

'Don't rush things. Just let her work her way through it and then be there to listen to her when she needs to be listened to.'

Nick nodded. 'Thanks, mate.'

Don sipped his pint. 'No worries. As regards depression, y'know, I see kids in this parish who, by any definition, are clinically depressed, due to things happening at home and school and bad diet and just, everything...and they're sleepy in class and are just not functioning properly. It amazes me that it's not addressed. People will say, "Oh, he's a lazy kid and doesn't try" when really, what he is, is depressed. So much bad behaviour and so many problems could be addressed if we recognised mental illness more readily. I hear people casually bandy words like "retarded" around about them and it is really very patronising and quite offensive, I think. These kids need more understanding, not less.'

'Yeah, when I think back to so-called bad kids at school, it's clear to me now, that there were problems in their life and they were just really upset children.'

'Hmm. This demonising of kids is easy to do - it's hard to love a destructive, evil little sod. But no kid is born like that. It's the grown-ups' world that's making them like that.'

Nick leaned back and crossed his legs. 'Well, we're putting the world to rights this lunchtime, aren't we?'

'One thing I've noticed about you, Nick, is you never chat about inconsequential stuff, do you? It's always the big issues. That's not a criticism, by the way.'

'Oh, yeah, that's true. Sorry. I can't do lightweight chit chat about white goods or TV shows. I'd like to, but I find it hard and quickly get out of my depth. I'm much more comfortable with philosophical questions or discussions about music.'

'No need to apologise. Why don't you write about that? Put it into a novel, maybe.'

'I am thinking of writing a novel, actually. Try and put another string to my literary bow.'

'You should. You've got a really original way of thinking about things. Not normal. Ha ha ha...but in a good way. Ha ha.'

'Not normal is my normal.'

'Exactly. Well, hopefully there'll be room for a hip and cool vicar in them. Perhaps one who is slim, good looking and fabulously well endowed...oh, and can do a really good Evensong, possibly whilst pleasuring his congregation's prettiest women. Ha ha ha. I say that as though I have any idea what it might mean, which I really don't.' He flung his head back and roared in laughter.

'The rock 'n' roll vicar? Yeah, I'm sure that could be arranged,' said Nick.

'Shall I put my suit on?' said Nick, as they got ready later that day to go out to Big Fish's launch party. 'It's supposed to be a smart do.'

Julie came out of the bathroom wrapped in a towel and plugged in a hair dryer. 'Yeah, why not? You've actually only worn it once - for the Northern Writers Award, remember? Oh, and I suppose you almost got married in it last summer, as well. About time it got another outing. I'm looking forward to this, we've not had a smart night out for yonks. Not since that awards do in fact and that was...god, over three and half years ago. Time flies.' She let out a small, tense gasp of air. It made Nick tense to hear it. It had become a literal representation of the upset they'd been through.

'Dinner, drinks and a disco. All sounds very forty-something, doesn't it? What are you wearing? Emily is wearing a leather jumpsuit!'

'Bloody hell. Good luck having a piss in that when you're 10 drinks in and have to try and hover above a toilet in a small cubicle. I'm going in my rock 'n' roll lawyer outfit.'

She pointed to the hanger on the back of the wardrobe where a black pair of pants and tailored jacket hung with an elaborate gold and red brocade waistcoat.

'Ah, yeah. Nicole Farhi, isn't it? Cool stuff, man.'

'I know you were probably hoping I'd wear the cream suit, but I'm saving that for the wedding in August. I'll just get red wine on it and ruin it. You know what I'm like.'

'I do like you in that.'

'Aye. Too bloody much.' She thrust her groin at him cartoonishly. 'You'd be dry humping me all night given half a chance. I know you.' She grinned at him and sighed heavily. 'Not that I'd mind. You've always been a quality dry humper.'

'I had a lot of practise as a teenager. I love the dry hump. Sex while wearing clothing is underrated. I was just saying that to Jeff yesterday. Sex when I was 17, despite involving no nudity at all, was brilliantly exciting.'

She yelped out a bark of a laugh. 'When I was 17 sex involved at least *some* nudity, lad, so I'm a traditionalist, I'd go for being naked every time. Unless I'm doing it in the bogs of the Royal Oak, of course. You've got to have standards.'

She began to dry her hair into long, loose ringlets. It had been highlighted into half a dozen soft shades of blonde, from platinum to sunshine yellow to strawberry.

'I love what they did to your hair,' he said, as he returned from the shower. 'It's classy but quietly freaky. Just right for you.'

'To think I had it all respectable and fair and straight for so long in my old job, like a sensible career girl. Very boring. I much prefer this.'

Taking a plastic bag from the bed, she looked inside it then looked at him a bit awkwardly.

'What is it?' he said, picking up on her expression, right away.

'Well you know how since...since it happened...we've not...' she paused for a while and sighed, annoyed at her own inability to say the words she wanted to say, '...we've not...'

'...made love?'

'Yeah.' She wouldn't look at him. 'Is there a reason?' she said, casting a quick glance at him with sad eyes.

He shrugged, not wanting to say the wrong thing. 'I thought you didn't fancy it and that you'd want to be left alone...like that, I mean. And I thought you'd just not be in the mood. You've not been, have you?'

'Well, no. I've not really been in the mood, which is very upsetting for me 'cos I like that side of things.' She was so awkward with him and that was really upsetting. Normally, they could talk about anything. 'But I meant, do you not want to?'

'I don't want to if you don't.'

She let out an exasperated groan and threw her head back. 'Oh, Nick, man! Stop being polite with me. I hate it when you're polite and daren't say what you really feel in case it's not what I want to hear. Tell me the truth. Has the...has it put you off me?'

He was shocked to hear her say that. 'Jules, man, of course it hasn't.' He tried to say it with maximum sincerity, but was worried that made it sound forced.

'Are you sure?' Her face was scrunched in a deep frown.

'You know what I'm like, I don't often initiate sex. I figured you'd tug at my coat for it when you felt like it. I'm happy to wait until then.'

She slapped her hand on the side of her leg, in a frustrated and tense way.

'But I don't want you to be happy to wait...I want you to want me.'

He had the feeling he wasn't really understanding what was in her mind and that this was one of those situations where no matter what you say, it will be the wrong thing.

'Nothing has changed, Jules. I was just trying to give you space after the...you know.'

'Are you sure that you're telling me the truth?'

She never usually questioned his honesty. That was another horrible little barb in his heart. 'I'm certain. I'm not just saying that. When you were bending over the car the other day, I...I felt like I always do. You picked up on that, I know you did.' It was his turn to be embarrassed and awkward. They were never like this with each other and it was awful - inhibited and uptight.

Then she smiled her nice smile and wiped a small tear from each eye. 'Yes, I did. That was good. I needed it.'

'You *needed* it?' It seemed an odd choice of word.

Wearily, she slumped forward. 'Oh, you don't understand. Why would you?' Another tear fell and she dabbed at it with a finger. 'It's about who I am...my self-identity.'

He smiled but he didn't fully know what she was talking about, even though he really wanted to, also fearing that asking her more about it would just upset her more. He also knew that talking about how you felt was often impossible, or at least, it seemed impossible to find the right or accurate words.

She sniffed loudly and opened a carrier bag. 'Now don't laugh, right? I'm going the whole hog tonight, mind, posh suit, posh waistcoat and new bra and pants.' She held up some underwear. 'Bought them in town today. Have a guess how much?'

'£40?'

'Try again.'

'£65?'

'Bloody hell, I'm not made of money. They cost a total of £6.50 from that cheapo shop in Wellington Square.'

'£6.50? You were robbed. They almost don't exist! I'm impressed.'

She held them up to her eyes. They were a black lace and mesh fabric and in a small bikini style. 'They absolutely scream woman having a mid-life crisis and any feminist worth her salt could easily argue that they're conforming to patriarchal and sexist expressions of female sexuality.'

'If that's the case, you didn't have to get them just for me, Jules.'

But he'd misunderstood. She made a tutting noise.

'I didn't get them for *you* - not primarily, though I knew they'd appeal to your sense of aesthetics. They're mostly for me and my mid-life crisis, or whatever you want to call it.'

He thought about that for a bit.

'Bollocks to the mid-life crisis, I say. We're the generation who never grew up. If we can't pull on tiny knickers and sex ourselves up, who can? I noticed you'd given your pubes a short back and sides, judging by the hair in the plug hole.'

'Had to tidy it all up for these, didn't I? Got to do the job right.' She unwrapped the towel, put the underwear on, pushed up her breasts and made a corny seductive pose. 'Any good?'

Just a bit. Whatever it is that gears what you find attractive, wherever that is rooted in your psyche and whatever sublimated desire drives it, Julie was the perfect expression of it for him. Her body shape had changed a little over the years and she was perhaps a little broader in the hip than she had been when they first met, but it made no difference. How she was, was always just right to connect with his sexual self. One look was all it took. One look, except when he'd been depressed, was all it had ever taken, from the first moment she'd stood next to him at Jack & Danny's bar in Harrogate. And he often saw the same look in her eyes towards him, at least until recently. It was a connection that seemed part of something quite spiritual in the way it worked, even though it manifested itself in sheer lust. He often told her how much he fancied her, aware those words sounded shallow, but those words were nonetheless meant as a profound appreciation of who she was. At least, that was the intellectual and political reasoning and he truly believed in it, but the fact also remained that even in her mid 40s, she still had what he considered to be a magnificent arse.

'You look lovely, Jules.' He went across the room to her, wanting to show some physical affection and hoping she'd be receptive.

'No being too rude,' she said, giving him a light hug. Again, it was not something she'd normally say.

He ran his hands over the soft, fine underwear and looked in to her eyes. 'I think you're so doing so well.'

'What for wearing skimpy, cheap new underwear? It really isn't that difficult. You just put one leg in and then the other and pull them up till they cover about 50 percent of your vital bits. Easy.'

She went quiet and rested her head on his shoulder for a little. She was working up to saying something. Instinct told him; the quiet told him. There were so many layers to her upset, and probably to his, too.

'I think what it is, right, is I just want to feel sexual. I want to feel vital and not clapped out...do you understand? Please try. Not sexual for you, but for me. I haven't felt like sex since it happened...and that scares me. It makes me feel old and useless.' She peered at him through squinting eyes, like she was looking into the dark. 'That side of life is a big part of my identity and it has been since I was about 15. Do you get me?'

'But you do know it's who you are that really turns me on, don't you? It's not just a physical thing. It's your brain and your body together.'

She raised an arched eyebrow a little quizzically and wandered around the bedroom, messing with her hair. He watched her closely as she did so, realising that this was a big moment in their relationship. This was a time to understand and not to judge or assume anything.

'I do know that and I know you mean it and that's all very admirably PC...but after...you know, the big M...I need to feel like I'm still...well...like I say, still vital and...' she sighed heavily, '...and still a sexual, desirable woman. I know it's probably shallow, but there you go. I've always feared being dried up and middle aged and now I do more than ever. I'll be 46 in a couple of months. I've had two miscarriages and there's absolutely no way I'm having a third. We're going to use contraception until I know there's zero chance I can ever be pregnant again. So that's it. That part of my life is done. They already told me I'm peri-menopausal, so it's all over. Can you see how that feels for me? You're still the same man you were before it happened, but I'm not the same woman. I'm changed. I can't just be the old Julie because she could have had children and I can't now.' She rubbed the lines on her forehead in a frown. 'It all feels like a really big shadow hanging over me and I can't see beyond it.' She sighed so heavily that it wrenched at Nick's heart.

Nick considered what she'd said for a while, trying to work it out.

'Is it because being fertile - being able to give birth - is one of the defining things about being female, even if you didn't want kids for most of the time? So when that stops, it's like you stop being female, in some psychological sort of way?'

She turned to the mirror, flicked at her hair and tugged at the cheap clasp in her bra, to stop it digging into her.

'That's exactly it. *Exactly.*' She took a dab of hair wax from a pot on the dressing table and rubbed it into her hands and onto her hair to give it soft gloss. 'I can't help like feeling my usefulness has dropped by about 50 per cent. For all my feminist reading over the years, it does just feel like I'm diminished. And the worst thing is I'd hate to hear any other woman say that, so to feel like that myself is just fizzin' horrible. I feel like I'm letting myself down. I'm so messed up.' She said the final sentence quietly, almost under her breath.

He went over and stood behind her with his hands on her shoulders, looking at her in the mirror.

'But, at the risk of stating the obvious, you're much more than just the ability to reproduce, aren't you? That's just a small part of Julie Wells.'

'Logically, yes. Emotionally, though, it feels like a massive thing. I don't know where to put this feeling of...of...of loss. It's not just the loss of little Joni, it's the loss of who I am and of who we are...or were...we had the hope of children before, now we don't.' She groaned again at being unable to cohere her feelings better. 'Anyway, that's why I want to feel sexual, even if that just makes me seem shallow or weak. That's why I'm worried that you don't want me the way you used to want me.'

'It's not shallow. Being sexual is a fundamentally important part of being human.'

She made a flat smile. 'I'm glad you understand that. I should have known you would.'

'I think you're being really brave about it, but you don't have to be...you can let go, Jules. Don't bottle up all the emotion about losing Joni forever.'

She shook her head, but wouldn't look him in the eyes now.

'No, I'm not being brave. Bravery is when you take a hard or selfless choice. I had no choice to make, but dwelling on it changes nothing. Like mam has always said, "Who said life was going to be easy? No-one." She was right all along. Life had taught her that it was a lot of failures and occasional successes. She had to cope with dad walking out. She didn't know if he was alive or dead. It was bad enough for us kids but it must have been 10 times worse for her. She couldn't get on with life.'

They went quiet for a minute. How were they going to get over this pain?

She came over to him and pushed his hair behind his ear - a little affectionate tic she had with him. 'I'm fed up with talking about myself. What about you, darlin'? How are you?'

'I'm good. Yeah. Sad. I keep thinking - oh, what if?...but I'm coping. I'm stronger these days. I'm just worried about you, Jules. I want to help but I don't know what to do. Maybe you should take Phenibut to help with this depression.'

'I'm not depressed. I don't think so. I'm just upset. I can't settle into myself and just feel really ruffled inside and tense, as well.'

'I can tell.'

She pecked him on the lips. 'I'm pleased you've still got the light in your eyes.' She glazed with tears again as she looked at him and then rubbed his cheek with her thumb. 'I'm so sorry that I'm like this. I love you so much. I do...really, I do...'

'I love you with all my heart, Jules. And you don't have to say sorry. That's my territory.'

With a firm nod she seemed to make a decision not to dwell on things any more. That's what she'd been doing, every time they'd got close to talking at length about the miscarriage and its effect on them. She tried to play her way out of it, so she licked his nose and then glanced downwards. Her voice lightened a little. 'My top-notch crotch observation skills tell me that for all those fine PC words of yours, the underwear thing is still doing some business for you in the downstairs blood flow department.' She jiggled her breasts at him in the new bra again.

He must have looked a little sheepish, as he often felt like he shouldn't react so predictably, even though he didn't seem to have a choice. It all seemed to work almost independently of his brain. Even if he told himself not to react like that, it made no difference.

'Sorry, Jules. See, I told you apology is my territory.'

'No, no...don't feel guilty, luv. You know I don't mind it - quite the reverse. If it didn't happen, I'd feel even worse about myself, right now.' Again she spoke the last sentence almost under her breath.

'It just makes me feel so typically male,' he said, 'that's why I flinch at it. I hate the thought of being like every other bloke.'

'Typical of you, that is. Don't overthink it.'

She patted him on the cheek again and they rubbed noses, her beak smooth and tender against his. These small acts of intimacy, especially the non-sexual acts, were the beautiful little moments that he cherished. Sex was driven by animal lust but intimate affection was based in something else, something really good, maybe something even holy. He'd often thought that while sexual infidelity would be hard to cope with, it was less the physical sex act that would destroy a relationship, it was in the small acts of delicate affection and intimacy with someone else that would be where the real betrayal would lie.

'Is there anything I can do for you to help you through this?' he said, as they were nose to nose. She went into joke mode.

'What? Like wear sexy underpants?' She laughed loudly now and pulled back. The thought actually seemed to cheer her up, in fact. 'Ha ha...I don't think so.' She shook her head. 'No. That's not my thing. Never has been.'

She squeezed his manhood tightly through the towel. 'That funny bashful look you get on your face when you're feeling randy is enough to get me going...so stop looking at me like that. We've not got time to consummate your lust and especially not to consummate mine.'

'Ah, so you do feel like it?'

She looked almost bashful herself, which wasn't one of her default expressions at all.

'Maybe. A bit.' She drummed her fingers on him. 'Let's save it.' Nick knew that she didn't. Not really. It was just Julie trying to be Jules. Trying to be the woman she had been. He tried to just go along with it because rejecting it wasn't what she needed, either.

'Am I on a promise, then?'

'I was going to ask you the same thing. Am *I* on a promise?' she retorted, pulling on the black trousers and smoothing them down, then pulling on a tight, stretchy black vest.

'For future reference, you're always on a promise, Jules - a permo-promise. At least while I'm on the drugs.'

'Good. Because, the thought of you and me having it off really does make me feel a bit stronger. At least in theory.' That was the crucial and probably accidental truth. 'I feel like I shouldn't rely on male approval in that way, but this is all very hard-wired stuff for me.'

'I know what you mean but surely it's not male approval, per se. It's my approval. That's sort of a bit different.'

She shook her head. 'You're a right emotional smart arse these days, aren't you?'

'I seem to have access to my better self at the moment. Did you really think I'd stop fancying you after...you know?'

One of these days they'd have to say the word *miscarriage*, but neither could face it yet.

'It worried me because I know you wouldn't admit it, maybe not even to yourself. It's not the craziest notion. It did look like a frontline battle unit in Vietnam at one point. I wouldn't have blamed you for being grossed out and thinking, well I don't want anything to do with that end of her any more.'

'Don't be daft. I'll always love you, you know that...in all ways.'

'Well, I'm just being honest with you. It was hard to go through all of that and come out the other side feeling good about yourself.' She stood in front of their full-length mirror and turned to look at herself side on. 'Have I got a knicker line showing?'

He leaned over and looked at the close-fitting trousers. She bent over a little and felt around the top of her buttocks.

'Nope. No VPL at all.'

'Good. I got the right size for a change then. I like these pants, they're smart black cotton but they're cut like jeans. I could wear them with a crop top in the summer. I might get my belly button pierced if I do, just for the full mid-life crisis look.'

They were tight to the curve of her thighs and sat low cut under her hip bones. She put on the waistcoat, cinched it into her waist and buttoned it up.

'You look cool, Jules. Hippy lawyer is right.'

'I saw a woman in Santa Monica who was dressed like this when we were on holiday there last year. I always liked it as an idea. Smart but a little bit freaky.'

She let out a heavy sigh, involuntarily, it seemed.

'Come on then, get yourself ready,' she said. 'Have you ironed a shirt?'

'Yeah. White one OK?'

'Your linen one?'

'Yeah. It won't show my inevitably massively wet arm pits. I always end up sweating so much in public.'

That amused her. 'Yeah you do, why is that?'

'Nerves. I'd rather talk to 1,000 strangers than one.'

'Mad bugger. When we first went out, you were wringing wet by the end of the evening. I remember thinking how unusual it was. It was oddly sexy. Like you were a bit wild.'

'I've always been a sweater, right since puberty. I used to have huge salt rings around my armpits at the end of every school day. It looked like the shoreline on the Black Sea.'

'Eugh. You're generally very profuse with emission of the old bodily fluids, wherever they're coming from. I'd never seen the like. Proper shocked me the first couple of times we had it off. Had no-one ever mentioned it before?'

'Yeah. I took it as implicit criticism, though there's nothing I can do about it. I had no idea it was unusual. There was no way I could have known until a lass at college mentioned it. She was this German woman. She said she was 21 but me and Jeff always thought she was in her 30s. She was certainly an experienced woman of the world.'

'You've never said about her. So she taught you a few tricks, did she?'

'Dagmar, she was called. Yeah, she did rather.' He laughed to himself at the memory.

'What? Tell me. I like hearing your sex stories,' said Julie, patting him on the chest and taking hold of his hands.

'Are you sure?'

'Yeah, go on. I'm always telling you things from my sordid past, aren't I?'

OK, well, it was in the first term at college and we just got it together one night, you know the way you do, and I'd never received, ahem, oral attention before...' He raised an eyebrow at her.

'Oooh, that must have been a bit radical for you in 1979.'

'I thought so at the time...but then I was hardly Warren Beatty, was I?'

'Aye, you were - Jeff's told me all about your rampage through the virtues of women at Newcastle Poly. So let's not have this "poor me" rubbish.'

'OK, well, she's...y'know...' he gestured with his hand.

'...I know how it goes, man, aye.' She nodded with a laugh in her voice.

'And I rather quickly physically reacted the way the younger male of the species traditionally reacts in such situations.'

Julie was laughing now. 'Was it a spit or a swallow?'

'Well, that was it...she got a bit caught by surprise by the...ha ha...the power and the volume...ha ha...and...this is so gross...but it was very funny...she breathed in just at the wrong moment and somehow inhaled half of it up her nose and nearly choked to death on the rest!'

Julie pulled away and howled a high-pitched hyena cackle. 'Get out of here - she did not!'

'God's honest truth. I went off like a garden hose, as per normal and it flew right up the back of her throat and came out of her nose. It wasn't a little cough...this was a proper choking and retching.'

Julie was bent double, gasping for breath, tears of laughter rolling down her cheek. There was nothing fake about it, nothing forced or exaggerated. 'Eee, fizzin' hell, or should I say jizzin' hell...the poor lass. You should've warned her in advance.'

'Well you can imagine my embarrassment. I didn't know where to put myself. Briefly, I was worried she'd pass out or something. She went a funny colour.'

'What did you do?'

'I offered her a tissue to blow her nose, didn't I? I'm not an animal, Jules,' he said, giving her his best innocent look.

That just set her off again.

'I don't know, oh, dear me...what a very special man you are. You're a loss to the adult movie business. There are techniques she could have employed to stop that happening but they do take a bit of practise! Why have you kept that from me for so long? That is a brill story. Oh, it's cheered us right up, that has.' She cackled a bit more and wiped her eyes. Tears of laughter, not tears of sorrow. There was such a difference.

'It came back to me when Jeff mentioned her the other day. There are other stories I could tell you. He was reminding me of a few.'

'I want to hear them all but nothing will top that...nearly drowning a lass in that way...that's a classic.'

She went to brush her teeth, still laughing. Nick felt happier that she seemed in better spirits. It was an echo of her normal self.

He rolled on some deodorant and fastened up the shirt. She came back in from the bathroom and patted him on his bare backside.

'Give us look at you. Eee, fizz me, you're looking quite the sexy beast, aren't you? This is a good look for you, naked from the waist down but with a white shirt on.' She put her hands on his cheeks. 'And the white brings out your tan. Aren't you gorgeous?'

'If you say so, Jules.'

'I do.'

He pulled on the rest of his outfit and Julie brushed his shoulders with the flat of her hands, almost chuntering to herself.

'Nice soft shirt untucked, tight dark pants, single breasted jacket, unshaven but smelling of something nice and musky, yeah, you look properly rugged and handsome in your sort of hapless, trampish sort of way.' She wet her fingers and stroked at his wispy hair to smooth it down, then pushed it behind his ears, again with gentle affection.

She fastened her fine silver necklace, pulled her hair over her shoulders and shook it a little. 'God, you know what the worst thing about getting dressed up is?'

'Is it actually getting dressed up? I feel like I'm in another man's clothes, somehow.'

'It's that you end up so bloody self-conscious about stuff you don't normally care about. Is my hair alright? Can you see my knicker line?

Should I wear make up? All of that. Tedious. As I get older I just want to be a jeans and jumpers lass.'

'You don't usually wear make-up.'

'Well it's such hard work keeping it all maintained throughout the night. It's just another thing to worry about. Should I bother tonight?'

It was his turn to put his hands on her shoulders and look at her. The lines on her forehead seemed a little deeper, the crow's feet around the corners of her eyes a little more marked, the bags under her eyes a little heavier than they once were. Life was leaving its marks on her, the way it does on every single person. But in its own way, it was a lovely thing. Beauty is not the preserve of the young, smooth-skinned and unblemished. There is so much beauty in life experience and the scars that it leaves. She still made his heart beat a little faster and he felt certain she always would. These moments were very important moments in their lives. Important moments of reassurance and reconnection that all relationships must go through from time to time. You couldn't just tell someone you loved them, they had to see it in your eyes and you had to see it in theirs. Words only got you so far, the crucial aspects of relationships are contained within the non-verbal moments.

'I reckon make-up just hides your natural beauty, Jules. You should go *au naturel*.'

She relaxed her face and gave him a loving tilt of her head. 'Aw, luv. Aren't you nice? Aw...I'm keeping you.' For a moment, he thought she was going to cry again but she pushed it back down. 'Mind, Big Fish will just think I'm a lesbian. He thinks any woman not in full war paint is a lesbian.'

'That should be good enough reason not to bother with any, then.'

She leaned forward, slipped her hands around his waist, and put an index finger in the gap between his shirt buttons and found his belly button, rubbing it in a slow circle, in the full knowledge that it was hard-wired to his libido and knowing exactly what it would do.

It wasn't an unusual thing for her to do, because she knew he liked it, but it wasn't for real. It wasn't really what she wanted to do. You can tell when someone has that sexual feeling and when they're just going through the motions and Julie never normally did that.

He took her finger out of his shirt, kissed it and grinned. 'Jeff will be here soon.'

Now she kissed him. Not just a peck this time, but a proper, wet, passionate kiss. She was trying hard, bless her. He pulled her tight into him, his hands rubbing the inside curves of her buttocks and up between her legs, pressing at her in the hope that it would communicate his lust for her.

She whispered in his ear. 'We'll have big fizzin' one soon. I promise.'

'When you're ready, I'll be ready,' he said, not knowing if it was right thing to say, but hoping it was some reassurance.

Again, her look was one that revealed tears close to the surface, but the door bell went. She pecked him on the lips and he went to buzz Jeff in.

'Your carriage awaits, Prince Nicholas of Guymer-land and Julie of Wells-shire,' said Jeff, appearing at the door. 'I say carriage, I mean slightly odd-smelling 1992 Ford Mondeo driven tonight by an expert purveyor of humans called Wiffy Smiffy.'

'Cool. We'll be right down.'

'You look all done up like a pox...'

'...doctor's clerk. Aye, I feel like it.'

'Ha ha...you look like one of those blokes in a Calvin Klein ad - all dilated veins, muscles, artfully dishevelled clothes and very, very, very...and I shall say it again...very, gay.'

'Yeah, that's me all over. I'm certainly the gayest man standing here. Anyway, you can talk, you're smoother than velvet in your dinner jacket. Is that a cummerbund?'

'It is. Fresh from Oxfam. I like to think of it as a sort of fancy version of a truss, which will be handy if I have a hernia tonight.' He pulled at the green, blue and black woven silk.

'Hiya, Jeffrey!' Julie called out as she pulled on her best black and silver trainers. 'Eee, look at you.'

'He's wearing a cummerbund,' said Nick, pointing at the big man, holding his dinner jacket open.

'Is that for soaking up your cum, then?' she said, hooting a laugh.

Jeff feigned shock. 'I have no idea what you mean, Ms Wells. I have no bodily fluids, due to being a low-rent robot, as you well know. Are we set to go, then?'

'We are. Let's rock 'n' roll,' said Nick, closing the flat door behind them.

CHAPTER 4

Emily and her boyfriend, Matty Rhodes, were already in the cab. She sat on his lap so Nick and Julie could squeeze in the back, while Jeff took the front seat.

'Now then. How are my two favourite rock 'n' roll love birds?' said Julie as she squeezed in.

'We're good, aren't we Em?' said Matty, a well-spoken middle-class boy from Linthorpe who played lead guitar in a very good rock band called Metal Road and who usually wore a bit of eyeliner with expensively distressed-looking hair and clothes.

'We are indeed. This is nice us all having a night out together.'

'I love your black leather jumpsuit,' said Nick, as Emily stretched her little legs out across them all, her arm around Matty's shoulder.

'If he starts humping your leg, just give him a kick,' laughed Julie.

'Do you like leather, then, Nick?' she said.

'Put it this way, if I got a jumpsuit like that, I'd never get out of the house. He'd be all over me like vinegar on chips.'

'At least it's a wipe clean fabric,' chipped in Jeff from the front. They all laughed.

'And you're wearing tight velvet pants, Matty!' said Julie, rubbing his leg. 'This is very good. Black velvet, too. Very old school rock 'n' roll.'

'He's going for the Chris Robinson in 1990 look,' said Emily, happily playing with his long hair.

'Oh, he was gorgeous back then. I fancied the arse off him something rotten in that "Hard to Handle" video. Pity he turned into a smelly-looking hippy,' said Julie.

'How's the band doing, Matty?' said Nick.

'We're stuck in a rut. Can't get bigger gigs. We really need some proper exposure, a support slot on a major tour.'

'When I start my record label, we'll put out a live EP or something,' said Jeff.

'Your label?' said Julie. 'You never said anything about this.'

'It's just another idea. If I get this club off the ground, a label would make sense too. It's all synergy, innit?'

'Is it?' laughed Nick. 'Are you sure?'

'It does sound like the sort of thing a 23 year old who's done Business Studies and now works in Barclays pushing buttons on a computer would say. And as you know, those men are my role models.'

'Your hair is ace, Jules. Have you just had that done?' said Emily, reaching around and pulling a long, loose curl of it.

'Yeah. I was just saying it's the nicest I've had it for ages.'

'I think we'll easily be the most glamorous troop of bad-ass rock 'n' roll muthafuckers at Big Fish's thing. What do you reckon, Smiffy?' said Jeff to their driver.

'I'd agree if I had any idea what the bloody hell you're on about, like,' said Smiffy, a fat man in his 20s with hair that had been washed at some point in his life, but quite when, was harder to say. He spoke in an accent born and bred in South Bank. 'Are youse lot all on summat? Pills 'n' that, like?'

'We're just high on life, Smiffy, that and your cheap air freshener,' said Jeff, wafting his long hair up and down like it was two big ears.

'Except those of us who are coked up to the eyeballs,' said Matty, throwing a peace sign at the driver.

'Eee, well, I never, you youngsters are very naughty,' said Julie, wagging a finger at them.

'If you've got any spare, I wouldn't mind a beak full of that, like,' said Smiffy, who looked an unlikely consumer of Class A narcotics.

'Hey, Smiffy man, I never had you down as a drug fiend,' said Jeff, who often got his cab home.

'I'm not a drug fiend. I've not got the money, have I? Everyone needs summat to get them through, don't they?'

'Call me old fashioned if you like but I prefer my taxi drivers not to be fucked up while going at 80 miles an hour down Newport Road,' said Jeff.

'Ah, you bloody puff,' said Smiffy, as he sped along, seemingly excited by his car being full of party goers.

Middlesbrough Ballroom was a grand Victorian building near to the station which must have been home to many society parties in the great industrial era.

'Come on, let's have a photo of us all,' said Jeff, as they got out. 'Take it for us, Smiffy.'

Jeff stood in the middle, his arms out wide over their shoulders, with Nick and Julie on one side of him and Matty and Emily on the other.

Smiffy took Jeff's phone. 'Say massive tits, then.'

'Massive tits!!' they yelled. The flash went off.

'Have a good night then, you lucky people,' said the cab driver.

They were greeted at the door by two, broad bouncers, one short, one tall. Nick showed them their tickets.

'I'm the Big Fish's brother,' said Jeff, to excuse his lack of ticket.

'Oh, yeah? Right,' said the tallest, cynically. He sounded East European.

'He is,' said Nick, 'he wouldn't lie about something like that.'

The shorter man held Jeff up with a hand on his chest.

'You four are good. Not this one.'

'This one? I am not A One!' said Jeff, with mock indignation.

'Owee, lads, he really is the BF's brother,' said Julie.

Jeff, ever keen to avoid confrontation, got out his phone and called the big comedian. 'No worries. These lads are just doing their job. I'll sort this out. You lot go in and I'll join you.' The ballroom was set up with two bars. The smell of hot fat and cooking meat was in the air. A stage had been set up at the far end under a huge chandelier. An equally huge photo of Stevie Salmon, the same one that was also on the invite, hung on one wall. It made it seem as though it was a celebration of a dictator.

'That's very distracting' said Nick. 'It's like he's looking down on us all.'

'Well, he does look down on us, doesn't he?' said Julie.

Matty and Emily went to the bar. Jeff came up.

'Ah, you got sorted, then?' said Nick.

'Yes indeed. BF came up and slapped the two bouncers down. "Don't you know who this is?" - all of that. But they were only doing their job. Couple of right hard buggers those two, eh? There are loads of them around. He seems to have employed a whole team of them to run this place and do security.'

Julie said 'They're East European lads, I think. Some right big sods amongst them.'

'Aye, they look bad ass, don't they? Ukrainians, according to El Fishio.' He looked across the room. 'He must have hired them from some gang master on the cheap, knowing my brother. Still at least old dead Elvis would have approved - they're not Russians.' He looked up at the giant poster. 'Bloody hell, it looks like some North Korean-style cult of personality rally in here. "Don't Cross The Tees". We're going to be hearing a lot of that in the coming months.'

A woman circulated with sheets of paper and little Biros.

'The Fish wants everyone to write something down that you want on his manifesto,' she said. 'Someone will be around with the ballot boxes later and he'll read some of them out.'

Julie took a sheet and wrote in neat capital letters, 'All penises to be removed and only handed back once the owner has proved themselves to be a decent bloke.'

'He'll like that,' said Jeff. 'Bet he reads it out. This'll be his big theme for the tour. The Big Fish Manifesto.'

After an hour or so, the place was full of about 200 people. Big Fish took to the stage. He looked odd shorn of his beard; like a big baby, in some ways. He held out his arms as though he was Jesus in front of his disciples.

'Lovely Teessiders. Can I have your attention, please. I won't keep you long. We'll soon be serving the parmos, and I know that's why you're all here, but first I'd like to pay tribute to a man some of you will have seen working with me. Teesside's best Elvis, Jim George, died in a car crash two days ago. He was a funny bloke and he did a helluva Elvis tribute act. Can we just have a minute's applause, please?'

Big Fish led the appreciation.

'That was surprisingly humane,' said Nick to Jeff, who nodded as the clapping rippled around the hall.

'I think he might have been a bit of a mate of his. Or an acolyte, anyway. The BF sees little difference between those two things,' said Jeff.

After an hour of eating and drinking, Big Fish previewed 20 minutes of his new 'Manifesto' material, reading out suggestions people had written and improvising jokes around them.

'Ah, we've got a good one here,' he said, as he scanned a piece of paper. 'It says, "all penises to be removed and only handed back once the owner has proved to be a decent bloke". Yeah, nice idea that, but that means it'll be women who keep them all and every woman I know has already got a dick at home. She's usually married to him. Am I right, ladies?' He did his wide eyes and mouth open look, a look that wasn't a million miles away from Jeff's way of expressing himself when he thought he'd made a good point. As always, he got a big cheer.

It was about as good a joke as he made. Somehow, it was always disappointing to be amongst people who thought he was hilarious. Then again, they were all drinking and eating for free because of the money his work generated.

After the BF had left the stage, Nick made his way to the toilets. They were, like everything the Victorians did, large and grand with ornate jade green and white tiles everywhere. There was a long line of urinals but with only one man voiding his bladder. But that was one too many. Nick went to find a cubicle but they were all occupied, presumably by men like him, all with paruresis. This was where it was awkward. You had to hang around and breathe in more stench.

Eventually a bloke emerged and Nick followed him in, only to be confronted by something approaching a dirty protest. He backed out. Beyond disgusting. Fortunately another cubicle became free and this one was clean. But he still couldn't piss. Now there were drunk blokes banging around the place and singing. That was too off-putting. He put both fingers in his ears and began to hum to himself. This was another technique he deployed to allow himself to do this most basic of acts in public. Eventually, after much pushing of his bladder, a thin dribble leaked out, thus uncorking the dam and allowing the rest to flow freely.

He emerged from the cubicle after nearly 10 minutes, sweating heavily with the tension and effort it had required. This simply had to stop. It was no way to live.

As he returned to the ballroom, Big Fish was talking to Jeff and Julie.

'Now then, Nick,' said the big comedian. 'Crackin' bogs in here, eh? Victorians knew how to build a shit house.'

As usual, the BF dominated the conversation. It was as though no-one else was allowed to say anything unless it was about him. His life was all about him, all of the time. A waitress came up with a tray of free glasses of Cava. She was wearing a short, tight, black-and-white polka-dot silk dress and had clearly been chosen, probably by the BF himself, for her role tonight on the basis that she had large firm breasts and legs that, as the old blues songs would have had it, 'just wouldn't quit'.

'Thanks, darlin',' he said, plucking a glass off her tray and then watching her go. 'Dear me. Lovely piece of sweet meat in the little black dress, eh, boys? No offence, Julie...' He held up an apologetic hand, as though that would have excused him her arched raised eyebrow and a disapproving stare. 'Right. I'll be off for a parmo. Catch youse later.'

Jeff turned to look at the waitress carrying drinks and then looked back at Nick and Julie. 'He missed the chance for a spotty dog joke...' Julie raised both eyebrows '...believe me, he would have if it had popped into his tiny mind.'

'The stupid thing is, he's technically a really good comedian. If only he'd use his power for good,' said Nick.

Emily came back with a bottle of Smirnoff Ice. 'Who are you talking about?'

'Big Fish,' said Julie.

Emily shuddered. 'Sorry, I just can't stand him. He's the opposite of everything I like in a human being.'

'He's a man. Are you saying you only like women, Emily?' said Julie, with a laugh. 'Is this your big lesbian confession? It might be a shock to Matty.'

Emily giggled, reached out and squeezed Julie on the backside. 'Only with you, baby. Oooh, they're playing Chic. Come on, let's dance.' She put her drink down and dragged Julie by the hand onto the dance floor.

Jeff raised his eyebrows at Nick, and Nick raised his eyebrows at Jeff as they took a seat at a table.

'I'm saying nowt...' said Jeff '...but can you *imagine*?'

'I could, but I'd better not or I might have a heart attack,' said Nick.

Julie just couldn't dance. She could move and move vigorously. She shook her arse and bounced up and down and thoroughly enjoyed herself, whooping and clapping, but if any of this happened on the beat, it was all purely coincidental. It was as though she couldn't actually hear the music. It seemed to pass through her ears and never once anchor her to its rhythm. It was quite a sight to behold.

'You know that bit in *Seinfeld* when Elaine dances badly? They must have seen Jules dancing. That's just what she's like,' said Jeff, sipping at a double vodka, watching her frug her way around the dance floor with Emily. 'I'm no John Travolta, but I look like a ballet dancer compared to her.'

Nick felt drunk. He couldn't help but laugh. 'And it's made to look even more offbeat by the fact that Emily is so in time. She's right on the 1 and the 3. Look at her go, man.'

'She's metronomic. I've noticed that in the shop. She doesn't have to try. Some people have perfect pitch, she's got perfect rhythm. No wonder young Matty is such a happy boy, wherever he's gone.'

Nick held up his finger and pointed at him. 'Ah. No. See, it doesn't affect the downstairs dancing.'

Jeff cast him a quizzical, wizardy look and flapped his hair up and down. 'Does it not? Tell me how so, oh wise man.'

'Ha ha...I don't know, man, but it doesn't. On top or underneath, makes no difference, when it comes to, what she likes to call, the mucky fucky, Jules could drum for Sex Zeppelin.'

'Sex Zeppelin? Ha! I dig it. See, looking at her there, moving around like a badly loaded spin dryer, had I not known her, I'd have assumed she was one of those lasses who'd push up whilst you're pulling out and then pull back when you're pushing, and do it to no particular rhythm and you'd keep slipping out and not get a good piston action going.' He held his hands up. 'I am aware that in saying that, I am making out I am some sort of shag monster, as opposed to a former fat man who didn't have sex with a human female for 20 years.'

Nick swilled his drink around in the glass. 'Yeah, you were almost monk-like, weren't you?'

'Not by choice, son. Anyway when you're huge, it isn't the most practical of things to be doing...I won't go into details.' He made a zipping gesture across his lips.

Nick patted at his old mate's arm and blinked slowly. 'Glad you lost all the weight and, y'know, everything. Argie and that, like. Everyone deserves some sex, at least occasionally. Sharing it with someone, even if it's a one-night stand, is one of the great joys of existence. At least in theory, anyway.'

Jeff gave a resigned shrug. 'You'll not find me arguing with you. I wouldn't mind a bit more.'

'Talking of arrhythmical women, did I ever tell you about that Irish lass I went out with at the Poly? You missed her off your list the other day. Can't even remember her name now. She was one of those off-beat shaggers. Two in, one out, three in, two out, it was impossible to keep it in her. It was very off-putting. I make absolutely no claims to be especially wonderful but I *can* keep a decent rhythm if needed. You can rely on me to go in and out for a few minutes, without so much as a brief wonky time signature or free-form jazz interlude.'

Jeff squinted in recollection.

'I remember her. Hold on, her name will come to me. Yes, she was called Marie. A nice pink-faced girl. Liked Adam and the Ants, so it was never destined to last.'

'Well recalled. You're good with facts.'

'It's the record shop brain. It needs to have good name and title recall.'

'She *was* very pink - had those almost invisible pale pink nipples that, in the dim light of the bedroom, made you think she was entirely nipple free. But she was easily the worst at sex I ever encountered. It was like trying to have it off with a paper bag as it was blowing down the street. She was never in the same place for more than a couple of seconds.'

'Lasses get a free pass at bad sex. Bad sex is the cultural province of the male. Unfair that. Same with the size of genitalia. The under-endowed male has to put up with cultural ridicule whereas the lose-a-side-of-beef-in-it, baggy vagina woman gets off without any degree of disparagement.'

Nick laughed, enjoying himself. 'Oh, yeah...remember big Wendy?'

'Tall girl with curly permed hair, yes? Worked in the Poly library.'

Nick pointed at him. 'The very same. She had a huge vagina.'

'See, I can believe that. She had a big mouth...I mean - it was like a cave.'

'Maybe that's the sign. Big mouth, big fanny.' He sat tapping his foot to Chic's 'Le Freak'. 'Yeah, I got off with her at a party in Elswick flats...'

'....yes, you did and I was going out with Rachel Tilley. Aw, I loved Rach, at least until she went off with the brother of someone who played for Blyth Spartans. Cow.'

'...and we went back to her place. Honest, I couldn't even tell whether I was in or out. I swear it didn't touch the sides and, y'know...it usually did.'

'Maybe she went on to have a career in drug smuggling?!'

'She'd only need to fill it up once to be minted for life. Mind, the off-beat shagger *is* better than the lump of dead meat. You know her? The lass that just lies there and expects you to just do it *to* her and not *with* her. At least the off-beat shagger is giving it a go. The dead meat one is always the one who, when you ask what they like to do, will inevitably say, "oh, nothing special" or "just the usual" with little enthusiasm. Call me old fashioned but I liked my lovers to actively enjoy sex. Even in the sexually unenlightened 70s, I thought that should be the norm.'

Jeff made whooping noise. 'You're nothing but a crazy feminist with talk like that. Sex is to be endured, not enjoyed. That's what we were brought up to believe was women's role in life, wasn't it?'

Nick sank more vodka. 'Even going back to the dry humping, it was always done with maximum passion by the lasses I went out with. All of them really went for it, big style. Maybe I just picked the right Teesside girls.'

Jeff laughed loudly and threw his hair back. 'You always did have a good eye for the passionate girls, you.' He sank his vodka, pushed it to once side and started on another by clinking it against Nick's glass. 'This is a bloody good thrash this and you're on good form, sunshine. Hey, but if Jules's downstairs pleasure zone has got good rhythm, it must be her legs that don't. Look at them, she's wobbling around like her legs are made of jelly spanners.'

'That's probably the gin doing that. She's half cut, like me and you. She loves a good boogie, though, and admirably has absolutely no shame about looking like a robot dancing in metal boots on a magnet.'

Jeff bellowed out a laugh again and held up his hand to high-five him. 'Nice one, Poet Boy.'

'She's going to get me up to dance soon, I know it.'

'Oh, no. That's *never* any good. Why can't we dance?'

'I *can* dance. I just feel very self-conscious about it.'

'I might be able to, but I fear if I get my groove on, it may appear as though a bear has been released into the room and is being tasered. Anyway, a man who grew up on Uriah Heep and Rush should not be expected to be a disco dancer of any flavour. Me and dancing don't go together - like chocolate chip fudge and sprouts, you could put them together, but it would be a terrible waste of both and lead to unpleasant digestive distress.'

As the Chic song finished, Julie and Emily came over to their table and sat down.

'It's like a school disco this, all the lads sitting around watching the lasses dancing,' said Julie, sitting down with a groan.

'We have our cool street credibility to think of,' said Jeff.

'You looked like you were having a good time,' said Nick, happily.

'Emily was showing me up,' said Julie.

'Where's Matty gone?' said Emily, looking around.

'I think he's talking to someone near the bar. Tell him to get another couple of rounds in, we're on a roll here,' said Jeff. She went to find him.

'Eee, well, I'm knackered. I'm sweating like a fat lass in a pie shop. You don't realise how old you are until you've got to keep up with a 23 year old. Have you seen the way she dances? It's like she's a professional. Talk about being shown up. God, I remember being like her, I could go all night and the next day as well. Not any more. I'm already looking forward to my bed and it's only 11.30. Anyway, what were you two talking about? I saw youse both laughing.'

'Ah, we were talking about sex...' said Nick.

'Again?! You dirty get. Tell me more...' she said, sipping at some white wine.

'...and a woman called Wendy with a huge vagina.'

She took another drink and nodded. 'Oh, yeah, you told me about her.'

'It was like putting a cheese straw in a pint pot,' said Nick. Jeff laughed loudly and hi-fived him again.

'He's on top form tonight, Jules, isn't he? We've come up with a theory. See what you think of it. You know how it's said the length of your feet and hands tells you how big the bloke's trouser snake is?'

'...that's rubbish, by the way,' she interjected. 'How big are your feet, Jeffrey?'

'Size 12s, my dear,' said Jeff, in a posh voice. 'I always carry a shoehorn,' he added cryptically. 'Well, we reckon the woman's mouth indicates the vagina volume.'

She spluttered into her wine and laughed, then opened her mouth wide, revealing a lot of fillings and a wet, pink tongue.

'I've got quite a big mouth, me. Does that I mean I've...'

Nick held up his hands.

'...I'm taking the fifth on that, Jules. You're no Wendy, I'll say that, though.'

'I'm glad to hear it. I think. Does it matter much if you've got a glove compartment instead of a velvet glove?'

Jeff applauded. 'Quality expression. It's like sitting with Dorothy Parker, this.'

, 'As I was saying to Jeff, it's nice to touch the sides, if at all possible. It's just having it off with warm, damp air otherwise.'

She threw her head back in a deep rolling laugh. 'The big man is right, you've got quite a turn of phrase on you tonight. Have you not considered the fact that Wendy may have been normal-sized and you were the small one?' She raised an arched eyebrow.

'Obviously, I would have assumed that, had she been my first lover, but even my limited experience told me she was unusually dimensioned.'

Julie gestured for both of them to lean in, as she kept her voice down.

'If your theory is right, boys, Emily must be tiny down there because all her features are petite sized and she's got a tiny mouth.' She looked from one to the other, conspiratorially.

Nick nodded sagely. 'Oh, yeah, it'll be like the neck of a shampoo bottle.'

She yelped in laughter and slapped at him. 'My god, you'd make her eyes water, then.'

'...unlike with Wendy. There's nothing more dispiriting than the "are you in yet?" question,' said Nick.

Julie flinched. 'Ouch. That *is* a bit of a passion killer. I only had one bloke like that, back when I lived in London but I never actually said anything. You've got to make the best of it, whatever. It's not like there's anything he can do about what he's batting with. It's not his fault.'

Jeff tapped the table with his hands in approval.

'Very nice of you, that, Jules. Good manners to not insult a chap's genitals.'

'That's also why, with Wendy, I didn't actually say, "hang on, I think I've lost me watch in here",' said Nick.

She howled in laughter again.

Jeff got to up to go the toilet.

Now that they had a moment alone, Julie squeezed Nick's hand. 'This is good, isn't it?'

'Yeah, we've not had a piss-up for ages, have we? Do you feel like the shadows are lifting a bit?'

She looked away from him and out at the people dancing, thinking for a moment.

'I want to say yes, but I'm not sure they'll ever go away for good. I'll always be haunted by those four hours in the hospital. I'm just blotting them out at the moment...which is fine. What else can I do?'

He inspected her nails, squeezing her fingertips contemplatively. 'Life leaves its marks. That's the way things are. You're doing well, though, lass.'

'I am having a good time, like. I'm pissed, like. All the dirty talk is funny.'

'I thought you'd like it. It's one of your specialist areas of life, remember?' As soon as he's said it he wished he hadn't. The smile dropped off her face.

'It was, but not any more.' She said it morosely, but as soon as Jeff returned she faked a happy face. 'I intercepted Matty. He's met some musicians he knows, so I left him and Em to it. Doesn't do for the old man to hang around trying to pretend he's down with the kids.'

'You're a cool dude, Jeff, cooler than those thrusting young bucks,' said Julie.

'Oh, aye. I know that. But they don't.' He pointed across the room to his brother, who was talking to a woman in a gypsy skirt and long floral shirt.

'See her? She was with the BF when he was sorting out my Ukrainian problem. I think she might have been Elvis's partner slash girlfriend. He was saying he'd do a little tribute to him.'

Nick took a long look at her. 'I'm not being funny, but is there something a bit off about her?'

'I thought that,' said Jeff. 'Her face looks like a shaved squirrel and it's frozen in one expression.'

Julie squinted. 'Well, it must have been a terrible shock for her, him dying like that.'

'True. That wouldn't make you so shiny though, would it?' said Jeff. 'She actually looks varnished.'

'Maybe she's just hot,' said Julie.

'Aye, that or it's a terrible seizure brought on by talking to the big kipper, which can happen to even a partially sentient animal,' said Jeff, turning away. 'Anyway, cheers!'

As they took another drink, a fight broke out on the far side of the room. In classic style it involved a couple of swings and then a lot of pulling and pushing and noise.

'Shall we intervene, Mr Evans?' said Nick, as no-one seemed to be trying to stop the two men.

'No need, old boy. Look...' Jeff pointed at two of the Ukrainian bouncers who were already on their way over to the skirmish. They plucked them apart - a fat, beery 20 something and another older, solidly built older bloke - and hauled them away like they were nothing more than couple of carrier bags of shopping, dragging them across the floor by the scruff of the necks, and out of the back of the building.

'Bloody hell. They're hard buggers, them,' said Jeff.

'I know, wouldn't like to get into a fight with them,' said Nick, watching them go.

'Not without the aid of a tank,' added Jeff, draining his glass again. 'Cheers everyone!'

CHAPTER 5

'Hello, Brian,' said Jeff, as the old man opened his door.

'Ah, Jeff. Thanks for coming by...oh, Nick, you're here, too.'

He seemed disappointed at this. Nick gave a small wave. 'Hi, there. Long time, no see, Brian. You look well-tanned.' The old man was a deep chestnut colour, acquired from spending most of the last nine months in the Bahamas.

Brian Salmon gestured for them to come in. It was the first time Nick had been in there since the bomb had gone off last summer. It held a lot of ghosts and made him feel cold in his heart to be there again. The devastation the bomb had caused was still all so obvious. The room it had gone off in was being totally reconstructed. The deaths in that space still haunted him. The sound and vibration of that damn bomb going off was stained on his DNA now. He could still feel its profound resonance and it didn't take him much effort to re-see the bloody disembodied limbs, either.

Brian led them away from that side of the house to the wing that had been untouched by the explosion and into a living room that looked like a gentleman's club. Leather books lined one large wall, several leather armchairs were placed around a large fireplace. A green leather Chesterfield sofa was set in the centre of the room. A red leather-topped desk sat in front of one of the two large Georgian paned, sashed windows that started near the floor and ended near the ceiling.

'I like the tie, Brian,' said Jeff. 'Very...err...intense.' He gestured at his multi-coloured blue paisley silk tie.

'This? It's just an old plain blue thing,' said Brian, looking down at it dismissively. 'Can I get you coffee?' he said, rubbing his hands together a little nervously.

'That'd be good, thanks,' said Jeff.

Brian went out to make it.

'He loves his leather, Brian,' said Nick wandering around the room. 'This place seems very masculine. How long is it since his wife died?'

Jeff went and stood at the window, looked out and then turned around. 'About nine years, I think. These old Georgian houses are nice, but a bit imposing. Hard to feel cosy in a room like this, with such tall ceilings and massive walls.'

'Yeah, you're right. Not sure I'd like it, really. Jules loves a bit of Georgian, but you only need so much space, and after that, it's all superfluous. A man like Brian could live in a two-room flat very nicely.

The fact he owns a house with...how many rooms is this?'

'Twelve, I think, maybe more.'

'...a 12-room house for one man, is...I don't know...I think it's wrong when there are people homeless or living in squalor. I'm not sure anyone has the right to such overconsumption.'

Jeff held up his hands. 'Woah there, Communist Boy. We're not going down an "all property is theft" trip are we?'

'No, but you know what I mean. The idea that one man can have so much should be challenged on a moral basis as well as an economic one and not just lauded as, basically, the thing we should all be striving to achieve. I hate the way wealth is so respected. Gets right on my wick. Wealthy people are not better people than the rest of us. The rich need the poor to be poor in order to be rich; we all forget that, but the rich don't.'

Jeff gave a little sneer. 'Maybe. Not sure that's how Brian sees it.'

'No, but why would he?'

Brian came back in with a tray on which were two cafetières and three white china mugs.

'I hope you don't mind me bringing Nick over with me to talk about Argie. We've been best mates for 35 years, so I really trust him, y'know...god knows why, I mean look at him, he's little more than a poorly shaved gibbon.'

Nick made a dopey expression. Brian smiled. He looked tired, though. Nick imagined how tired he'd have been if he had no money and still had to work to make his mortgage or rent. The rich could afford to be weak. God help you if you were poor and didn't have the stomach for the fight.

'Of course. It's always nice to see you, Nick, and one must take the advice of one's nearest and dearest. As I said on the phone earlier, there is something I'd like to talk to you about, as well as little Argie. A delicate matter, actually. Perhaps Nick might be able to help with it, too.'

Nick put his thumb up, wondering what that could be and what on earth 'a delicate matter' was. It sounded vaguely salacious. Hopefully, anyway.

Jeff leaned forward and put his hands together. 'Well, first things first, Brian. I've had a good think about things. I'm quite keen for Argie to grow up as a normal lad. You've been very generous with your financial offer, but I just can't accept a trust fund for him. Sorry.'

This clearly surprised the old man. His grey eyebrows shot high up onto his head, very much as Jeff's did when surprised.

'Are you absolutely sure? It's a hard world, an uncertain world.'

Jeff nodded. 'Yeah. It is those things but, as mad as it might sound, my shops do well and we'll be fine, financially. If, when he's a grown man, you and him want to sort out a financial arrangement then that'll be between the both of you and nothing to do with me, but right now, when he's my responsibility, I really can't accept your money or the offer of a share of the land.'

'Well, in 18 years' time, when he's an adult, I'll be nearly 90, Jeff, so it's not likely I'll be around to give him anything.'

Jeff was in full sensible mode. It was an impressive thing to see, especially as, for most of his adult life, he'd lived like a dissolute student.

'I can't tell you how to dispose of money and assets in your will. If you choose to leave him anything, I can't change that, nor would I want to. It's nothing to do with me how you organise that stuff. All I'm saying is I'd like to bring him up like any other regular kid, not as a rich kid and not as a kid who knows he'll never have to work for a living. I don't think any good would come from that. When he's older, he can work it all out for himself, but booking him in now for a life of wealth and privilege is just against...I don't know...it's against my values, Brian. I'm not having a go at you. I'm just telling you how I feel. Is that OK?'

He sat back and wiped the corners of his mouth. Nick felt like applauding. Jeff had rejected Brian's generosity very diplomatically, but by the look on Brian's face, the news had rather upset him. All he had was his wealth. It defined him and was all he had to give in the world.

Jeff went on. 'I want you involved in Argie's life, of course. I want him to know his granddad well. That doesn't change. We're not going to be strangers. That's more important than money, isn't it?'

'Well. I understand, of course. I was brought up to accept one's responsibilities in life and I naturally feel I must provide for my grandson. My only grandson, at that.'

Jeff nodded and cracked his knuckles one at a time, then picked up the coffee mug.

'Yeah, I totally get that. But where I'm from, "providing" means a tenner at Christmas or a new bike on his birthday. It doesn't mean making him a millionaire or a landowner. The way I see it, money doesn't make a happy man happier and it won't make a miserable man happy, either. As long as you've got enough to pay your bills and live somewhere safe, after that, does it really all make that much difference to the quality of life? With all due respect, Brian. I don't think it does.'

Nick's chest swelled with pride again at his old friend's words. They spoke to a greater truth about the nature of life and showed a deeper understanding that Jeff, more often than not, kept hidden under his bluffness and propensity to joke around.

Brian drank his coffee and rubbed his neck in contemplation, puffed his cheeks and blew out air.

'Well. I respect your choice, Jeff. Of course I do. So I won't press you any further. You've made your position clear and I appreciate straight talking, I always have. So we'll say no more about it. Needless to say, if you have a change of heart, my door is always open...well, my door is always open, regardless.' He glanced towards the actual door and looked awkward and unsure, which was not like Brian at all. His life of inherited money, property and land had given him the innate authority and confidence that almost all the rich, established upper middle class have by default in Britain, an authority which, in many, manifested itself as obnoxiousness or smugness, rising to arrogance, though not in Brian, or not much, at least. He was a decent man, a gentle man really, but like a lot of wealthy people, the money only gave him material freedom and sometimes, that's the least important freedom a person needs. Life has to be about a lot more than mere money. As Nick knew all too well, no matter how much money you do or don't have, you still have to live with yourself, in your own head. There's no escaping who you are, no matter your income.

'Err...well...as you're both here, I have another issue I need to discuss with you that's just come to light this morning. A very odd business.' Brian's face was a study in stress and contemplation.

'Fire away. We're all ears, aren't we, Nick? Well, ears, hair and a few other limbs.'

'Obviously, you are aware of the Blakeston racing stables?'

'Yes, of course,' said Jeff.

'Of course you are...well, our most successful horse is called The Tees...'

'....oh, err...right,' said Jeff. 'Have you heard of that one, Nick?'

'Not really. I don't follow horse racing. I don't get it, really. Not as a sport,' said Nick. It was the truth. He had never seen the attraction.

'He was a fabulous horse. Swift as lightning. Retired last season.'

'Is lightning swift?' asked Nick, apropos of nothing and then felt embarrassed that he'd voiced it.

'The main characteristic of lightning is speed, I suppose,' said Jeff, always keen to go off on a tangent when it came to words or expressions. 'That and the electricity and general fry-your-head properties of it. Swift sounds too slow for lightening...sorry, Bri...go on.'

'The point is, he was a great horse. As I say, he's retired now and he's being put out to stud.'

'Much like myself,' said Jeff, pulling a face, then putting the palms of hands up in apology for the interruption. Nick grinned a little.

'Actually, this will be easier if I show you what has happened. Follow me.'

Brian got up a little unsteadily and marched out of the room. Like two schoolboys, they followed on behind, walking out of the study, turning right and walking down a long corridor, past a substantial kitchen and then right again. Brian took out a key from the pocket of his pinkish red trousers and unlocked a large Georgian door. Jeff raised a quizzical eyebrow at Nick.

They were led into a room, smaller than the study, but nonetheless a large room by normal standards. It also had the same two big, sashed, Georgian paned windows as the study, with thick, heavy green velvet-type curtains, tied back on each side. The carpet was also a dark green. On the walls hung lots of paintings of jockeys on horses. An especially large painting dominated one wall. It was of a race to the tape, crowds of racegoers throwing hats into the air as the horses and jockeys strained to win. The place exuded old-school money and a culture which was entirely alien to Nick and yet totally familiar at the same time. This was the Establishment and this was what they did when at play and this was where they did it.

A large, old, oak, glass-fronted cabinet was filled with various silver trophies of all shapes and sizes from cups to plates and little bronze statuettes.

'So this is your stables' trophy room, is it, Brian?' said Nick, hands on hips, looking around the room. He'd always thought silver trophies were ugly things right up to and including the jug-eared FA Cup and Champions League trophies. Big stupid things with absolutely no style or class about them. Who had decided trophies were even a thing? Why not anything else? A silver hat or a pair of boots, why a useless pot?

As he browsed the ones in the cabinet he noticed there was a central space where, quite clearly, one was missing. A small, dust-free circle revealed where it had stood.

'Have you had one nicked then, Brian?' he said, pointing to the space and laughing a little. Brian didn't laugh.

'Yes.'

'Eh?' Nick looked up at him, puzzled.

'You've not, have you?' said Jeff.

Brian wasn't joking. He nodded. 'Yes, we have. At some point this morning, the Sir Walter Francis Cup disappeared. Someone has walked off with it.' For a tanned man, somehow, he looked pale on saying this. 'It is very upsetting.'

Nick stood back and looked around the room. Everything was in its place. It wasn't just tidy, it was neat and precise, as though laid out for visitors, the way a stately home was. In fact, so pristine and precise was everything, it simply did not look lived in, probably because the reality was, it was not lived in. Not in the way regular people live in their homes. It certainly had not obviously been subjected to a typical burglary. No drawers were pulled out and nothing at all was out of place.

'Is that why you had the door locked?' asked Nick.

'What?' said Brian, looking at him with narrowed eyes.

'Had you locked the door after you discovered it had gone?'

'This room is always kept locked - for obvious reasons. There are a lot of silver trophies in here.'

'Who has a key?'

'Just me and Malcolm.'

'Who's Malcolm?'

'My housekeeper. But he's away just now.'

Of course he had a housekeeper. The only surprise was that it wasn't some large-bosomed, bustling woman in a mop cap and apron, but instead, a man. Was he really a housekeeper or actually, a butler, a gentleman's gentleman? Nick couldn't help but feel riled by this, somehow.

'Is it valuable?' said Jeff, peering at the place where the small trophy had stood.

'Yes, it's valuable.'

'How valuable?' said Nick, who suspected Brian's grasp of what was valuable and what wasn't was somewhat tenuous.

Without hesitation Brian said, 'Well, err...I don't look at any of them that closely but it's a small plain silver cup. Its value is in its history. The Sir Walter Francis is one of flat racing's oldest cups. After The Tees won it in 2009 for the fifth consecutive time, it was retired in his honour. It's clearly been stolen to order. A burglar would have taken all the others too, but no, they've walked off with the most prestigious.'

'What does it look like?' said Jeff. 'And how big is it?'

'Like I say, it's small. Little bigger than the palm of my hand.'

'Easy to walk off with, then?' said Nick.

'It would fit in a pocket,' said Brian.

'And it's just plain silver?' said Jeff.

Nick twirled a strand of hair around his finger and looked at Brian. He was frowning heavily. 'Yes, just a small plain cup, I think.'

He walked to the cabinet and looked in it, as though to confirm it was still missing.

'You *think*?' said Jeff. 'Aren't you sure?'

Brian returned to face them. 'Yes, yes, it was a small plain cup. I was looking at it only the other day because, as I say, you don't inspect these things very often.'

If it was famous then it couldn't be sold, so it'd be melted down at scrap value, but it was small so wouldn't get a thief much money. Why not choose one of the bigger silver trophies, then? Why not take all of them? He had to be right. It was stolen for what it was, not for the money it was worth.

'Have you called the police?' said Jeff, looking at one window and then the other.

'No.' He shook his head with certainty. 'And I don't want anyone in authority to know about this.'

Jeff spread out his arms wide.

'Eh? Why not, Brian? If it's been stolen...they could come in and dust for prints and interview all the workers that are here. I mean, the other wing of the house is full of builders and such. Anyone could have taken it.'

'I already know who has done this,' said Brian, twitching his pale lips and looking out of the window and across the fields.

Nick and Jeff stared at him. The old fella was sweating a little on his grey hairline in the sunny, warm room.

'Err...sorry, Brian, I don't get you. You *know* who's stolen it?' said Jeff. 'How do you know?'

The old man paced around the room, hands in pockets.

'It's complicated. But I need your help to get it back, Jeff.' He turned around. 'And you too, Nick. I need some proof of who has taken it.'

'You want us to get proof of who took it, so you can get the cup back?' said Nick.

'Yes. I'll pay you, of course.'

That annoyed Nick, immediately. He held up a hand.

'Hold on, hold on. Life is *not* all about money. If I do help you, I'll help you for free because out there in the real world, that's what decent people do.' He pointed into the distance, back towards Stockton. 'We don't need paying to help people. Get me?'

75

Brian held both hands up to his face, palms outwards, in a defensive gesture.

'Sorry. Yes. Yes, of course. I meant no insult.'

'Surely you'd be better off getting the police in, since you say you know who took it,' said Jeff, casting a disapproving glance at Nick's aggressive tone.

'There would be other implications if I did that. Trust me.' He went quiet.

Nick was still pissed off and it must have showed because Jeff gave him another very stern look. Nick turned away in annoyance. He couldn't relate to Brian at all. Maybe he should have been able to, but he couldn't. It was all one-sided, anyway. All you did by respecting the wealthy elite was to enshrine them in their position. A bit of disrespect was needed if the status quo was to ever be challenged.

'You go out to the car, Nick. I'll have chat with the boss here,' said Jeff, realising the situation needed diffusing.

Nick nodded and with a wave left the room. Jeff closed the door behind him.

He stood in the corridor, his pulse racing a little, and looked around. Instead of going back outside, he took a right and tried the next door. It was locked. The passageway took a left; he followed it around and, looking out of a small window, realised he was heading eastwards towards the stable block. There was a small door on his right. He pulled at it: a cupboard. In it was a vacuum and a few pots of paint and other decorating odds and ends. Closing it, he heard voices outside. Glancing out of the small window he saw the unmistakable large form of Steve 'Big Fish' Salmon. He was talking to a small bloke, presumably a jockey, as they passed the window. There was a slam of a door somewhere. Bugger. He really didn't want to run into the BF here, let alone try to explain why he and Jeff had turned up. The inheritance thing was off limits and maybe the cup theft, too. Running away or hiding seemed the easiest thing to do.

Their voices got nearer as they came in the back door and began to walk through the house, perhaps headed for the kitchen. Nick pulled open the cupboard door again and stepped inside, closing it behind him.

It smelled of polish and dust and was pitch black. Womb-like, it immediately put Nick in mind of the cupboard under the stairs in his parents' house in Palm Grove where he'd hidden as a small boy when he was upset. That confined dark space had always felt comforting and was both physically and mentally a place to hide away from the hurt the world inflicted. As he stood in the small space, a wave of tingle washed him from head to foot with pleasure. The still, lightless space felt secure and also made him want to move his bowels. That had always been the case when he was a kid, too. It also happened when he was in a library, or in any quiet space at all. It must have been the inner relaxation the peace brought. He smiled to himself, almost laughing. He was *so* messed up.

Just deep enough and tall enough to accommodate him, he stood stock still as footsteps approached, the shudder of Big Fish's huge frame making the floor vibrate. Nearer, nearer, nearer. And then...they stopped. Right outside the door.

BF's voice was its usual boom. 'Bollocks to him, Mickey. He's nicked it, no matter what he says.'

A small, reedy voice replied, 'I know he has. He's been after it for ages. And he's always on about me pulling the whip. I said, why would we pull the whip in any race? It's just ludicrous. I don't know why he's saying it. Macca is just furious because I've won more races than him.'

'He's a shit stirrer who is just trying to make trouble. Just ignore him, Mick. It doesn't matter. It's just an auld trophy, isn't it?'

'I bloody won that fair and square. I'm not having him nicking it. I just wanted you to know what he was saying'.'

They walked on and out of earshot just as Nick's phone vibrated. It was a text from Julie. He took it from his pocket and flicked the screen.

'Martha has just offered me a job! A paid job! Women's Support Worker. Starting next week. They think I'm ace!'

His heart surged and he gripped his fist. Get in! God knows, she deserved some good news and she'd volunteered there for well over a year for zero money, so had paid her dues. This might be the lift she needed to bring her back to herself. He texted back.

'You are brilliant. Now you can afford to buy more expensive underwear!'

He laughed to himself. What a bloody situation to get that news in. He looked up, nodded and said some words in his head, as a kind of prayer to God or maybe it was a psychic thank-you note to the universe, which, maybe, was the same thing. It would be a welcome bit of financial velvet between their vertebrae.

Still standing in the dark, he looked up the Sir Walter Francis Cup on Google.

The Sir Walter Francis Cup was named after the 4th Earl of South Durham. The race is one of the oldest flat races in England, dating back to 1885. The trophy was made by Carl Fabergé in 1886 and was presented to Walter Francis during his stint as Anglo-Ukranian Ambassador in the Disraeli government. It was widely regarded as one of Carl Fabergé's finest pieces of work. It is crafted from fine silver in an early Art Nouveau style that later became Fabergé's signature.

Held at Teesside Park racecourse from 1880 to 1980, it was moved to Redcar racecourse in 1981 and is raced in the first week of May every year. The original trophy was controversially retired in 2009 in honour of Blakeston Estate-trained horse The Tees, who won the trophy five years consecutively, a feat unequalled in flat racing.

Fabergé. Bloody hell. Anything Fabergé cost a fortune. Brian had undersold it by saying it was just plain. By the sound of it, it was a proper work of art. So why the hell wouldn't you report that theft to the police when this was obviously an important and valuable piece? The small photo alongside the entry showed a lovely, delicate, early Art Nouveau thing, no bigger than a large hand. It was a piece so distinctive that you could never sell it, except to a private collector who asked no questions.

Curious. Brian was surely lying about the nature of the trophy and Nick didn't like people asking for his help whilst simultaneously lying to him. Something odd was going on. Rich people's games? Yeah, maybe.

An ear to the door told him all was clear, so he emerged from his hiding place and went the way Big Fish and the jockey had come from, hopefully to avoid meeting them. Around the next corner was a small utility room, with a line up of boots and shoes. A big white wooden door led out to the stable courtyard. As Nick pulled it open and walked out, a very familiar tall, broad man came striding across the yard holding two planks of 4 by 2, wearing a tool belt and overalls.

'Alright, Conrad, what are you doing here?' said Nick.

'Bloody hell. I might ask you the same thing, kidda,' said the big Geordie. Everything about Conrad was big. Feet, hands nose, chin, ear lobes. He was built to last.

'Jeff's talking to his dad in there. Are you working here?'

'No, bonnie lad, I just never leave the house without me two planks, do I? What does it bloody look like, eh?' He rasped a smoker's cough and gave him a look which said, "are you daft or what?" 'The lads doing the building job just got us in as a chippy, didn't they? Best in the business, me, like, and I've not had any regular work since last year's bit of trouble.'

'There must be a lot to do in there.'

'Aye, there is. Basic structure of that wing of the house is knackered after that bomb. But you know what they say, one man's piss is another man's gravy.'

'Do they say that?'

'Aye, 'course they do.'

'I never heard anyone ever say that.' Nick grinned at him. Con grinned back.

'Why, you're not listening hard enough then, bonnie lad. Hey, how's your Jules?'

'She's good, ta.'

'Poor lassie. Terrible thing what happened to her. Mind, between you and me, I was glad I was down the club at the time. I'm a bit squeamish when it comes to women's things in that region. I'll happily hit a six-foot bricky in the face with a chair but a spot of blood from anywhere below the waist on a lass and my god I'm outta there, me!!' He rasped another laugh with a voice that was three parts asthma, two parts brick dust and one part broken ashtray in the face. Nick had often thought if Brian Johnson wanted to retire from ACDC, Con could have walked right into his shoes. Same accent, same sort of voice.

'Hey, Con. Have you been in Brian's trophy room?'

'What, Brian Salmon, who owns this place?'

'Aye.'

'What trophy room is that, like?'

'It's a room in the house where all the trophies the stables have won are kept.'

'That does sound like a trophy room, aye.' Con did sarcasm very well. 'Nah, never seen it, like. I know nowt about the nags, me. All I know is they run around in a circle for a bit and then the brown one wins. Boring load of shite for poshies and pricks, if you ask me. Gambling is for mugs. Anyway, I've gotta get on...come around the house soon, Jackie'd like to see Julie. She doesn't like to make a fuss - y'knaw what she's like, kidda - but she worries about her bairn, like any mother does.'

'OK, I'll tell her,' said Nick, 'Have you heard this rumour about some cup being stolen from the trophy room here?'

The big man raised an eyebrow. 'Someone had it away with one of his silver pots, have they? No, bonnie lad, I've heard nowt. When did this happen, like?'

Nick shrugged. 'This morning, I think.'

'I bloody hope it wasn't one of the lads. The whole team will likely get laid off, if it is.'

'Best keep it quiet then, eh.'

The big Geordie put his thumb up.

Nick walked off across the yard and as he came alongside the trophy room windows, he stopped and took a look in. The windows, which went nearly to the ground, were the obvious way anyone would gain access. They were Georgian sashes, all you had to do was slip a blade in the space between each sash and flip the metal slider that held the window locked and you were in. He went on tip toes and checked that it was locked. It wasn't and there was a scrape of paint recently removed from the edge of the sash. A curl of white where a knife had been slid in and caught the angle of the woodwork. There was your entry point. That's how they got in. You can lock as many doors as you want but an almost floor-length window like this was an absolute gift when it didn't have a window lock on. Anyone could have been in and out of here in less than a minute; the trophy cabinet hadn't even been locked.

It was all pea gravel in front of the window, so there was no way anyone could even leave a footprint in that stuff. They'd just walked up here, probably dressed as a workman and could have been in and out without anyone seeing.

Jeff was sitting on the BMW as he got around to the front.

'Where've you been?'

'I just met Con.'

'Jackie's Con?'

'The same. He's working as a joiner here. Subcontractor, like.'

Jeff nodded and folded his arms across his checked shirt, staring at the ground.

'Look Nick, you were well out of order in there. Right? You were a proper arsey get. That was the wrong time to get holier than thou about being paid. I mean, he's still a bloke, for all the money and that...and he was upset at being robbed. Him being rich doesn't change that, does it?'

Nick felt decidedly unrepentant.

He cleared his throat and bit his bottom lip. He felt like arguing the point but knew Jeff wouldn't have said anything at all unless he was properly pissed off at him. That didn't happen often, so, in deference to his old mate, he shut up.

'OK. Sorry, man. Do you want me to go in and apologise?'

Jeff shook his head.

'No need to do that. I excused you on the grounds of being upset after your...y'know...loss.'

'OK, but before you get too far up on your high horse, there's something you should know. Brian lied to us in there about that trophy.' Nick pointed towards the house.

'Eh? What? Are you saying it wasn't stolen?'

'Oh, I think it was stolen. In fact, I know it was. Someone flipped the window catch. You can see where they did it. But it wasn't a tin pot. It was a Carl Fabergé silver Art Nouveau patterned cup. Fabergé is usually worth a fortune.'

He took out his phone and showed him the Wikipedia entry with its photo.

'I've never even heard of this thing,' said Jeff, stroking his beard in contemplation. 'And even given my total lack of interest in the nags, if it was super-valuable, I probably would have. So it can't be that big a deal.'

'Neither had I, but then I've not heard of anything to do with racing. It's all a closed world to me. There's probably loads of cups and trophies dished out. Unless you're in the game, or are big into betting, you've no reason to know. In fact, I wouldn't mind betting Brian doesn't know what half of them in there are even for. He seemed a bit vague about it, at one point, and I'd never even heard of his record-beating horse...well, I probably had, but it's just not stuck in my head. It's not important to the non-gambling, non-horsey world.'

'But why would he lie about the cup? I don't get it. Brian's not one for lying. He's got no reason to lie. Even if the cup isn't valuable, it's still been stolen.'

'Well, he damn well knows it's not a plain silver cup. Unless he's going senile, he's lied to us. Maybe he's embarrassed that it's so valuable and he left it so vulnerable. Maybe he doesn't want to make out it's as important as it really is. But that doesn't make much sense because it's all online, isn't it? There's this picture of it. It was only a matter of time before we found out it was a Fabergé. He must've taken us for fools. He wanted us to help find a cup but lied to us about what it was like. That's weird. Makes no sense at all.'

Jeff understandably wanted to defend his dad, but there was something Nick found very uncomfortable about Brian. He was nice enough in one way, but the money and everything that went with it really got in the way for Nick. Maybe there was a large chip on his own shoulder...maybe it bloody well should be a large chip. Brian was just a man. No more special than any other. No more worthwhile. A man who had inherited land and property and had sucked on the tit of public EU farming subsides, ridden the wave of ever-rising land prices and grown richer and richer and still they were supposed to respectful, like he was some self-made man, who had pulled himself up by his bootstraps. It just didn't feel right. For all that he was apparently a nice-enough man, he embodied the grotesque inequalities at the heart of the modern world.

Nick started up the BMW. 'So why was it stolen and who by?'

He drove off down the long gravel drive and back towards Norton.

Jeff straightened out his long beard. 'A place based up in Middleton called Regency Stables. That's why he doesn't want to report it.'

That rang a bell with Nick. 'I don't get you. Why does he not want to tell the cops because of that?'

Jeff tugged on his beard and then looked out of the window. 'Because then the whole thing will go public.'

'What *thing?* And why does it matter?'

'There's a big dispute between the Regency Stables and the Blakeston Stables.'

Nick drove down Junction Road. Roadworks meant they had to sit at some lights.

'What dispute?'

'Regency have accused Blakeston of rigging races. I've not heard of it before. But you know what the racing world is like, it's an alternative society, populated by tiny people, red-faced men and women with large yellow teeth. They don't mix with the real people, they're too busy shooting things and doing nude badger watching...or whatever else the term "countryside pursuits" means.'

'Ha...yeah...the nights are long and lonely up in Teesdale, the only way to survive it is by encouraging wild life to pleasure you,' said Nick, with a glance at Jeff.

Jeff laughed his booming laugh. It seemed to break the simmering mood between them. 'And because they're all super-posh people, they don't want the hoi polloi seeing them doing their dirty washing in public. Bad form, innit? Also, it'd bring both stables a bad reputation and maybe put off rich Arabs from using them for their horses.'

'Is that how it works? I know nothing about racing, apart from the fact that they go round and round and then the brown one wins.' Well, it was good line from Con, one worth passing off as your own wit.

'Oh, man, it's a whole thing in itself and it's sort of sealed off from the regular world, like you said. These Arab dudes pay fortunes to have their precious nags given the full bed and board and then the stables get a cut of the winnings and such. I mean, it's a huge business.'

'So that horse, The Tees - is he foreign owned?'

'No. That was...whatever the term is...hand reared from birth by the Blakeston Stables. So they coined it big off his winnings. He was the fruit of the loins of two winners in their own right, so it's all genetics.'

'Ha. So even in the world of racing, the money keeps the money. Those with the right breeding have a better chance of succeeding. Sounds familiar.'

'Aye, I suppose so. Trust you to put a left-wing slant on horse sex. What's up with you these days? All this bloody socialism and that...I expect it from Jules because she works with lefty PC lesbians...'

'...Jeff, man...she doesn't. Or at least, you don't know that. That's just an easy cliché. They're good, mostly working-class people, who do a bloody hard and much-needed job for sod-all money. They're not walking stereotypes.'

'I don't doubt it, but there are no right wingers in social services and abused women organisations. That's the way of the world.'

'It's dangerous to make such assumptions, even if, in my book, one of the basic criteria to be called right wing is a lack of human empathy and understanding.'

'See, there you go again. I'll tell you something, right? In the 60s and 70s in this country, the left wing unions were stuffed full of racist bigots. The dockers went out on strike so they didn't have to work with black people. Lack of humanity is not the preserve of the right wing. Your trouble is you're always too keen to go off on a romantic notion about this sort of thing. Power to the people and all that, giving it the full Citizen Smith, even though you bloody hate most people. You sit in the Royal Oak and take the piss out of every baggy-arsed, grey trackie-bottomed loser, no-mark who comes in for a pint of strong cider. You're no more a man of the people than Brian is, not really. You're an arty, fucked-up weirdo with a huge record collection which you obsess about, you read books of poetry and write for a living. The oppressed masses of the working class that you're so keen to be a part of would, by and large, look at you like you were an exotic creature and certainly not one of their own. Look at how Jackie Wells treats you. She thinks you're a bit of a ponce just for being able to write. God knows what she'd think if you told her about all those volumes of Gary Snyder poems you've got on your shelves. There's nowt wrong with that, as far as I'm concerned, but give the man of the people bollocks a rest, eh, 'cos it's not right coming out of your gob.'

The lights changed and Nick pulled away. 'Have you finished having a pop at me?'

'For the time being. I thought it was a quality speech though meself. Thought I'd pretty much nailed you with it, even if I do say so myself.'

'It was a decent soliloquy, but I already know you're right. That is what I'm like. But that's not the point. I'm not trying to make out I'm a regular bloke. I know I'm not. But as I get older, I feel like I'm changing. I can't tolerate inequality like I used to. Maybe it's how the pregnancy has affected me...I started to see beyond myself and what might make a better world. All those years we lived for 5.30pm and the first drink of the day...'

'...first drink? 5.30? *Fourth* drink, I think you mean.'

'Well, exactly. Don't you think about the world you want the Argmeister to grow up into? That's what is at the heart of all this for me. I'm sick of things getting more and more unequal and unfair.'

'Yeah, sort of. But I'm not you. I don't worry about things. I never have. I'm a doer, not a thinker. And if I'm not doin', I'm not endlessly thinking about stuff the way you do. Get on, live life, see what happens. That's me.'

'Yeah, I get that, but don't you think that how society is organised gears all of that? That's where politics comes in and I'm sick of having to suck on the corporate dick and having everything geared around profit maximisation. We've dehumanised society and turned everyone into units of profit generation. It's wrong and it makes people unhappy.'

Jeff shook his head and drummed out a beat on his lap.

'Pfft, I have no idea what any of that means. It's all beyond me. All I know is, you'll never make everyone happy and you'll never get anywhere trying to run things by committee. There'll always be bosses and workers. You need innovators and thrusting types like me to do things like setting up a rock club to employ all the thick people to work in. I'm not saying they're bad people because they can't do anything other than work in a bar, someone has got to do it. I totally respect their graft. But I'm not exploiting them if I employ them. Am I? Not really. If they'd got a good degree they'd have a chance at getting a good job. They didn't. So they'll work in my club. It's not a perfect system, but it's the only way that works, most of the time. This country is a bloody good place to live compared to a lot of places. I know the posh twats get on our wick, but at least we're not all trying to ethnically cleanse each other or whatever...you know?'

Nick sighed. He knew they were some way apart on this and he wasn't even sure what he was trying to say, anyway. He was just pushing ideas around, trying to sort the idealistic wheat from the pragmatic chaff. All he knew was that things felt like they were going wrong and that the values of caring, sharing and community were getting destroyed by the focus on making money and exploiting every last penny of profit...and for what? Being happy was only about money to a small degree - after that, it's all about the world you live in and the people you live with.

'So why have Regency Stables stolen the Sir Horsey Henry Cup then? Just to piss Brian off? They can't sell it unless it's to a dodgy collector.'

'Because they consider he won it unfairly and twice cheated their horse out of wins. It's a sort of punishment. Or, at least, that's Brian's theory.'

'Petty revenge? Seems unlikely.'

'Aye, it does, but horsey horsey is a mad world. It's a soap opera. You and me both know what jockeys are like, for a start.'

'Piss heads of the first water. Do you remember when we did that tour of East Anglian car boots and ended up in Newmarket?'

Jeff pointed at him and wagged a finger. 'I was going to mention that. Lots of very tiny aggressive rat-arsed people. All the pubs had those "no jockeys allowed" signs up. Fierce bunch. I suppose you don't need big bouncers on the door, though. A fat 13 year old could out-muscle a jockey. Throw them away like a small bag of potatoes. Almost all of them were Irish, as well - even the ones who aren't actually Irish, are really.'

'So I take it that Brian denies fixing the races.'

'Totally.'

'Explain how he's supposed to have fixed them?'

'You pull the whip on your best horse for a few races beforehand. In other words, you don't drive it to the max.' Jeff mimed galloping on a horse and made the appropriate clopping noises with his tongue. 'So you get the price on your gee-gee up and make everyone think it's off form or no good. Then you unleash it on full power, in the race you want to win.'

'Pull the whip? That's the second time I've heard that expression in the last hour. In fact, I was going to say earlier, I heard something about this stolen cup in the house.' He told Jeff about overhearing his brother whilst hiding from them, not thinking for a minute that it might sound a bit odd. It was a typical oversight for Nick, who for a lot of his life had made a bit of a specialty of saying things without realising they'd be regarded as strange.

Jeff looked at him with an expression of amused amazement. 'You were hiding in a cupboard?! Hiding. In. A. Cupboard?!' He broke into a woody cackle and punched him on the top of the arm. 'What are you like? You don't even know why it's bonkers, do you?' He looked askance at Nick.

Nick didn't, but wasn't about to say so. 'Laugh all you want. I would take even more evasive action than that to avoid speaking to the Giant Kipper.'

'You're proper weird, you are. Ha ha. You're getting worse, I swear. You'll be going into the Royal Oak and setting up screens to hide behind so you don't have to speak to Jock behind the bar.'

'Don't you ever cross over the street or duck into a doorway, so you don't have to speak to someone?'

Jeff shook his head in an exaggerated manner. 'No. Earth to Nick. Normal people don't do that.'

'Well normal people are weird. There's nothing wrong with that, man. It's good manners to avoid an awkward meeting. Better for everyone. I'm doing it for the greater good.'

'I might have known it would be driven by your newly heightened sense of social justice and altruism. Anyway, I suppose being accused of pulling the whip is one of the worst things you can accuse a jockey of. Questions their integrity, y'see. But it sounds to me like this Macca bloke is the one who's stolen the cup.'

'OK, so Brian thinks his big rivals have stolen the Sir Scrotum Cup...what is he going to do about it, if he isn't getting the law involved?'

Nick drove into their car parking space behind the Georgian Green Dragon Yard. Jeff had gone a bit quiet. Nick turned to him. 'What?'

'Well, I sort of promised we'd, well, sort of get it back for him or get proof of who stole it.'

'You did what? Why did you say that?!'

'Well...I felt like I had to help him.'

'Why did you say "*we'd* get it back" then? I thought we were just supposed to find evidence of who's stolen it?'

'It was just a slip of the tongue.'

'Yer bollocks it was.'

They got out.

Nick looked out over the Tees below, the Millennium Bridge spanning it; the bridge he'd tried to jump from only a few months earlier. The bridge Jeff had plucked him from to save his life. It was all too clear sometimes. The upset, the fear, the weariness with life. He didn't feel like that now, but he could recall all too easily what it was like. The bridge brought it all back to him every time he saw it.

He owed his life to Jeff and Jeff never even mentioned it. Not once.

'Alright, man. I'll ride shotgun for you. We'll see what we can do.' They hi-fived.

'Good lad.'

'And I have some big news,' said Nick, locking the car.

'Ah. Is it big news? Really? That's setting it up on a pedestal.'

'Ha ha. Jules has just been given a job at the TWC. Full-time, paid work as a Support Worker. Happy days, eh. We'll feel like we've won the lottery when she gets paid.'

Jeff whooped and picked Nick up off the ground. 'Get in! Glamorous and Crazy Socialists 1, Big Bad Capitalist World 0.'

'The good thing about being skint is, that when you get a bit of money, it feels like a shit load. Like when you support a football club that never wins, when you do, it feels brilliant, whereas the club that only loses four games a year, they take winning for granted. It's the same with money. Brian will never feel how brilliant it is to have a little extra money. He can't ever feel that and probably couldn't understand what it means. In such ways are small wins actually big wins.'

Jeff pointed at him. 'Now, that I do understand. And you're right. And you didn't even mention redistribution of wealth or lesbian social workers - let's keep it that way!' Jeff grinned at him and strode off towards the shop. Nick called after him.

'Jeff! How do we go about finding proof that Regency stole the Fabergé cup?'

The big man turned around. 'Haven't a clue. I'll have a think. In me head, like.'

Nick got in the flat, took two packets of steak out of the freezer and put them into warm water to thaw out and prepared some vegetables. Then, layering thick vanilla cream with cherries and strawberries and shaving some 70 per cent dark chocolate over the top, he put the dessert in the fridge.

He'd just sat down with a mug of tea when Julie came home.

'Hiya!' she said, full of smiles, tossing her bag onto the sofa, arms out wide.

'Who's a clever girl, then?' he said.

She galloped up to him and fell into his lap. 'Me me me me...it totally came out of the blue. I went in for my assessment and Martha said they were impressed with my work and their funding had finally come through and they needed two more Support Workers and would I be interested in being one? I nearly screamed. Oh, man, it's made all the training and volunteering worthwhile.'

'Your dedication really paid off. Good work, Wells.'

'It did, aye. To the tune of just over £20 grand a year. Not the big bucks, but it'll double our income.'

'We should celebrate. Can you get off work at short notice?'

'I'm off anyway. The new job starts on Monday.'

'Cool. Let's go up into Teesdale and do some walking, then. Have a little break, like. The forecast is for dry and sunshine over the next three days.'

She kissed him and stood up. 'Brill. Why don't you book the Village Hotel in Middleton for a long weekend? That's a nice place. And more importantly, it's cheap at this time of year. They usually have a weekend break deal on.'

While she took a shower he went online and booked a double room dinner, bed and breakfast for Thursday, Friday and Saturday night on a deal where you got the third night for free.

Over dinner he told her about the missing cup and what Brian had said.

'The Regency Stables are just on the outskirts of Middleham. I remember seeing them in the past, though I didn't know that's what they were called,' said Julie, scooping a cherry and some cream onto her spoon. 'I think you're right to be a bit wary of Brian. I do like him, but that shouldn't get in the way of the fact that he's a rich bloke who lives a life about as distant as it's possible to be from people like us. The fact he wasn't honest about the cup doesn't say much for him. He's obviously scheming something.'

'I wonder if, as he's an old bloke, he didn't realise or think that we could just look it up and discover it was a unique thing.'

'He said it was plain silver but Fabergé things are stunning Art Nouveau and, even to a lay person, don't look like a plain silver cup.'

'Well, it is a lovely little thing. It makes no sense at all. Maybe he's getting a touch of the Alzheimers?'

'Yeah. Not the least unlikely thing.' She pushed her clean plate away. 'God, that was delicious, luv. Thanks. You're a good cook, you.'

He cleared the plates away and poured them each a glass of white wine and took them through to the lounge. Sitting at his laptop, he did a search for Regency Stables while Julie lay on the sofa, flicking through the TV channels to find some football.

'Ah, German football. I like the Bundesliga. It reminds me of what top-flight football used to be like here before it became more like going to IKEA to eat pizza,' she said.

Nick glanced up at the Borussia Dortmund game. 'I love their manager,

Jurgen Klopp. He said he likes his team to play "heavy metal" football.'

'Did he? Brilliant. He's a proper dude, isn't he? Very shaggable.'

'None more shaggable dude in football, I'd say...hey, listen to this, Jules. It says on this horse-racing site that Regency Stables are owned by Yuri Chekov, a Russian oligarch. Made his money in oil in the early 90s. One of Yeltzin's old mates. He bought it last year from Cameron Baxter-Smythe. It had been in his family since 1821.'

He sat back and took a drink of the Chablis. She looked over at him. 'Hey, Russians love Fabergé. They love any Russian art. They're driving the market, right now. I was reading about it in the paper the other week. Them and the Chinese are mad for all their old stuff. Since Brian had a special Fabergé piece...well, put two and two together and it looks like maybe he's had it stolen for his own collection, just as Brian suggests. There's your crime solved. Next!' She clapped her hands together triumphantly.

'This Baxter-Smythe man is in the House of Lords. He's Lord Thirsk, apparently. How the hell is he Lord Thirsk?'

'Funny that, isn't it? A rich man from the landed aristocracy with a seat in parliament. What a coincidence.' She gave him a weary, cynical look. If she could have spit after saying it, without making a mess on the carpet, she would have.

'We're still a feudal society in some ways. Why wasn't my dad in the House of Lords? Why wasn't yours?' said Nick.

'Because they were common, that's why. And, in my dad's case, drunk. But then being a drunk seems to be one of the qualifications for the job, so he'd have fitted right in. Funny how being a piss head, if you're the aristocracy is part of your loveable eccentricity, but if you're off the Hardwick estate you're just a drunk loser.'

'Was he always like that? Your dad, I mean.'

'No. Not really. Only after he got laid off from British Steel. Don't think he took it well - looking back. Even so, he was a bastard to us. He took out his demons on us.'

'What did he do, exactly?'

'He'd fight with Ricky and Kev, I've told you that before. And he'd shout and curse at mam and at us. He'd come in so drunk he hardly knew his own name. He'd be sick on the walls. We'd find him passed out in a puddle of his own puke in the hallway when we came down for school.'

She bit her lip and shook her head.

Nick read on. 'Baxter-Smythe's grandfather's brother was the Walter

Francis the trophy was named after. That's it, then. It's not Chekov who's stolen it. It's the posh bloke. He thinks Brian has got it under false pretences and he's had it stolen to return it to the bosom of the Baxter-Smythe family. We should go to the police about this, really, even though Brian doesn't want them involved.'

Julie blew a raspberry. 'You think that'd make any difference? He's old-school aristocracy. He'll be totally protected from the gaze of the law. If you're high up in society, you have to try hard to get arrested for anything. Look at how many of them were paedophiles, rapists, even murderers. They get away with all sorts. Someone has a word to the local Chief Inspector, evidence is lost or ignored and everything is brushed under the carpet, if at all possible. We live in a very unequal society. The law isn't applied evenly and it never has been. The Establishment isn't called the Establishment for nothing.'

'I know what you're saying, but DI Colin Harcombe wouldn't behave like that. He's as straight as a die.'

'He might not have a choice. He's a DI, he's not the gaffer. He has to do what he's told or be out on his ear.'

'Even so. I can't see him colluding in that sort of business. He's a man of principle. He'd rather resign than let a villain off the hook.' Nick turned back to his computer. 'Mind, this Chekov fella sounds hardcore. There have been two attempts on his life by Mafia types from the Ukraine. They're at each others' throats, aren't they - the Russian and Ukrainians? His wife was once kidnapped and he had to pay a ransom. He has houses in London, New York, Paris and Moscow.'

'I wonder if he'd swap all his money for peace of mind and security? I often wonder if rich people realise that people without much are just as happy, if not more so. Life is about passion, love and friendship, not money.'

Nick looked up and smiled. It was a very Julie-ish thing to say.

'No rich person wants to believe that - it devalues the thing which aggrandises them. He'll be buying a football club soon, I should think. That'll bring him up short. Football is a great way to lose money and be publically hated or ridiculed by thousands of ungrateful people.'

Julie pulled her knees up and hugged them with her arms. 'We've met Brian, and he just seems like a posh old bloke. You'd never really imagine the circles he mixes in as a hugely wealthy landowner, with a successful stables. He's right up in the top 1 per cent or more, rubbing shoulders with Russian oligarchs and royals as well. He's probably got friends in very high places.'

'Yeah. He'll have been to the palace a few times, I should think.'

She nodded. 'Funny how we've not been invited there, too, isn't it?' She groaned. 'It all stinks. I hate anyone lording it over me and that's what it feels like.'

Nick put his computer away. They watched the Dortmund game and were just about to go to bed for an early night when Nick's phone vibrated. He picked it up and looked at the screen. It was a text from Colin Harcombe.

'Speak of the devil...it's Col.'

'What does he want at this time of night?' said Julie, looking over his shoulder.

'For me to give him a quick call.'

'His ears must have been burning.'

'Ha. Yeah. Did your mam use that expression, too?' said Nick. 'It made me a bit paranoid. I thought my ears could actually tell when I was being talked about, like they were an emotional radar.'

She laughed and shook her head and went to the toilet.

He dialled Colin Harcombe's mobile number.

CHAPTER 6

'Hello, Nick. Thanks for being so prompt in getting back to me,' said Harcombe, his tone always clipped, formal and old fashioned.

'How are you are, Colin?'

'Fine. I've not seen you and Julie since the New Year. I hope you are both keeping well.'

'Yes, thanks. Well...just so as you know...Julie lost the baby.'

Harcombe let out a shocked gasp. 'Oh, damn it! So sorry to hear that.'

'Yeah, last month. After 18 weeks this time.'

The policeman tutted. 'Bad business. Is she well?'

'On the mend, yeah. Thanks.'

'Good. Give her my best. Very disappointing for you. Still, life has a habit of being unsatisfactory.'

His no-nonsense tone was always a relief. You never had to worry Colin would go mushy or weepy on you. He was always in control of himself and his emotions and, Nick always suspected, he was vaguely contemptuous of those who weren't.

'So how can I help at this late hour, Col? Is it something urgent? I presume it is.'

The policeman cleared his throat.

'Something came across my desk earlier today. A road accident in Oxbridge that you were witness to. Chap in a Metro died...'

'...dressed as Elvis, yes, that's right. Awful, really. He'd just been on the allotments. Me and Jeff had been talking to him, in fact.'

'Ah, really? What did he have to say for himself?'

Nick outlined what he could remember of their brief conversation. 'It was all inconsequential stuff, really, Colin. Why are you asking?'

Harcombe ignored that question. 'But you didn't see who hit his car?'

'No. It all happened very quickly. A woman in the bungalows said it was a Range Rover.'

'Interesting. Yes, I have her comments here, too.'

'Whoever hit him must have been driving away as I ran down, but I just didn't notice them. I was focused on the Metro. I could see he was slumped over. I thought he'd been knocked out, but he was dead.'

Harcombe cleared his throat. 'Hmm. Indeed. I just had the medical report on Jim George, your Elvis. It's a bad business, Nick.'

'Why?'

'Strictly between ourselves. I know I can trust you with this. Two things.

First, Jim's neck was broken.'

Nick winced. 'Poor fella. He was certainly dead when I leaned in. He must have hit his head on the steering wheel or something.'

Harcombe made a negative sound to contradict him.

'No. That's not what happened. Someone broke his neck. He didn't do it in the accident. No evidence of that. He was dispatched. Murdered. His neck snapped in one violent movement.'

'What?!' exclaimed Nick. Julie came in from the bathroom, made an inquiring expression at him and mouthed the words, 'Is everything alright?' Harcombe continued.

'I'm afraid so. I think this is what is likely to have happened. The Range Rover deliberately hit the Metro, knocking it off the road. The driver or a passenger got out, went to the car, leaned in and snapped Jim's neck. Murdered him. Just like that. They may have quickly looked in his attaché case, as that was open, then returned to the Range Rover and drove off.'

It wouldn't sink into Nick's brain. 'That...that's just incredible. Are you sure? Is it even possible? How could someone just do that so quickly? I didn't realise you could break someone's neck so easily.'

'Not difficult if you know how. Well, I say it's not difficult, it is - and you need to be very strong to do it - sort of thing that is taught in the SAS.'

'...so you think he was killed by the SAS?'

Julie's jaw dropped.

'I didn't say that. Someone who has been in the forces, or special services, possibly.'

'Bloody hell. But he was just a fat Elvis impersonator. Why would anyone murder him?'

'I don't believe that is all Jim George was. This goes deeper and wider. He was *someone*.'

'Someone? Someone significant?'

'Absolutely. There is a file on him.'

'What does that mean?'

'It means security services were interested in him and were watching him. Hold on...'

Harcombe went quiet as he turned some papers, then tapped away at a keyboard briefly.

'He's a strange one. They're clearly concerned he was an agent for a foreign government.'

'Why would they think that?'

Harcombe read through some details.

'He's born in the old USSR. Seems to have had contacts over there when he was working as a biology lecturer at Sunderland Poly.' There was more turning over of papers. 'Have you heard of BioResearch International in Hartlepool?'

'No. What is it?'

It sounded like Harcombe was reading out a synopsis.

'It's an R & D company developing drugs to fight various diseases. They're leaders in bacterial analysis, apparently. Hadn't heard of it myself. Our Jim was seen there on several occasions.' Harcombe hummed a contemplative noise.

'What was its name, again?' said Nick.

'BioResearch International.' Harcombe made a somewhat amused grunt. 'They have an in-house magazine called *Bacto - The Future*. Very witty. Ish.'

That jogged Nick's memory. 'I saw a copy of that on the passenger seat beside Jim when I looked in the car. It had spilled out of his leather case along with some other stuff.'

'When you spoke to him, did he talk politics at all?'

'No. Nothing like that. We thought he was a typical moaning Teesside gadgee...a bit down on the region and on the people.'

'Can you be specific?'

'He was saying how local people were dossers. A bit anti-foreigners. Just the sort of thing that is commonly said, y'know.'

'Indeed. Anything else?' Harcombe was obviously taking notes. Exactly how you can tell someone is taking notes over the phone is hard to say, but you definitely know when someone is doing it, in the same way you can tell when someone stops listening to you and has had their attention distracted. There's a palpable sense of 'going away'.

'He seemed to like the Big Fish.'

'He's not alone in that,' said Harcombe, in a way which left Nick in doubt he wasn't a fan, himself.

'Yeah, he said at least he wasn't employing any Russians, which he seemed to think was a good thing.'

'Russians? What had he got against Russians? He was from Russia, wasn't he?'

'We just ignored that comment. Some people get weird bigotries, Col. My dad really disliked the French.'

'Sensible man. That *was* a joke.' He added quickly, speaking flatly and without humour.

'I actually thought there were Russians on the door when we went to the Big Fish's launch party - but Jeff reckoned they were Ukrainians. Big lads. High cheekbones - powerfully built types. Ideal bouncer material.'

'Ukrainians? I see...hmm.' Harcombe took more notes.

'He was a strange-looking man, though. We both said so, and Jules, too.'

'Strange?'

'Yeah he looked sort of fleshy...tight skin...like he had allergy, maybe.'

Harcombe shuffled papers. 'Again, this is just between you and me, the toxicology report says he had a high concentration of botulism in his system...' Harcombe spoke rhetorically, almost under his breath '...what on earth have you been up to, old son, eh?'

'Botulism?!' said Nick, hissing out the word with increasing disbelief. Again, Julie pulled an astonished face. 'Isn't that a fatal thing to have in you? Has he been poisoned with a dart or something?'

'I couldn't tell you...not my area of knowledge at all. He wasn't killed by that, though...but it suggests he's been up to something.'

'Botox!' said Julie, clapping her hands together. 'That's why he looked like that. Botox is actually botulism. That was why he looked odd. His girlfriend looked the same way, too.'

'Did you hear that, Col?' said Nick.

'I did. I've noted it. Good thinking from Julie. OK. Thanks for this, Nick - a big help, as usual. Sorry to disturb you so late. Some things just won't wait in this business. I'm getting in touch with Jeff also to make him aware of the situation.'

'Well, if I hear anything at all that might be useful, I'll let you know.'

'Appreciated. Thank you, Nick.' He cleared his throat again. 'Call it a copper's sixth sense, but I don't like this at all. This isn't a normal crime of violence and there *are* outside forces at work on Teesside, right now.'

Nick furrowed his brow. 'Outside forces? What does that mean?'

'I'll be getting a more thorough briefing soon, I should imagine. We've got MI-5 on our patch right now, and let's just say it's my guess; no, it's my belief, that somehow this is part of wider, more international and more dangerous situation that is unfolding as we speak. It's important you stay out of the way...'

His formal tone made him sound like a 1950s detective in a black-and-white film.

'Blimey, Col. You make it sound like international espionage or something.'

'Hmm. You are a very perceptive man. Stay safe. My regards to Julie.'

Julie had been standing in front of him. 'Murder?! Botox?!' she said, a look of astonishment in her eyes.

He looked at her for a moment, tugging at his stubble a little nervously. 'I think, judging by what Harcombe is half-telling me, some very big shit is about to go down on Teesside and the death of Elvis is just the start of it. What were a middle-aged couple having Botox injections for?'

'It irons out your wrinkles. Maybe he thought he'd get more work as a younger Elvis.'

That had to be it. And you did hear about some people suffering terribly when the injections went wrong. What was the point in trying to pretend you were younger than you really were? The worship of youth only leads to heartbreak because it's a battle no-one can win. It is all the more ironic that when you're young, you actually want to be older.

The drive up to Middleton-in-Teesdale the following afternoon only took just under an hour on the A66 and A67, finally joining the B6282 into the small market town. They arrived in the middle of an azure blue Thursday afternoon that was as clear as a Californian swimming pool.

After checking into the old country hotel, they took a three-mile circular walk through and around the market town. Julie tied her hair back, pulled on a baseball cap, hitched up her walking trousers and clapped her hands together. She seemed very cheerful and that made Nick feel good.

'C'mon on then, big boy. Let's get a pace going.' She looked up at the sky. 'What an afternoon. You wouldn't want to be anywhere else on a day like this, would you? It's gorgeous up here.'

Nick pointed across the marketplace as they set off.

'See that building over there, with the green door? That's Leslie West's offices.'

'Oh, yeah, your dad's lawyer?'

'Aye. My lawyer too, for that matter. Amazing that he's still even alive. I've never seen a more purple man. They must have to use a special high blood pressure gauge on him. 400 over 270 or something.'

'I like Leslie. He's the sort of man who you hope all old blokes will be like. Sensible and sort of fatherly but not in a creepy way.'

'Well, I hope we don't have cause to see him any time soon.'

They walked south out of town and stood on the small stone bridge that crossed the River Tees.

'Funny that this is the same river that flows into the North Sea, isn't it?' said Nick, staring down at the dark water lapping onto a small bank of pebbles, the sun glinting off the moving water.

Julie looked down. 'When we say we're Teessiders, this is why. This modest little river. This is such a big part of our identity.' She tossed a pebble into the water below.

They walked on and took a footpath left and down to the river itself, walking through trees and rough grassland, the Pennines rising behind them to the west.

'This is so beautiful. The only sound is birdsong,' said Nick, as a robin hopped in front of them, followed by a blackbird in full late spring voice. 'Now it's not far from the start of summer, you can feel the sap has risen and life has returned to things. There's no stopping it now.' A warm glow of relaxation and goodwill to all living things spread over him, the way it does when you feel privileged to witness the annual rebirth of nature. We take it for granted sometimes, but the yearly transformation is perhaps one of the most naturally spiritual experiences we have.

'Aye, it's all about breeding now. Nests to make, eggs to lay,' said Julie, as they stopped to watch a pair of swallows swooping over the water to catch flies.

Their own loss, as they watched nature going about its dance of reproduction and renewal, was all too obvious. They both felt it powerfully. Feeling tears rising, Nick reached for her hand, just as she was reaching for his. They gave each other a look that was somewhere between a smile, a grimace and a sob.

He sucked in some clear soft air to settle his emotions and pointed across the river and into the middle distance.

'See those horses? That must be where the Regency Stables are.'

'Oh, yeah. I wonder if that cup is in there. I like horses, but they scare me. They're too big.'

'It's the same with horsey women. They frighten me more than the horses, actually.'

She made an amused noise. 'They're always all big foreheads, teeth and big side of ham-like thighs, aren't they?'

'At the risk of sounding paranoid, one always feels as if your typical male would not measure up to the horsey woman's early life experiences of male animal genitalia. I fear being compared to a stallion.'

She clucked a small laugh. 'Does everything have to come down to that, like?'

'It's never far from the male mind, trust me. Anyway, you can talk. You're the one who always notices which side men dress.'

She flicked her head to one side. 'Ah, but that's just quality observational skills. Nowt wrong with that,' she made a small grunt. 'The bloke who showed us to our room was a righty.'

He turned to look at her. 'You're making that up.'

She gave him a shrug and held out her hands. 'Check him out later if you don't believe me. Most men are leftys, like you. Though, you're left handed so you should be a righty, really.'

'Ah, but I'm right handed for most things except writing and ball-throwing.'

'...and for the self-pleasuring. You're instinctively left handed at that.'

He shook his head, a smile on his lips. 'You're incorrigible, you are.'

They walked on holding hands again, connected together, being by themselves with the nature of the north for company. Funny how the smaller, modest gestures and the quiet moments can speak the loudest to the human soul.

'You know when I went to see Don? He told me you were a great public speaker at college. He mentioned some speech you gave about destroying the hegemony of international capitalism. Sounded very impressive.'

She hooted a laugh. 'Oh, yeah, I remember that. I was a proper little Miss Che Guevara. Life knocks that sort of naïve idealism out of you, though.'

'Yeah. It does. But that got me thinking. Why don't you do anything like that any more?'

'What, public speaking? I don't know. I'm channelling all of that into my work now.'

'Don said he thought you'd go into politics.'

'I did think about it but when I left Uni with my degree, I immediately got offered that job at Chase and Carlisle in Middlesbrough and the starting pay was 18 grand, which was a sodding fortune back in 1986 and I did that classic working-class thing of chasing the first decent pay cheque that came my way and I just got on that escalator. When they sent me to London in the 90s, I thought I was going to rise up their corporate legal ladder. I was PA to a partner and on good money and living the weekend high life, during which I'd blow all the money. I did that for bloody years. Seems like a different person did all of that, now.'

'I'm impressed that you didn't save any money.'

'That's because underneath all the so-called aspiration, I was a Northern working-class girl, born and raised in the shadow of industry and under clouds of pollution. It coloured everything. I'd meet middle-class

Southerners and they were so different. They had...they had plans...and careers...and they knew what they wanted. But I never trusted the future. I couldn't see the long term. I lived for the nights and for the weekend. I lived in the moment. If I had money, I spent it because, who the hell knows what tomorrow is going to bring?'

'That is quintessential poor kid, working-class thinking. Teesside is predicated on that notion and why wouldn't it be? Industries have come and gone in a generation. The iron ore boom of the 1800s barely even made it into the 20th century. The steel we both grew up with is still around but not like it once was. As an industry, it was never as strong or permanent as the steel itself, nor of the buildings and the bridges all across the world that the Teesside working class built so well and so proudly with its bare hands. And the pits...well...there are no pits at all anymore, but 35 years ago there were over 50 in County Durham.'

'But when you meet people who are from leafy places, they usually just don't get it. It doesn't make them bad people, but they don't understand why the industry, the factories, the river, the pollution even, why it lives so strong in our hearts and they don't get why when you run into someone from the region, somewhere else in the country or overseas, the strength with which they grip your hand really means something. We are a sisterhood and a brotherhood. I see that now. But for years I just wanted to be divorced from it and that took me away from who I really am. I only realised that later in life.'

'It's not a crazy idea to live for now. All we've ever got is now, Jules. No-one, no matter how rich, has ever had more than that.'

She pushed him affectionately as they walked; it was something she always did in normal times, but hadn't done since the miscarriage. 'For a daft bugger, you're much too clever, sometimes. Oh, god, I wish you'd been in my life then.' She grabbed his arm and pulled him in for a short hug and sang, 'I'd have "come to you, with open arms". I used to love that Journey track so much. Y'know? "Open Arms"? Steve Perry, my god, now there was a man who dressed to the left. Those early 1980s tight pants, they left nothing to the imagination.'

'Journey were epic. Jeff will tell you their proggy first albums are the best, but you don't sell that many records without properly touching people and those late 70s and early 80s ones are brilliant. "Separate Ways" is another superb track.'

'Oh, god...' she bent a little at the knees '...I totally loved that. Perry was so awesome. He didn't sing like *anyone* else. I can't tell you the amount of times I'd put "Open Arms" or "Who's Crying Now" on at parties all pissed and maudlin and wondering why no decent man would love me. And when it came to "Don't Stop Believin'" I mean, I really was "just a small town girl", wasn't I? And I "smelt of wine and cheap perfume" as well and I did my fair share of "searchin' in the night" too. That song could have been written for me. Though, truth be told, I did stop believing I'd fall in love.'

'If "Who's Crying Now" has never made you shiver, you should be disqualified from being defined as human. Such a brilliant solo from Neal Schon. Mind, for me it was always Whitesnake ballads. I'd be drunk and scowling at people who didn't like the music and didn't understand why you did. Those years seemed to go on forever.'

'Yup, been there, done that, got the tear stains on the t-shirt.' She ticked an imaginary box on a list.

'I was talking to Jeff about this the other day. When we first went to college, I went out with quite a lot of girls and sowed a lot of wild oats and it was funny to recollect them, y'know. Me and him had a laugh going back over all these women, most of which he can recall better than I can, he's got such a great memory, but even as I was talking about them, I remembered just how at the end of these one-night stands, and brief liaisons, in a way, I was really lonely. They were all people I liked, but that's as far as it went. It was great for a while...I mean when you're young and women want to sleep with you, you can't not feel good about that...but by the time I was in my 20s I was really ready for something that didn't end after breakfast, y'know? But she just never came along. And by the time I was in my 30s, I stopped even going out with women much because it always ended the same way. Until I met you. Then it all changed. And you forget - or I forget anyway, what that was like...that yearning for someone who you really connect to...we shouldn't ever take that for granted, Jules. Understanding is such a rare thing in life.'

'Oh god, you're so right. All those years when you longed to turn to someone who would just know how you felt about even small, trivial things and there was no-one there, or no-one who really got what you were on about.'

Both of them had tears in their eyes now, at the recollection mixed with the upset of recent weeks.

They went quiet for a minute or two. Then Nick spoke again.

'Don't you regret dropping all of that career stuff? I mean, you were working for a firm that was focused on employment disputes and equality legislation and all of that...so it's not like you were just being a corporate lawyer's right-wing suck-up.'

She shook her head from side to side. 'I don't regret it for even a microsecond.' She looked around herself in contemplation. 'Looking back now, it feels like it was an island that I was stranded on, a long way from my real home.'

He had to say something which had always bothered him since they'd got back together but which he'd never found the words to express before. 'Sometimes, I worry that meeting me again was a bad influence on your career - that I took you away from being successful.'

She took no time to reply. 'Don't be daft. I already had half a foot out of there when you came knocking on my flat door in Norton with Stanley, that day. I'd had enough. I'd got away from myself for too many years and I knew it. Going back to University was always going to be my escape route. I'd planned it on and off for a while. It was nothing to do with you. Not really. Education was my way off that particular hamster wheel.'

They climbed over a low gate into the next pasture.

'You weren't always unhappy though, were you?' said Nick. 'I can't bear the idea that you were this lost and lonely person in London. I've seen pictures you from back then, you were quite glamorous in a Stevie Nicks circa 1987 way.'

She pursed her lips together.

'Pat Benatar, please. I've never been floaty enough to be Stevie. Not with my shite dancing. No. Not on the surface, I had a lot of laughs. You make the best of things, don't you - even while inside, you're dying. That's how life is for millions of people. You can't force the love of your life to arrive, so you plug away. I went out a lot and drank a lot and shagged a lot...but you're right, after a while you just tire of it.'

'At least you'd got away from home and everything that meant.'

'I wanted to be as different from my family as possible. And as different as possible meant having a job that paid well and that was concerned with the law and justice. That's why I went out with good-looking but soulless, respectable men who had gold credit cards and drove fancy cars and had expensive houses. In a way it was all rebellion against my upbringing. But it didn't make me happy. Not really, which, looking back, is why I never had a major relationship under my belt until I met you in my mid 30s. A couple of months was always enough with those men because being pissed on champagne in a room full of jerks is sodding lonely, no matter how good the champagne is. And there's only so long you can keep your rock 'n' roll self down. Mine was bursting to get out again, one way or another.

101

It used to rise up out of me when I was drunk and I'd be at clubs or parties in some fashionable part of London which loved itself more than it had any right to love itself, and I'd be shouting in the full Hardwick voice, "Have youse got any fuckin' Sabbath, like?" and generally being a gobby Northern cow.' She smiled to herself.

Nick laughed. 'God, I'd have fancied the knickers right off you if I'd seen you shouting that. I'd have been your ally in that fight. When I first met you in Harrogate you said you'd only just returned to the northeast, so me and Jeff both thought you had to be some sort of high-powered executive. You looked very respectable. I'd never have guessed you were a party girl.'

She turned to him with a big smile. They stopped walking. She took his hands and leaned back.

'Meeting you was the *best* thing that ever happened to me. You were the exact opposite of those blokes I'd dated in London.'

'Skint and not respectable, you mean?'

She smiled and squeezed his hands. 'Yeah, you were arty and funny and odd and poetic and full of unusual thoughts and ideas that I'd never heard anyone say before. And you rented that lovely flat overlooking The Stray. I was impressed by that.'

'Aye, but I could never really afford it. It soaked up so much money.'

'Coming back to Teesside at that time was the start of a return to my roots and reconnecting to who I really was. If that makes any sense. It took a long time, though. I held on to yuppie Julie for longer than I should have.'

In the warm sunshine, their hands were getting sweaty, so he put his arm around her shoulder instead and they walked on.

'I totally assumed, when you walked up to stand beside me in Jack & Danny's, that you were some posh bird who was loaded. You had your hair in that neat Jennifer Aniston style and wore a dark suit, you were so not the sort of woman I ever dared talk to. I dated scruffy, arty women, if I dated anyone. Not smart women in Nicole Farhi suits.'

They stopped to sit on a fallen tree, looking out across the slowly moving water, the sun just starting its descent into the western sky behind them.

She laughed and put her head on his shoulder. 'You know what? When I think back to that moment, I think I fell *totally* in love with you right there and then. Just like that. In an instant.' She clicked her fingers. 'I walked up to buy two glasses of wine and you were talking to Jeff about Grand Funk Railroad.'

'And you leaned in and said, "*We're an American Band* is their best album because it's produced by Todd Rundgren". Who you love.'

They smiled at each other in recollection.

'And I looked at Jeff first and then I took one look at you.' She paused as a bee flew around them. 'And I lost my heart to you, in that instant. It leaped up into my throat, as though I'd had a big electric shock. I remember it clear as day. All those years of dating blokes...I'd met and been out with so many that when I met you, I knew it was like nothing I'd ever felt before. It scared me and excited me, all at the same time.'

'That's a bit Mills and Boon, isn't it?' he said, kissing the top of her head.

'It does sound like that. But, honest, my heart really did leap as you turned to look at me. I got this tingle of electricity all over and I knew I didn't just fancy you...it does sound ridiculous...I went back to my seat with the drinks and I said to my friend Annie, "There's a gorgeous bloke at the bar, there", and she said give us a look, went to the toilets, came back and copped a look at you. "He's nowt special", she said...I thought she was crazy. She couldn't see it. I thought you were the lushest thing I'd ever clapped eyes on and that even in a few words there was a connection between us.'

Even the recollection of the moment in their lives made Nick feel excited all over again.

'It usually took me ages to get the courage up to ask someone out but I couldn't let you walk out of there and out of my life. I actually saw it like one of those corny movies where the man chases after the woman he's only just met. When you got up to go, you looked over at me and smiled...'

She interrupted him with a push to his shoulder.

'Hey, I didn't just smile, I gave you the full, "Come on big boy, I want you to get my pants off" look...which was traditionally how I secured a man's affections, back then. You were so nervous, you could barely get the words out to ask me for a date. You got your words all mixed up. "Err, w-w-would you like to drink something to eat?" It was so lovely and un-macho. I couldn't say yes quick enough...and then when you said where you were from and it turned out we'd actually gone to the same school, I was amazed...it was all kismet.'

'Jeff said I had no chance with you. That you were out of my league. When I told him you'd said yes, it was the proudest moment of my life. I had pulled a proper cracker. Ha ha...don't look like that. It's true...you were out of my league. Honest. Me and Jeff both said it.'

'Well, I'm not sure about that. At all. You looked like my idea of a sex god. Little did you both know what a common cow I was!'

He smiled and took her left hand. 'You know, I still loved you when we split up. I thought I'd blown it. I knew I'd been a bad partner. I knew I'd struggled with being who I was and with being messed up in the head. I thought I'd ruined it forever. But...' he swelled up with tears again '...when I saw you standing at the top of the stairs, that day I came round with Stan, I knew I still loved you so much.' She squeezed his hand tightly. 'It had never left me. Like it was a seed that lived on inside. How does it happen? Love, I mean? You can't plan it or force it. It's the strangest of things.'

The sun played out on the water, casting shattered flashes of jewel-like light, as though it was a mirror ball.

'You can lie to yourself that you feel love, but you can't deny it when you really do feel it. It's a bit like great music. You hear a lot of stuff and you think, "oh, that's good" and then you hear something brilliant and it puts everything else in the shade and you end up wondering how on earth you thought the other stuff was any good. Until I met you, I didn't even know I was capable of that depth of feeling. Not when you get to your mid 30s. You think you've been through it all.'

He nodded. 'I think it's a sort of psychic or spiritual connection. There's affection and warmth and that...but on top of it is this other mystical thing where you feel connected, so connected that I feel you're with me even when you're not.' He kissed her lightly on the lips. 'Just saying "I love you" doesn't do it justice. There are no words that really work properly...I suppose that's what music and art is for - to express complex, amazing feelings.' He made an amused grunt. 'I suppose that's why we have Journey.'

They sat quietly for another minute. This was a deep moment in their lives, one of those moments that would live on, that would define who they were to each other. They would look back on this and see it was in these times that they reconnected to each other and understood who they were, both in themselves and as a couple. Slowly but surely, she was coming back to him, reconnecting properly. It was a tangible thing brought on by understanding where they'd come from, emotionally.

Nick took her hand and kissed it.

'You've got to understand that's why not having our Joni couldn't make a difference to how I love you. Me and you...it goes beyond the ups and downs of day-to-day life...' he left a long pause '...and I still fancy the arse off you, as well. You do know that, don't you?'

She made a flat smile, and after another long pause, she said, 'We might not have children, but we'll always have each others' love...we should be grateful for that.'

That touched him so deeply. He let it sink in. A connection between two humans isn't a thing which gives itself up to analysis. But Nick knew this was as close to a union of souls as anyone had ever felt.

'Come on, let's walk some more,' he said, pulling her to her feet.

'Thanks for saying that - about fancying me. I shouldn't need to hear it from you, but I do.'

'Wanting to feel desired is only natural, Jules. You wanting me, the way you do, physically, I mean...that has given me the chance to climb out of my depression and my self-loathing and believe in myself. It's been a long climb from a dark place...a long climb into the sunlight, but you helped make it happen...so I do understand, really, I do.'

She closed her eyes slowly and reopened them. 'And I still do desire you, darlin'. Even if I haven't shown it much recently. I really do.' She narrowed her eyes and looked into the middle distance. 'Do you think we fancy each other so much because we're so in love? Or is the physical thing on a different level?' she said, as they walked on in the quiet of the rural afternoon.

'Good question. The connection between the physical and spiritual is a hard one to call because you can lust after someone purely physically.'

'Yeah, totally. I mean...for all I went through some dodgy relationships, I did have a good time with some blokes in and out of bed but it wasn't anything like us being together. That's like...' she drew an imaginary high mark above her head '...and they were all down here,' she swiped below her waist.

He bit his bottom lip, swatting away a large black fly.

'When I first got that flat in Harrogate, I met this lass called Jemma. She was a teacher at the girls' school. Harrogate Ladies College.'

Julie pushed her nose up in the air with her index finger.

'Aye, she was a bit stuck up, but she seemed nice enough at first and more importantly she had all of the physical attributes a shallow man relishes. We went out a couple of times and she stayed over at the flat.'

'By stayed over you mean, you shagged her, Guymer, you dirty get?' She nudged at him.

'Oh, yeah. You'd have been proud of me. I brought my A game for her.' Julie laughed and threw her head back so the sun caught the yellow in her hair. 'And it was all perfectly...you know...'

She laughed again at his hesitation. 'You're so coy, sometimes. You can tell me what it was like, I'm not going to be jealous, am I?'

'Alright, well, she was totally into me, physically, I mean...couldn't get enough...if you know what I mean. She said the blokes she'd been with weren't...well...you know...not as good...that's what she said...I dunno if it was true.'

'Eee, lad...Still with the coyness...well she wasn't that daft, then.'

'I mean, I don't know about that. She was just saying it, y'know, the way people do. To be nice, like. I don't think I was anything special...' he shrugged.

She let out small exasperated sigh.

'You've got to get out this annoying habit of not believing in yourself, y'know. Have at least a small bit of ego.'

'I wasn't being down on myself - just realistic. I really don't think I *was* anything special.'

She tutted, though not harshly. 'Do I have to say it?' She peered around and looked into his eyes. 'I do, don't I?' She shook her head, as if in wonderment.

'What?' He had no idea what she was saying.

'Nick, man, you're *really* good in bed and you always were - partly because you're not selfish and you think of who you're with before yourself. You've *never* realised that just being a bit sensitive and thoughtful was a sexy thing in itself. And if I thought that from day one, I'm sure other women have. It's not something you've learned, it's part of who you are.'

'Aw, thanks, Jules.' He genuinely had no idea that it might be true.

She pushed his hair behind his ears and pecked him on the lips. This was all natural Julie stuff. The kind words and the affectionate gesture - all done with a bit of a laugh in her voice. The melancholy that had shadowed her for so many weeks seemed to have, at least temporarily, gone.

'You're most welcome, luv.' She grinned widely at him. 'And you know, you're very physically passionate when the mood takes you - god knows, you gave me a proper big shagging on our first night - and you know where a lady's tingly bits are and what to do with them...and you've got good control of yourself, so it's not over too quick.' She laughed at her own words. 'Eee...I don't know how I've kept my dirty paws off you for so many weeks, when I think about it.' She rubbed his tummy and gave him a silly, toothy look. 'So what about this Jemma lass?'

'Oh, yeah, she'd come around the flat and we'd do some horizontal dancing and she'd do a lot of screaming. This went on for a couple of weeks then one day, after we'd had it off, we were watching football on the TV in the bedroom and she made an idle racist comment about a footballer. "What a lazy bloody nigger", to be precise.'

'Eee, my god. Did she? A Big Ron-ism?'

'The full Big Ron, long before Big Ron had said it. And I wasn't having that...so I admonished her for it.'

'You admonished her! Ha ha...oooh, will you admonish me, darlin'? Ha ha...it sounds like it might involve being spanked lightly with a wet slipper, which, for future reference, I am not entirely opposed to.' She bent over slightly in front of him and slapped her backside. Now that was something she hadn't done for a long while...*that* was Jules.

'Well, she apologised, but those words just made me see her so differently. It showed what she was really like and the physical attraction I'd had for her just evaporated. All I could see was an ugly racist. Just didn't fancy her at all after that. I ended it the next day.'

'Aw, aren't you the wet pinko liberal? That sounds like how a woman would feel about a bloke. I thought all men were slaves to their libidos.'

'All men except me, perhaps. The thought of having sex with her after that became almost physically repulsive to me. So the connection between lust and love - between the physical and the spiritual, it must exist. You can't totally divorce one from another.'

'...or *you* can't. I've known men who could cheerfully ignore what a woman was like, as long as she'd do it with them.'

'Yeah, I guess so. But you know what you were saying about wanting to be sexual and desired after the miscarriage...'

She interrupted him by touching him on the arm.

'...you said the word...'

'...miscarriage?'

'Yeah, that's the first time you've said it since it happened...'

'Is it? What am I saying? Of course it is. I do know that.'

'I've not said it, either.'

'Said what?'

She took an audible deep breath and spoke the word with a tense gasp. 'Miscarriage.' She gulped a sob down as she did so.

Instinctively, he hugged her tightly for a moment, the images of her miscarrying in the hospital still fresh in his mind.

'You don't need to worry about that. Right? The connection between us - what we've just been talking about - that's unbroken.'

She pulled away from him and rubbed some moisture from the corners of her eyes.

'I know...I really do. I suppose I've just needed to feel that within my self-identity. Knowing you're there for me is brill, but I have to recharge my own batteries, ultimately, don't I? And this is all helping massively, by the way. Talking about us and everything...it's not something we do much of...'

'I know. Well, we're repressed Northerners, aren't we?' He stopped her and looked into her eyes. 'Whatever you need from me, I'll give it, if I can. Body or mind - whatever I have, I'll give it to you.'

She just hugged him.

'Come on. Let's walk further down - there's some big stones we can cross the river on. Then we can walk around and see those horses up close,' he said.

As they walked on without talking, it felt like the reconnection between them that maybe had begun in the bedroom before they'd gone out to Big Fish's party, was now starting to be completed. The distance that had been between them had been bridged. It's impossible to say how, but you do know when it has happened. You can't take such a metaphysical thing as affection and love for granted. When it disappears, you feel it like a loss, but when it returns, the warm glow in your heart makes losing it, however briefly, almost seem worthwhile.

She stopped him after they'd walked a little further, put her arms around him tightly and hugged him without saying anything. He breathed in her musky strawish-honey smell like it was nourishing food.

CHAPTER 7

The gallops were a lush, brilliant green that must have stretched over half a mile. Three horses came flying along on the other side of a white rail, as Nick and Julie stood watching. The ground thundered underneath their feet as they sped past.

'What amazing animals,' said Nick, as the jet stream they left in their wake blew his hair off his forehead.

'The speed they get up is amazing, isn't it? I don't think I've ever seen horse racing up close,' said Julie.

They walked back towards the town, coming to the end of the gallops and hopping over a fence to walk around a large stable block. Horses poked their heads out and nodded up and down. It was hive of activity, with stable lads grooming the animals and jockeys standing around with men in quilted green jackets.

A group of half a dozen men stood around in army green t-shirts and combat trousers, talking in a foreign language. They turned to look at them as they passed by, staring for a few seconds. For a moment, Nick thought they were going to object to them being there, as they stared in such an accusatory way.

'There's a proper uniform to some of these sorts, isn't there?' said Julie. 'They love a quilted, sleeveless jacket.'

'Not those blokes. They sound German or something; wonder what they're doing up here? Thought one of them was going to come over and have a word. But aye, the country type normally likes a gilet and jodhpurs. They were prototype leggings, jodhpurs.'

'Yeah, they remind me of when you've got a pair of leggings and the fabric gets perished and goes baggy and hangs off your arse, like you're wearing a nappy: tight on the legs, big sloppy bum. The hunting girls like it though, don't they?'

They walked on past the stables and around the front to a big gated entrance. Regency Stables was obviously a large organisation.

'The money invested in this place must be huge. It can't be cheap to look after this many horses. It's got to be a very big business,' said Nick.

'I wonder if they did steal Brian's cup?' said Julie, as they walked on. 'It might be near to us, at this very moment.'

'I can believe they did. Like Jeff said, it is all a massive soap opera between these competing stables; a world within a world. But how Jeff's thinking of finding out, I just can't imagine. He can hardly walk in there and take a look in their trophy cabinet, if indeed they've even got a trophy cabinet.'

'That was just the stables, there's no house attached, like there is at Brian's. If it's anywhere, that's where it'll be.'

They walked on a little way and turned a corner. 'And that's where Cameron Baxter-Smythe lives, I bet,' said Julie pointing to a large, rambling four-storey early Victorian Gothic mansion, set in its own grounds. 'That has to be the biggest house in this area. It's bound to be his.'

A pair of tall wrought-iron gates that protected the entrance to the large house were shut. Set onto tall stone pillars, in the centre of each was a shield and a Latin expression: "Cuius habet potestatem in terra".

'What does that mean? Any idea?' said Nick, pointing to it.

'Err...something like...' she squinted at it. 'My Latin is terrible, I only did it for a year at Uni. Terra is land...so it says, he who owns the land has the power.'

'Bloody hell. Are you sure?'

She mouthed the Latin words again to herself. 'Yeah, deffo. He who owns the land has the power.'

'Seig bloody heil, eh. All bow down to the great landowner. I wonder if anyone around here knows it says that. It's very heavy-handed and arrogant.'

'Aye. It's saying I'm the boss, quite nakedly; though, it has to be said, they're right. He - and it is almost always a he - who owns the land does have the power over those who don't. The richest and most powerful people in the country are landowners. The land generates more and more wealth for them, and with that money comes power.' She stopped and pointed to a sign. 'This place is called Regency Towers. Sounds like a girls' boarding school in Enid Blyton.'

Nick took a photo of it on his phone and entered the name into Google.

'Here we go. "Regency Towers, Middleton-in-Teesdale, is the family home of the Baxter-Smythes"...'

'Can you be any more posh than being called Baxter-Smythe?'

'Were there no Baxter-Smythes on the Hardwick Estate, then, Jules? I find that hard to believe. It says here they're major landowners in the area...and owned the Regency stables until 2009, which we knew.'

'This pile must have been built at the same time they set up the stables in 1821. Classic cheesy Victorian Gothic, right out of a horror story. Ugly as shite, if you ask me. The Georgians would have been disgusted if they'd saw some of the pretentious old tut the Victorians put up. This will have been the finest expression of the nouveau riche's lack of class, in its day. It's the equivalent of the footballer's mock Tudor house on the new estate.'

Nick looked up from his phone.

'Yeah, so in landed aristo terms does that make the Baxter-Smythes new money? Less than 200 years old - that's nowt when it comes to these families. When does Brian Salmon's money date back to, can you remember?'

'Around the same time. I seem to recall him telling us it was his great great grandfather who had made the money in merchant banking and had bought all the land. So that must in the 1820s or 30s.'

'In that case, I wouldn't mind betting the two families have known each other ever since. Both big players in landowning and horse racing. So this rivalry goes back decades, maybe even centuries. Maybe that's also behind this dispute between them.'

'Aye, it makes the likelihood of one wanting to screw over the other all the more likely. When you're rich you've nothing to worry about in life except the trivial shit, so it wouldn't surprise me at all if they obsessed over a small cup.'

Nick looked at his watch. 'C'mon, dinner is at 7.00pm; we'll be late, if we don't make tracks now.'

They walked at pace back to the hotel. After a quick wash, Nick changed into his white linen shirt and dark, fitted suit.

'I'm bound to get gravy down this,' he said, tugging at the shirt.

Julie emerged from the bathroom. 'You'd better not. That's a mint shirt, that is. Here, zip me up, will you?'

She turned her back to him and he carefully fastened the fine black zip on the vintage 1920s dress she'd bought four years ago.

'You look like something out of a costume drama in this,' said Nick, patting her on the backside and spinning her around.

'Seemed appropriate for this old place, though. I know it's quite cheap here at this time of year, but it's still quite posh, or as posh a place as we get to go to and I've not worn it since that awards do.'

'I love all the black embroidery on the taffeta, silk and lace. Aw, you look ace. God, I fancy you.' It was out of his mouth before he'd even considered whether to say it.

She flicked at her hair happily, so it spilled down over the front of her shoulders. 'Aye, I make a decent Lady Muck, I reckon. And it matches the underwear! Wahay!' She lifted up the dress to show him the cheap black underwear.

'And that is the most important thing,' laughed Nick, feeling a stirring below the waist.

She sat down to pull on a pair of low-heeled black velvet shoes. 'I never wear proper women's shoes these days. I lived in them when I had my old job. That was another good reason to leave. At least I can do my job in trainers these days. Don't think this dress would work with them, though, somehow.'

When they were both ready, Julie set their camera on a delay, placed it on the dressing table and they stood together, arms around each other, to pose for the photo. She looked at it after it had been taken. 'Aw, that's a lovely one of us. I'll just put that on my Facebook page. We could almost pass for respectable members of the middle class in this. Almost, but not quite.'

He looked over her shoulder. Arms around each other's shoulders, heads leaned in together, Julie in low heels made them the same height. They looked like they were in a wedding photo.

She pointed with her index finger at him. 'And, note, dressing to the left.'

'Ha. Oh, yeah. It's quite obvious in this suit, isn't it?'

She raised an eyebrow at him. 'There's not much you can do about it, luv. Not in close-fitting pants like those. You could tuck it up between your legs and pretend you're a woman, if you like.'

'Only if you're a *very* good girl.'

'Oh, I don't think there's much chance of that, not tonight.'

'Is there not?'

She grinned at him. 'Oooh, no, darlin'. Almost none at all.'

They went down to the restaurant and were shown to a table by the window overlooking the substantial grounds.

'Shall we order some reassuringly expensive booze?' said Nick, looking at the drinks menu.

'Oh, aye, go on. Not champagne, though. It's overrated. Everyone knows it is an' all. I've had the most expensive and half of them taste like white cider. This could be because I'm common, I suppose.'

'I never got the obsession with it. Spend 50 on champagne and you get something OK, spend that on a bottle of red or white and you get something mind-blowing. How about a Californian Chardonnay?'

'Great. As long as it's very oaky.'

'Why very oaky?'

'Because people who are wine snobs all think yer oaky chardo is

112

common and mass-produced and basically a bit vulgar, whereas people like me who just like wine as long as it comes in a massive bottle, just like it 'cos it tastes nice. It's a blow for unpretentiousness.'

'I like your logic. There's a Russian River one here, it says it's rich and oaky. We'll have that. Only 40 quid.'

She opened her mouth and screamed in silent horror.

'Well, it's all going on the last bit of credit we have access to, so we might as well push the boat out and go down all guns blazing into the ocean of debt.'

'Ah, well, bollocks to it. Life is all about now. Tomorrow can take care of itself.'

He pointed to it on the menu to the waiter. 'I bet you never used to say that when you were a thrusting career woman in London.'

'I wouldn't have said it, no, but I always thought it.'

The waiter poured the wine into their glasses after Nick waved away an opportunity to taste it, an entirely pointless task as no-one ever sent a bottle back for being corked. In this case, it was delicious.

'My philosophical musings must be rubbing off on you...and let me just stop you there before you make a rubbing off on me joke.'

She threw her head back and laughed. 'Oh, darlin', you know me so well.'

They ordered a smoked salmon starter, followed by roast pheasant and a dessert of chocolate cheesecake. It was brought to the table by a tall blonde man with an East European accent.

'He's got amazing bone structure, that fella,' said Julie as he went away. 'You could slice meat on his cheekbones.'

'I think he worked on the parmo catering at Big Fish's party.'

She nodded. 'Yeah, I think he did. In fact, the bar staff look familiar from the Boro Ballroom, too.'

'Probably hired them at the same gangmaster that the Fish used.'

'Nah, these lot are too well-fed looking to be typical illegals. The blokes are positively buff. Look like body builders. Funny seeing them up here in Teesdale, though - there were some working at the stables as well, wasn't there?'

After eating, they ordered another bottle of wine and took it through to a large bar area, at one end of which was a log fire. Nick poured them each half a glass, as they sat alongside each other on a soft chenille sofa.

'By the time we've had this, I will be pissed as a fart,' she said. 'I feel proper lush, all full and warm and nice.'

'Yeah, nice to get out of Teesside. Maybe we made a mistake to move into town. Being out in the countryside again reminds me of how nice to was to live in that old farmhouse.'

'It was nice, apart from the armies of mice. But the flat is handy and it's cozy, too. I really like it and we've got the allotment for a bit of gardening and that...it's a nice combo, I think.'

As she spoke a red-faced man in a green tweed jacket came in. He was wearing voluminous gold jumbo cord trousers. In a booming voice, he ordered a pint of a local ale.

'Have you noticed your rural poshy does very little to dilute the cliché or archetype?' said Nick.

Julie cast a vaguely contemptuous glance at the man at the bar. 'Well, they're not bothered, are they? They dismiss any criticism of them by townsfolk as being due to our funny urban ways and not understanding country ways.'

Nick tutted. 'It's all bollocks, that. There is nothing special about country ways, unless they're still ducking witches out here - which actually wouldn't surprise me. It's all a false distinction, if you ask me. They just like to think of themselves as different.'

'They probably do the nude badger watching that Jeff is always going on about. You could nettle a nipple or sting a scrotum doing that. Very painful.'

'Do you think he's Baxter-Smythe?' said Nick, sipping at his wine.

'Yeah. Deffo. He thinks he's king cock, him.'

'Though those trousers are too huge and loose to tell if he's king cock or not.'

'Probably hasn't got one. Lost it in a threshing machine accident or it was bitten off by an angry goat in a bestial tryst.'

He pushed at her playfully and they collapsed into a drunken fit of the giggles.

'Right, I'm going to see if I can get to and from the toilet without falling over,' said Nick. 'I've got no tolerance for drink any more.'

He weaved off and found the gents. Thankfully it was empty. That meant he could use the urinal rather than a stall. Even when drunk his paruresis wasn't improved. Thankfully, he had just begun to relieve his bladder when someone came in. The weird condition meant that as long as he'd started to go, the presence of someone else didn't dry it up; it only prevented it starting in the first place. What a crazy condition it was to suffer from. Maybe he should get hypnosis for it. Yeah. He'd seen a local advert for someone who did hypnotherapy. It was time he got over it.

Any man knows that when sharing a relatively small space with other men, all of whom are passing water, you don't look around. At least you don't in the northeast of England, not if you wanted to avoid getting hit or worse, getting someone else's piss on you. So he didn't even glance at the other man, but even so, Nick could sense that he was being looked at. You always know when it's happening even if you don't look across, the perception that someone is looking at you pissing is strong and it's not a nice feeling; in fact, it felt intrusive. After he'd done, Nick zipped up and walked over to the sink to wash his hands. It was then that he noticed the man looking at him was the big man in the voluminous corduroy trousers.

'Lovely sunset tonight, wasn't it?' said the big man, in an upper-crust accent, washing his hands alongside Nick.

Nick nodded. 'Really beautiful. We were walking down by the river and then crossed the stepping stones and went up by the stables. We saw some horses going at a hell of a lick. Very exciting.'

'Ah, yes, well, we've got some absolute thoroughbreds.'

'Oh, they're yours?'

He put his hands under the dryer.

'Well, yes. I run the place.'

'Ah, the Regency Stables. Great. I don't know much about racing, I'm actually a football writer, but I love horses. Marvellous animals.'

'A writer, eh. Who do you write for?'

'Anyone who pays. The *Northern Echo* and the *Yorkshire Post*, mostly.'

The man nodded and then pointed a thick finger at him.

'Nick Guymer. Right?' He grinned at Nick, annoyingly confident of being right.

That was weird. Too weird.

'Err...yeah. How did you know?'

'From your byline in the *Echo*. Never forget a face.'

That was a lie for a start. He didn't have a picture in the *Echo* next to his pieces. He didn't have a byline photo anywhere. Nick had to try and get some sort of psychological retaliation in.

'And you're Cameron Baxter-Smythe.'

But the fact that a stranger knew who he was didn't seem remarkable to Baxter-Smythe. He probably assumed everyone knew who he was. In his world, he was well known.

They shook hands. Although he'd washed them, the thought that 30 seconds ago he'd been holding his...with it...urgh. But it was a chance to get on the inside of the Regency operation and maybe find out more about the dispute with Blakeston and even where the Walter Francis Cup was for Brian.

'OK, Cameron. Why don't I drop by one day and do a piece on the Regency Stables? The paper always likes a story about a successful business in the area. I could highlight your winners and prospects for the future.'

'I don't see why not. Splendid idea. How about Tuesday?'

They left the toilets.

'Fine. 11am?'

'Good with me. Just call in at the stables. I have an office there.'

It didn't sound like there'd be a trophy cabinet actually at the stables.

'Actually, I'm a bit of a fan of architecture and I love your house. Is there any chance we could meet there? Bit of an intrusion, I know.'

Baxter-Smythe nodded. 'Fine.'

They walked back into the bar.

'So what are you doing up here on a Thursday night?'

'Oh, me and my missus are having a long weekend walking in Teesdale.' He nodded in Julie's direction.

'Ah, yes. I see. Well, nice to have met you, Nick Guymer. See you next week.'

Nick sat back down next to Julie.

'Don't tell me you were chatting him up in the bogs?'

'I was.'

'How? From inside a cubicle. That'd be a bit weird.'

Nick explained what had happened.

'Good work, that. Well done, you. You've got inside the enemy camp, so to speak...or you will have on Tuesday,' she said.

'He knew who I was, though. Said he'd seen my photo in the paper, even though I don't have one.'

'How odd. Maybe he just was mistaken.'

'Maybe. Or maybe he was lying.'

She shook her head. 'Don't get paranoid, luv. Now, shall we take the rest of this bottle to bed?'

They made their way up the old, creaking wooden stairway.

'Have you ever been too drunk to have sex?' said Julie, kicking off her shoes as they got in the room.

'Oh, yeah. Loads of times. Actually, technically, no I haven't. I can always start...' he put the bottle down on the dressing table with their glasses beside and slipped off his jacket, draping it around the back of a chair.

'Ha ha, that was a quick change of mind. Unzip us, will you?'

She turned around and he pulled the small zip down to the small of her back.

'Ta. What a gent you are.'

'Eh, why?'

'See, you don't even know why, do you?'

'If I've done something good, I'll pretend it was totally a conscious decision. If bad, I blame it on being conditioned by the patriarchal society.' He put both thumbs up at her and pulled a goofy face.

She laughed and took a drink of wine, the dress hanging off her shoulders.

'A lesser gentleman would have taken the unzipping as an opportunity for a grope.'

'Oh. Would he? And that would have been wrong, right?'

'Not necessarily, but it's nice to have the choice.'

'I did think of doing it - obviously - but my hands are cold off the wine bottle so I thought I'd let them warm up a bit. Anyway, the difficult bit with sex when drunk isn't getting started, it's the finishing.'

She laughed and went into the toilet.

'Same for us lasses. We've all laid there and almost nodded off, whilst he's going hell for leather on your bones. That was pretty much my late 20s, right there.'

He went into the bathroom. She was sitting with her cheap underwear around her knees.

'Do you ever suffer from paruresis?'

'What's that again?'

'Can't wee in front of people.'

'I never have to test it, do I? I can wee in front of you. I am now!' She made a straining face, one eye half closed and then laughed as it hissed into the pan.

'What about if you're being rushed or put under pressure to do it quickly?'

She squinted up at him and shook her head. 'Nah. I can piss for Britain, me. Why, like?'

'I'm getting worse for it and it's starting to get right on my wick.'

He went back into the bedroom.

'Aw, must be a pain, that,' she said, following him out.

117

'The more you want it to not happen, the more it happens.'

She patted him on the backside. 'It's because you think so much about everything, innit? Have you never had any trouble with the old hard on for the same reason?'

'A couple of times when I was younger, mostly when I felt under pressure or got massively self-conscious. For years it was always in the back of my mind that it *might* happen. So don't go putting ideas in my head.'

'Nah, with me you've been the opposite, if anything.' She giggled a little. 'You're like the John Lewis of sex. Never knowingly under-hard.'

They both laughed, both drunk.

'I've been unable to finish but always been able to start. In such circumstances it's always best to fake it. I became very adept at faking it at one point.' He tried to focus as the wall slipped sideways a little. 'I actually started that early - even during the teenage dry humping years.'

'Dry humping, indeed. We should do more of that, if you like it so much. I just like being naked with you, though.' She snorted and shook her head. 'You're a funny bloke, you. Why did you fake it?'

'I seem to recall I just couldn't get to the end game and that seemed like it'd be an insult to the girl, so I faked it. It was easy, we were fully clothed.'

She went for a wash and called out to him as she was doing so.

'I'm impressed. Very. So much easier for us girls to do a bit of groany-groany, shudder, pant and the job's a good 'un.'

She came out of the bathroom again with a towel, drying her face. 'I was ace at it, me.'

'I bet you think no-one ever faked it with you,' he said.

'I'm certain not even one did,' she said with the confidence of a drunk.

'No woman ever imagines the man has faked it. Not one. Sometimes I enjoyed the faking more than the rest of the sex. It felt like more of an achievement.'

She took off her watch and let the dress fall to the floor, bending over to pick it up and put it on a hanger.

'And are you going to fake it tonight?' She gave him her arched eyebrows, wicked grin.

'Fake it? No need. There. I've already done it.' He make a panting expression at her as she stood in her underwear, hand resting on one hip, sipping at her wine.

'You'd better not have, I don't want to have to get that suit dry cleaned.'

He laughed, took the pants off and draped his shirt over the back of the chair.

She walked unsteadily over to him. 'You know what?'

'That we're both drunk, again?'

'We are. Very. Come here... this is important.' She put her hands on his shoulders as he sat down on the bed, swaying a little in front of him, then sat down sideways on his lap. He held her around the waist, feeling his lust rising with her warm body pressing into him. Her pale skin reflected the low yellow light. 'I'm sorry I've not quite been myself. You've been very patient with me...especially about sex and that...'

'I don't know about being patient. I know you've been struggling a bit, but you've still been great, man. Still a lot of fun. Still beautiful. And we had a good night out at the ballroom. That was nice.'

She squinted in thought. 'I know, but I've sort of been trying to make myself be myself, rather than just be myself. Does that make any sense?'

'I know you have. I could tell.' He stroked the small of her back down to her buttocks and with the other hand made a circular rubbing motion on her belly.

'Of course you could. You're not so daft, you. But our long talk today, it's helped me reconnect to myself and to you and me. I feel more normal and I've not felt normal for ages.' She let out a big sigh. 'Oh, god, it feels nice. Really nice.'

She unfastened her bra and threw it onto the floor and kissed him, rubbing his ear as she did so.

'Thank you for being a lovely man,' she whispered. 'Oh, and if you're interested, I fancy a really massive fuck,' she said it, as though it was just incidental, then gurgled her dirty laugh. It was the laugh he'd missed. It was the real Julie, with a look of lust in her dilated pupils. 'What shall we do first?'

He lifted her up, laid her on her back on the bed and kissed her.

'It's me who should be thanking you. I'm the luckiest man that ever dressed to the left,' he said, removing his underwear.

She drew her legs up and spread them wide, grinning up at him. 'Not so much to the left now, as straight up the middle. Just the way I like it. Come here, darlin'. She was breathing quickly, her heart racing as they clung together, skin on skin, wrapped around each other, breathing each others' air. 'Oh, god, I want to do it with you all night,' she whispered in his ear, in between little passionate moans, as she writhed under him, relishing their intimacy. He gave his whole body to her now, all the love in his words translated physically.

'I actually had a weirdly filthy dream last night,' said Julie after they chose bacon and eggs and sausages from the breakfast counter. 'Strange really, I never have those sorts of dreams.'

'Did it involve me?'

'Of course it did.'

'It doesn't have to. I don't mind if it didn't. It doesn't count as being unfaithful.'

'Is that your way of telling me you dream about other women?'

'I don't dream about women at all, as far as I can remember. I'd like to, but it never happens. More usually I'm being found doing something somewhere that I shouldn't be doing it. Much like waking life, in that regard.'

They got a table and ordered some coffee, both feeling a little hung over and tired.

'It was very odd. You were a centaur with hairy hind legs with your thingy just hanging there like a horse.'

She shook her head in surprise.

'Blimey. What happened?'

'You were instructing me on how to have it off correctly because I'd been doing it wrong all these years,' she said, in a low whisper, cutting into her bacon.

'Me? Instructing you? It was definitely a dream. You've forgotten more than I'll ever know.'

'Don't be daft, man. There's nowt much to know, is there? It's hardly quantum physics. But it got *very* rude,' She actually look embarrassed. 'I can still see it in my mind's eye. When you're being given a good seeing to by a half horse, half human, you know things have got weird.'

'That or you're having a Friday night out in Hartlepool.'

She yelped a laugh.

'It was *quite* an education, let me tell you. Very vivid. I woke up at 6am in a right lather. I nearly woke you up to sort me out, but I feel back to sleep.'

'Ha ha...sadly, I never get rude dreams.'

'No, but you got a lot of very rude reality last night. I hope we didn't make too much noise. I thought the woman on the desk was giving me a funny look when we came down.'

'We were quite quiet, I think, or muffled at least,' he said, in a whisper. 'We were at it for *ages*, though. You were on top form, Jules.'

'You think? You can talk, cor, lad, that was proper seeing to that you dished out to us. We both had a lot of fuel stored in the tank, didn't we? I nearly bit that pillow in half, trying to keep quiet.' She had a wide grin on her face. 'It was ace.'

'So, shall we have a day of walking up by High Force, get back for another meaty dinner, some more drink and another night of passion followed by some in-sleep bestial porn?'

She grinned at him. 'Oh, alright then, if you insist.' For half a second, she rested her lips on a sausage, let her tongue lick the top of it and raised an eyebrow, her sapphire blue eyes electric. Yeah, the full Jules was back. Nick could have wept with relief. Where she'd put the bad feeling and upset, he didn't know. Maybe it would find an emotional release at some point in the future. But the shadow that had been cast on her for so many weeks seemed to have finally gone - disappeared by the sunshine of their love.

It was a clear, mild, bright morning as they drove up to High Force, parked and then climbed right up to the top of the famous waterfall, looking down into the powerful plunge pool before walking a further five miles up to Cow Green Reservoir, set high on the moors. This was the rolling moorlands of the upper Pennines, wild and windy; a land that many Northerners have a deep connection to, especially in how its resolute, bleak magnificence is reflected in the character of the people.

Taking a rest, looking out over the cold, blue reservoir whilst drinking green tea from a flask, Nick pointed to a line on the near horizon.

'What's that up there?'

They both squinted at a ridge of isolated moorland to the north.

'It's some people, I think. Yeah, a line of people.'

They ran down a slope and then peeled to the left and right. Nick took out a pair of birdwatching binoculars that they always carried on their walks.

'I think it's an army exercise. They're all men. Some of them are in camouflage fatigues. They seem to be practising a routine or something.'

'They're always yomping around on moors. We once saw them up at Otterburn, didn't we?'

'Yeah, these have got guns. Someone is being timed setting up a machine gun. They've got a stop-watch on him.'

'That'd be useful for quickly shooting a lot of game birds!' she laughed and made a rat-a-tat-tat sound.

'Ha, yeah. They've picked it up now and are running off with it.' He watched them for a minute. 'Jules? This is weird. I think two of them are the bouncers that were on the door at the Ballroom. The ones that stopped Jeff and later broke up that fight.'

'Really?' She was puzzled. 'No...can't be...gettaway. Are you sure?'

'I'm not totally sure, no. They look similar, though.'

The dozen or so men ran over the ridge and down the other side and out of view.

'Come on, let's get back.' Nick drained the cup of tea, shook out the dregs and they walked along the single-track road. A large black Range Rover with big silver bull bars was parked up on a bend lower down. As they approached, it did a three-point turn and drove away from them.

After the 11-mile walk and dinner, they were tired and turned in early but still couldn't keep their hands off each other. Their sex bottle had been well and truly uncorked. It made the abstinence seem almost worthwhile.

Saturday repeated the pattern, with, if anything, even more lust.

On Sunday morning Nick looked out of the hotel room window onto open countryside. Even though it was late May, it had been a chilly night because it was so clear. A low mist shimmered above the land like silver smoke. Julie was still fast asleep so he slipped downstairs to take the air.

It was just after 6am but some staff were already up and about. He nodded a smile at a woman on the desk.

'It's a lovely morning,' he said.

'It would be if I hadn't only got to bed two hours ago,' she said with a weary smile.

He'd loved his early morning walks when they'd lived south of Yarm. The early morning invigoration and daily reconnection with nature was cheering even to a depressive soul, he had discovered.

Birds were already busy, diving at speed across the hotel gardens and into dense shrubbery. He walked out into the marketplace, jammed his hands into his walking pants pockets sucking in crisp, cold air, feeling cheerful; a weekend full of sex, walking, eating and drinking can do that to any man. Walking a little out of town at a brisk pace to get his heart rate up, he was soon approaching the Regency Towers house.

A pair of riders came trotting out of the stables and waved a hello to him, the chestnut brown horses very self-contained and calm. Beautiful.

As he approached the gates of the house, he noticed that they were now wide open. They'd been closed on the day they'd arrived. He stood and looked down the driveway. It swung around to the right and ended beside the front of the house. Inevitably, a large black Range Rover sat outside. You couldn't live in a house like this, in a place like this and not have the top-of-the-range Range Rover. It was probably a local bylaw. All that guff about them needing an off-road vehicle, yeah, being on the driveway was the nearest this one had ever been to off road, judging by its pristine condition. Probably still wouldn't stop them writing it off against tax as a business expense, though. The richer you are, the richer you stay.

A black Range Rover had been seen forcing Jim George off the road. The top of the range were especially huge, heavy cars. It wasn't hard to see how one could make a mess of an old 1980s Mini Metro. By comparison, it was a tank. This one was absolutely pristine. It looked fresh off the forecourt and had big silver bull bars, the same as the car they'd seen up on the moors watching the army people training. My god, they were ugly cars. A symbol of where mankind was going wrong.

The house, like the car, was a big, vulgar pile with gargoyles peering down at various locations on the architecture. It was an expensive house and yet, in some ways, there was something cheap about it, culturally if not financially.

Nick stopped. There was a distant noise. A radio, possibly. He'd already walked on along the road when some raised voices blew on the breeze and then louder shouting punctured the Sunday morning silence.

He stopped again. It was coming from behind the Regency Towers wall. Quite a commotion.

Reversing up, he peered around one of the big pillars on which the wrought-iron gates were hung. Two men were going at it on the lawn, swinging punches at each other, then one dived in and grabbed the other by the waist, pushing him over and punching him on the ground. Big, hard, violent, raking blows.

What is it about seeing two people fighting that makes you want to intervene? It just seems to be something that shouldn't happen, which is kind of ridiculous because humans fighting is one of the basic defaults of our existence. All the same, out of instinct, Nick ran up to the two men. It wasn't until he was close that he realised they were both small blokes so it seemed likely they were jockeys. One was certainly under five feet and the other not much taller. They can't have each weighed more than 100 pounds wet through.

'Hey, hey...pack it in, you two,' said Nick, as he reached them, realising as he did so that he had no idea what words to use when confronted with two men fighting. As ever, you tend to rely on what you've heard in movies.

'Come on - break this up. It's no way to solve anything!'

He grabbed the bloke on top by the scruff of his sweatshirt and hauled him off without much effort. In fact he had to pull back a little to stop himself just throwing him away like he was a sack of rubbish.

Small they may have been, but they'd really hurt each other. Each had a busted, bloody nose and red marks on their faces from the punches. Both were in considerable pain. This wasn't, in football parlance, handbags, these two had been going at it hammer and tongs.

The man that had been getting the worst of got to his feet, wiping at his bloody swollen mouth.

'Thanks, mate,' he said toward Nick, then turned, hockled up phlegm and spat it out along with a broken front tooth.

'Are you alright? You've taken a bit of a pounding, mate. Do you need an ambulance?'

'Aye, he'll fucking get some more an' all,' said the other belligerent, smaller, sweatshirted man.

'Hey, hey...calm down, you,' said Nick. 'Whatever this is about, beating the crap out of each other won't help.'

'It won't fuckin' help him,' said the smaller man again and flew at his opponent in one, two, three strides and a leap, kicking him to the ground with a grunt and a bellow.

Nick plucked him off again and dragged him away in a tight grip. At a foot taller, four stone heavier and a lot more muscle, it wasn't hard to subdue him; nonetheless, he was powerful for his size. Jockeys were all muscle. He tugged and pulled to get free from Nick's grip, still absolutely raging.

'Look, you've got to calm the fuck down, lad,' said Nick, half pulling, half dragging him away from the other man.

But he wasn't for calming down at all. 'Get off me or I'll fuckin' have you an' all!' You had to admire his ambition. Nick could have broken him beyond repair.

'No, you won't. If I have to hit you, you'll stay hit - so calm down.'

Seeing his opponent was helpless under Nick's grip, the other man took the chance to run around and kick him in the balls, making the smaller man howl in pain.

'Fucking hell, will you pack it in!' yelled Nick. 'Stop sodding fighting!' He pushed the man well away. The sweatshirted man was bent double, holding his groin. 'You stay here. If you so much as move I'll knock you into the middle of next week.' Turning to the taller of the two, who was fiddling with his broken teeth, he yelled at him. 'Now, you walk over there to the gates and cool off.'

At last, the man did as he was told.

Sweatshirt yelled more abuse but seemed physically subdued by pain now.

'Do I have to get the police here?' Nick said, hands on hips, looking down at him.

'I don't give a fuck if you do. You think they'll do anything?'

'Last time I looked, beating the crap out of people was against the law,' said Nick.

'You're not from round here, are you?' he said, spat again and laughed at him in a mocking sort of way, like Nick was stupid.

'Oh, no, don't tell me this is part of some rural tradition that townies don't understand. Don't give me that bullshit,' said Nick.

He turned to look at the other bloke. He was squatting on his haunches, also in some pain, mopping at drops of blood from his nose.

'Nothing that happens in here is illegal. Nothing. If you report this, as soon as you tell them where it happened, they won't want to know. Try it, sunshine. Just try it.'

'What's he talking about?' said Nick, turning to the other bloke. 'Do you work here?'

'Do I fuck?'

'He's a Blakeston bastard, aren't you, son?'

'Don't kick off again, for god's sake,' said Nick, wearily.

'I'm going.' The Blakeston man jabbed a finger. 'This isn't over, Macca. You know you've got what's rightfully ours. You prick! I know you're a thieving bastard. I'll fucking 'ave you, sooner or later I'll 'ave you and if you ever say I've pulled the whip on an 'orse again, I swear I'll kill you.'

'You pulled the whip on General Johnson last week. There. You gonna kill me now, you fucking no-mark?!'

It was then that Nick realised it was Mickey, the man he'd seen with Big Fish at Blakeston Stables. This was a fight about the stolen cup. It had to be. The other man was Macca, the man who had, allegedly, stolen the cup. Bloody hell, these two hated each other. This was a personal battle.

Macca turned and was about to go back in the house.

'Hey. Was this all about the Sir Walter Francis Cup?' said Nick.

The man stopped, turned around and flew at Nick, grabbing him by his jacket. 'How the fuck do you know about that?' His grip was strong. It was like being attacked by a sodding weasel - small, but vicious and powerful.

125

'I'll take that as a yes, then,' said Nick, pushing the man to arm's length with as much strength as he could muster. The jockey staggered backwards and nearly fell over.

'Who the fuck are you, like?' said the man, so aggressively that Nick took a step back. This fella's fury was impressive. He could muster it up and spit it out like a ball of fire, almost at will. 'If you know what's good for you, you'll walk out of here and forget you ever saw anything. You get me? You're out of your depth, son. Way out. We make our own rules up here at Regency. We do what we want. Go on...jog on...you've not seen nothing.'

'Not seen nothing? You mean I have seen something? That's a double negative,' said Nick, aware it would anger the man some more.

'Don't try and smart arse me. There's trouble coming your way. You have no fucking idea. Don't say you weren't warned.' He jabbed a tiny finger at him.

He gave him such a fierce look that it imprinted itself on Nick's eyeballs. It was a look that you'd have to describe, given its violence and dark anger, as evil.

The wee man marched back into the big house. Nick turned and walked back to the hotel. Bloody rural nutters. You didn't get this sort of trouble off the smack heads hanging around Stockton High Street.

He got back to the hotel and told Julie what had happened. She looked amazed.

'Did you get hurt, luv?'

He shook his head. 'No, but it was the most vicious bit of fighting I've seen for a long while. They were both furious at each other.'

'Will you mention it to CBS on Tuesday?'

'Eh? CBS? The record label?'

'Cameron Baxter-Smythe. I'm not wasting good working-class breath on a posh name that long.'

'CBS, I like it. Jeff will enjoy that, too. Yeah, I'll have to, I suppose. It'd be odd if I didn't. The weird thing is still that CBS already knew me.'

'Yeah, you said, from your byline.'

'As I don't have a byline picture, he can't have done. So he lied about that. Why lie?'

'Do you think he's been checking up on you or something?'

'Yeah, I think so. I'm sort of connected to the Blakeston Estate through Jeff. Do enough internet searches and you'll find me and Jeff linked together. See, that's what that fight was about. They think Blakeston has been cheating and we know Brian and by extension Mickey thinks that Regency nicked their Sir Wotsit Bollock and Prong Cup.'

Julie laughed a deep chuckle. 'I think I should have won the Bollock and Prong Trophy this weekend.' She made a wince and squeezed herself between the legs. 'I'm actually a bit bruised.'

'Sorry, Jules. I did get a bit carried away. I got a bit...ha ha...vigorous.'

She laughed. 'We both did.' She bit her bottom lip and shook her head a little. 'Eee, dear me, the things we get up to when we've got the horn.'

She finished packing her bag.

'There's a Range Rover with big chrome bull bars at Regency Towers. Looks like the same one that was watching those men training on the moors.'

'Well, he probably owns all that land up there, doesn't he? He was probably pulling a "get off my land" trip.'

After checking out, they went to the car park to the blue Porsche.

'I bet in the future, we look back at this weekend as a significant one in our lives,' said Julie, looking up at the old hotel.

He ruffled her hair. 'Yeah, I think you're right. It's been a really lovely three days...'

'...and nights,' she added, and kissed him.

Julie drove the Porsche out of the hotel car park.

She had just begun to accelerate out of the town in a low gear, when a large black Range Rover zoomed up behind them and without stopping tried to ram into the back of the Porsche. Julie, watching in her rear view mirror as the car approached far too fast, had anticipated it and was already stepping on the gas. As a result it nudged them, but did no damage.

'What the fuck's that doing?' yelled Julie. 'Look, it's a black Range Rover.'

'It's not the one at CBS's house,' said Nick, turning to look. It didn't have the bull bars on. 'The jockey made some sort of threat to me, saying we'd walked into a lot of trouble. Is this what he meant?'

It tried to ram them again, approaching at speed, but Julie had more revs under her foot and pulled away again, swinging the car into a tight bend. It had magnificent handling and could outrun the bigger car.

'The windows on this are tinted, even the windscreen is,' said Nick, and even as he spoke the words, it came back to him. As Jim George had passed them at the allotment gates to go to his car, a Range Rover with tinted windows had passed them outside the allotment. It was an observation that had been sitting in his unconscious and now it returned to him. He hadn't consciously known he'd seen it and even when the old woman who witnessed the car being rammed said it had been a black Range Rover, it still hadn't registered but now, seeing it here in real life, the memory was strong and clear. Was this the same one that rammed Jim George - the one that had contained the person who had then snapped his neck?

She looked in her mirrors again. 'That's illegal. You're not allowed to have your windscreen blacked out.'

Every time the road straightened out, the Range Rover came flying up to them, gaining ground only to lose it again as the Porsche gripped the corner like a cat and pulled away. It was 35 years old but if you thrashed the old girl, she could still really shift off the mark, roaring from 30 to 110 in seconds.

'It's a private plate, 33RM91,' said Nick.

'RM? That's a military plate. Fucking hell. Didn't Colin say the killer was SAS, or something? It's him, Nick. He's trying to fucking kill us.'

CHAPTER 8

His heart was pounding in his chest. They were in trouble here. Someone wanted them dead. He'd got too near some sort of truth in Middleton, just as Macca had said.

She looked in her mirror again. 'Why the fuck is it a military car? Are they out to get us, or just anyone? Is it a psycho? Shit. He's getting closer again.'

She dropped the gears and took off past a farm vehicle, dramatically swinging it back in as an oncoming car came towards them. Accelerating again, she overtook a Ford and then another tractor. The Porsche probably wasn't as quick as a top-end Range Rover given a long distance race, but when it came to weaving in an out of traffic, its fantastic handling and ability to accelerate so quickly guaranteed the Rover couldn't get near them again, not least because Julie was good at flinging it around corners and building revs to get the most out of the release of the power.

'Something is very wrong about this. Who joy rides in a military car with illegally tinted windows? No-one.' He turned and looked behind again. The Range Rover was two vehicles back. It overtook. Now only one.

'Can you see the driver?' she shouted.

'No. The windscreen is too dark. This is serious shit. Have we got any weapons?'

'Weapons? Err...there's a toolbox in the boot. There's a fucking big wrench in there.'

'This is very fucked up. It's coming for us again. The road is like this for miles. We'll never get away from them.'

The Range Rover overtook the car between them and accelerated. The road was too twisty with too many corners to risk overtaking the car in front. This was going to end in a smash, one way or another. Julie chewed on her bottom lip and, looking in her rear-view mirror as the Range Rover sped up to them, at the last moment, she swung the Porsche left and into a lay-by, coming to a halt in a cloud of dust and gravel.

The Range Rover had been too close to follow them in and sped past.

'Nice move Jules! Fuck me, you're like a racing driver.'

She swung out into the road again, now behind the Range Rover.

'And now the hunted becomes the hunter,' she said. 'Look, this road goes into Barnard Castle and from there we can get onto the A67 home.'

As they got onto the A6278, the Range Rover put its foot down and flew off into the distance.

'Should I follow them?'

'No. We can't just drive behind them forever. They're not going to lead us anywhere. They'll know we're tailing them. Let them go.'

The black car disappeared around a bend and out of view.

The both blew out tense breaths of air.

'This is totally crazy. I just don't know why we're being picked on like this. It must be something to do with that fight I broke up. It's not just a random crazy in a military car, is it?'

Julie took a long curve. 'No, it can't be.'

As she spoke, the Range Rover came out of a track on the right at speed and accelerated so it was alongside and parallel to them, driving closer and closer, trying to force her off the road and onto the verge. She screamed an obscenity. Nick prepared for the smash that seemed inevitable. The road up ahead was straight and clear. She eased off the gas, letting the bigger car move ahead, then she dropped the gears, picked up speed again, burning past the slowing Range Rover. 'Bloody try and catch me, you twat!' she yelled. But it wouldn't be shaken off. It dipped in behind them as a car passed on the other side then, with the road clear again, it came alongside and slammed into the driver's side of the Porsche. Its huge weight was too much for the Porsche to resist. It lifted up briefly onto the two left-side wheels.

'We're going over at this rate.' said Julie, swearing again, hitting the brakes, shifting the car to the left and skidding into a lay-by set back from the road. She stamped hard to prevent them going through a hedge. The Porsche bucked and screeched and came to a halt in squeal of rubber. The Range Rover pulled over, blocking their exit from the lay-by.

'Fucking hell...get that wrench!' yelled Julie.

Nick leapt out of the car and pulled open the boot. As he did so, a man of similar height and build to him got out of the driver's side of the Range Rover and ran towards him. There was no time to even pull open the toolbox. Nick turned to face the man. No point in waiting around here. As soon as he was within reach, Nick set himself and unleashed a right hander to the man's face, raking it into him, once and then a second time as the man staggered back. Two solid hits.

Julie had got out of the car, ran behind the man and, in the manner of an old-school defender, kicked the him in the back of the leg, giving him a dead leg. Never mess with an aficionado of 1970s football, in a fight.

He let out some sort of guttural expletive as he fell to the muddy ground.

Nick leaned over him and hauled him up by the camouflage army jacket he was wearing. Julie ran to the boot of the car, opened the toolbox and took out a huge wrench.

'You want this in your face? You fucking bastard?!' she said, her fury and fear being whisked into a hurricane of emotion. 'What the hell are you doing, man?'

Nick pulled at him and flung him against the side of the Porsche, weighing up whether to give him another dig. He was a clean cut, short back and sides bloke. Could easily pass for a typical army officer.

'Did you kill Jim George?' he said.

'I'm not telling you anything. That's not my job,' he said, spitting out some blood from where Nick had split his lip.

'So what the hell is going on?' said Julie, jabbing at him in the arm. 'Why are you trying to force us off the road?'

In a swift move that looked like some aggressive form of ballet, he grabbed the wrench from her, pulling her over as he did so. Julie screamed as she hit the ground but he had pulled himself up at the same time he had pulled her over and quickly straddled her across her back, grabbing at her hair and yanking her head backwards.

'I can snap her fucking neck right here and now. Is that what you want?!!' he yelled at Nick, who had instinctively advanced on him to protect Julie, cursing himself for not spotting the move coming.

'Leave her alone!'

The man yanked on her hair again but she didn't scream this time. Her face set in bitter fury at this attack.

'Nope. Don't think I'll do that,' he said, nastily.

'Why us? What's this to do with us?' said Nick.

'Shuttup. Listen to me. This is a warning. Right? One. Stay away from Regency Stables and Regency Towers. Two. Tell your mate Jeff Evans the exact same thing. Three. Do not bother telling Colin Harcombe or any other police officer about this. It will do no good. I am above the law. Four. Anything Brian Salmon has told you is a lie. Understand? If you believe him, it will get you killed. Understand?'

'What? Who are you?'

'You don't need to know who I am. You already know too much. You just need to listen to me. Right? This is your one and only warning. Next time, you're dead. You, her, your mate. Dead. No. Second. Chances.'

He released his grip on Julie, stood up and walked briskly back to the Range Rover. He got in and started the engine, pulling away with a screech. As he did so, Nick took a photo of the vehicle on his phone.

The whole incident had totally ruined their lovely weekend. When you're going through a shit time, you can handle some evil more easily because that seems to be what life is throwing at you and it's not exactly a deviation from the norm. But when life has been full of love and sunshine, the ugly aspects of existence seem even more intrusive.

And it had been absolutely terrifying. The man was so cold and vicious. The way he'd pinned Julie down and grabbed her hair was certainly the act of someone who was not unfamiliar with murder.

When they got home Nick sat and made some notes of everything to do with CBS, his house, the stables and the fight he'd broken up. He also made notes on what they knew about Brian and the missing cup.

He drew a family tree to express all these connections and studied it whilst sipping at a vodka and fizzy water. It was obvious that the dispute between the two stables extended from owners to jockeys and had been festering away for some time. It also seemed not exactly unlikely that because of that, Cameron Baxter-Smythe had known who he was, partly through name recognition in the *Northern Echo* but just as likely through being connected via Jeff to Blakeston. The army hard man had also obviously known who they and Jeff were. Someone had done work on them, either before he'd broken up the fight, or after.

The jockey from Regency had made similar claims to the Range Rover man about doing what they want and the police ignoring them, as though they had immunity. But surely none of them were above the law.

'Jules. When you said that the plate was a military plate, what does that actually mean?'

She came in fastening an old denim shirt and hitching up her comfy old ripped jeans, hair tied up in a colourful scarf. She hooked her thumb into a bra strap and adjusted it a little.

'It means whoever is driving it is in the armed forces or at least the car is registered with the MOD.'

'But it can't be for top-secret people because it *is* obviously a military car. Only people who wouldn't be a target would drive them.'

'Yeah, just regular MOD workers, I suppose. It is a bit odd really, in these days of terrorism, anything that identifies a car as being part of the state would be a target, you'd think. I really don't see the virtue in it.'

'But why would the military - presumably the army - be involved in the Regency Stables?'

She went into the kitchen, poured herself a big gin and tonic and cut a slice of lime, returning with her lips pursed together in a pout of contemplation. 'Actually, we don't know he really was in the army, regardless of the plates. They could have been illegally made up plates, even though they looked right 'cos they were non-reflective black plates with white lettering. He might be one of these fantasists who likes to play at being in the SAS and goes everywhere in full army gear but is actually on the dole in Dormanstown.'

Nick tapped at the picture of the car on his phone. 'Nah. He wasn't one of those. He was too sure of himself and too cold. He'd killed before. I stiffed him with two cracking right-handers out of the blue. He didn't even go down and he wasn't fazed by it. He'd been in fights, he knew how to handle himself. I think he *was* SAS. The way he caught hold of you and turned your threat into an attack was the work of a pro.'

'I agree. He was a professional hard man.' She hissed quietly. 'I'm fucking furious about it. How dare he do that to me?' She rubbed her sore neck. 'I'm havin' him for that. No-one does that to me.'

'We have to be careful, Jules. He wasn't pissing around. I know you're angry and rightly so...but this is serious shit. He killed Elvis. I'm certain it was him. Jim George knew something or had done something in relation to the Salmon and CBS dispute. That means there is some sort of conspiracy going on and the police are complicit in it at some level. Colin almost told me as much. He said "forces" were at work in the region and that this all had an international dimension. Another weird thing is, CBS gave me his card with his office and mobile numbers on. He wouldn't have done that if he didn't want me around the house, would he? So that attack was something to do with me breaking up the fight or he'd never have given me the card.'

'Or he doesn't know about the army man. Maybe the army man is working against him. Why don't you call him in the morning, just to confirm the interview is on, see what he says? He'll put you off if he's behind the attack.'

'Yeah, I will. The other option is to give Colin a call. That's not Cleveland Police's territory up there, though, is it?'

'No, but the bloke said not to tell the police about it, didn't he?'

'Sort of. He said not to bother telling Colin or any other cop because he was above the law.'

'I'm not sure you should tell Colin yet. Not until we know more about this.'

Nick agreed.

The front door buzzer went. 'Oh, that'll be Shawn,' said Julie, padding to the door to buzz her in.

'Shawn? Shawn Yeadon?'

'Aye. She texted me earlier. We're going out for a drink. Don't worry, I'm not going to say anything about what happened. I don't want her to know anything about it. Being attacked like that is horrible and abusive and isn't the sort of thing you really want to talk about.' She opened the door and waited. 'Hey lady, how are you?'

Nick looked up as his old schoolboy crush came into the living room dressed in a blue floral blouse, dark blue trousers and flat shoes. She smiled nicely at him with blue eyes and wore a little blue eye shadow, red lipstick on thin lips, her hair cut into a longish bob and coloured to a close approximation of the fair to blonde it had been when they were all a lot younger. She was what Jeff would call 'straight', meaning she didn't have any rock 'n' roll freak in her. Nick wasn't so sure. He thought he saw a spark in her eyes which hinted at a more exotic private life.

'Hello, Nick.'

'Now then. You look good, Shawn. How's life treating you?'

'Good, ta.'

'I'm just having a substantial gin. Do you want one?' said Julie.

'Ooh, yes, please.'

She went to the kitchen, leaving them alone together.

Nick let out a little, tight breath, feeling stressed out by the attack on them and also feeling a bit awkward in Shawn's company. Though why he should feel awkward, just because a woman he had spent a sizeable amount of his teenage years privately in love with was in the room 30 years later, he couldn't work out. It was just the same when he'd met her the previous summer. Despite the lines age had put on her, despite the fact her eyelids had sagged a little, despite the fact her neck was creased with age lines, she was very evidently still the same lovely lass he'd been daft about. Maybe those early flames never quite burn out; not unless there is a good reason for them to do so, anyway. Life had taken them in entirely different directions, but now here they were again.

'You're looking in good shape, Nick. Very tanned.' She smiled, making the lines around her mouth and eyes more defined.

'Oh, we just spent a long weekend up in Teesdale walking. It was ace weather.'

'And how are you keeping? Julie told me about what happened before Christmas. I felt dead sorry for you.'

'Ah, yeah. My leap for freedom? That was just due to some dodgy drugs. I'm good now. Best I've been for years, in fact. Thanks for asking.'

She looked away from him, and then returned to his gaze.

'Not at all. We're old friends, aren't we? I was upset for you.' She smiled her smile again. Yeah, it was just like when they were 16 and it felt like time hadn't passed at all. Oh, god.

'Yeah. Yeah, we are. How's work?'

'Good. I heard about Jules getting her new full-time paid job - really pleased for her. I said I'd take her for a drink to celebrate.'

'Going anywhere nice?'

'There's a wine bar opened on Yarm Lane called the Vine. Thought we'd try that out. All the places we used to drink in as kids are all long gone now, aren't they? The Vic, the Berni, Dovecot...'

'...yeah, it doesn't seem long ago, does it?'

She gave a little shake of her head.

'No, it all passes so quickly.'

'The Garrick has survived, and the Castle and Anchor.'

She pulled a face. 'Not over keen on going in there.'

'Aye. I know what you mean.'

Julie came back in and handed her a drink.

'It's nice in here, isn't it? I've never been in these flats,' said Shawn.

'Yeah, it's snug and much cheaper than our last place,' said Julie, sitting beside Shawn on the sofa.

'How are your neighbours?'

'We don't see them, do we, luv?' said Julie.

'They're a young married couple, but we never hear a squeak out of them.'

'The only downside of living here is we have to keep our noise down a bit so as not to disturb anyone,' said Julie, taking a big drink of gin. 'But it's not great hardship. Just involves a bit of pillow biting from time to time, doesn't it?' She gurgled her dirty laugh.

Shawn laughed a bit. 'Is he a groaner?'

'No, he's not much of a groaner, he's more of a screamer, like. Same as me. Ha ha.'

Shawn laughed and looked over at him. 'Aw, look, he's blushed.'

'Yeah, he does that. He's a bit shy, really. You'd think he was 16, not 48, wouldn't you?'

'Aye. He always was a bit shy, like, to say the least. Couldn't pluck up the courage to ask me out for years, even though he knew I wanted to go out with him.'

Julie laughed. 'Oh, yeah, you mentioned that. Ha ha. He was a bit messed up, poor lad. You should've asked him.'

'I should have done, but you didn't do that back then. You always waited for the lad to ask you out.'

'Oh, yeah. It was painful, sometimes. You'd be standing there silently urging them to ask you out. The daft thing is all the nicest lads were always the most shy at asking you. All the macho idiots just steamed right in.'

Shawn shrugged in a resigned way. 'I think we all learned that the hard way by going out with too many lads, just because they asked us. I liked your Nick because he was the opposite of that.'

'Aye, the one thing he isn't is a macho idiot. An idiot, yeah, but not a macho one!'

'Can you not talk about me like I'm not here?' said Nick, pretending to look at his computer, but not being able to concentrate at all because of their conversation.

The two women laughed. 'Owee, Shawn, we'll go in the kitchen and leave the sex bomb to explode in here on his own.'

Shawn gave him another nice smile and followed Julie out.

There is a powerful pull of nostalgia for someone from your past, from a time when you were young and had your whole life ahead of you. They were still connected to that feeling of youthful optimism, preserving it in some sort of emotional aspic, especially as, in this case, he'd never had a cross word with her. Never had a relationship that had soured. Old girlfriends that you'd broken up with on bad terms, you didn't think much about them. They were the long-expired firework that lay in the garden of your life, but for those that wasn't true of, maybe it was natural to still feel, at least to some degree, the warmth you had once felt for them, at least in abstract. It's hard to emotionally dismiss people with whom you've had many happy times and not many bad, especially when they're right there in front of you and seem to be the person you had always known.

He went back to his notes.

'We're off,' said Julie, putting her head around the door, a bit later. 'Won't be too late.' She blew him a kiss.

Once alone, he picked up the card that Baxter-Smythe had given him and dialled the mobile number, being careful to mask his number before he did so.

'Hello?' Even with one word, the upper-crust baritone was very distinctive.

'Is that Cameron?' said Nick, affecting a bluff, posher voice than his own.

'Indeed. Who's this?'

Nick dropped into his normal voice. 'Hi, there. It's Nick Guymer.'

'Hello, Nick. What can I do for you?' His tone didn't change. He wasn't surprised.

'I'm just calling to confirm our meeting at 11am on Tuesday morning. I've got a memory like a sieve these days and I didn't write it down.'

'Ah, I sympathise. Old age, old boy. Old age. Indeed, it's 11am Tuesday at the house.'

'Great, I look forward to it.'

'Toodle-pip.'

Toodle-pip? Who says toodle-pip in the 21st century? Did he think he was living in a P.G. Wodehouse novel or something? But there was no sign of him backing out or of not wanting to meet him, in which case it meant that the army man didn't want him to meet CBS, rather than the other way around...either that or CBS wanted him to turn up and be killed.

It had been the Regency jockey, Macca, who had been the most aggressive, the most in his face. Maybe a way into this was through Mickey, his opponent from Blakeston. It was 8.30pm. A lot of the Blakeston Stables people drank in the Horse and Jockey on Junction Road, which was probably the nearest pub to their workplace. If he just happened to be in a pub with a jockey, so what? Army man had said to stay away from Regency and to not believe Brian, he didn't say anything about not talking to jockeys and he seemed very clear about what Nick should or shouldn't do.

Actually, now he thought about it, that was a significant point. He'd spelled out his points very clearly: Don't go to Regency Stables or the house; tell Jeff the same thing; don't bother to tell the cops; and believing Brian would get them killed. Nothing at all about jockeys, or estate workers, or even about actually talking to Brian. Army man's instructions were clear. Don't believe anything Brian *said* or they'd end up dead. That wasn't the same thing as not talking to Brian. That can't have been a slip of the tongue or an omission.

He took a drive over to the Horse and Jockey pub. Big, inky black clouds began to spit rain as he pulled into its car park. It was once a bit of a Stockton institution for those who had grown up on the Hardwick and Roseworth estates, but those days felt long gone. Whereas it had once been a place for everyone to meet up, society seemed more fragmented now and people drank at home, something they'd rarely done in the 70s when Nick was growing up. The habits of life had changed and places like the Horse and Jockey had been forced to diversify into selling food and trying to attract families in, which was once something that no self-respecting boozer would ever have done. Back then, food was a bag of crisps or nuts, or, if they were hugely progressive gourmets, a cheese toastie. Children were barred on the basis they were children and had no place being in an establishment which served mind-altering substances. Plus, they made noise and annoyed people who had gone to the pub precisely to get away from the noise and annoyance of children in their own homes.

As he walked in, a boy of about seven or eight was sitting at a wooden table outside with bag of crisps. He was wearing a Boro shirt, his hair all messy. What was a lad that age doing there on his own? Anything could happen to him. The boy looked up at him and gave him a small, sweet smile, then began peering at a spider that was crawling on the table with the restless interest that every young kid has. Nick cast a backwards glance at him as he went inside. Children and alcohol always seemed to be a bad mix. The boy looked back at him with big eyes. He was such a young boy. He needed to be at home at this hour and tucked up in bed, not sitting outside a pub at a busy junction as the rain began to fall. Wasn't there a law against this sort of thing? What did you do? If you went up to him and asked if he was alright, someone would think, sure as night follows day, that you were a pervert, call the police and report you. Then you'd have to explain that you were only doing what any citizen worth their salt would do in making sure a vulnerable youngster was alright. He sighed and growled in his throat. As he did so, a bloke walked past him with a bottle of coke in one hand, a pint of lager in the other. He was in his mid 20s, thick set, beery and unhealthy-looking in sagging grey tracksuit bottoms and a red polo shirt. If the 21st-century loser had a uniform it was surely the ill-fitting, grubby grey trackie bottoms. Athletic gear worn by the least athletic people in society always looked like some sort of bitterly ironic joke. Nick let him past and then reversed up. Sure enough, he was the boy's father, or he was with him, at least. He gave the kid the pop and then lit up a fag.

It was awful. What chance did that young lad have with a father who wanted to be out drinking so much that he'd had to take the lad out with him? And he looked like such a dirty, scruffy bastard. A waster. The sort of waster you saw too many of in the area. In their 20s, out of shape, smoking and poorly educated. Probably destined for a drug habit or prison or both. The sort of man who'd never had a job, had never really wanted a job, let alone any responsibilities but who had nonetheless had a kid by the time he was 18. The sort of man who had not grown up. A boy in a man's body, wasting his days ducking and diving and drunk. How you got these people back into the fold to make them decent, productive people, was hard to see.

They were not even the grunt labour who could use their broad backs to beat pig iron and lay tarmac. They were just out of shape and useless and underneath the aggressive, often abusive male bravado that was second nature to them in order to survive in a hard world, they knew it, too. They'd given up on life and the world and the world wasn't much bothered about it, at least not until he robbed them to pay for a drug or drink habit or punched your daughter in the face when she rejected his drunken, groping advances.

You wanted to defend these people because it was obvious that the system wasn't working for them and that they were pissing their lives away. But they made it so hard. Stuck in a cycle of self-loathing and negativity, a mutual hatred between the waster and everyone else had become endemic and never the twain would meet. If only they could stop reproducing the species. By all means be a waster. In a cruel world, hell bent on exploiting the labour of the masses for the profit of an elite, it was a destructive but understandable lifestyle choice, but please don't bring a little innocent life into your devastated, chaotic, unstable one, because surely even a stupid sod like you knows it's not going to work out well for anyone.

He wished he could just scoop the boy up and take him to live somewhere where he'd have a chance of being loved and well educated and having his potential nurtured. It seemed so unfair that some kids grow up with love and support and others are all but abandoned. It seemed unfair that he and Julie wouldn't get the chance to give a child of their own that support and love. Then again, there were so many kids that needed good people to look after them. Maybe, sometime soon, they should look into adoption.

Please let him be alright, God. He said in his head. Though it a seemed a futile plea as, if there was a deity to hear him, it had surely put the kid in this position in the first place.

He went to the bar and ordered himself a tonic water and perched on a stool.

'Do you still get a lot of jockeys in here from Blakeston Stables?' he said. A barmaid with a face that looked carved out of granite and tobacco nodded. She looked like the sort of woman for whom fighting on the cobbles in the back lane after too many milk stouts would have been a way of life if she'd lived in the 1930s. With big forearms on her, she had what Jeff often called chicken choker's hands.

'Aye, plenty get in here, like.'

'I thought they might have been barred. A lot of places ban jockeys, don't they?'

'So I hear, like. We need the trade, though. If we barred everyone who gets in fights we'd have no bloody punters at all! We don't get no trouble off them, really. Only little lads, anyway, aren't they? Soon sort 'em out.'

She would as well. By god, aye. She could throw a jockey around like they were a small bag of potatoes.

'Now then, Nick. What are you doing in our neck of the woods?' He turned around. Julie's brother Kev Wells had come in. Dressed in a tight, short-sleeve blue checked shirt, with close-cropped greying fair hair, a look of cold blue steel in his eyes, a big gut and with huge arms covered in tattoos, he looked bloody terrifying. If Nick hadn't known him, he'd have run a mile.

'Alright, Kev. How are you?'

'Ah, you know what they say, I'm only in trouble if they catch me.' He laughed. 'Get you a pint?'

'No, ta. I'm OK.'

'Jules not with you?'

'She's out with a mate. Tell you what Kev, I'm after a jockey.'

Kev narrowed his blue eyes and stared at him.

'Why, what's he done? You need someone sorting out?'

That was always the first thing Kev Wells ever thought about. Conflict.

'No, man. Well, not yet. Actually, now I think on, there are two things I can pick your brains over. I'll buy. Lager, is it?'

'Just the one to be going on with.'

They took a seat by the window. Nick glanced out and saw the man with his boy. The bloke was still smoking and the lad sitting drinking coke. Both just sat at the wooden table staring at the traffic as the sun set. Neither looked happy. It was just a snapshot of life, but it was nonetheless heartbreaking on many levels.

'Are you meeting anyone?' said Nick. Kev shook his head.

'No. I often come in here for a quiet pint, as long as the Blakeston racing boys aren't in, anyway. They're fucking mental, that mob.'

'Funny you should say that, I was just saying to the barmaid how they get banned from pubs - jockeys, I mean.'

'It's always been like that. Worse in places like Northallerton or Ripon after race days. Youse can have a proper tear up if you fancy it down there, like.'

Nick nodded. 'You know me and Jules just spent a long weekend up in Teesdale.'

'Aye, our mam said, like.'

'I had to break up two jockeys who were fighting, right? Early in the morning, too. They were really going at it.'

Kev laughed. He loved any story about fighting. The scars and scabs that littered his fists, hands, arms and doubtless every other limb on his body were testament to a life spent brawling. It was in his DNA now. Fighting was his culture.

'Vicious little cunts, aren't they? Did you have to twat them? Given you've dumped our Ricky on his arse before now, a couple of lively short arses should be no problem to you.' Even if Nick became a Pulitzer Prize-winning writer, he'd never get any respect from Kev for it, at least not in comparison to the respect he got from him for being able to throw a decent right hander.

'Nah. I just kept them apart. Had to threaten to break one of them, obviously, and I nearly threw him away like a bag of shopping when I was hauling him off the other.' He mimed it. Kev liked that, laughing in his deep fag-ash rattle.

'Aye. It'd be like dwarf tossing. I always wanted a go at that. Can't believe the PC brigade have banned it.'

'I'm not sure they have. I think you can still toss a dwarf, if said dwarf is consenting. This jockey was just a five footer, though, so not an actual little person. Was light as a feather.'

'Sounds little enough to me. So what was it about?'

Nick shrugged. 'I don't know, exactly. But the one from the Regency Stables was really arsey with me. He said there was no point in reporting it to the police because they do what they want up there...'

'...giving it the big I Am, like?'

'Yeah. The implication was that the police gave them a free pass.'

Kev turned his mouth down and sank a third of his pint.

'Would not surprise me. Rural coppers are all bent. Make city coppers look like angels. He'll be right. They could probably murder someone up there, bury them on the moors and no-one would ever ask any questions.'

'You reckon?'

He nodded. 'Aye. Think about how many country boozers have lock-ins. That's all done with the copper's knowledge. They're all up each other's arses out there, literally. And up the sheep an' all. Dirty fuckers.' He seemed to mean it.

'Alright, well, the other lad in the fight was from Blakeston. I saw him over there with Big Fish one day. I was wondering if he drinks in here, y'see.'

'Probably does. What does he look like - short, obviously.'

'Small features. Quite boyish. Little hands. Slightly balding, maybe. Not that distinctive. He's called Mickey.'

'Why do you want find him, then?'

Should he tell him about the army man? Why not? Kev's world was one of threats and violence. He was more at home with it and they might need a nutter as an ally in this.

'Well...the thing is Kev, some weird shit happened to us on the way home. On the way back, we got rammed by a big Range Rover with tinted windows.' He told him about the battle they'd had on the road.

'Twockers, was it? Joyriding? Did it knack the car?'

'No, Jules put her foot down and got away...she was amazing at outmanoeuvring it...'

'Always been a good driver, our Jules. Used to go out on the old airfields when she was 15 to do handbrake turns.'

'...but it wasn't having it. It waited for us on a blind bend and forced us into a lay-by.'

'Fuck. Did you get some bother, like?' As if by instinct, he flexed his right hand and rubbed his knuckles. Or maybe it was just rheumatism.

'Aye, the fella got out and came straight for me, but I didn't hang around and I sank two stiff right handers into his face, but he took them. Then Jules dead-legged him. That was what dropped him.'

Kev gripped his hand into a big fist. 'Get in. She's always gone for the dead leg. Used to knack us when we were kids. Then what happened? What did he want?'

'That's the weird thing, Kev. The Range Rover had military plates and the bloke was army. Or he looked army. He had a camouflage jacket on and army pants and was all short back and sides.'

He showed him the photo he'd taken of the car.

'Top of the range, aye. And deffo military plates.'

Nick told him what happened next. On hearing that the man had straddled Julie across the back and pulled her hair, threatening to break her neck, it was possible to see Kev Wells's rage tank filling up in his eyes. Both the brothers were like this. Their defence of family was total, unquestioning and absolute. When he'd floored Ricky at Christmas, he'd only got away with it because, through Julie, he was considered family and thus allowed to administer rough justice, if necessary. Had he not been, Kev would have come round and beaten the shit out of him, or if he felt he couldn't do it all by himself, would have brought a couple of big mates to finish the job. It wouldn't have mattered how justified it was, or what Ricky had done. Any violation of the family had to be avenged.

'He's a fucking dead man,' he said with a quiet certainty. 'I'm not having that. Literally no-one has ever treated her like that. Not once. Not allowed. That will not stand. Right?' He jabbed a finger into the table. 'I'll hunt that cunt down and make the fucker pay. He knew her, so he must know me. He must know what will happen to him for this. And yet still he does it? Pfft, the fella is either very stupid or he's very fucking evil. Either way, he'll get a severe cunting for this.'

Nick was often shocked by Kev's language but it was pointless to admonish him for it. 'Yeah, well, that's what I was going to say. You're not dealing with a common or garden punk, Kev. This was a man who looked to me like he was used to violence. I think he was an SAS killer. I think he killed Jim George by snapping his neck.'

'He's not met me yet. I'll fuckin' snap his neck.'

'Didn't you hear me? He's a killer. He'll kill *you*, Kev.' Nick tried to impress the seriousness of the situation on him.

'The fuck he will. I'll not give him chance.'

'Think about it Kev. He's obviously either working for the military or he's an-ex army SAS whack job doing contract work. Either way, you're on a hiding to nothing. If he doesn't get you, someone else will. See? Think about it. You're not stupid. Ricky is stupid. You're not. Think, man. Yes, let's get revenge on him for abusing Julie like that. I want that as well, nothing would give me greater pleasure, but we have to be careful and do this right. We need to find out who he is and where he's from, who's he working for and why. Get me? Harcombe told me Jim George was murdered and I saw that blacked-out Range Rover just before the crash. No-one kills someone by snapping their neck, no-one except a trained killing machine. And like I say, I twatted him twice with my best right cross and it was like he could easily deal with the pain from that. He was used to fighting and violence. He kept his cool and took his chance.'

Kev said nothing for a bit, sank his lager and went to the bar for another.

As he sat down he jabbed a finger at Nick.

'You, son, are right. A proper cunting up is a dish best served cold. Isn't that what they say?'

No, it wasn't what anyone said, but Nick wasn't going to contradict Kev.

'Right, so, what's going on? Why does he want us to stay away from the Regency Stables, not tell the police and to disbelieve anything that Brian Salmon tells us?' Nick explained about the Fabergé cup. The name Fabergé didn't seem to mean anything to Kev. It wasn't in his cultural universe. His cultural universe started with lager and ended with a glass in the face.

'What? So this trophy is worth a load of money?'

'Sort of. It's priceless. You couldn't sell it on the open market. It'd have to be bought by a collector on the quiet.'

'And this stables is owned by Russians who'd buy it?'

'Or just Russians who want it.'

Kev sat and tried to work things out. It was almost possible to hear his brain whirring into gear.

'See, the thing is, right? That car is too expensive for regular army. It's top of the range and it's got illegal blacked-out windows. You'd soon get pulled up for that. Pigs would think you were a dope dealer.'

'He said the police wouldn't stop him. That's what this Macca bloke said, as well.'

'So why did he tell you not to go to the police?'

'He didn't say not to go to them, he said it wasn't *worth* going to them because he was above the law.'

'I'll tell you this. If he's above the law, then he's *not* a copper and he's *not* army. They've all got to stay right side of the law. The only ones above the law like that are secret service.'

'MI-5? Colin said MI-5 are on Teesside, right now.'

'MI summat, aye. Fuck. What have you walked into, Nick?'

'I don't bloody know. I can't work it out. It was just a fight between two arsey jockeys, as far as I could tell. I thought if the Mickey fella was in here, I could question him a bit, like. Obviously, he's pissed off at this cup being stolen and he thinks Macca has taken it, but it feels like something much bigger is going on.'

Kev drank more lager. Maybe it fuelled his brain. 'You know what I think, right? I think you must've seen something that someone didn't want you to see. That or something that they *think* you've seen, even if you haven't seen it or don't know that you've seen it. Get me?'

That made a lot of sense. When it came to being accused of things, Kev was an expert. Nick should've realised that.

'Well, I saw the Range Rover before Elvis was killed. Maybe that's it.'

'Maybe it is. He's trying to put the shitters up you, though. That much is for sure.'

'Well, he succeeded.'

Kev sank his pint in three more gulps and got up to buy more.

'My shout,' said Nick, putting his hand in his pocket. Maybe if he plied Kev with enough alcohol he'd turn into a Stephen bloody Hawking.

As he returned to the table with the pint, Kev was sucking on his bottom lip, in just the same way his sister did when contemplating something. 'Thing is, right. Just say he's MI-5, the only reason he's in that car is so the cops won't pull him over. It's his get out of jail free card. If he was working undercover, there's no way he'd have a car that was so identifiable. That probably means he's on the move all the time. It also means that he's likely to be in a hurry. He needs a free run all the time, so he must be *really* important. He's a last line of defence, if you ask me.'

His brain really did work better half pissed.

'Aye, I can see what you mean.'

'I reckon he's a Shadow. That's what he is.'

'He's what?'

'A Shadow. Like I say, he's a last line of defence. He's got a free pass off the authorities - he can basically do anything with im...err...y'know...

'...impunity?'

'Aye. He'll never get held up by plod pulling him in for speeding. They look him up and they know he's got to be left alone. Fuck me, I'd love to rob that car. You could crank the fucker up to 190 and no-one could stop you!'

'Thing is, I've got an interview with the stable owner on Tuesday but the army man said not any more, I didn't, but when I rang the posh bloke, he was still up for it.'

Kev blew out his cheeks. 'Wouldn't fancy that, if I was you. Might be setting you up to whack you.'

'You reckon? I did wonder that, myself.'

'They call people like him Shadows because it's like they don't exist. They can do anything they need to do. He's off the radar; anonymous and untraceable but working for the government. They give them one General to report to and no-one else even knows what they're doing. Deep undercover, like. He could probably kill you without every having to justify it to anyone, so you'd better watch your back. You want me and

Ricky to ride shotgun for you?'

Nick's instinct was to say no because hanging out with those two lowered your IQ by 50 per cent and he wasn't convinced that Kev hadn't just watched too many spy movies and was letting what imagination he had run away with him.

'I'll give you call if I need you, alright?'

Kev seemed to just ignore that. He was in now, whether Nick liked it or not.

'I'll get the boys in the Grid onto your picture. I know a few ex-army. Big bastard drinkers, mostly. They might know who this is. We'll hunt the fucker down, don't you worry. He's not getting away with owt. Did he have anything obvious about him? A scar or a limp?'

'He's probably got a bruise on his cheek where I hit him twice.'

That made Kev grin. Any report of violence clearly gave him joy, the sicko.

'...which side did you give him the dig?'

'His left.'

Kev nodded. 'OK. If he's still around the region, we'll spot him. Teesside's a small place, you can't hide for long. I should fucking well know.'

'Don't do anything stupid, Kev.' That seemed like a vain hope. 'Remember, if he is a Shadow, he can kill you with impunity, too.'

'I'd like to see him bloody try,' said Kev with typical bravado. It was as though he could never take a backward step. A hundred years ago he'd have been the first one out of the trenches, walking into enemy fire. And he'd be the first to be cut down.

'Well, I'd better get off. Hey, any idea who that bloke out the front with the young lad is?'

Kev looked over. 'That's Trev Jones. He's with his little Billy.'

'Is the kid alright, Kev? He'd been left out front on his own.'

'Was he bleeding or summat?'

Christ, what a thing to think first. Was he bleeding?!

'No...he just looked miserable and he'd been left on his own.'

'Trev's alright. His ma has just snuffed it. He's taken it bad.'

'Ah. Right. You just worry when you see a young lad on his own like that.'

Kev gave him a hard look. 'Don't be soft, just because you lost your kid before it was even a real kid doesn't mean you have go dopey over other people's kids. Just get on with life, son. It's not like you've any choice have you? Our Jules will.'

Maybe you had to be a good reader of people when you lived a life on the edge of criminality and violence. You had to be able to tell what people where thinking, who was screwing you and who might want to beat you to a pulp. Kev's quick perception caught Nick by surprise and reminded him how easy it was to underestimate people, even people who, by most measures, seemed pretty stupid most of the time.

'Yeah, you're right. OK. I'll be in touch, Kev.'

'Good lad.'

Nick walked past the boy on his way back to the car. He was playing with empty crisp bags while his dad was on the phone. Poor lad. He still felt an urge to scoop him up and take him to a better life.

Back at the flat he took a shower, feeling tired and introspective. The vicissitudes of adult life, you could deal with those to one degree or another, but seeing children getting a raw deal was something else. The boy just looked like he was so isolated and so deprived of affection and stimulation. His little lost face, looking to him for approval, kept returning to his mind. But what could you do? You couldn't save every child from a less-than-perfect life, no matter how much it broke your heart.

CHAPTER 9

He was in bed when Julie came home, peering around the door and waving.

'Hiya, luv.'

'Hey, Jules. Nice night out?'

'Aye. Not exactly an evening of carnal rock 'n' roll excess. Just two glasses of wine and a nice chat. I do like Shawn, though. She's a canny soul. One of those people who are just really nice. No side to them.'

'Does she live on her own still?'

She nodded and took off her denim shirt. 'Yeah, no man in her life. She's not interested.'

'She's not interested in men?'

'Not interested in a relationship. She's been burned once too often.'

'Poor lass. She did something along those lines when I met her last year.'

'If I hadn't met you, I'd be the same, I bet. I told her that.'

She went into the bathroom and emerged drying her face on a towel after a wash.

'Really? But you had a steadyish boyfriend when we met.'

'*Ish* is the word. I would have bailed out of that. Nice bloke but too boring.'

'Well, someone might come along, she might meet someone...you don't know...you never know.'

'Yeah, but she's 49 now and I'm not even sure she's open to the idea. She's set in her ways and used to living on her own. Hard to change from that as a way of life.'

Nick felt sad to hear that. 'But everyone deserves someone's love, Jules.'

'She's got her kids, so she's not starved of love. Better to be on your own than in an unsuitable relationship, I reckon. I think she's got it sussed. What's the point in throwing yourself into something on the off chance? It can cause so much disruption and hurt in your life. Easier not to bother.'

She unbuttoned her jeans and sat down to take them off. 'She said she has blokes stay over occasionally...so she still gets a bit of naughty and as she's not auditioning them for a relationship, I think it's all fairly free and easy. I told her I thought she had it sorted.'

Nick put his hands behind his head. 'Yeah, sounds like it. It's always easy to assume that a couple is happy and in love, but I bet many aren't really and they'd probably have more fun on their own. Too much emphasis is put on pairing up - everything from literature to music is about it, but the fact is, a lot of people are with other people out of habit or convenience or fear and not because of some deep connection. I definitely would be on my own if I hadn't met you. I know that for a fact.'

'Throw us my pyjamas.'

He took them out of the bed and watched as she took off her underwear and put the nightwear on.

'Yeah, well, for what it's worth, she stills fancies you, y'know.' She glanced at him as though assessing how that news would be received.

'Eh? How do you know that? She didn't tell you that, did she?'

'No, but I can tell by the way she looked at you.'

'Are you sure?'

'Uh huh, and by the way, she asked about you.'

'What did she say, like?'

'Just this and that,' she said coyly.

'What's this and that, when it's at home?'

'Well, I was talking about the miscarriage, or rather, she asked about it. And I was saying how insecure I'd felt and that...y'know...that I was worried you'd go off me...'

'...can't believe you thought that. Daft bugger.'

'...and how I needed to get back to feeling sexual and desired and not a dried-up menopausal old bag.'

'Yeah...?'

She ran a long-toothed comb through her hair.

'I sort of said that we'd always enjoyed each other, physically, like. Honest, I don't make a habit of seriously talking about our sex life to other people. It always seems a bit tacky.'

'I don't mind if you do. Not in that context, anyway.'

'I hope you don't talk about us with Jeff.' She frowned at him, her fair eyebrows knitted together in admonishment.

'With Jeff?! God, no. He wouldn't want to know. One of the great omertas in male relationships is the silence we maintain about the details of our sex lives with the missus.'

'Eh? Why?'

'I don't know why. It's just one of these male things that you learn. I think it's because you tend to know the wife or girlfriend as well, so knowing that she likes to be spanked with a wet copy of the *Radio Times*, or has nipples the size of saucers, whatever, is too embarrassing for everyone. Being able to picture your mate having sex is also too close to being gay. I think that's what drives it. So no, you don't have worry on that score. We're far too inhibited and repressed to discuss such a thing, other than acknowledge it happens and thus we are Proper Men.'

'But if you picked a lass up for a one-night stand, you'd be all over that with each other?'

'Of course. Beans would be spilled right down to the smallest detail.'

'And you talk about what old girlfriends were like in bed?'

'That's allowed, too.'

She shook her head. 'You men are absolutely bonkers. So anyway, while I was telling her about this, she was asking little details about you. I mean, she didn't come out and ask about the size of your bits, but it wasn't far away. I told her about that infamous night in Laguna Beach after we'd had all those tequila sunrises and in...err...quite...well, graphic terms...y'know and a girl can tell when her friend's interest is a little stimulated by the thought. She said something like, "Eee, well it's a shame I missed out on a good time with your Nick, didn't I?" So there's another feather in your self-esteem cap, kidda.'

That made Nick feel rather good about himself, especially as it was from Shawn. It wasn't a feeling he often enjoyed, so he embraced it while it came to visit.

'But for all your teenage crush on Shawn and then going out with her when we split up, I'm not sure you'd have been suited at all, long-term.'

'No? Why not?'

'She'd have found the way you go on too annoying.' She grinned at him and poked her tongue out, playfully. 'Your hi-falutin thinking and musing. It's not her thing at all. Also she's not a big rock music fan. She just listens to the radio, so you sitting and playing UFO for four hours wouldn't have gone down well. And she said she couldn't bear having the house cluttered up with records.'

'Bloody hell. I didn't realise she was that much of a philistine. That does it, I'm not marrying her, nor will I pleasure her with my body.'

She laughed. 'Having one of your only three rooms full of records is most women's idea of a nightmare, and most blokes' too, come to that.'

'What would they want to fill it with, then?'

She got into bed alongside him.

'I dunno, do I? Cushions, probably. Some women are mad about cushions. I don't know why. Never understood the cushion and pillow thing, myself.'

'I like a cushion but I don't wish to put them on a bed, nor go to IKEA and browse them.'

'I would only go in IKEA these days if I was drunk or heavily sedated. I can't think of many places I'd like to go less. I swear fumes come off their furniture which make you feel sleepy. I can't stop yawning in there.'

Nick put his hands behind his head again.

'I'm sure you used to love all of that though, when we first met. You were all about interior design and stuff...that flat in Norton you had was done out really posh.'

'It bloody was. I spent nearly 10 grand doing it up. That was the old yuppie Jules, though, or what was left of her in 2006. It was all part of the woman who didn't want to be her mother's daughter. Not sure my heart was ever really in it, though, and it certainly isn't nowadays. There are more important things in life than soft furnishings. Working at TWC has shown me that.'

'The less you worry about buying stuff, the less you worry in general, I reckon. All pain comes from attachment, as the Buddha said...or was it Donovan? Same thing.' He shrugged.

She kissed him quickly, her wine and toothpaste-tinged breath on his cheek. 'That is true, O wise one. So what have you been up to?'

He explained about meeting Kev and his theory of the Shadow.

'Kev does love a good thriller - so you're right to take anything he says with a pinch of salt, but on the other hand he does have a lot of mates who were in the army and he does know a lot about that world, plus he's got access to what he likes to call the Grid.'

'The Grid? Oh yeah, he mentioned that. I didn't ask him what it meant.'

'The Grid is just his network of mates and villains all over Teesside. You know what they're like. It's like a version of the internet only instead of packets of information on servers, you've got packets of crisps eaten by fat beery tattooed men with mobile phones, sitting outside of pubs, smoking. They keep an eye open for anything that's been nicked or anything they want to be nicked. If someone has gone awol and are spotted in Seaton Carew, the Grid will kick in and report to whoever wants to know. So when he says he'll ask his mates to look out for that Range Rover, they actually will - they won't make much of an effort - but if they're sitting outside the Builders Arms and they see it, they'll let Kev know.'

'I like Kev, in a funny sort of way. I don't like Ricky at all, but Kev is alright, even though he scares me a bit. I always feel like he could just snap and do anything. It's a bit like that with Alsatians. They seem nice enough but one day they go for you and give you a right good savaging.'

'Yup. That's him, Very perceptive.' She nodded, taking a dab of moisturiser from a pot on her bedside table.

'How's your neck?' said Nick.

'It doesn't hurt as much as my pride. Being held down like that...feeling so powerless. Horrible.'

'Try not to fret about it.'

'I'm not fretting. I just want to see him brought to account for doing that. No-one has a right to do that to anyone.'

'Kev has his own form of justice in mind. I told him he might be out of his depth with this bloke, but that only encouraged him to go after him more.'

'You should know what he's like by now. It gives me no pleasure to say this but it will get him killed one of these days. All my life I've expected to hear one or both of them have been killed. The worse thing is, he knows it too, underneath, like. He knows one of these days he'll walk in, chest puffed out, playing the hard man...being the hard man...and he'll just get a bullet in the head and that'll be that. Sometimes I think that's what he wants. He'd rather die in a hail of gunfire than live a peaceful life.'

'He must be clinically insane, then.'

'Oh, yeah. He is. And he always has been, at least since my dad left us. But even so, it's a decision both of them have made. They could stop being aggressive nutters, but they don't. It might have been dad's fault at first, but they've carried it forward all these years. It's like they don't know how else to live and I've given up hoping they'll change.'

'No, that'd be futile. Their kind of semi-psychotic mindset must have some use, but I'm struggling to think what it might be.'

The following morning, on his way to the allotment to plant some tomato seeds into seed trays, Nick stopped off at a newsagents in Oxbridge and picked up a copy of the *Northern Echo*.

Opening the allotment gates, he was met by Jock, the man who had the next-door plot.

'Alright, mate. How are you?' asked Nick. 'I've not seen you for a couple of weeks.'

'I've not been in the best of health. Cold went onto my chest.' In his late 60s, he spoke with a west of Scotland accent, despite having lived on Teesside for decades.

'Sorry to hear that.'

'Aye. Feeling better now, though. I missed all the fun down here, then.'

'Fun?'

'With Jim George. What happened down the road...did you know him?'

'No. I only saw him on that day. Had he kept bees on here long?'

'Just since last year. A lot of growers had a terrible crops of fruit the previous year - I didn't get one pear. And we all put it down to poor pollination. So we thought if we had a hive in here, that'd help. Someone knew him. He'd kept bees for decades so we got him down about a year ago and it worked well. Much better crop last year.'

'Make sense. I mustn't have seen him before because the bees are all asleep in the winter, so I suppose he wasn't here much.'

'Aye. Strange chap, though, I thought. Had a funny look about him.'

Nick watched a male blackbird chase another, making a clucking noise as it did so.

'Yeah, he seemed a bit odd. He was sort of shiny...we think he might have had Botox injections to make himself look younger. They found a high level of botulism in him, apparently.'

'Botox? Like a celebrity, you mean?'

'Yeah. Him and his girlfriend.'

Jock pulled a face. 'That's downright weird, that is. Someone said he was originally from Eastern Europe, or his family were.'

'He sounded more like he was from Billingham than Moscow to me, but yeah, he was born in the old USSR, apparently.'

Nick wandered down to the makeshift shed constructed out of parts of an old railway carriage, along with odd bits of wood and glass. He took out his flask and poured himself some coffee and put his feet up to read the paper. He found his latest column. Nope, no byline photo. So how had Cameron Baxter-Smythe known who he was?

The allotment was lovely for reading. Quiet and somehow away from the bustle of life, it encouraged quiet contemplation. He'd just finished drinking when his phone buzzed. Jeff.

'Hey, Big Man.'

'Now then. Did you have a good time out in the green and pleasant lands of Teesdale?'

'We did...I need to talk to you about that, actually. Was going to call, but I got busy last night. It was quite eventful.'

'Eventful? The countryside? Are you sure? Are you at home now?'

'I'm at the allotment, just thinking about starting to think about doing some work.'

'It's a hard life, eh. I'll come down, then. Is it OK if I bring the Argmeister?'

'You don't need to ask that. Of course.'

'I found out something interesting about dead Elvis last night,' said Jeff.

'The singer or the beekeeper?'

'The latter. Did you know where he's from?'

'Eastern Europe?'

'Oooh, lucky guess.'

'Not really. Col told me.'

Nick had just finished planting seeds when Jeff arrived, pushing Argie in his big pram. Nick leaned in and tickled the little lad under the chin. He'd started smiling a lot and looking, somehow, very Jeff-like. He had big eyes, rosy pink cheeks and was very expressive. He'd even started sitting up on his own and looking around himself, as though just beginning to properly appreciate the world around him, like every day was a miracle. It was a joyful thing to see, or at least it was when you didn't have to get up at 3am because he was screaming the house down.

'How's you then, Argie? Eh? You look pleased with yourself, don't you?' said Nick.

'A bit of off-road pramming, Arge. How do you like that?' said Jeff. The little lad barked a squeaky noise that Nick hadn't heard him make before.

'What does that mean, Arg?' said Nick, laughing a little.

'I think he's working up to saying Uriah Heep.'

'It sounded more like he was saying Mick Box.'

'That'll do for me. As long as his first word is rock 'n' roll-based I'll be happy.'

Jeff unfolded a chair and sat down.

'I look like a giant sitting in the little people's furniture on this,' he said, his large frame crammed into the cheap garden furniture.

'They don't make big dude's foldable chairs, do they?'

'So what happened up in Teesdale?'

'Plenty.' He went over the fight and then the attack by the Range Rover and his subsequent meeting with Kev. Jeff sat and listened, taking Argie out of the pram and sitting him on his knee as he did so. After Nick had finished, he shook his head.

'That is some story. Is Jules OK?'

'Yeah. Angry at the attack. But not physically hurt.'

'I can't keep it all in my head. There's a lot to this. Clearly, this bloke...what did Kev call him?'

'A Shadow.'

'Creepy. Well, he's not done what he's done for no reason. He wasn't some random lunatic. I'm not happy that he knows me, either.'

'It's all very strange. The thing I've kept coming back to is that we know Brian lied about that cup and our Shadow Man said not to believe anything he said or it'd get us killed.'

'How could that be the case? Even if we accept that he's lying to us about the cup being a plain thing...how could it get us killed?' Jeff pulled a face.

'Maybe if we try and help him get it back...that's what will get us killed. That's what he asked us to do, after all. Maybe this bloke wants that thing as well.'

Jeff stroked his beard in contemplation. 'Aye. That's what he must mean. What do you reckon? We're not ones to run away from a fight, usually.'

Nick looked his old mate in the eyes. 'I'm telling you man, this bloke was a killer. He wasn't just hard, the way Kev Wells is hard. He was ruthless and cold. He would have killed Jules, I just totally believed that. And I'm sure he killed Jim George.'

'Ah, yes. Jim George, or Iacov Yuri, to be more precise.'

'How did you find that out?'

'Tommo. You remember Tommo?'

'Of course. Club Fiesta archivist and man of a thousand smells.'

'The very same, though in fairness, he seems to have taken to washing occasionally, so his whiff is somewhat less whiffy recently, mostly because Emily, God bless her, has bought him some clothes from a charity shop...and he seems to like them. She's trying to wean him back to a life within society and not isolated from it, due to being a stink bag.'

Nick grinned. A kind act reverberated out into the world and made everyone who was open to it feel good. 'That's so nice of her, isn't it?'

'I know. She thinks it's her Christian duty to help poor old Tommo. He was in the cafe yesterday and I was talking to him about Elvis. He actually knew him. Says he came over from Kiev when he was seven and grew up in Billingham.'

'Kiev? Really? You'd never have known to hear him talk.'

'A Billingham accent is like a linguistic nuclear bomb; it wipes out all before it.'

Nick thought for a minute. 'Think about what this means. Elvis was born in the old USSR. And he was murdered in a ruthlessly efficient manner by a man who told us not to trust anything Brian said. Brian told us his cup was stolen. We know that cup is originally Russian and that the Regency Stables, who Brian had said had stolen it, is owned by a Russian oligarch.

Are any of those things in any way linked, do you reckon?'

Jeff put the baby back in his pram, pulled his hair back into a ponytail and fastened it with a hair band and sat without speaking for a minute or two, making humming noises in contemplation. Cocking his index finger at a right angle, he leaned forward. 'Right. Let's think outside of our trousers for a moment and invent something wild and improbable...'

'...inventing something wild and improbable is what you usually do. So surely that wouldn't actually be outside of our trousers, it'd be inside...'

'...good point, Captain. Let us take our trousers off and not be inhibited by them...symbolically, I mean. No actual trouser removal is required.'

'I'm pleased to hear it.'

'Right. Let's say somehow our Elvis knows the man who bought Regency...what's his actual name, this oligarch bloke?'

'Chekov.'

'Does he have a cherry orchard or a starship *Enterprise*?'

'Very literary of you, Jeff.'

'OK, so somehow Chekov knows our Elvis and he sends him out to steal Brian's cup for him because he badly craves old Russki artefacts and then Shadow Man, for some reason, doesn't like this and so gives our Elvis the old Vulcan Death Grip.'

'The problem with that is that if we're to disbelieve anything Brian says, that would mean the cup wasn't stolen at all, which makes your theory fall apart totally. Apart from that, it's good...'

'We can't trust what Shadow says, though, can we? He's got his own motives...he might just want to scare us off.'

'True. OK. Elvis was obviously murdered for *some* reason, so we need to find out a lot more about him and see if that uncovers any reason why he met his untimely end. How do we do that? Do we know anything about him at all? Does he have a family or kids? He had that girlfriend with the shiny face.'

'I don't know anything about him, but old Tommo does. Like I say, he knew him.'

'How well did your brother know Elvis? He worked at his clubs and he had that minute of applause for him at the launch party.'

Jeff twizzled his long beard hair into a point. 'I don't know, I'll text him and if you've nothing much to do today, we'll go on an Elvis hunt. Emily is in the shop with Matty, so I don't have to go in until later. We can find out as much as we can about him. Then once we've done that, we might have a better idea why old Shadowski snapped his neck and exactly what the threat to us is.'

'OK, but say we do find out why it happened - what do we do then? We can't tell the police.'

'We could anonymously tip them off...Shadow Man wouldn't know if it was us or not...' said Jeff.

'He might not care. Any chance that it *was* us, he'll come and break *our* necks, won't he?'

Jeff went quiet again and checked on a now-sleeping Argie.

Nick spoke again. 'But then, thinking about it, he just said not to bother to tell the police anything because they wouldn't believe it or wouldn't want to know...he didn't say he'd kill us if we did. So actually, that leaves us in the clear to find stuff out, it's just that it'll be pointless to do so, from his viewpoint, anyway. The big threat was for believing what Brian says. He said that would definitely get us killed. He was really insistent about that.'

Jeff stopped, looked at him and jabbed a pointing finger. 'Ah ha! Do you hear what you just said? *Believing* Brian would get us killed - but he didn't say it'd be *him* who killed us, did he?'

'Err...well...that could have been what he meant. I assumed it was.'

'But you know what they say, assumption makes an ass of...err...things...whatever...bloody stupid saying, anyway. From what you said, he wasn't one to make things ambiguous. He'd have said, "I will kill you", if that's what he was going to; thus, the threat to us from believing Brian must come from elsewhere. He's actually trying to protect us. I know it doesn't seem like it when you had a fight with him and because of what he did to Julie, but that is in effect what he's doing. He's warning you of danger. So his role is protective.'

You couldn't argue against Jeff's logic. It all made sense. 'OK, agreed. Owee, then. Let's go round to Tommo's and then go and see Big Fish.'

Nick packed away his tools, watered all the seedlings in the cold frame and locked the shed. They walked up to the gates. Away on their right were Elvis's three large white beehives, set in one corner. A few bees wafted around them.

'Let's have a quick look at these. I wonder what is going to happen to them,' said Nick, striding over. As he approached, he broke into a grin and pointed at a sign on the front one. Painted in black on a small, white board, it said 'Welcome to Graceland'. 'Even his bees were an Elvis tribute act.'

Jeff laughed. 'I wonder if there's a pretty little thing, waiting for the King, down in the jungle room?'

They stood and watched the bees crawling around the entrance. 'I'd like to see a bee in a jumpsuit.'

Jeff pulled a face at him. 'Bees in jumpsuits? What are you on, son?'

'Sorry.'

'Everyone knows bees prefer to wear leather jackets.'

He wafted at two as they buzzed around his head.

'They seem to like the smell of your hair, Jeff. Is it some sort of honey shampoo?'

'You must be joking, I'm not a homosexual - I use Fairy Liquid and bleach.'

More bees emerged from the hive and flew around them. It was very quickly intimidating, especially when they buzzed in your ear. It was hard not to think of them as aggressive.

'Owee, let's get out of here,' said Nick, walking away at pace. Jeff yelped and came galloping up behind him.

'They're after me!' said Jeff, pushing the pram on the grass path at speed, yelping comically as he did so.

By the time they got to the gates, the bees seemed to have given up their chase.

'We're a right couple of wusses, us, aren't we?' said Jeff, checking on the baby. 'That was what happened to Elvis as well. They seem to get angry.'

'Do bees get angry?'

'Those bloody bees do. Those are the bee equivalent of the 1970s Boro Aggro Boys.'

'They did seem agitated, but only when we were near the hive. They must be defending the queen or something.'

'Aye. Probably think we're going to steal their royal jelly. I say that like I know what it is. What exactly is royal jelly?'

Nick unlocked the allotment gates.

'Trust me, you don't want to know, man.'

'It's not the male bee's sex wee, is it?' said Jeff with a look bordering on fear.

'Ha ha...not as such, no. If I remember right, it's some sort of secretion from the head of the worker bees and they use it to feed the larvae in the hive, just for a few days, like. And the queen gets it as well. She hoovers up the top-notch nosh all her life.'

Jeff looked at him, appalled. 'Christ, I think I'd rather it was sex wee. Head secretions sounds unsanitary and sci-fi weird. What are they doing that for?'

Nick closed the gates behind them.

'Who knows? They're far-out things, are bees. They've got a complex gig going on in there.'

'I have a theory...' Jeff said with a cocked index finger as he unlocked his van.

'...you usually do...'

'...it is this: there's something about nature that we just don't get. Something we've never discovered. Something really important, in the same way knowing about gravity is fundamental to working out why everything on earth works...it's something like that. I mean, how did bees work all that head milk business out? How do birds know when to migrate and to where? Why do eels all go to the Sargasso Sea? How come Pandas are shit at sex? Why do cats look so gormless when they're pissing and yet so alert the rest of the time? All these questions could be answered if we only knew the One Big Thing.'

'Maybe it's God? Maybe that's the answer?'

'I think it probably is,' said Jeff putting the pram in the back of the van and placing the baby in his carry cot.

'Do you? Really?' said Nick.

'Yeah. That's the great thing about the whole God business. It's a big theocratic bin you can pour everything we don't understand into. I hope you're writing this down, words boy. I was especially pleased with "theocratic bin".'

Jeff drove them to Bishopton Court, a circular council estate in Fairfield, the suburb of Stockton that Nick had grown up in and where Tommo lived.

'Hey up, lad,' said Jeff, with an armful of Argie, as Tommo pulled open his door, dressed in a vivid green, red and yellow floral print Hawaiian-style shirt, clearly one of Emily's charity shop purchases. It made him look a bit healthier. The last time Nick had seen him, he was ashen grey and didn't look in good health. Now, he had a bit of colour to him.

'Now then, Jeff. Ah, you've brought the bairn. Hello, young fella. He's getting big, isn't he?'

'Aye, takes after his dad. You remember Nick, don't you?' said Jeff, jerking a thumb at him.

'Aye. Alright, son. I don't normally get visitors. Are youse lot coming in?'

They stepped inside. The last time Nick had been there, the smell of sweat and something worse was overpowering. Today, it was much better and didn't coat the inside of your mouth with thick stink anymore. Emily's ongoing campaign to bring him back from the edge of a hermit existence seemed to be working.

They went through to the back room which was covered in memorabilia from the Club Fiesta in Norton, where Tommo had worked on the door for over 20 years.

'By heck, it's cracking in here,' said Jeff, who had never seen it before. Tommo was pleased. 'This should be on display somewhere. Hey, why don't we use some of it in the new cafe? Posters for Slade and that...not so much for the Barron Knights, like.' He pointed at the black and orange posters in frames.

'They were hilarious, them lads. Aye, well if you want owt, just say, Jeff. I never thought anyone would be interested. Is that why you've come over?'

'Not really. We're interested in Jim George. You were talking about him in the shop, and said you knew him a bit and that he was originally from Kiev.'

'Jim, eh? Aye, he was. Yeah. He was born in Kiev. Iacov Yuri was his original name. I think that's Russian for James George. His mam and dad came over here in the late 60s. What a poor lad, dying just like that.' He clicked his fingers, then wiggled them at the baby, who seemed to find his bright, floral shirt fascinating.

'So what brought them over here?'

Tommo jingled the change in his pocket and sucked his teeth a little as he tried to recollect.

'Not sure, boys. Oh...hang on...his dad worked at Sunderland Poly and Jim went on to do the same thing.'

That was what Harcombe had also told Nick. 'He lectured in biology, didn't he?'

That's right. Then he moved on to Newcastle Poly, or whatever it's called now.'

'Northumbria University,' said Nick.

'Aye, that's it. He lived in Rimswell for years. He moved there from his parents house in Billingham. I used to drink in the Rimswell pub with him and a few others.'

'When was that?'

'He only moved out about four months ago. He went to live on a new estate in Thornaby. Seemed to have come into a bit of money, or that's what I thought, like.'

'Was he doing his Elvis when you first knew him?' said Nick.

'Nah. He only started that a year ago, just before he moved. He got a bit carried away, if you ask me. He was never out of that manky white jumpsuit 'round town. He could do a passable imitation, I suppose, but...y'know...he was a fat sod...people just laughed at him. That's why he got work - he was just a joke. He must have known that. Why are you asking, anyway?'

'We just wondered if he had any family that needed to be told about his accident,' said Nick. 'I was first on the scene, y'see.'

'Oh, right. Bloody hell, Nick. That can't have been nice. His mam and dad are long gone. He had a woman in tow, she was from that Thornaby estate.'

'Did she have a shiny sort of face, by any chance?' said Jeff.

'Aye, that's her. Looked like she'd been polished.' Tommo laughed and waved at Argie again. 'She was nice enough. I only met her once. Now I think about it, like, he hooked up with her just after moving.'

'Where would we find her, any idea?' said Nick.

'I know exactly where. The make-up counter in Binns. That's where she worked. Probably where she got...you know...buffed up with the moisturiser and that.'

'So what did he do for a living?' asked Jeff. 'How come he wasn't still a lecturer?'

Tommo looked at them from one to other and scratched his balding head. 'Y'know what? I don't know. He just said he'd packed it in one day. I don't actually know what he did. Maybe he just did the Elvis thing?'

'That couldn't pay enough money, surely?' said Nick. 'Not enough to buy a new house, anyway.'

Tommo shrugged. 'Sorry I can't be of more help, lads. I feel bad for him, though. You never know what's around the corner, do you?'

'Very true. Well, thanks, matey,' said Jeff. 'Hey, I just bought two huge boxes of 1950s singles. You should come in and have a look, bound to be some Marty Wilde and such in them. Might be something you don't have.'

That pleased Tommo and he grinned, revealing yellowing clothes peg teeth.

'Oh, right. I will. I like your little lassy, Emily. She's a bright spark. You see so many miserable buggers around town, but not her. Always got a smile on her little face and she's been a right little angel to me. Do you like the shirt she got us? Flash, eh?' He held it out like it was the poshest shirt you'd ever seen in your life.

'Aye, you're a fashion guru, you, Tommo,' said Jeff.

'It's right nice 'avin' a lass like that to look out for you, like. Means a lot to us. Will you tell her that from me? I'm no good with words, like.' The old geezer was actually almost blushing.

'Yeah, 'course I will,' said Jeff, nodding. 'I've got a good team in there. Drop in and see us soon, Tommo.'

As they drove away, Nick said, 'I really like him. Feels like he's got more to his life now than when I first met him.'

'Yeah, I do, too. He seems to have perked up a lot. I was worried he was isolated and depressed when he first came into the shop. He walked around like there was a cloud over him and he was permanently in the shadow of it. You see a few old lads like him...well, they're not that old really - just in their early 60s, but it's like they've become invisible. He can't get work because no-one would give him a job, but he can hardly retrain for a new job just two years before he'll get his pension. When they've no family to speak of and not much money, what are they supposed to do? I reckon between Emily and my boxes of old singles, we've saved the state from having to pick up his care bill for a few years.'

Nick rolled his watch around his wrist. 'It must be easy to get like that on your own. No-one looks out for you and soon you stop caring for yourself and go days without even speaking to anyone. I can imagine being like that myself. I'm a hermit waiting to happen.'

Jeff nodded and flicked his hair over his shoulder, then wafted his beard at Argie in his carry cot. 'Not many of Emily's age would have taken the time and trouble to pay a stinky old gadgee like him any attention. You meet a lot of people who are full of fine words, but she's one for the doing rather than the talking. She's brought him back into the world, really. Actually, it was her who sort of inspired me to open the rock club. I want it to do that, as well. It should be a place for people to come on their own, male or female, and find a friendly welcome, as well as some serious aural pleasuring. See, I was thinking about this. Society seems so fragmented compared to when we grew up and everyone is so busy grafting for sod all, or looking at their phones or whatever, so the Tommos of the world fall through the cracks. We've got to change that 'cos it doesn't help any of us if there are people cut adrift, and you do see a lot who are like that around town.'

Nick smiled.

'What?' said Jeff, casting a glance at him.

'Nowt. It's just incredibly good of you to think like that, especially as you think you're not one for the deep thinking. Sounds to me like you do plenty of thinking.'

Jeff winced and shook his head. 'See, I hate that. Shouldn't even be necessary to say it's good of me. Should just be part of our everyday duty. I don't want bonus points just for being decent with people. It makes it seem like you're trying to make out you're some sort of saint, when it's just a matter of being decent. And don't start saying it's political, because it's not.'

'It is, though. The personal is political.'

'Oh, god, here we go with the t-shirt slogan politics. Have you been reading Jules's Germaine Greer books again?'

'What we do in our own lives has a political dimension, it must do. Just think about it. How you live and what you do or don't do feeds into society, and society has to be organised and run in some way. That's where political philosophy comes in.'

'Aye, but that isn't the same as political parties and all of that...'

'But that's how it finds its expression. Admittedly, there's not much of a choice any more, as the last election just proved.'

Jeff half nodded, half sneered.

'I just hate politics. It divides people into factions unnecessarily. Red v blue. That's what I dislike. I'm just not tribal like that.'

'Or maybe it just highlights the divides that already exist.'

Jeff groaned and then sighed.

'Aye. Maybe you're right.'

It was time to change the subject. Jeff would never be convinced about the rights and wrongs of politics. 'So where do we find Big Fish?'

'He's rehearsing for his tour at the Purple Room in the Boro.'

'Rehearsing? He actually rehearses standing with a microphone and shouting catchphrases?'

'It's a big show. He's got to get the lighting organised and this time he's doing little sketches and stuff, god help us. So he's got to get the whole thing set up right. It's not just a stand-up tour this time.'

They drove into Middlesbrough on the A66, turning off by Newport Bridge and heading into Acklam where the Purple Room was located. An old red-brick Victorian warehouse, it held club nights and DJ-based events and during the day was a rehearsal room for bands.

Nick and Jeff pushed open the doors and peered in.

'Hey, this is smart, Jeff,' said Nick, looking around. 'It's basic but cool. Stripped back brick, old oak boards on the floor.'

'Aye, this is what I'd like my club to be like. It's a bigger version of that old hall we saw, isn't it? Probably dates from around the same time.'

They walked into the main space. Windows had black blinds pulled down and at the back of the hall was a lighting desk. On a low stage stood Big Fish and two other younger blokes, one of whom was dressed in a red foam tomato-shaped suit and green tights, for no obvious reason.

'Now then, Jeff. Alright, Nick,' said the BF. The big man sat down on a small chair and blew out air, mopping at the dew of sweat on his head with a white towel.

'We'll take 10 minutes out, lads,' he said to his fellow performers. They walked off. The tomato man waddled along like a giant haemorrhoid, which was probably what he was supposed to be, knowing the BF's sense of humour.

'How's it going?' said Jeff.

'Alright. It's a lot of bloody work. I hope the fans think it's worth it.'

'It's not just stand up now, though, is it?' said Nick.

'Nope. It's more like a rock show. Lights, pounding music and dry ice and blokes dressed up in comedy fruit suits. It's all added value, though. If people think they're getting more, they're not so bothered if you hike up the prices by 10 quid. Anyway, I got your text, what can I do you for?'

'How well did you know Jim George?' said Jeff.

'Jim? Elvis?' He mopped a fresh veneer of moisture off his buzz-cut head. 'Didn't really know him. He played at the GC a lot in the last year, and I've used him as a daft warm-up act a few times at club dates.'

'Was he primarily a comedy turn, then?' said Nick.

'Not on purpose. But a fat middle-aged bloke in a manky jumpsuit doing a passable imitation of Elvis Presley makes people laugh. Punters liked him and he was no threat to me and he worked cheap. It's not like he could tell jokes. People thought he was being clever - what's that poncy expression?'

'Post-ironic?' speculated Nick.

'Yeah, I have no idea what that means, but they thought he was being a shit act on purpose, but I knew he wasn't, which was why he was so funny. He thought he was brilliant, plus he looked weird - like someone had hit him in the face with a cricket bat. People laughed at that, as well. What brings you here asking about him, like?'

'We were the last to see him alive,' said Nick.

'Aye, but...so what?' said Big Fish, who didn't seem to own an ounce of sympathy, empathy or anything ending in -pathy.

'It's just we didn't know anything about him, did we, Jeff?' said Nick, looking to his mate for support, not knowing what to say, really.

'Aye, and we heard he was actually Russian, did you know that?'

'Jim? Gettaway. He was from Billingham. He wasn't Russian...'

'Aye, he came over when he was kid,' said Jeff, 'from Kiev.'

The BF shrugged, unconcerned. 'Wonder why he never said. Thought he might have mentioned it when he was over at the stables with me and dad.'

Nick leaned forward a little. 'At Blakeston? Jim went over there?'

'Aye, a few times. He liked the gee gees, didn't he? I showed him around the place. Weird he never said about being an Ivan. Me and dad even had dinner with him. Weird.'

Nick glanced at Jeff, who had an eyebrow raised. He cleared his throat.

'Brian told me about the Sir Walter Francis Cup being stolen...'

'...did he? Aye, thieving gets. We'll get it back at some point...'

'...from Regency Stables?' said Nick.

'Well, it's them who's stolen it, isn't it? Macca. He's a little toe rag, that one.'

'Do you know that it was him for sure?'

'Has to be. No other fucker would want it. Him and Mickey hate each other.'

'But given that the cup was so valuable, how come you didn't have it locked in a vault?'

'Well, it wasn't that valuable, was it?' Big Fish squinted at them, his face red and moist.

'It was made by Fabergé. That means it's valuable,' said Jeff.

Big Fish made a bark, which suggested he didn't believe this for a moment.

'It is, man. We looked it up,' said Jeff and took out his phone and brought up the Wikipedia entry with its photograph. 'See...that's the Sir Walter Francis Cup.'

Big Fish took the phone and held it right up to his eyes. 'Aye, that's it. Small plain silver cup. I'm sure it's just worth a few grand at the very most. They've just nicked it because they think we cheated them out of it a couple of times. Looks like the sort of thing that you might win playing darts. I knew it was a Fabergé - but not all that shit is mega-valuable. Mind, you can't trust Wiki-bloody-pedia. Someone rewrote mine and said I was well known for having sex with goats...everyone knows I only fuck sheep...I'm not a bloody pervert.'

He delivered it like it was a joke in a gig - the indignation, then the pause before the punchline, right on the beat, and the final pay off, perfectly dead pan. It wasn't an original quip at all, but delivered by someone who knew what he was doing made it more funny than it had any right to be. That was his art. You might not like his jokes much, but they were always impeccably timed. Less successful comedians had more original material, but few could match the Big Fish when it came to comedy technique.

'Did Jim George ever see the trophy room, BF?' said Jeff.

'What? You think Jim stole it?' said Big Fish, with a look of astonishment.

'Just wondering. Our dad asked me and Nick to try and find it.'

'Did he? Why you?'

Jeff looked at Nick. It was a fair question. Why had he asked them? 'I don't really know, BF, but I said we'd help, if we could. He doesn't want the cops involved, does he?'

'Christ, no. The less the old bill sniffs around our business, the better.' The comedian shrugged. 'I did show him it, along with everything else - 'course I did, but that was weeks ago, long before it was half-inched.'

A technician came over and tapped his watch. 'We need to run through the dog farting section, BF.'

'Right. Is that all you wanted me for, Jeff?'

'One last thing, BF,' said Nick. 'You remember your launch party? Where did you get the staff from? The Ukrainians?'

The big man looked at Nick with his mouth open, breathing heavily. 'Just from an agency in Darlo. Er...what's it called, now? It was a good name. Oh yeah, The Jobs Worth. Why do you want to know that?'

'Some of the same people were working up in Middleham at a hotel we stayed at,' said Nick.

'Yeah well, that's what your Ivans do...'

'Technically, they're not Ivans,' said Nick.

'They're all Russians, aren't they?'

'Nope. Ukraine isn't in Russia,' said Jeff.

'Is it not? Well, shit me. Look, I've got to go. Top-quality laughs don't happen by accident. I'll see you around, eh.'

They watched for a couple of minutes as a stuffed dog on wheels was pulled across the stage on a rope. It was Big Fish's duty to light a strategically placed Bunsen burner as it passed by him. To call it broad humour would be to suggest it had more sophistication than was true.

'Owee, I can't stand to watch this witless crap,' said Nick, turning his back and pushing the door open.

They walked back to Jeff's van. 'Was he lying about the cup, do you think?' asked Nick.

'Nah. El Massive Kipper is too arrogant to even want to lie. In fact, now that I think about it, if he knew it was a valuable cup, he'd have shown off about it. He'd have been unbearable about it. You know what he's like. He can't stop boasting about awards and his assets.'

Nick nodded. 'Yeah, that is a really good point, Jeff. A very good point. When it comes to showing off, he's a world beater.'

'But the one in the photo wasn't plain, even though he said it was. It looks top-end Art Nouveau. Why didn't he acknowledge that?'

Nick scratched his head. 'He seemed to think it *was* the right one. Maybe *he* just thinks it looks plain. He's into cash for flash and it isn't that.'

'No, it's not, but even if for some reason he did think it *was* plain, Brian wouldn't. Brian can tell plain from Art Nouveau patterned. It's mad. It makes no sense at all. Why are they both lying about it?'

They drove back to Stockton, still trying to work it out.

Jeff drummed on the steering wheel. 'Him and dad must have conspired on this, right? They want us to think it's a plain silver cup.'

'Have they? Brian called *you* to the house. Then you gave him your Argie speech, but he'd got you over there. I was just there because you wanted moral support. So he can't have planned to tell me. And your brother hasn't volunteered any information at all. We turned up and asked him. So that's not much of a conspiracy really, is it? Also, if you think about it, he wasn't even bothered about the missing cup...not really, not like his dad and he didn't even know that Brian had asked us to get evidence of who stole it. OK, he could have been lying, but there'd be no advantage to him doing that in any circumstances.'

'Hmm. Even though it seems they have to have known what the thing looks like, I can't help but feel like they don't or didn't, just from both of their attitudes.'

Nick agreed. 'Aye. Me, too. It's all very weird. Still, we did learn that Elvis had been in the trophy room, if nothing else. My money is on him. Maybe he's a thief - that's how he supports himself - that's how he afforded the new house in Thornaby.' He looked out of the window at the river as they went across the Tees flyover, which he always felt was at the central core of Teesside. 'What's this all about, Jeff? Come on, give it to me with both barrels. As mad as you like.'

Jeff took the Portrack turn off and headed to the High Street.

'As mad you like, eh?' said Jeff, giving him a wild look.

'As mad as you like.'

'Alright. Jim was a Russian spy and he stole the Fabergé cup for the Regency Stables which is owned by the oligarch, Chekov, because Chekov is an old friend of Jim's family.' Jeff looked at him and flashed his eyebrows up and down.

Nick took some time to let that all sink in.

'That's actually not that weird, man - that actually makes potential sense. Well, almost. It doesn't tell us why Brian and Big Fish think it's plain and not patterned.'

Without hesitation Jeff said, 'That's because they're hypnotised.' Then he laughed manically, like a comedy horror movie.

'Eh?' Nick laughed. 'Hypnotised?'

'Yeah. They've been hypnotised into thinking that the cup is plain and not patterned.'

Nick kept laughing. 'Who did that, then? And why?'

Jeff shrugged. 'I don't bloody know, do I? When in doubt blame the Lizard King, he can do anything. That or black helicopters flown by the new world order...or the Queen.' He made a comedy trumpeting sound. 'There you go, that's the whole thing solved.'

Nick laughed as Jeff parked the van.

'Mind, if you're dressed as Elvis, you'd not make a good spy, though, would you? You'd be too memorable.'

Jeff tugged on his beard and turned the engine off.

'No, I think you're wrong. You'd be a great spy exactly *because* you're dressed in a manky jumpsuit. No-one will take you seriously. Most people would think you were a bit bonkers and give you a body swerve.'

'You mean you go undercover by being in full view? Being distinctive makes you more covert. Interesting theory. I like it, man.'

Jeff nodded and pulled a mad face at him.

'Aye. I'm pleased with it. It's just a pity Jim wasn't a spy and was, in fact, just a slightly bonkers fat Elvis impersonator.'

'Well, I suggest for our own sanity and safety, we just pretend like we've never heard of the Sir Walter Francis Cup, nor of Elvis or Regency Stables. I'm going to cancel my interview with CBS. There's no way I'm getting mixed up in whatever is happening with Big Fish and Brian. The games of the rich and powerful are nowt to do with me or thee and I can't see what we gain from trying to find it.'

Jeff put Argie in his pram. 'I'm inclined to agree. I mean, poor

Jimbo...but it's not like we knew him or even met him for more than about nine minutes in total. If he hadn't been playing at being B.B. King - see what I did there - we'd never even have spoken to him.'

Jeff went back to the shop and Nick went home. When he got there, inspired by Jeff's crazy notion, he called Ellie Gold, a hypnotherapist. He'd looked her up before but had never had the courage to call. Now was the time to do it.

CHAPTER 10

'Hello, Ellie Gold speaking.'

'Ellie. My name's Nick Guymer and I'd like your help.'

'Certainly, Nick. How can I help?'

He took a deep breath. It was embarrassing but he was sick of suffering. 'I have paruresis and I wonder if you can hypnotise me to cure it?'

Impressively, she knew what the condition was.

'I think I can help you. It's fundamentally like a lot of phobias. I have a high success rate with this sort of thing.'

'Great. When can we start?'

'Well, I've just had a cancellation this hour, if that's any good to you?'

'I'll be right over.'

Twenty minutes later, he'd driven over to Upsall Grove in Fairfield where Ellie Gold worked from an office in her home. On the way over, he'd imagined she would be a middle-aged woman, maybe a couple of stone overweight. Hypnotherapy all sounded a bit alternative and the sort of thing that would attract hippies and new age types with Herdwick hair and tie-dyed skirts. But it was all he could think of doing to get rid of this condition. He'd suffered with it on and off for well over 10 years now and it was getting worse and worse.

When an attractive woman with wavy blonde hair, in cream-coloured trousers and top, opened the door, he briefly wondered if this was someone else. She bore a strong resemblance to Jenny Hanley, who had presented *Magpie* when he was kid and had been a common teenage fantasy, especially for Jeff. Nick had Paula Wilcox, Stevie Nicks and Linda Rondstadt, Jeff was mad for Jenny.

'Hello, I'm Ellie,' she said. Not a typical new age, whale music, tie-dye lentil worshipper, anyway.

Was it going to be easier to do this with a good-looking woman or harder? Maybe he'd get distracted and wouldn't be able to concentrate on being hypnotised. She showed him into a front room in which were a couple of armchairs. It was decorated in neutral colours with nothing on the walls to distract your attention. It smelled of vanilla.

'Now, why don't you just tell me a little bit about yourself and your problem?'

'There's not much to explain, Ellie.' He rubbed his hands together, they were sweaty. 'About 12 or 13 years ago I just stopped being able to have a wee when anyone else is present - in public toilets, most obviously. It was just occasional at first but has got worse over the years. Though if Julie, my fiancée, is waiting for me - say before we go out - and I'm under pressure to perform, as it were, I can't do it then, either. It's as if the gate has been tightly closed and hermetically sealed. It doesn't matter how full my bladder is, I just can't do it. I've tried waiting until I'm bursting but it still makes no difference. Sometimes it's so bad that even if I can get a stall, the noise of other people coming and going still prevents me from doing it. I've even had it so bad that I've driven home to use a toilet and then gone back to the pub.'

He couldn't even look her in the eyes as he told her. It was too embarrassing. It wasn't like she was a doctor who was used to seeing bodies that didn't work. But she just sat opposite him with a notepad on her lap and seemed remarkably unmoved and just nodded a little. 'I've no idea why it started but now I'm so self-conscious about it, it happens every time. It's self-perpetuating.'

'But you can pass water normally if you're on your own or are not under pressure?'

'Yes. Also, if I have my iPod on, listening to loud music, that frees me up and I can do it then. But if I put music on just before going into the toilet, that doesn't work because I know that's what I've done - does this make any sense? It is mad. Whereas, if I'm around town with my headphones on, need a wee, and then go into a toilet with music playing in my ears, then I can do it...because I haven't just taken action to stop myself from drying up.' He laughed nervously and let out a sigh. 'I am very messed up, I know.'

'Hmm. Well, that is quite a complex layer of psychological issues you've got there, but this is not a rare condition, let me assure you of that.'

'I've tried lots of techniques that are supposed to help but they've not worked.'

'This sort of thing is self-perpetuating, as you said. Because you suffer from it, it guarantees you keep suffering. We need to break the thought processes you've built up by using the power of positive suggestion to bring about subconscious change of thoughts and feelings and behaviour. The process itself aims to alter our state of consciousness in a way that relaxes the conscious part of the mind, while simultaneously stimulating and focusing the subconscious part. This heightened state of awareness - reached using relaxation techniques - allows me to make appropriate suggestions to relieve you of this condition.'

'Sounds good. Right, well, let's crack on. I'm all yours.'

'Have you suffered with erectile dysfunction on a similar sort of basis? Because if you have, I can build that into this session, too.'

'No, I haven't. In those respects, I seem to, err, well...function correctly.'

She smiled a non-smile of acknowledgement.

'Good. Have you been hypnotised before?'

'No. Does it hurt?' he smiled. She smiled back, properly this time.

'Not if I'm doing it right. Some people are more susceptible than others.'

'I bet men always think they're not susceptible, don't they? The macho thing.'

'That would be a fairly accurate gender generalisation,' she said with a bemused look.

He lay down on her soft couch, a pillow under his head, hands resting on his belly. This was such a weird thing to do, putting yourself in someone's hands like this. Still, she was welcome to abuse him whilst he was under her spell. She *was* very attractive. You could be fiddled about with by someone worse, that was for sure. Now shut up with the sexist nonsense. Why does it always come back to sex for you? Determined to give himself up to the process, he closed his eyes.

She began to talk low and soft in what felt like lush chocolate and honey words, telling him to imagine relaxing all of his limbs one by one, feeling lighter and lighter and picturing lying in the sun by a gently flowing river at the happiest time in his life. Feeling more and more weightless. More and more relaxed.

This was turn off your mind and float downstream territory and from the first seconds it was pushing at an open door. Nick absolutely loved it. Grateful to be free of his regular consciousness, he let his mind slip its moorings and drift back to being a young boy, playing in their garden in the summer, sometime in the 1960s, back before the adult world meant anything, back before the pain of life had begun to imprint itself on him, back when all you had to think about was the next moment of being alive, back when he was always his mother's 'happy laughing little boy'. It was so familiar, like a long-lost picture that you came upon in a long-forgotten attic. This wasn't a mere memory, this was something bigger and more profound: it was a re-experiencing. It was *being* a child again, not as an observer, but actually reinhabiting the existence. He surrendered his adult male 48-year-old body and became his 6-year-old self and everything seemed amazing and wonderful and huge beyond imagining. There were no boundaries to his mind and all was joy.

Her voice was like the drone of summer insects, of bees and birds singing by the river on those long summer afternoons that never seemed to end, with the day stretching out long and free and blue, when nowness was all you knew and your mind was pure and clean and nothing wasn't fascinating. The womb of childhood held him in its embrace one more time and all was only soft happiness.

Breathing slow and deep and feeling like he had just had warm bath, Ellie's voice said '...and as you wake and become aware of your feet and your hands...you can open your eyes and look at me.'

He did as she said. She was smiling.

'Wow, that was so beautiful, Ellie. Thank you.'

As his child mind once again evaporated like a cool mist on a mirror, unable to withstand the heat of adult consciousness, he waved goodbye to it and felt a sob rise up and out of his chest. Not being a small boy again, was, if only for a second, almost unbearable.

'Sorry...' he bowed his head and cleared his throat.

'That's OK, it can be quite emotional for some people.' She seemed so kind and he felt quite vulnerable, as though his adult defences had been stripped away.

'It didn't last long though, did it?' he said, reaching for a glass of water on the side table.

She pointed at the clock on the wall. It said 4pm. 'You were under for 25 minutes, Nick.'

That seemed impossible. It had been nothing but a fleeting dream, a brief sensation.

'Bloody hell. Really? It was so intense, though.'

'If it's any comfort you are...' she smiled sympathetically '...by some measure, one of the most suggestible people I've hypnotised in a long time. It was like you couldn't wait to leave this consciousness!' She clucked a little laugh in her throat.

He rubbed an eye. 'Am I? Is that good or bad?'

'Well, good for our purposes today, but may also be why you suffered with paruresis to begin with. I think it may be the case that you're very sensitive to ideas and notions and they quickly embed themselves in your subconscious, for good or bad.' She nodded at her own words, her head on one side, sympathetically.

'That does sound right. My mind is a bit of a mess, to say the least. I suffer, or have suffered from depression, during which I do get fixated on issues and problems. I get locked into reactive states of mind which I can't break out of.' He closed his eyes. 'I used to self-harm a bit, just to cope with it.'

She blinked slowly and nodded. 'I understand.' And it felt like she did. He looked into her mottled grey-blue eyes for just a second or two. Some people think angels walk amongst us; emissaries from a purer, more beautiful existence. Ellie Gold could have been one. But then again, his mind felt wide open in that moment and even at the best of times, he was always vulnerable to overly romantic notions.

'So am I...you know...cured?' he said.

'Well, we won't know until you next want to use the toilet in public...my feeling is that it was a successful session, but do come back again if you need me to reinforce it for you.'

'I feel like I've had a really nice nap.'

'Good. Like I say, you went under in seconds.'

'I went to a beautiful place. A place I never thought I'd go to again.' He felt very emotional again, his voice breaking a little.

'Do you want a hug?' she said, arms open.

He accepted it without embarrassment, just for a couple of seconds.

She tapped her head with her right index finger. 'Powerful thing, the mind. It holds so much we think is forgotten.'

He put his hands in his pockets. 'So what did you actually do while I was hypnotised?'

'Once you were under, I placed some trigger words in your mind to free you from your inhibitions in that specific circumstance. I can't tell you what they were but they should help direct you to a positive outcome.'

'Will they work, even though I know you've done that? Does that sound daft?'

'Yes, they will and no, it doesn't.'

'Can you do this, at least in principle, for anything, then?'

'Oh, yes, especially to someone like you.' She smiled her nice smile again. Man, she was something. Attractive in mind and body.

A silly notion came to his wide-open mind. 'Could you hypnotise someone to see something that wasn't there?'

'In theory, yes, or to see something as different to what it really is. Much stage hypnotism relies on exactly that.'

After he'd paid her and walked out into the suburban Stockton afternoon, he still felt emotional, as though coming back to and settling in his adult self was taking some getting used to. When home, he began writing a text to Jeff: 'I've just been hypnotised. I know you were just joking, but I think you were right. I've got an idea about Brian and the cup...' but then the phone rang. It was Julie.

'Hiya. We're going to mam's for our tea,' she said.

Nick's heart sank slightly. This was the adult world again, that was for sure, and it was always hard work at Jackie's.

'OK, then.'

'I said we'd be there for 6pm. We'll only stay an hour. I've not been there since the miscarriage, have I? I should show my face.'

Funny that she could say the word now when only a few days ago she just couldn't face it. 'Yeah. Fine. I might walk over rather than drive. The weather's so nice.' There was no time to tell her about the hypnotherapy.

He sent the text to Jeff and then sauntered up Durham Road towards the Hardwick estate. His route would take him past the Horse and Jockey pub. It seemed a shame to have to face Jackie entirely sober, so he went in for a quick double vodka.

The pub was quite busy. He perched on a stool at the bar. No sign of any jockeys; rather, it was full of people who looked like they were strangers to working. Mostly scrawny men in their 20s with overweight women in overtight leisurewear revealing their folds of fat. It was funny how they often went together.

How did they manage to afford to drink in pubs when they weren't working? Stupid question, really. They got by, one way or another, by fair means or foul...more usually foul. Worklessness had become endemic in some areas of the northeast ever since the 1980s and had become accepted as the natural state of things. It never used to be like that in the 60s and 70s. If you were off school and you had to go up to the shops with your mother, you'd just never see an adult male, except an old gadgee. Men worked during the day, they didn't sit around in sweatpants, drinking lager with their girlfriends. These were very different days. When you stripped away everything, it was a sad state of affairs, all of this life just sitting around being unproductive. It did no-one any good, but no-one seemed to care.

He was weighing up whether to have a second drink when a short man came in, dressed in a polo shirt and grey slacks. He recognised him immediately. It was Mickey. Would the jockey recognise him as the man who had broken up his fight, though?

Nick gave him the nod and half-smile, half-grimace that you always give other men when you're sitting at a bar, finished his drink and pointed to the empty glass, so the barman would give him another. Should he buy him a drink so that he could engage him in conversation? No, that'd be weird. You didn't buy strange men drinks. The fact Nick had to consciously think these things illustrated to him just how outside of normal social interaction he really was.

The jockey also ordered a vodka.

'Nice evening, isn't it?' said Nick, as causally as he could, looking out of the window as if quite disinterested in the man's answer.

'Uh huh.'

Nick didn't look at him. Surely he'd recognise him. He feigned a yawn and sipped at the vodka.

'Hey, do you have any idea when the next race day is at Redcar?' said Nick, taking out his phone to give him a reason not to stare at the man.

'Two weeks today. I'm racing in it.'

'Yeah? You're a jockey, like?' he said, affecting a much thicker Teesside accent than his own, feeling out of instinct that this situation required pretending to be more working class and rough.

'Hmm. I am.'

'Up at Blakeston, like?' he said, pronouncing it with a long, drawn-out Teesside vowel: 'Blaaaykstun'.

'Yeah.'

'Do you know that famous fat comedian lad, then? He's summat to do with all of that, isn't he?'

'Big Fish? Yeah.'

He wasn't a chatty sort, but at least he hadn't seemed to recognise him. Nick gave him a quick glance, he had a black eye from the fight and a scab on his lip where it had been split, a swollen ear and bruised neck. My god, he'd taken a pounding.

'Did you fall off your 'orse or summat, then? You look like you've been in the wars.'

'Aye. That's right.'

'There was something in the *Gazette* about a trophy or something getting nicked up there,' said Nick, attracting the attention of the barman as he said it. 'Did you hear about that?' he said, nodding at the bloke behind the bar.

'What's that, like?'

'Some trophy got nicked up at the stables. Someone will probably come in and try to swap a round for it.' The barman laughed at his joke.

'Aye, that wouldn't surprise us at all, like. I've had people trying to pay with metal buttons before now.'

Gettaway, you've not, have you?' said Nick, doing his best to be a

Hardwick bloke and not a slightly poncy, well-educated Fairfield man.

'Was it worth much?' said the barman.

'I dunno. Was it?' said Nick to the jockey.

'I don't know, but I know who stole it,' said Mickey. 'It was a twat called Mick McCartney. Macca, they call him.'

This was more like it.

The barman leaned opposite Nick. He was about 40 with a heavily lined forehead and thinning hair.

'Which cup was it, then?'

Nick pretended to be thinking hard. 'Err...The Henry the Horse something...'

'Henry the horse?!' The barman laughed. 'Henry the bloody horse...'

'Ha ha...no, I got that wrong. It's something Henry...'

The barman rapped on the bar with his knuckle. 'The Walter Francis trophy. That's the old one, innit?'

'That's it,' said Mickey. 'We'll get it back one way or another. It's in that big fucking house in Middleton. They think we've won it by cheating. They're fucking crazy and the Macca bloke - I fucking hate him. I wish he was fucking dead.' The bitterness clearly still lingered, to say the least.

There was no disguising the fury that was still in him.

'How are you going to get it back, then?' said Nick, slurring a little to try and seem less educated and more...more...more something.

'By fair means or foul,' said Mickey, cryptically.

'Hey, did you hear about poor old Jim George?' said the barman, looking to keep the conversation going to stop himself going out of his mind with boredom.

'Never heard of him. Have you, mate?' Nick said to the jockey.

'He was the fella that died in a car crash the other day, wasn't he? He was a mate of Stevie Salmon - the Big Fish,' said Mickey.

'Was he? He used to drink in here sometimes. Used to dress as Elvis. Was a bit of weirdo, like,' said the barman.

'Was he dressed like that up at the stables, then?' said Nick.

'Aye, I saw him up there a couple of times.' Mickey gave a small laugh, the first emotion to crack his face so far. 'I heard he'd died, like.'

It was a quarter to six. Nick had to be making tracks. 'Gotta go and see the missus, see youse two, then,' he said, draining his glass.

Walking out of the bar, he spotted the toilets and went in. One of the 20-something wasters was in there, hosing a ceaseless stream of piss into the urinal, holding himself with one hand, cupping a crafty ciggie in his other.

Nick stood at the far end from him and, as though in competition, released a satisfyingly powerful jet of water himself. Just as it began, he realised he'd not thought about going into the cubicle. Or had he? As he'd pushed the door open he had...or he thought he had...then he'd seen the urinal and just used it. It was all over so quickly. Was this the hypnosis at work already? As he finished, he realised it simply had to have been. With a bloke standing there smoking and pissing he wouldn't normally have had a chance of releasing a drop.

It felt absurdly magnificent, like it was an almost unsurpassed achievement and also a very familiar one. It wasn't something that had bothered him at all until he was in his late 30s, so, in a way, it almost made him feel younger again.

The other bloke walked out without washing, placing his cock hand flat on the door to push it open. After Nick had washed his own hands, he kicked open the door and walked through without having to touch it, feeling extreme bladder and mental relief. That Ellie Gold, she really had been an angel. She'd messed with his brain beautifully.

Julie's Porsche was already outside Jackie Wells's house as he walked up the path. He knocked and let himself in. Julie was in the hallway.

'Hello, luv,' she said with a smile. 'Did you walk?'

'I did indeed.' He was keen to tell her about his hypnotised achievement but there was no opportunity. He wasn't about to talk about it in front of her mother.

Jackie Wells appeared in the kitchen doorway. 'Now then, Nick. How are you, son? You alright?'

'Yeah. How are you, Jackie? Is your hip alright?'

'Stiff every morning,'

'Are you talking about me again, Jackie?' said Conrad, coming out of the back room.

Jackie Wells burst into a hoarse, phlegmy rattle of a laugh. Julie pulled a nauseous face at Nick, her back to her mother.

'And how are you, Julie?' said Conrad.

'Fine. I'm really good now, ta. So what's for dinner, mam? Smells like roast chicken.'

The four of them sat down to eat. It all felt very like when he was a kid, sitting around the table with the grown ups, all of them in too close a proximity to each other. Literally within touching distance. It was awful. Eating with people was never any fun. How do you do it? You can eat or you can talk but you can't do both and concentrating on saying things meant you couldn't even enjoy your food. Your mind was too preoccupied to focus on the taste. All his worst rows with his parents had happened over tense dinner tables and it was buried deep into his psyche, always ready to re-emerge at any time, such as this. Maybe he should get hypnotised about it. Maybe hypnosis was the answer to all of his social phobias and tensions.

Julie chatted away, making small talk while he found himself gobbling his food down to get it all over with quickly, but then just sitting there with a clean plate while everyone else ate was embarrassing too, so he tried to slow down. Still, at least he had a couple of vodkas between his eyes, another one wouldn't go amiss.

As he ate his last slice of breast meat, the doorbell rang. Instinctively, he took the opportunity to get away from the table, even for a few seconds, just to break the awkwardness.

'I'll get that,' he said, getting to his feet.

'It might be Elsie for her catalogue money,' said Jackie.

A catalogue? Who used catalogues in these days of the internet and credit cards? Even the word sounded like it belonged in the 1970s. His mother used to have a Kays catalogue and it was where many teenage boys were first exposed to pictures of women in underwear, with, if you were lucky, a just discernible glimpse of pubic hair though some self-consciously sexy lingerie. Well it was that or, as in Nick's case, the cover of *Country Life* by Roxy Music, which could always be guaranteed to raise the pulse, amongst other things.

He pulled open the door. A bloke about his own height stood there. He had thinning white hair swept back over his head and down to the white collar of a blue rugby shirt, a tanned, leathery face and really striking blue eyes.

'Oh, hello, mate,' he said and smiled. He looked very familiar. Then again, people often did look familiar on Teesside. It often felt like you'd met everyone, if briefly, at least once.

'Hiya,' said Nick and smiled.

'Err...I was wondering if Jackie Wells lives here, mate.' He spoke with a strong Teesside accent but with a twang of something else laid on top of it.

'Yeah. She does.'

'Really? Right. Does she live here on her own then, mate?'

Australian, that was his additional accent. It blended well with a Teesside twang, somehow.

'No. She lives with Conrad.'

'Is that her husband?'

'No. He's...well I don't know what he is...' Nick laughed and shrugged.

'And are you her son?'

'Me? No. I'm Nick...Julie's fiancé. Jackie's daughter.' Who was this bloke? Why did he want to know?

'Julie's fiancé, eh? Oh, yeah, of course you are.'

The man smiled at him. Again, he looked so familiar. Maybe he sat near him at the Boro. You saw the same people near you for years but never spoke to them. There was probably something you were supposed to say or do in a situation like this, but Nick couldn't think what it was. Who was he? He looked in his mid 60s, maybe and was in decent shape for an older dude. He had a deep tan you didn't ever get in the UK, let alone on Teesside. Not unless you'd been involved in an explosion at a chemical plant.

'Err...do you want me to get her?' said Nick, turning to shout through just as Julie came out of the back room and up to the door. She glanced around Nick and looked at the man, with a smile.

'Hiya...do you want mam?'

Then she froze as though gripped in ice.

All colour dropped from her face.

She let out a short airless scream and held her hand over her mouth, as though to stop herself from being sick. For a moment Nick thought she was going to faint.

Nick glanced at her, worried. 'What's wrong?' He looked back at the man. He had a sheepish smile on his face.

'Hello, our Jules...good grief...good god...you haven't changed a bit, you turned into a beautiful woman...you really did.'

Julie seemed paralysed, just staring at him. Her eyes filled with tears and a huge sob came out of her and she rushed at him, arms wide.

'Dad...oh, my god...dad...where the hell have you been?'

Nick stood aghast, unable to compute the situation. Julie hugged the man and he wrapped his thick, tanned forearms around her. Jesus Christ, that was why he looked familiar, he looked familiar because he looked like Julie. Same eyes, same smile. And that was because he was her father.

He'd walked out one day in 1977 and never returned and nothing was ever heard from him again. Until now. Until this minute.

'How have you been?' he said.

'How can I even answer that?' she replied, pulling away from him. 'Why are you here? Why now?'

'I'm just back in the UK. I've been in Australia since the early 80s.' He rubbed at his neck and looked up the street. 'I wanted to make things right with you and your mother and the lads. I've wanted to for a long time. I can't believe I'm seeing you in the flesh. I'd looked at your Facebook page - the both of you. You're just like you were when you were 13, Jules. You've hardly changed.'

'Neither have you. Except now you're an old man. A very tanned old man at that.' She spoke softly and affectionately, then looked over her shoulder in the direction of her mother. 'Go back in the room, Nick, make sure she doesn't come out.' She pushed at him and he had to go despite having no idea how he would stop Jackie leaving the room if called upon to do so. Bloody hell.

She closed the door and he did as he was told. This was some serious shit and there would be repercussions. He could already see it. This would change their lives in a major way; whether for good or bad, it was impossible to tell. Ah, well, rock and roll, this was what life could do. Just when you thought you'd got used to how things were, something happens to mix it all up again and, y'know, sod it. Why not? If everything was unchanging and predictable, life would be very stale. He took a deep breath as he walked back into the room.

'Who's at the door?' said Con as he returned.

'Just someone Jules knows,' he said, sitting down and picking up the bottle of wine and topping up their glasses. Alcohol could usually anchor Jackie to her seat. Now was the time to learn the art of meaningless conversation. How did you do it? Just ask questions. That's what Julie had told him often enough. Just ask things about people, because most people like to talk about themselves. He didn't. But most people did.

'So, how's the house coming along up at the stables, then, Con? Have you been up there, Jackie?'

'No, luv. I don't like the countryside. It makes us feel like I'm miles from civilisation. Snobby country types - I bloody hate them.'

Con laughed. 'It's only about four miles from this house, Jackie.'

'I don't care. It stinks of shite and there's loads of animals that want to bite you. When the bairns were kids, we once had a week in the Lakes. I hated every minute of it. There was literally nowt to do, man. Me and their dad got shit-faced for the full week.'

Bloody hell. And that man was about 20 feet away from where they sat. 'You could've gone walking,' said Nick, trying to be casual.

She gave him a scowl that could have scorched paper.

'Why do people want to go walking? What's so good about walking?

181

You walk everywhere when you're at work, why do it when you're on holiday?'

'It's enjoyable. You get to see things. Me and Jules like it.'

Jackie wasn't convinced and she pulled a face as though she felt the whole idea was about as ludicrous a notion as she'd ever heard. Con laughed again. He did a lot of laughing. It wasn't proper laughing, it was more like a punctuation noise to acknowledge a point being made.

'So are youse two having a holiday?' Always ask about holidays. It's what hairdressers did.

'We thought we might go to Spain, Con's daughter's got a villa out there.'

'A villa, eh? Very nice.' Now what else could you say about that? 'Err...you'll get the sun, anyway.' That was shite. You can do better than that.

'Aye, cheap drink an' all. Champion,' said Con.

'Is there a pool? I...I...err, I love a pool. Me and Jules did a lot of swimming in California.'

Jackie knocked back her wine and began to get to her feet. Shit. She was going to leave the room. Why? Did she need a piss? Urgh. Awful thought. He scanned the room quickly for a way to stop her. He could hardly rugby tackle her.

'Do you need something, Jackie? Sit down, I'll get it for you.' He said, jumping to his feet. 'Don't want you hurting your hip...or...you know, walking...I know how much you hate walking now, eh?' He laughed at his own joke. Con did one of his barks.

She looked at him and narrowed her eyes, just as Julie did when she knew he was saying something with an ulterior motive.

'Alright, son. If you insist.' Her words were full of knowing. She sat back down. 'I left me fags in the kitchen.' There was no fooling her. Old birds like her had a sixth sense when it came to being bullshitted. Who knows where they learn it, but it's as if they can smell obfuscation, lying and deceit.

'No worries.' He picked up his glass of wine and walked out of the room, closing the door behind him. He glanced to his left at the front door. Hurry the hell up, Jules.

Nick went into the kitchen, picked up the packet of Silk Cut from the table along with her small red plastic lighter and turned to go back in the room but Jackie was standing in the doorway looking at him, again with the narrowed eyes.

'I told you not to bother getting up, didn't I?' he said, handing her the fags and lighter.

'Just remembered, the lighter is buggered. I'll need to light it from the cooker,' she said, knocking a fag out of the packet and leaning over the flame from a gas ring. He turned to look at the front door. Julie was coming in. She closed it quickly behind her, pushed her hair behind her ears and took a deep breath just as her mother looked up at her.

'Who was that, our Jules?'

'Barbara Stainsby,' she said, plucking a name out of thin air, as though her mother would know her.

'Who's she?'

'You know Barbara.'

'I wouldn't have asked who she was if I knew her, would I?'

'She used to work at Carol's hairdressers.'

'Never heard of her. How did she know you were here?'

'She saw the car. No-one else she knows has got a 1975 Porsche, have they?'

It was all such admirably plausible lying, but Jackie wasn't having it. She knew her daughter all too well. This must have been what it was like when Jules was a teenager and she was keeping all sorts of secrets from her mother.

Jackie narrowed her eyes once again. 'I don't know why you're lying to us, Julie Wells, but I'll find out.'

'I'm not lying, why would I lie about that?' said Julie, her voice just a little too high to pass for being honest.

Jackie squeezed past her to return to the back room, stopped in front of her daughter, went up on her tip toes to try and make up some of the nine inches height difference between them and said, 'Bollocks,' square into her face.

As soon as she'd left, Julie raised an eyebrow at him and blew out her cheeks.

Nick's phone vibrated. He didn't recognise the number.

'Hello?'

'Nick. It's Kev. We've found him.'

'Found who?'

'The Shadow. The Grid's found him.'

'Where is he?'

'An industrial estate in Hartlepool.'

'What? Why's he there?'

'I don't bloody know. That Range Rover was spotted.'

'And he was parked up?'

'Coming out of a place called BioResearch International. Or the car was. Couldn't tell who was driving it.'

Nick's brain whirred into life. BioResearch? Harcombe had mentioned them. That's where Jim George had been seen. *Bacto - the Future*, the magazine, was on the seat next to him when he died. Shit. This had to be significant. What were they both doing there?

'Any idea where it went?'

'Not really. He was heading back into Teesside. It means he's still around though, doesn't it? He'll get spotted again in that car, then we can build up a picture of what he's doing and where he goes. We'll hunt the fucker down and then I'll have it out with him for what he's done to our Jules. I've got lads all over the place on the look-out for him. He'll not get away. We'll have 'im.'

Kev rang off. Nick stared into thin air. Was that really a good idea? This was all unknown territory. Kev wasn't hunting down a car thief or a scally off the estate who'd robbed someone. This man could be armed and dangerous and with a licence to kill...if indeed you could obtain a licence to kill, which seemed unlikely.

'What?' said Julie in a quiet, urgent whisper.

'Kev's lot have spotted Shadow Man coming out of this place in Hartlepool that dead Elvis used to go to.'

She rolled her eyes.

'What about the visitor?' he asked.

She made an expression of blank shock. 'I gave him our address. Said he should come round in an hour or two. Nearly actually physically shit myself when I saw him. I'm in shock.'

She put a finger over her lips and went into the back room.

'What are youse two plotting about?' said Conrad.

'Nothing interesting,' said Nick.

'Thanks for a nice dinner, mam,' said Julie, taking her grey hoodie from the back of her chair and slipping it on. 'We've got to be going.'

'I'm glad you're feeling better, lass,' said Con, with a big stained-toothed grin.

'Thanks, Con. It wasn't like I was ill, though. I just miscarried a baby. It's very common.'

Con visibly winced. It was all too 'women's downstairs bits' for the big old Geordie.

'Aye, well, even so...' he looked awkward.

'We'll go out for a drink one night soon,' said Julie. 'Up the club, maybe, eh, mam?'

'If you like. Aye,' said Jackie, pulling on her cigarette and looking up at them through a drift of blue smoke.

'She knows something's going on,' said Julie as they got into the Porsche. 'It's like she's got a psychic radar. I always thought that was the case when I was a teenager. She just knows when you're keeping something from her.'

'Only because when you lied to her, you tried to be too casual and your voice went a bit higher. It was totally not how you normally talk to her. You've got to keep your voice as it normally is when you're lying. It's a total giveaway to Jackie. She's heard you lie all your life, remember.'

She was a little indignant at that. 'Well, I'm sorry, I'm sure. I *had* just met my dad for the first time in over 30 years,' she snapped, pushing her hair back behind her ears and rubbing her face.

'He looked very like you.'

'I know...I'm confused...I don't know what to think. I'm full of resentment at what he did but at the same time, I want to have my dad back. And he seems nice.'

Nick thought about it as they turned down Durham Road. 'He was a boozer when he left, wasn't he?'

She nodded, her lips pulled together in a pout. 'He was always drunk when we got home from school. It was horrible, I don't even like to think about those days because it still upsets me. He'd shout and bang around the place and he was always fighting with Kev and Ricky. He's the reason they turned out like they did. They learned it all from him. He'd have drunken brawls with them even though they were just young.'

'So why has he appeared now?'

'He wants to make amends. He'd bloody emigrated to Australia! He's got two kids over there. I've got two half sisters!' She let out a sob and pushed at a small tear in each eye. 'I always wanted a sister so badly.'

She had to pull into the side of Durham Road to have a little cry.

He squeezed her leg. 'Aw, Jules. It is a bit of a mind blow, isn't it? For what it's worth, I thought he seemed canny enough. And he looked healthy, so he's probably not a drinker any more.'

'No, he's not. He quit 20 years ago...or so he says.' She took a deep breath and wound down the window. 'I told him to meet mam when she was on her own. I know Con isn't a brawler these days, but you never know...working-class blokes like them, from their backgrounds...well...it's not like they're going to have a philosophical discussion, is it? They'll be stripped to the waist and fighting on the cobbles before you know it.'

Nick chuckled. It was such an amazing thing to have happened. Now he had a father-in-law to be.

'So, is he living over here now?'

She got a bottle of water from the back of the car and took a drink.

'He's visiting but is thinking about coming home.'

'To Teesside? From sunny Oz? Why? I mean, Teesside has its good points but it's not hard to see the attractions of somewhere sunnier and less fucked up.'

She shrugged. 'He seemed much more intelligent than I remember. Very articulate. In my mind he was a rough-arsed fella and very sort of macho. But he doesn't seem like that at all.'

'Well, none of us are the same people we were in 1977 and he was drunk a lot...that does lead to stupidity and you were so young. You've got two top degrees. You must have got your brains from somewhere. It wasn't from your mam, that's for sure, so it seems likely he was a clever bloke who just went off the rails.'

'I always wondered if I was just a freak. Mam, auntie Sandra, my maternal gran and granddad, god rest them, none are or were exactly intellectuals.'

'There you go, then. What does he do for a living?'

She turned to look at him with upset but happy eyes.

'He runs a market garden...grows flowers. Can you believe that?' She let out another gasp of air as she suppressed another sob. 'How lovely is that? No man who does that can be all bad, can they?'

'His life will have changed him from the man he was back here. It'll have given him perspective. Like I say, I thought he looked cool. Even had a bit of old freak about him. Maybe he was mentally troubled and that's why he drank. Maybe he was depressed. When you're a kid you don't know. My mam had mental problems for years before it became obvious to me. I'd find her sitting and crying when I came in from school, just weeping, the way someone who is mentally unwell does. I thought she was just trying to get attention...which she was...but not in the vain way I had horribly, selfishly thought. I can't forgive myself for my lack of sympathy...'

'...but you were 11 or 12, or something. There's no way you can understand that sort of thing.'

'Exactly. That's what I'm saying. Who knows where he was in his mind? What did your dad do? I don't even know his name...'

'Robert. Everyone knew him as Robbie.'

'He looked like a Robbie...so what did Robbie do for a job?'

'He worked at British Steel and was laid off in late 1976, I think it was. That's when his boozing really got out of hand.'

'And one day he just upped and walked out?'

She nodded.

'Never said anything?'

She shook her head.

'Didn't he even send a postcard or a Christmas card?'

She shook her head. 'Literally nothing. We went to school one Tuesday morning and when we came home he wasn't in and he never came back. It was torture. We thought he must have been murdered or something.'

'God, that must have left a huge hole in your life and you'd not have known if he was just going to show up at any moment. That's some flavour of hell.'

She cried again.

'It was horrible and so upsetting. I used to think I could see him coming up the road. I'd virtually hallucinate him. Thirteen is such an important age.' She sighed and blew her nose on a tissue, then drove home. As they got out of the car in the car park behind the Green Dragon Yard, he put his arm around her shoulder, pulling her into him and kissed the top of her head.

'The reason I was so promiscuous as a teenager all stemmed from him walking out, I'm sure of it. Everything I've subsequently learned says that I looked for male approval that way because my dad had left me. Even now at the TW Centre, I've met women who went through similar situations and they ended up looking for the love they never got from their father in a series of unsuitable relationships, often with abusive or manipulative men who can spot someone with lack of self-worth a mile off. Yeah, that was me. That was me!'

She sobbed again. It was all too much to take.

He hugged her and held her hand on the way back to the flat.

Nick unlocked their door and threw his keys on the table beside the door.

'Parents fuck you up, as Philip Larkin said. Are you going to forgive him, do you think?'

'Forgiveness isn't just a word, is it? You have to let go of all the hurt and anger. I don't know if I can do that. It's right in the core of my soul. It made me who I am.'

She came to him to hug him again, seeking his reassurance and comfort.

He patted her on the back and she clung to him, perhaps in some deep psychic way, just as she would have liked to have been able to cling to her father, all those years ago. The way we are in our adult lives is formed from so many influences, but so many of them date from those couple of years around puberty when who we are to become starts to really take shape.

'How have you found a place to put all the shit from your teenage years? You were upset and messed up, just like me, only in different ways and for different reasons...but it amounts to the same thing, really.'

'What therapy has taught me is I've got to let it go. It is possible, Jules. Take the ball of rage and hate and negativity in your hand and just throw it as far as you can away from you.'

She gulped tears down once again. 'I want to but I think I might need it, just to be me. And I've only just come back to myself after the miscarriage. I can't just flip flop like that.'

'No, you really don't need it. Trust me. The pain likes to tell you need it to survive in the same way booze tells you that you need it to be funny and interesting, but you really don't. Pain just weighs you down and holds you back. It's all excess baggage and life is better when you let it go. I'm still carrying too much around with me, but releasing some of it has helped me so much.'

'I'm scared to let go of it, though. I want to hate him for everything...but he seemed so nice. Not just nice...he seemed like a lovely man to have as a dad.'

She broke down once more, into floods of tears now. He let her cry it out. Better to let the emotions bleed out. There's no way to staunch those sort of emotional wounds, you're better off just letting the poison drain from you.

She shuddered in a way that he'd never known her do. She was, almost always, so strong. Even when she couldn't quite keep up a powerful façade, she didn't let it slip for long. But this was somehow a bigger and deeper letting go of her troubled mind and once you let go, he knew better than most that it was a deep and powerful river that you had to cry.

They went into the living room and sat on the sofa. She buried her head into his chest and just wept simple tears of loss and hurt born out of childhood pain. It was an inversion of their normal relationship. He'd needed her strength to come back from his darkness. Many times she'd just held him as depression had gripped his soul with a black ice. Now, like in so many relationships, it was his turn to repay the favour and be the powerful, resolute and understanding one. He took it on as an instinctive duty of love.

'If you want to get over this, you can, Jules. It's all about how you want to see it.'

'What do you mean?'

She lay across him, a mess of red eyes, tears and snot.

'Well, you know I made peace with mam before she died. With dad, it was more difficult...I still wish he'd been able to more obviously love me...it damaged me beyond repair, but I choose not to be upset by it any more. As Marc said to me once, "he brought you up to survive without him", and there's something to that. Your dad left, but you and your mam and what he'd put into you in those 13 years allowed you to grow into the woman you became.'

She gulped down some phlegm.

'That's putting too much of a happy-clappy spin on it for me. Having your dad walk out of your life is a terrible thing and no dressing it up in psychobabble will change that. It shouldn't have happened and any man worth his salt wouldn't have let it happen. That's how I feel. He let us all down.'

He wondered how to say it right. 'The thing is Jules, what dealing with my upbringing taught me was that our parents were just humans. He'll know he let you down. But they're as lost and messed up as we are or were. They were scared and useless and helpless. They did loads of things wrong and they probably wish they hadn't, but that is the way of life. It doesn't always go right all of the time and none of us are perfect. If our Joni had lived, we'd have done some things wrong for her. You don't know how life might go. It drags you away from the right path or the best path, sometimes.'

Her body language was defensive. 'But I can't just let him off.'

'You don't have to. You just have to forgive him. That's different. I've done that with dad. He bore me no ill will but he couldn't love me like I needed to be loved. He probably wanted to but just couldn't access that within him. The fact that he should have been able to, in a way, makes no difference - he wasn't able to or didn't know how to and because of that, I've forgiven him. You can do that for your dad. You acknowledge the damage and you let it go and stop it hurting you any more. Forgiving isn't forgetting or pretending things were alright. It is just a letting go of the hate and upset. Don once told me that his faith had taught him that hanging onto hate stopped love, God's love, as he'd have it, from entering your heart.

Even if we strip the religion out of it, you can see how that works, can't you?'

She nodded and blew her nose again. 'You're right. Of course you are. I know that.'

'There's no right or wrong way to deal with it. You just have to find a way that sits right with you. So he's coming over in about 45 minutes, is he? Do you want me around for support?'

She sat up and cleared her throat.

'Do you mind if I say no?'

'No. Not if you're sure.'

'I almost don't want you to see me going through this. It's...it's almost embarrassing. I'd rather do it on my own, at least for now.'

'No problem. I'll have a walk up to Jeff's and get a coffee in there. Just text me when you need me.'

'Thanks, luv,' she smiled and kissed him tenderly on the lips, her hand on his neck.

'Just try not to get upset...I know it can be hard and this is all such a big shock...but life does this. It throws a curve ball. There's a lot to get your head around, not least having half-sisters who might have kids themselves - I don't even know what relation they'd be to you...'

'Oh, don't. It's all too much.'

'...so just take it easy. Him turning up like this isn't a bad thing. It's a new thing. Right? You're not obliged to see him again, if you don't want to. But the way I see it, he did a terrible thing to your family, not by walking out per se, but by never getting in touch and leaving it all so up in the air. That's the real crime he should be apologising for. But I'm sure he'll have had his reasons and I wouldn't be surprised at all to hear he'd had a breakdown of some flavour. He obviously feels strongly enough about it to want to make it right with you and Jackie now. But what will Kev and Ricky say?'

'Ricky will throw a punch at him. Guaranteed. Kev too, probably. They're not emotionally healthy enough to cope with it in any other way. I'm not sure I am, to be honest.'

He put his hands on her shoulders. 'You are. You've always been strong enough to cope with my issues. You can do this and, who knows, it may be a great new thing in your life - having a dad. He might be a cool older dude. He looked pretty cool to me.'

She sighed and reluctantly nodded. 'Well, we'll have to see,' was all she could muster.

CHAPTER 11

There was music blaring out of Jeff's shop as he approached; Budgie's classic track, 'Breadfan'. Although it was well after 8pm, Jeff kept the place open often until as late as 10pm, especially with the cafe now open. It just made sense to be available when customers were off work and could spend some time browsing. As a result he sold more records from 6pm than he did in the mornings. On a High Street that was so deserted it might as well have tumbleweed blowing through it after 5.30pm, it was a welcome oasis of activity.

The big man was behind the counter looking at a large computer screen. 'Hey, crazy dude!' he yelled. Nick saluted. 'How's it hanging?'

Nick looked down at his crotch. 'To the left, it would seem. Jules tells me it always does.'

'Aye, well she'd know, that one, wouldn't she? The geography and dimensions of male genitalia is one of her specialist areas of knowledge. She should go on *Mastermind* and answer questions about it.'

He turned the volume down so they didn't have to shout at each other. Two couples sat in the cafe at the back drinking coffee and eating muffins. Matty gave him a wave from behind the coffee machine. Someone was looking through Jeff's blues section and pulling out records with the eagerness of any collector who has found a rich seam of stuff that they must have.

'Some weird shit has just happened,' said Nick, perching on a tall stool by the counter.

'We've not got another dead Elvis impersonator on our hands, have we?'

'No. But it does involve a missing man.'

'The Shadow?'

'Ah, no and yes. The Grid spotted him coming out of a place called BioResearch International on an industrial estate in Hartlepool.'

Jeff looked askance at him. 'That's weird. You told me that Harcombe told you that Jim George went there as well.'

'Yup, is that just a weird coincidence?'

'It's not a bloody coincidence, it can't be. Why would either of them be there? What do Bio-thingy do?'

Nick looked it up on his phone. 'Research into bacteria and infection for the drug industry. Jim had their magazine in his car when I found him dead. It's called *Bacto - the Future*.'

'Nice pun, if you can forgive abbreviating *bacteria* in that way.'

Nick paused to think about it for a moment. 'I can't work any of this out. Shadow Man and Elvis - how do they go together? I just can't figure it. Actually, the missing man I was talking about was Julie's dad.'

'Old man Wells? What about him? He went Missing in Action in the 70s, didn't he?'

'He did, but he just turned up at the house while we were there for tea.'

Jeff gave him a confused look. 'Eh! Are you sure it wasn't someone taking the piss?'

Nick shook his head. 'He was the absolute spitting image of Julie. Quite a funky old dude. Looked a bit like a surfer. He's been living in Australia running a market garden, growing flowers.'

Jeff mimed a big 'wow' sound. 'He does sound like an old head. Julie must have totally freaked out.'

'Aye, you could say that. He had a touch of that about him. He was lean with tanned, leathery skin, white swept-back hair and the same blue eyes as Jules. Looked like he might have been the keyboard player in Country Joe and the Fish or someone like that.'

'Amazing scenes. So why is he back now?'

'Wants to make it up to the family for walking out on them.' He explained Julie was meeting him at the flat. 'She's been in floods of tears. I've told her it could be a good thing.'

'Yeah, you can never have too many hip older dudes in your family.'

Jeff pulled on his beard and went into the stock room to check on Argie, returning with him in his arms, the kid looking around with bright round blue-grey eyes.

'Hey Arg,' said Nick, wiggling his fingers at the little lad. He leaned over the counter and took him from Jeff, letting the kid sit upright in the crook of his arm. The baby reached out and put his tiny hand on Nick's cheek, exploring the world around him with that look of innocent wonder all babies have.

'It's funny that he can sit up now. I'm used to him just lying down,' said Nick.

'I know, one morning he just realised he could do it. Hasn't stopped since. The speed at which he's growing and developing is amazing to me. So, I suppose Jules is bound to be a bit weirded out by this turn of events.'

'She was really upset just now. I mean, I totally understand why. It goes to the roots of who she is.'

Nick handed the baby back to Jeff.

'Yeah, but he was a bit of a bastard, the way she tells it.'

'I know. He was a piss-head - sorry for the bad language, Arg...' Jeff put his fingers over the baby's ears. '...and a bully to the kids and god knows what he and Jackie got up to. I can only imagine the fights, because she'd not have given an inch in a row.'

Jeff blew out air. 'Sounds like classic tears before bed, to me.'

'Yeah, I'm not sure this is the best time for it to happen. She's still getting over the miscarriage, then we got attacked by Shadow Man, which really upset her as well...'

'...well, it would. Jules is tough, though.'

Nick wasn't so sure at all. She *was* tough, but there's only so much emotional upset anyone can stand in a short space of time before it crushes them or sends them to a very bad place. He knew that all too well himself. Your emotional batteries just get drained. He just hoped that she could keep on dealing with this stuff. Life has a nasty habit of delivering one test after another in groups of three or six. You go for ages without anything upsetting happening and then suddenly, it's as if the lever marked 'bad shit' has been pulled and you get hosed down with all the slurry life can throw at you.

'So is Kev playing at Dirty Harry with old Shadowski, then?' said Jeff.

'Given half a chance, yeah. He wants revenge. In other news...I met that jockey, Mickey. The one who was fighting the Regency jockey. He came in the Horse and Jockey earlier.'

'What were you doing in there? Not your sort of place, that.'

'I stopped off to have a stiffener before going to Jackie's.'

Jeff snorted, brought the pram out of the back and put Argie in, pulling the hood back so he could sit and see what was going on.

'Understandable enough. Didn't he recognise you?'

'No. Or if he did, he didn't let on. He came right out and said the bloke he was fighting - Macca - had stolen the cup. He seemed convinced and I don't see why he'd tell me or the barman anything other than what he thought was the truth.'

'Ah, right.' Jeff went quiet, thinking this news over, and drummed his fingers on the counter and then pointed at Nick.

'Hey, what was that text you sent me about hypnosis about? I couldn't make head nor tail of it.'

Nick explained about his trip to Ellie Gold. Jeff couldn't help but laugh when he heard about how easy to put under Nick was. 'And I went for a piss in the pub on the way to Jackie's and it was all fine...'

'...no stage fright?'

'None. It sort of only half-occurred to me that there might be but it didn't linger as a thought, so as a result, I could just whop it out and whazz away. Whatever she did, it really bloody worked and that got me thinking. Now, this might sound a bit weird, but you'll like it, because it's exactly what you suggested.'

'Weird is good. I am good. Therefore, this will be good.' He put his hands together and bowed as though he was a monk in prayer.

'OK. I was thinking, you know Brian and Big Fish both seemed to have no idea that the cup was patterned and not plain? You said, in jest, that they had been hypnotised, didn't you? Well, maybe that is *exactly* what happened to them. They were hypnotised into seeing patterns as plain.' Jeff's eyebrows shot up. Nick raised a hand. 'Wait on before you call me crazy...remember two things, other than their belief that the cup was plain. One. When we arrived at his house, Brian didn't seem to know what you meant by saying that multicoloured paisley tie was psychedelic, remember. He said it was "a plain old thing". Two. The BF was lusting after that woman in the polka-dot dress at the party, remember that...?'

Jeff slapped the counter. 'You're right. He was and he said something about her being in a little black dress...'

'...when it was actually covered in spots - you made that spotty dog reference, remember? He couldn't see that pattern. He saw it as plain black. So, given what Ellie told me, I reckon they were hypnotised into seeing something patterned as plain in the dominant colour. So the Art Nouveau cup just looked plain silver, the dress plain black, the tie plain blue.'

'I love this!' Jeff raised his arms in the air and hi-fived Nick. 'It sounds mad, but frankly, if she can cure you of your cock-block, then anything is possible. Alright, riddle me this, Batman...or is it Catwoman in those tight jeans?'

'Leave my jeans alone. If I could get away with wearing a tarpaulin tied around me with string, I would.'

Jeff laughed his deep rumble. 'OK, this Shadow fella - he might easily be trained in that sort of level of black ops.'

'Exactly, but why would he want to do that to them? Why let them think the patterned cup is really plain?'

'Hmm, not sure.' Jeff stacked some records into a neat pile while he thought about it. Then he filed some invoices, sharpened all his pencils and put them into a mug on the counter. Once he'd taken £10 for a Howlin' Wolf *London Sessions* album, he spoke up again.

'Running with your excellent and mad idea, one thing this would have achieved is - depending on when they were hypnotised - and I feel like an arse even saying that - they wouldn't know if the original had been stolen and replaced with a plain cheap cup the same shape and size. Even if they looked at pictures of it online, it would still presumably look plain to them. So someone could steal it, put an identically shaped plain one in itself place and they're none the wiser.' He wafted his beard up and down. 'Not bad, eh?'

'It's a good idea but there are two flaws in it. Firstly, if they'd read a description of the cup, they'd have known it wasn't the one they could see and two, we know it *was* stolen - or at least, there was a dusty space where it had been. Unless *we* were hypnotised into seeing a space when there really was something there.'

'Bloody hell. We can't have been...can we?'

'I don't think so. I think you have to be compliant in the process. It can't be done without your knowledge.'

'OK, so we're seeing things for real. Now, yes, if they read a description of the cup, you're right. But they obviously haven't or it'd have come to light before now. Second, yes, something was stolen - but I'll tell you what, here's a great idea - that was actually the replacement for the *real* Sir Walter Francis Cup. This Macca bloke took it, unaware it was a fake, right? Get me? The card was sitting in front of it said it was the Sir Walter Francis, so he just grabbed it because of that.' Jeff drummed on the counter with his fingers in triumph. 'The real one was nicked, a false one put in its place to hide the fact, which in turn was also nicked by someone who didn't know the difference.'

Nick felt excited. 'I really think we're onto something here, you know. Deffo.'

'Yeah, me too. So why would believing what Brian told us about the cup get us, according to Shadow, killed?'

Nick shook his head. Then it dawned on him. 'It won't, man! It won't! He's just trying to scare us away from Brian. Yes! That was all just one big scare tactic. There was no truth to it at all, Shadow was just putting the shitters up us to keep us at a distance from whatever is going on. You said yourself, he wasn't attacking us, he was defending us. The warning was for our own good. He didn't want to kill us, he wanted to keep us safe.' He clapped his hands together. 'The other day we said he hadn't actually threatened us - OK, he threatened Julie on the ground, but that was to make us listen and take him seriously - apart from that, as we said, his only threat was that us believing Brian would get us killed - not that *he'd* kill us. This whole thing, for whatever reason, is a scam. It's all bullshit. The Shadow Man put the wind right up us all, to keep us at arm's length from Blakeston, Regency and the police and it worked.'

Jeff applauded. 'Those tight jeans must be squeezing some clever juice up into your brain.'

'You know what we should do? We should try and bring some of this to a head. We should just ask Brian outright about the cup. You did say you'd try and find it, didn't you? So call him up now and ask him why he thought it was plain when it's an Art Nouveau Fabergé piece. Grill him about it. Tell him it's not plain and if he thinks it is, he's been hypnotised. Obviously, he'll think you're mad. Put him on speaker phone, so I can hear what he says.'

Jeff did exactly as Nick suggested.

'Hello, Brian. It's Jeff.'

'Hello, Jeff.' Brian's voice was as well spoken and measured as ever.

'Brian, me and Nick were wondering something. You know you said your stolen trophy was a plain silver cup?

'Indeed.'

'Well, we looked it up in the reference guide and it's not plain at all. It's a Fabergé Art Nouveau cup.'

Jeff pulled a face at Nick as they both leaned into the phone to hear his reply. Brian had gone quiet. The sense that he'd stopped listening and was now distracted was absolutely inescapable.

'Brian? Are you there?' asked Jeff. They listened again.

'Who's that?! Good god! What the hell are *you* doing here?! Oh, my lord!' His voice was shocked and frightened. There was a second voice and then a third and some noise.

'Brian?! Brian, what's wrong?!' shouted Jeff into the receiver.

There was a thudding sound, followed by a crash and some raised voices.

'Brian?! Brian!' yelled Jeff. 'Are you alright? Brian!'

They looked at each other in shock as the line went dead.

'Come on. We've got to get over there,' said Nick, making for the door.

Jeff shouted to Matty. 'Can you keep an eye on Argie and get Emily to lock up and then take him to her flat? I'll pick him up later. OK?'

Matty put a thumb up.

As they headed out to the Blakeston Estate in Jeff's van, Nick kept trying Brian's number but it just rang. It didn't feel good, any of this. Nick's stomach churned. All the elements of the last few days were swirling around his brain like leaves in a gale. They were all related somehow. The cup, the stables, Elvis, Brian, Big Fish, the fighting jockeys, Shadow Man.

'We've got to be really careful here, man,' said Nick as Jeff turned up the track to the farmhouse. The sun was setting but it was still really light as they drove up the long gravel track and swung around the bend in the driveway. Nick's heart banged right up into his throat as soon as he saw it.

'Jeff! Look! Fucking hell!'

Parked in front of the house was a black Range Rover. Its plates read 33RM91.

'The Shadow! That's his car! Shit.' He turned to his old mate, whose eyes were wide and wild. 'What's going on, Jeff? Has he come here to kill Brian, just like he killed Jim George? He must have.'

'His car's here, so he's in there. C'mon, there's two of us. We can take this fucker...I just hope he's not killed Brian...I hope we're not too late,' said Jeff, coming to a halt and turning off the engine.

'...if he hasn't got a gun, yeah, we can sort him.'

'If he had a gun he wanted to use, he'd have threatened you with it the other day,' said Jeff. 'He could have killed you both but he didn't, that means he doesn't want to. Or at least, it's not his first choice. You said yourself, he's defending us, not attacking us.'

'Agreed. He was trying to scare us, not kill us then, but things might be different here.'

'We'll be as well assuming so. I'll go around to the back door that goes in from the stables, you go in the front.' Jeff leaned forward and reached under his seat, bringing out two tyre levers.

'Take this. Try not to batter him too senseless, eh?'

Heart pounding, Nick got out of the van. Everything was totally quiet. This was dangerous shit. What the hell had they got caught up in here?

Jeff ran around the house to the stable block on the east wing. Nick stood by the large Georgian front door, his mouth dry, rolling the iron bar over in his hands. Trying to be as quiet as you can only makes every single noise you do make seem all the more loud. The door clicked as he turned the door handle. It wasn't locked.

Pushing at it gently, he slipped inside into the reception hall. It was all so familiar, he knew the layout of the house pretty well. He stood and listened. Nothing. Not a single sound. The whole house was in semi-darkness.

Jeff had called Brian on the land line, and the phone was likely to be in the main living room, so he walked silently towards it and stopped by the door, listening so hard for the sounds humans made that it almost hurt his ears. Listening for breathing, creaking or a digestive gurgle. There wasn't much light in the room.

Where was Jeff? He couldn't hear him. The house was so big, though.

Nick peered around the large living room door and strained his eyes to look into the gloom. No-one there.

He walked on to the trophy room, making each step slow and deliberate, pulling his foot up just before it pressed into the carpet try and minimise any reverberation it might make. The door was closed. He put his ear to the wood and listened, feeling sure that they must be inside. Silence. He tried the handle but it was locked.

Then...noise...at the back door. It had to be Jeff. With his heart beating so hard that it felt like it would burst out of his throat, he crouched down behind a hall table to hide, in case it wasn't.

The footsteps could be felt more than heard. The old floorboards seemed to vibrate with every step as someone came around the corner at a slow pace. They wouldn't be able to see Nick behind the solid Queen Anne table.

He pressed himself up against the wall, half kneeling, as the person walked past him. As they passed him, it was clear that it was indeed Jeff. His heart relaxed a little.

'Jeff!' he hissed. The big man visibly jumped and looked around and down at him.

'Fuck me. You scared the shite out of me,' he whispered.

Nick stood up. 'There's no-one around. The whole house is quiet.'

'Think about this. I just realised that out front is the Range Rover but Brian's Volvo isn't there, is it? They've gone somewhere in it. They must have.'

'I wouldn't be so sure. Let's check the other rooms,' said Nick.

It was better having Jeff with him. He felt more secure. Two men wielding iron bars are definitely better than one. But, as they slowly walked around the ground floor, it was clear that there was no-one around the house at all, which was odd because the doors were all open. Who goes out and leaves the doors unlocked? Someone who is in a rush to leave.

They stood in the half light at the foot of the wide central staircase and looked around. A large Indian-style brass planter was lying on its side on the floor, having fallen off its tall bamboo stand.

Jeff pointed at it with his iron bar. Nick turned around and looked back towards the living room. Beside that door was a small table on its side.

'Come with me,' said Nick, walking back into the living room and standing right in the middle of it. The land line phone was on a telephone table but the unit wasn't in its cradle. It was on the sofa. He looked at the wire from the cradle to the wall socket; it had been yanked out and lay loose on the carpet. He hadn't noticed when he'd first glanced in the room but a window was open. The Georgian window which went almost to ground level had been pulled up by about 18 inches.

'You know what has happened here?' said Nick.

Jeff nodded. 'Someone came in through that window while we were on the phone to Brian.'

'Yeah, but not just that...there's been a chase or a struggle. See - this china mug here has fallen over on the coffee table...the display cabinet to one side of the door has been clattered into.' He went over to the Queen Anne glass-fronted cabinet. Inside were various figurines. Most of them had fallen over or were askew. A couple looked broken. 'Someone has clattered into this, then out in the passage, they've hit the table by the door and the plant holder by the stairs.'

Jeff stood and gestured with the long iron bar. 'So someone comes in. Brian shouts "Who are you?", then as someone comes in the door, "What are you doing here?" There's a struggle between the intruder and the other person out into the passage. We heard two other voices, remember?'

They walked back out and looked around.

'One of them escaped or got free and either ran outside or went upstairs,' said Nick.

'Whoever won the fight was on Brian's side or Brian would be dead in there...'

'Only if whoever broke in wanted to kill him. Come on, let's look upstairs.'

They climbed the wide, thickly carpeted staircase as quietly as they could. As they got to the top floor, where Julie and Emily had worked during the blues festival, Jeff put a hand up and turned to Nick, pointing to a door to their left.

'That's Brian's rooms.'

'Rooms? Plural?' whispered Nick.

'Two connected rooms, yeah. One is a living space, the other a bedroom.'

Nick nodded. 'We better take a look. Shit, I'm bricking myself. Not sure my heart can take any more of this tension.'

'Don't go having a heart attack on me.'

They both listened at the door for any sign of noise. Everything was still silent. The door itself was slightly ajar so Nick pushed at it just enough to peer around.

No-one. He walked in a little way, stood and looked. At first he thought the dark shape on the sofa was just cushions. But it wasn't. It was a man lying on his front. It was a strange position to lie in if he was asleep.

Nick turned to Jeff and pointed.

'Not Brian, is it?'

Jeff shook his head. 'No. Too small. And I'll tell you this - he's not asleep. No-one sleeps like that. Fuck it, I'm putting the light on.'

The heavy click of a switch flooded the room with an intense yellow light. Their eyes were so used to the dark that for a moment it was blinding. The man on the sofa didn't move. Nick walked the six strides over to him and squatted down beside him.

'Don't touch anything, Nick,' said Jeff, pulling him back a little. 'He's obviously dead, isn't he?'

'Yeah. I think so. Dead or drugged.'

He got onto his hands and knees and looked up at the man. His heart leaped into his mouth again as he saw who it was.

It was Macca, Mickey's enemy. Gone to the big stables in the sky, he'd ridden his last race.

Nick got to his feet. 'I'm no doctor, but I bet he's had his neck snapped, just like Elvis. Look at how weirdly he's slumped forward. I think he's been dumped here. He was probably caught on the stairs, killed and dumped up here. And there's only one neck snapper we know of - Shadow Man. Come on, let's get out.'

They flicked off the light and went downstairs at pace, reached the front door, had opened it and just walked onto the gravel towards Jeff's van when a flash of headlights scanned cross the house as a car approached.

'Oh, fucking shit. It's a car coming up the track,' said Nick, frozen mid-step in the doorway.

'Can we make it to the van?' said Jeff.

'No way, it's too far. They'll see us. Come on.' He sprinted across the gravel and towards a row of five tall plastic wheelie bins at the side on the house, near the stable block. They were the only cover they could reach in time.

They sprinted fast and low and got down behind them just as an old Mercedes rounded the bend and parked to the side of the Range Rover. Nick and Jeff squatted right down so they couldn't be seen, staring at each other in a frozen, dry-mouthed fear. Who the hell was this?

A car door was opened and then slammed shut. There was another noise; the boot being opened, perhaps. Footsteps crunched on the pea gravel, two people by the sound of it. Then, suddenly and shockingly, came the sound of shattering glass, banging and crashing. Whack. Whack. Metal on metal. They were smashing up the Range Rover with some sort of bat - a metal baseball bat, maybe. If anyone was around, this would surely bring them running, but no-one came. Nick's heart beat so hard with adrenalin that it felt like it could break free of his chest. Then there was shouting. 'C'mon! Where are ya?!'

Jeff tapped Nick on the arm. 'I know what's going on,' he said in an almost silent whisper.

'So do I.'

'It's Ricky and Kev. Pound to a penny.'

'Eh? How do you know that?'

Jeff pointed to his eyes.

'I saw it was an old Merc. They've always got an old Merc. They get them from Alf's garage in Hardwick. The Grid tracked the Range Rover down and they've come for revenge. They'd have assumed he'd be here too and that busting his car would flush him out.' He held up a big, tight fist. 'But he's not here.'

Nick quickly stuck his head out from behind the bins for a second, glimpsed what was happening and withdrew immediately.

'You're right. They've fucking totalled it. Shall we show ourselves?'

Jeff shook his head. 'Let them do their business. We don't want them to know we're here.'

'They'll have seen your van.'

'One white Transit is like another. They don't know whose it is. If they start battering it, we'll jump out.'

It took Ricky and Kev only 10 minutes to break everything on the Range Rover that could be broken and severely batter the rest of it. They shouted again but of course, no-one came, then they drove off in a cloud of dust and gravel.

As soon as they'd gone, Nick stood up and took out his phone. 'Right, let's get the police here. Time to test our Shadow Man's assertion that they won't believe us. This is our story, right? We'd come to see Brian, hadn't we? We found the Range Rover smashed up and Macca the jockey dead and Brian and his car gone. OK?'

'That is what happened. I know no other truth than that. I'm just going to call Emily.'

Nick put in a call to Colin Harcombe's mobile. The voice mail picked up.

'Colin. It's Nick Guymer. Something terrible has happened. Me and Jeff just dropped in to see Brian Salmon but he's not here. The house was unlocked and empty except for one dead Regency jockey. Outside is the Range Rover with military plates that I told you about - the one that forced me and Julie off the road. It's been smashed to bits. By the look of it, the dead guy didn't die of natural causes. We'll wait for you and your team here.'

He rang off.

'Emily has taken Argie to her flat, so all that is cool,' said Jeff, putting his phone away.

'Is that alright?'

'Yeah, she's great with him and she's mad about the boy. Argie oozes love. No-one can resist him. As soon as he looks at you with big glassy marble eyes, you're under his power. We're going to be here for a long haul, y'know. They'll go through us like a dose of salts. Who eats salts, anyway?'

'Eh?'

'A dose of salts? Who's eating these salts? What salts are they, anyway?'

'Epsom salts - they move your bowels, I think.'

'Really? Epsom in Surrey? Mind, being in Surrey can induce that feeling, as can most of the southeast of England. Terrible bloody place.'

Nick grunted a laugh just as his phone vibrated. It was Colin Harcombe. 'Hello, Colin.'

No introductions. His voice was terse and tense. 'Nick, get out of there now! That is no place for you! You hear me? Leave immediately, both of you. You'll be killed if you don't!' He shouted his last line. Colin never shouted.

'What? But there's a body here.'

'That place is fucking dangerous. Go, man. Go!!'

The line went dead. Jesus Christ, time they were gone.

'We've gotta go, Col's orders,' he said, dragging Jeff by the arm.

He sprinted to the van, Jeff in hot pursuit behind him.

'Why? What's going on?' said Jeff as they jumped in.

'He said it was and I quote, "fucking dangerous".'

Jeff turned the engine. 'Fucking hell, he never swears. Shit.' He'd stalled the engine, coming off the clutch too quickly.

'Jeff! Get the pedal to the sodding metal, please!' yelled Nick, a nameless fear gripping both of them now.

He turned it again, fired the engine up and took off down the track.

'Watch out man! You're coming off the gravel here,' shouted Nick.

They rounded the bend and flew down towards the narrow tarmac road at the bottom. 'Who are we running from?!' yelled Jeff. But as he did so, an intense metallic noise rang out. It sounded like someone had rung a bell inside the back of the van. 'And what the fuck was that?!'

Nick turned around to look into the dark space behind the seat just as the noise came again. This time he knew exactly what it was because it passed right by his face and flew out of the windscreen. It was a bullet. The windscreen cracked and shattered, leaving a big hole in it with concentric circles of fractures outwards from it.

'Fucking get the fuck out of here!' yelled Nick. 'They're after us!'

Jeff slung the van onto the road travelling over 60mph and stamped on the brakes to prevent him flying across the road and into the opposite field. The back end of the van skidded out from under his steering. It was perfect drift, aligning him with the flow of the road. He dumped the gears and hit the gas with all the power in his right foot. The engine howled in protest, the rubber screeched as the torque built.

Another shot rang off the back door of the van, this time not penetrating the vehicle. As it did so, Jeff released the clutch and took off at speed. Transit vans, being the choice of rock 'n' roll bands since time immemorial, can shift like shit off a shovel when they need too, and they're hardy beasts too, another reason why rock bands have favoured them for so long. Many had ended up in a ditch after being driven by a roadie out of his mind on cider and amyl nitrate, who yet had lived to tell the tale. This was certainly not the first time a Transit van had been shot at and it would no doubt not be the last.

Driving on pure instinct and adrenalin, Jeff gunned the van down the narrow country road, lights off, even though it was starting to get dark, just praying that nothing was coming in the opposite direction, almost waiting for the next bullet to take them down, ready to swerve off the road and into a fence, a wall or a ditch.

There was no time to say anything. No mental room to accommodate rational thought. The powerful bullets had come through the metal of the back door at head height and had passed right between them. Had Nick sat nearer to the driver's seat, he'd have got it in the back of his head, JFK-style.

Without meeting any other traffic, they roared down Blakeston Lane, braking heavily at the T-junction with Junction Road.

'We must have got away from them by now. There's no-one behind us,' said Jeff, looking in his wing mirrors, panting from the adrenalin-fuelled stress.

'Shit. I think we had lucky escape there, big man. Nice driving.'

Jeff high-fived him and then pointed to the hole in the fractured windscreen. 'Primitive bloody air-conditioning, that. I'm impressed it hasn't shattered into a million pieces.'

Getting back into town, they parked up at the back of Green Dragon Yard and inspected the bullet holes. They had to have been made by a high-velocity, high-powered rifle - not the sort of thing someone out shooting rabbits would mess around with.

'I'll have to get someone to fix that windscreen. It has to be Shadow Man who shot at us,' said Jeff as Nick unlocked the flat door. 'He killed little Macca and then tried to take us out.'

Nick wasn't sure. A note was on the table they put their keys on, by the door: 'Gone to Royal Oak with dad.'

'Fancy a bloody good drink?' said Nick.

'Too bloody right I do. Hopefully none of it will leak, cartoon-style, out of bullet holes in our bodies.'

They walked up the High Street, feeling sodding jumpy.

'Do you think they - whoever they were - knew it was us? Why didn't they shoot at Ricky and Kev?' said Nick.

Jeff took a rubber band out of his plaid shirt pocket and tied his long hair back. 'We'd run to the van, got in, I'd stalled it, then drove off, before that first shot dinged off the back of the van. That must have taken at least a minute and a half for all of that to happen. Yet those shots came right in the back of the van and out of the window.' He made a straight line in the air with his right index finger. 'So they had to be right behind us.'

'True, so what was right behind us?'

'Nothing. It's the western side of the house. The part that is under all the sheeting where all of the building work is happening. There's no cover there. No trees. They had to be standing to the side of the house, a rifle to their shoulder, taking shots at us from the open.' He held his index finger in the air again. 'They can't have known we were there *before* we drove away, because they'd have shot us, just like that. That means they only just got there as we were offski...we'd been parked up out the front for 20 or 25 minutes, hadn't we? Then Kev and Ricky came and broke the car up. That was another 10 minutes at least.'

'Yeah, that's right. And if the shooter was there when you stalled the van, they'd have taken us out right then.'

'Totally. But they didn't. So they were *not* there. They have to have just arrived at that side of the house as we gunned down the gravel. So what's behind the house on that side? They had to have been on foot.'

Nick thought about it as he pushed open the door to the Royal Oak. 'It's a field that leads down to the house on a low slope. It doesn't lead anywhere in particular but they must have come down there.'

'Sounds like something someone in the army would do. Running down a field, gun on their back, shooting at a van...crazy, man.' Nick stopped in his tracks. Jeff turned to look at him. 'What's up?'

'When me and Jules were up at Cow Green Reservoir, we saw some army lads training or doing manoeuvres. They were running up and down moorland slopes, they had rifles on their backs - what you just said, brought it back to me. They even did this thing where they set up a machine gun.'

Jeff scrunched his face up. 'Nick, man, think about it, the army doesn't do manoeuvres up there. How many where they?'

'About a dozen.'

'A dozen? They definitely weren't army. The army do huge exercises with a lot of troops. Twelve of them don't just run around on the moors of Teesdale.'

'Well, who were they? I thought two of them looked like the bouncers at the Ballroom at BF's gig.'

'No. Can't be. Surely.'

'I was probably mistaken.'

'Hold on...I've had a thought.' Jeff took out his phone and skimmed through the photos, holding one up at him. 'Remember that? Whiffy Smiffy took it of us all outside the Ballroom. Those two bouncers that gave me a hard time are right behind us. Was that the men you saw on the moors?'

Nick took the phone and made the picture bigger, squinting at the screen. 'Shit. Yeah. It was. It was them. One tall, one short, both of them really broad and with high cheekbones.'

Jeff nodded and took the phone back. 'Colin told us to get out...' he stopped mid-sentence and looked back down the High Street at the old town hall, thinking, '...he's already said about there being international forces in the region. Say there's some sort of private army here - the men you saw up in Teesdale - maybe they were sent to get Brian, and Colin knew. Shadow Man knew as well and they got him away...but we were there and they tried to take us out, thinking we were Brian.'

'...but where does Macca fit into that?'

'He doesn't. He was there by accident at the same time. Shadow Man killed him. He was there to protect Brian from the soldiers who shot at us. They'd come to get him, but saw us and tried to take us out. Like I say, they probably thought we were Brian.'

Nick looked at Jeff, feeling scared. 'That would mean Brian is...something...something of interest to the British state...'

'Maybe he's a spy. He's been out of the country for months.'

'Come on - Brian?!'

'I know it sounds mad but...getting shot at with high-powered rifles isn't exactly sane and that just happened,' said Jeff.

CHAPTER 12

Nick finally pushed open the door of the Royal Oak. Julie and her father, Robbie, were sitting in the far corner, each with a glass of white wine. She looked up and gave him a relaxed, full smile that told him everything was going well. He knew her smiles. The shape and degree of them were always the best indicator of her mood.

'Bloody hell, like daughter, like father,' said Jeff as they stood at the bar. 'Two more?' he said; she put her thumb up. 'He looks like he should have played drums in the Peanut Butter Conspiracy in 1968. Got a real old hippy look about him.'

'Great reference, big man. He's from Hardwick, though. No hippy ever came from Hardwick.'

'I think you're wrong. One thing being in the record business has given me is a very good sense of when I'm in the presence of some flavour of alternative freak. He looks like a man who will have an album collection worth buying. I can smell it on him. It's a sixth sense every second-hand record shop owner has. Trust me.'

Nick wandered over and sat down opposite them, holding out his hand to Robbie as he did so.

'Great to meet you properly this time,' said Nick, pushing his hair behind his ears.

'Nice to meet you, too. Jules has been telling me all about you. All good things. I'm glad she found a good bloke. I saw the photo she put up on Facebook of you two up in Teesdale. Thought you looked like a good bloke.'

'Yeah, well it took me a lot of searching to find him,' said Julie, with a wink at Nick.

Jeff brought over the drinks.

'Mister Wells, I believe. I'm Jeff Evans, proprietor of Jeff's Records and this fella's gay lover.' He slapped Nick on the back and kissed him on the cheek. They all laughed. 'So here's to you, man.' He raised his glass. 'Are you back in the UK now?'

'I'm thinking about it, Jeff. Maybe time for me to come home.'

'Sounds crazy to me. All that sunshine, the beach and liberal use of the word *drongo*. All brilliant,' said Jeff.

They all laughed again. 'Yeah. True. But I'm an old guy now and I feel like...I don't know...sometimes you just get a feeling in your heart.'

'I think you'll find that's indigestion brought on by drinking the wine in here,' said Jeff. More laughter.

Robbie passed his oak-coloured hands through his soft, thin, white hair. His scalp, visible through the thinning hair, was also tanned deep and brown. He looked in great shape; slim and broad and eyes that were clear and turquoise blue. Looking at him made genetic sense of Julie. The physical familiarity felt almost weird. He even seemed to share some of her mannerisms such as lightly biting her bottom lip when listening to someone talk, pushing his hair behind his right ear, arching his eyebrows as though always slightly bemused. It was all pure Julie. She was his girl.

There were obviously a lot of big questions to deal with here, primary amongst them, why did you walk out on your family in 1977 without a word and never even make a phone call since? Julie must surely have asked him that already and it certainly wasn't Nick's place to do so in the Royal Oak. She hadn't been crying though, that much he knew. Her eyes were clear and not red at all now. Given all that had happened to them with losing the baby, maybe she was just able to keep things in perspective. It seemed unlikely, though. The return of her father was about as big a thing as you could have happen in your life, except perhaps losing your own baby. Maybe the way the universe worked was to take away with one hand and give with the other. All things in perpetual balance.

'So where are you staying?' said Nick.

'I've got a room at a Premier Inn. I just landed yesterday, so I'm a bit jet lagged, to say the least.'

'We don't have a spare bed or you could have stayed at ours,' said Nick.

'It's fine. Thanks.'

'You could have stayed at mine if *I'd* actually had a spare bed. I'd offer to share my bed with you but that would be a cruel and unusual punishment,' said Jeff.

'So, are you going to go and see Jackie and the lads?' said Nick.

'Well, that was my aim but Jules reckoned it'd be best if she paved the way for it, first. Feel sick that Kev and Ricky have been such bad lads. That was my fault. Boys need their dad around to keep them in hand.'

'And girls do, too,' added Julie, eyebrows arched. He squeezed her bare arm.

'Did you think they'd have grown up to be academic, like?' said Jeff with a laugh in his voice.

'No. But look, to go inside for acts of violence and robbery isn't what I expected at all. I do blame myself. I'm sure I put the seeds of that behaviour into them. There's no escaping that, mate.' At times the Australian accent took over and he sounded like a cricketer being interviewed about the Ashes.

'You did...' said Julie, rubbing her forearm, '...but nothing is inevitable. They made bad choices. So did Terry, when he was young, but he's grown up now. Him and Jaz are a nice couple. You'll like them. Ricky and Kev have, at some point, made a decision to be as they are. You're not *totally* to blame for that.'

'What did you think would have happened to Julie?' said Nick.

Without hesitation Robbie said, 'To be honest, Nick, and don't take this the wrong way, I thought she'd have a rich bloke and be swanning around the place in fancy clothes and a big car.'

Julie laughed. 'There was a time in my life when I thought that's what I wanted, to some degree.'

'She was always bright, even as small girl.' He said it with a degree of melancholy at the recollection. 'I also sort of assumed that at least one of the four of you would have had kids as well.'

'Urgh...well...therein lies a tale of woe, I'm afraid,' said Julie, curling her lip up. 'And we think the lads are all infertile - well, Kev and Ricky, anyway. They're really irresponsible men, so if they've not knocked someone up, it must be because they're impotent or infertile or both. I think Terry and Jaz will have kids soon. They're talking about it, anyway.'

'So what happened, man?' said Jeff. 'Why walk out and never come back or stay in touch?'

It was the big question. Typical of Jeff to front it up like that.

Robbie didn't say anything immediately. He took a drink of wine and looked beyond them.

'Well...it's like this, mate. I'm not making any excuses. I could...but it isn't right to do that. I did a bad thing, a wrong thing. I could say what was in my head at the time, but that still wouldn't make it right. As I've been telling Jules, it's eaten away at me over the years...'

'...but a phone call wouldn't have harmed,' said Nick.

'I got locked into it as a mindset. I felt guilty and didn't want to confront it, at least not until recent years. I also thought I'd just get a mouthful off Jackie - and rightly so, like...I wasn't sure I could cope with that. I haven't got err...like...a ready-made answer or excuse. Nothing glib or snappy to say.'

'You were a drunk,' said Julie. 'That doesn't help anyone make good choices.'

'Guilty as charged. I was a drunk because I was unhappy, Jules. I felt trapped in that house with your mother and, I know it sounds terrible, but with you four kids as well...I felt like I was going insane. Then I was laid off from British Steel...they were dark days. I just felt I had to get away from it.'

Nick nodded. 'Do you think you had some sort of breakdown?'

'As I was saying in the flat, I definitely did. I'm not sure what it was. But I went sort of awol in my head and nothing seemed to matter. I don't even really remember the next few months after walking out. I don't know what I did or where I was. I must have done something to survive. I just...it's all gone.'

That sounded all too horribly familiar. But back then, mental illness wasn't something anyone knew anything about and the way it was treated ranged from the brutal to the careless.

'But how did you get Down Under?' asked Jeff.

'I was living in London doing labouring and someone was going out there to work on a big development in Sydney. The company was recruiting labour. I just flew down there and I never came back. Not until now. That was in 1979. I went through loads of jobs, but from the late 80s, I was working at this garden centre in Sydney and I loved it. I built up a bit of money and when the chance came to buy it because the owner was retiring, I gave it a go. That was in 2004. It's doing well. Not bad for an old steelworker, eh?'

He smiled but it was weak smile, a smile that betrayed a lot of deeply buried hurt behind his eyes. His was a story that would take a long time to unravel and understand, if indeed it ever could be. Our lives pass quickly and are a bumpy road upon which we travel, often losing our way and taking wrong turns. Sometimes we crash, sometimes we break down and ultimately, there is no destination to reach. We keep moving in order to experience the journey; the journey is all we have. Even if you want to tell someone everything you've seen or heard along the way, after over 65 years, there's no way you can do much more other than dig over the topsoil. Too much life has been lived to speak much about it.

Jeff spoke. 'Hang on, though, if you were offski, you can't have actually got divorced from Jackie, can you?'

'Mam filed for divorce in 1982,' said Julie.

'I assumed she'd do that,' said Robbie. 'I remarried in Oz in 1989 to Sharon. We had two girls, they're 21 and 19, both at Uni. Erin and Carly. We're very happy...we...we get on...me and your mother never got on, really, Jules. Not on...the right wavelength...I don't know...' He seemed unable to find the words to finish his sentence.

'Eee, god, I can't believe I've got two half-sisters,' said Julie, shaking her head.

Robbie took out a wallet and produced a family picture of the four of them taken on the beach. Sharon couldn't have looked less like Jackie. She was tall, blonde, tanned and good-looking with huge breasts crammed into a swimming costume. Their daughters were also attractive, tall, slim and blonde, just looking very Australian, somehow - all outdoorsy with white teeth and the Wells blue eyes. It would be pretty much impossible to say that they hadn't had a better quality of life out there than any of his kids in Hardwick ever had, even the biggest fan of Teesside would have to admit that.

'Anyway, where did you two get to?' said Julie, sipping at her wine.

'Us? Oh we had a bit of adventure didn't we, Nick?' said Jeff and then pointed with both index fingers at Robbie. 'We live a dangerous life on Teesside, Robbie...' He quickly went over everything that had happened. Julie let out a yelp as he told about being shot at, her hand over her mouth.

'Bloody hell. What's going on up there? What did Colin mean?' she said.

'He knew something was wrong up there...that's for sure,' said Nick. 'Jeff thinks those soldiers we saw up on the moors - they're a private army and they came for Brian, and shot at us.'

'Jesus Christ, is this your normal lives?' said Robbie with a bemused look. 'It sounds more like Bonnie and Clyde.'

They looked from one to the other. 'Err, yeah, sort of. We do get into a few scrapes from time to time, like,' said Jeff. 'What can you do? Teesside's the Wild West, except it's in the northeast. It'll make your life in Sydney look a bit tame in comparison, that's for sure.'

'Well, the old place looks exhausted compared to when I left, the bits I've seen. It's quite shocking how much of it has gone.'

'Aye, the old girl needs a good makeover, doesn't she? There's talk of an upgrade - but the problem is all the industry that was here when you worked at British Steel has shrunk right back or totally gone,' said Jeff. He glanced at his watch. 'Look, I've got to go and pick up Argie from Emily. Nice to have met you, Robbie. If you're staying around I shall see you again soon enough.'

They shook hands.

'He's quite a character,' said Robbie after Jeff had gone.

'Yeah, me and him go way back to school days. So what's your plan for tomorrow?' asked Nick.

Julie spoke. 'I'm going to go and tell mam and if she wants to see you, I'll arrange it. She might not, though. I wouldn't blame her if she didn't, really.'

'No. I wouldn't either.'

'Same goes for the lads. Terry will be alright but Kev and Ricky might want to have a pop at you, so I'll deal with them after you've met mam.'

After finishing their drinks, Robbie headed off for his Premier Inn room and Nick and Julie walked home arm in arm.

'Well, to understate things a little, that was an eventful day,' said Nick, feeling exhausted.

'Just a bit. Are you OK? You must have shit yourself in the van.'

'There was no time for that. Something weird is going on up there. Something...I don't know...not just criminal. Jeff reckons Brian is a spy or something. I reckon your brothers were very lucky to get away from there without being shot in the head. Whoever was doing the shooting must just have arrived as we left.'

'Where has Brian gone and who with? The Shadow Man?'

'That's what it looked like to us. He killed Macca and then disappeared with Brian in Brian's car.'

They got in and she took off her sweat top.

'I am utterly, utterly, exhausted. I can't take all this in. None of it. I need to go to bed.'

Nick lay in bed, and, as was his habit, after Julie had fallen to sleep, he let himself think think think. There was some grit or insight or knowledge in the back of his brain, working its way to the front. He could feel it. Eventually, the tide of serotonin washed in and took him to dreamland.

When he awoke, Julie was bringing Sencha green tea in.

'Hands off cocks, hands on socks.' She put tea on his bedside table, lifted up the duvet and looked at him, naked. 'Why do you men grip your tackle so much when you're asleep? You all do it. Is it for pleasure or comfort?'

'Maybe for both,' he said, yawning. 'Also, I need a piss. But can't until things soften up a bit...which doesn't happen for ages because your bladder presses on your erection button, for some reason. Why does nature do that? It's cruel.'

'Does that happen to people who are impotent?'

He got out of bed and padded to the toilet. 'I've no idea and hopefully I never will find out.' After some effort and a brief imitation of a garden sprinkler, he managed to drain his bladder, then cleaned up the floor.

'I hope you mopped up after yourself,' said Julie as he returned to bed.

'It's like a garden hose left unattended, that thing.'

'I think I'll take mine back to the shop and get a new one.'

'Oh, god, no. Don't do that. I like this one. It fits me like a glove.'

'It can't fit you like a glove. You fit it like a glove.'

'Ha. Oh, yeah. Either way, you've ruined me with it now, so you can't swap it for another one.' She pulled a face at him.

'Alright. I'll keep this one for the time being at least.'

He gratefully drank his tea and slaked his overnight thirst.

'Do you like it?'

'Aye, thanks, it's lovely tea.'

'No, not the tea, your garden sprinkler.'

She laid back on her pillow and ran a finger down her centre-parting.

He looked at her. 'What an odd question to ask a chap when he's just woken up. Why ask me that? Is this some sort of psychological test?'

'It ties in with some work I'm doing...' she picked a sleep crust out of her eye '...about self-identity.'

He thought about it for a bit. 'Yeah. I suppose I do like it, or at least I don't have any loathing towards the poor old thing, if that means anything. But I don't think about it that much, except when I have to have a wee in front of people...I don't like it much then, I'll tell you that...or I didn't...'
She interrupted him before he could tell her about the hypnosis.

'Good. That's healthy, I think. Explains a lot about you.'

'Does it? How?'

'Some dodgy attitudes are tied up with men's attitudes to their downstairs bits and pieces. Being positive but not overly proud or aggressive about it...that's probably as healthy, psychologically speaking, as you can be.'

'That's the first time the words *healthy* and *psychologically* have been used about me simultaneously...'

'Don't go putting yourself down. You know fine well you're in a good place with all of that.'

'Well, I make no claims for the aesthetic value of my trouser jewellery, but I'd hate to be without it and it's seen me through a lot of good times and even more bad.'

She nodded. 'You've got to like your love bits, I reckon, be they male or female. Important to self-respect. I was doing some work on this for TW.' She sipped at her tea again and rubbed her other eye. 'One of the ways abusive men put women down and break their self-respect in order to control them is to be insulting about the most sensitive parts of their body, to make them feel worthless or inadequate. One of the things *we* have to do is to restore that self-confidence and help rebuild self-respect.'

Nick tutted. 'There seem to be no depths that some men won't stoop to...it just appalls me. Lack of self-respect and self-belief is so destructive. It messes you up on all levels. So if people start insulting your body, it must impact on your whole life...well, just to be clear, I love and cherish your, what did you call them? Your love bits. They're beautiful and...err...ideally suited to their task in life. As someone once said, "every vagina is a unique snowflake - made of gammon".'

'Ha ha...thank you, darlin'. I won't ask you what my pineapple ring is.'

He finished his tea. 'As we're talking about such things, something happened to me yesterday that was both brilliant and amazing. I just didn't get the space or time to tell you yesterday, what with everything.' He explained what Ellie Gold had done. Julie looked over her mug at him with raised eyebrows, murmuring her approval at the whole process.

'And the best thing is, Jules, it actually worked.'

'Gettaway. Did it?' Her mouth turned up into a big smile.

'Yeah. First test was in the bogs of the Horse and Jockey before I met you at your mother's. I walked up, lopped it out and hosed it out like I was an normal adult. Brilliant. I know it doesn't sound like much, compared to the shit you hear about people suffering, but it's such a relief. And I'd just totally gone to her on the spur of the moment.'

'Isn't that amazing...eee, you should have had that done sooner. How ace for you. No more drying up.' She laughed a little. 'It really is a powerful thing, the mind, isn't it? We don't appreciate just how powerful, nor how much we can change.'

'Well, exactly and that's why I think Brian and Big Fish have also been hypnotised. I need to tell you about this, as well.'

She screeched a surprised laugh. 'Oh, now I have got to hear this...but I need to get ready for work, tell me in the shower.'

As they often did, they squeezed in the shower together and washed each other. It was a simple, intimate and usually non-sexual act.

'Do you remember what Big Fish said about the woman in the polka-dot dress at the launch party?'

'Oh, it was something sexist, wasn't it?' she said, as they got out of the shower.

'He said, "That's some sweet meat in the little black dress", to be exact.'

She pulled a face. 'Women really are just meat to men like him.' She took a pair of tweezers and extracted a stray long hair from around a nipple.

'Why pluck out nipple hairs?' said Nick, watching her do it. 'I've got nipple hairs, but I don't pluck them out, why should you?'

'Because I'm conditioned to think it's wrong and not feminine to have hairy nipples.'

Nick shrugged. 'But that's obviously rubbish. If it happens to you, a female, then it is de facto feminine.'

She smiled. 'I love that you've said that without even knowing what a lovely feminist thing it was to say.'

'Bollocks. That's making too much of it. It's just logical, isn't it? Can't get PC points for that.'

'OK, well, I'll leave the next one in. I've had that hair sprout out of there for about 20 years now, anyway. So what were you mentioning Big Fish for?'

He explained how you can be hypnotised to see things differently to how they really are.

'That is a weird idea, but you're right, it does explain some unexplainable things,' said Julie. She watched as he pulled on underwear, black t-shirt and old jeans and pointed as he did so.

'See, still dressing to the left...you didn't believe me, but it's always to the left...see?' she laughed and continued drying herself.

He inspected himself and sat down on the wash basket. 'I have actually started noticing now that you keep going on about it. You teach me things about myself that I didn't even know. You'll be telling me which of my bollocks hangs lowest, next.'

'Ha. The right one.'

'50/50 chance of getting that right. Not that I actually know the answer. So you're going to see your mam and tell her about Robbie?'

'Yeah, thing is, I really don't know how she'll take it. I'm dead nervous. What a thing to have to tell your own mother.'

'How long were they together for?'

'They got married in November 1963, less than a year after first meeting. I was their wedding night baby. Classic. He left in 1977.'

'That's still a long time to be with someone. Were they ever in love?'

'Yeah, early doors. But all I remember is them being daggers drawn, with each of them trying to turn us against the other. But 14 years is a long time, I mean, it's longer than we've known each other.'

'Well, it can't just be nothing to her, can it? He's the father of her four kids - surely that has to mean something. Who you had your kids with must be one of the most significant people in your life, even if it all goes wrong.'

'Yeah, but she was beyond furious about him leaving and her bitterness was so huge it probably had its own gravitational pull.'

Nick puffed out his cheeks. 'Well, give us a shout if you need support.'

'I will. Thanks, luv. What are you doing today?'

'I'm writing two pieces and plotting out my book.'

'Your book?'

'Aye. I decided I'm going to write a novel and see if I can get it published.'

She clapped her hands together in rapid applause, grinning at him. 'That's a great idea. What's it going to be about?'

'That's the hard bit. I don't know, exactly. I fancy writing about two lovers who get back together during the Boro's 2006 UEFA cup campaign.'

'Aw, like we did? A romance?'

'Hmm...sort of. A modern relationships thing, with added football and maybe a few second-hand records.'

'Eee, you big puff.' She looked at him affectionately and pecked him on the lips. 'Make sure the woman has a hairy pink nipple and likes Pat Benatar, and that he dresses to the left.'

'Those'll be the first things on the plot list, obviously.'

After Julie had left for work, Nick sat in their kitchen and made some notes on an A4 pad of paper, trying to draw lots of disparate people and things together to see if there was any sort of pattern to indicate why Macca had been murdered, why Jim George had met his maker and why someone had thought them worthy of being shot at. After he'd written it all down, the paper looked like a doodle of spaghetti and made little or no sense.

The one man that he was certain knew something about this, was Colin Harcombe. He'd known something was going down at Brian's house, so he must know more now than when he'd called him the other night. Nick dialled Colin's mobile phone, not expecting him to answer, but intending to leave a message; however, the policeman picked up after four rings.

'Yes?' he said, which despite being a single, short word was said in a tone which suggested extreme wariness. Surely his display would have shown who was calling. Was he suspicious that someone other than Nick Guymer had Nick Guymer's phone?

'Hello, Colin, it's just me, Nick.'

There was a detectable ease of tension.

'Ah. Hello, Nick. Are you OK?'

'I'm fine. How are you?'

'Good, good. Julie well?'

It was as if the last night hadn't even happened.

'Fine. Err...what was last night all about, Col? Off the record.' He listened but Colin Harcombe didn't say anything. Was he weighing up what to say? 'Col, we were nearly killed last night, me and Jeff. After I'd spoken to you, we drove off at speed and three shots were fired at us. One of them just missed me and shattered the windscreen.'

'Christ...is Jeff OK?'

'Yeah, he needs a new windscreen, but...you knew that was going to happen, didn't you?'

He replied quickly. 'No. No, I didn't. Not specifically. I really am not at liberty to comment much, Nick, not even in a private capacity.' He spoke in a very stiff manner, or at least more stiff than usual.

'Colin. We were nearly murdered in cold blood. I need to know who was trying to kill us and why. Come on, it's only fair you tell me, if you know.'

'Even so...'

'I don't understand...'

'...it's not for you to understand.'

That annoyed Nick. His temper rose in his throat. 'Don't treat me like a kid. The hell it isn't for me to understand! I'm not having someone trying to kill me, Colin. It's your bloody job to protect the public. I am the public. And more than that, I'm your friend...or at least I thought I was. It was only a year ago that I damn near got myself killed in Davey James's house, working for you...so let's have none of this bullshit, Col. You owe me big...I'm not going to tell anyone, you know you can trust me, now cough it out!'

Harcombe snorted into the phone with a mixture of admiration and derision. 'That was *quite* a little speech.' He went quiet, but didn't hang up, so he had to be considering what to actually tell him.

'If you can't tell me what you know, tell me why you can't tell me,' said Nick. That seemed to help.

'Two words. National security.'

'What?'

'You heard me. This is to do with national security. Way above my head. I'm just a humble DI, this goes right to the top.'

'MI-5? Is that what you mean?'

'That and beyond...to the upper reaches...beyond government, even. This is about international terrorism.'

Nick stared in front of him.

'Bloody hell. So how do you even know *anything* about it, then, if it's so top secret, I mean?'

'Because it affects plod on the ground. That being said, even we only know what we need to know. How much of the picture that is...well...that's something we just don't know. We're all on full alert for an incident. We've been told to prepare for...for the worst.'

'The worst? What the hell is the worst?' said Nick, scared by the tone Harcombe had taken.

'It doesn't bear thinking about.' He actually sounded scared himself. Jesus.

Nick searched his mind for what the worst thing could be. 'What? A nuclear bomb? Is that what we're talking about?' Harcombe didn't respond for five seconds.

'No. Biological weapons. A dirty bomb.'

It made Nick feel cold as ice. 'Is that what this BioResearch International place is doing? Is that what Jim George was involved in? Is that why Shadow Man was seen there?'

'Who?'

'The Shadow Man...that's what Kev Wells said his job was...the man who attacked me and Julie.'

'The man who what?' said Harcombe, with some degree of disbelief.

Nick explained briefly. 'And while I'm talking about that weekend, we also saw some soldiers up by Cow Green Reservoir doing some sort of exercise with guns.' He described what they'd seen.

Harcombe let out a deep throaty groan. 'Bloody hell. I wish you'd told me this earlier. Oh, my god.'

'It didn't seem that significant at the time. You do see the army around the northern countryside from time to time. Was it them who shot at us?'

Harcombe went quiet again.

'I'll take that as yes, then, since you'd have quickly said no, if it wasn't.'

'Again, I don't actually know, do I? I wasn't there. I deal in facts, Nick, not speculation. That's what my job is. I can tell you that group is almost certainly a terrorist cell of sorts. Damn it, why didn't you tell me this earlier?'

'I didn't know it was important, did I? Shadow Man warned me not to tell you anything. All of this involves Brian too, doesn't it?'

'Brian Salmon is involved, yes.'

Nick tugged at his stubble. It all had to mean only one thing.

'He's a spy, isn't he?'

Harcombe made a vocal flinch at the word *spy*. 'I've recently learned that he certainly has security clearance to a high level and has done for over 30 years, to my knowledge.'

Nick whistled under his breath. 'Does Big Fish know that?'

'Of course not.' He said it as though it was a ludicrous idea.

'So Brian has been taken from his house for his own protection by Shadow Man?'

'Indeed. Now, this has to stop, Nick. You've got to stay out of all of this. I can't protect you and there are some very dangerous people around.'

'Hold on...is this anything to do with the theft of the Sir Walter Francis Cup?'

'The what?'

'It's a racing cup that Brian asked me and Jeff to find. He said it was stolen by the Regency Stables. Was that part of his security work?'

Colin Harcombe went quiet. 'I don't know anything about that at all. I suggest you do nothing and stay well away from Blakeston or Regency Stables. In fact, if I was you, I'd take a holiday from Teesside until this blows over.'

'One last thing. Jim George had his neck broken by the Shadow Man, almost certainly. Why? What did he know?'

'Since I last spoke to you about him, things have become a lot more clear about Jim. The fact is, he was accidentally at the centre of all of this. That much I can say. He's muddied the waters considerably and, between you and me, he should never have been killed, though I now understand why it happened. Now, before I go, one last thing. Nick, those people you saw on the moors...they...they are almost certainly a crack team of Ukrainian terrorists. If you see them again, let me know immediately.'

'Well, there were a few Ukrainians working at the hotel in Middleton and some also worked for Steve Salmon at his party.

'Look, I don't have time to go into this. If you see Cameron Baxter-Smythe outside of the usual contexts, tell me that, too. Stay safe, Nick.'

He called Jeff right away.

'Yo, crazy momma! Hold on, I've got Argie puke on me...right...dear me, I think he's been out on the piss in the night...'

'Why do babies throw up so much?'

'Overfeeding, and as a sensible response to life.'

Nick told him about his call to Harcombe. '...and Brian *is* a spy...'

'Wow - that is a mind blow. Mind, they do always recruit these establishment figures, don't they? I wonder what he actually does? Must be why he's been away so long.'

'But Big Fish isn't in on it.'

'For obvious reasons.'

'Being an untrustworthy gobshite, primary amongst them. He did say Jim George was only accidentally at the centre of everything.'

'You know what, in sorting all of this out, we've assumed he was some important but weird character. But I reckon he really was just a weirdo who trod on someone's toes.'

'This dirty bomb, though - Colin was scared. I could tell. And I don't like hearing him scared. I want him to be in control and he's obviously bricking it.'

'It's bloody terrifying. But it might all just be gossip and internet chatter. There must be terrorist threats and plots all the time, we just never hear about them.'

'Yeah, I guess so. I tell you what. I'm going to go into the Boro and see if that shiny woman, Jim's girlfriend, is working in Binns.'

'Good idea. After you've done that, come into the shop. Mam's got Argie today, I'll just take him around to hers and then I'll be in. Tommo will be in for his usual coffee and cake at 10, we can see if he can help us any more about Jim.'

Nick ate some eggs and ham then drove into Middlesbrough, parking up on a meter just off Linthorpe Road. Places like Binns used to be so big and posh when he was young. They were big department stores where it seemed you could buy almost anything, and they were also quite individual, with their own character. Not any more. Binns had long been part of House of Fraser and as such, was like every other House of Fraser store. Then again, he was hardly their target customer, so it was probably wrong for him to even make a judgement. Still, it all seemed so not grand, when once it had seemed very elevated.

The make-up counters were at the front of the shop, as they always are, the women at each counter like heavily made-up guards, on duty to protect the rest of the store from under-made-up customers. The women who worked on these counters often seemed to be wearing all of their stock all at once. The first one he saw looked like an exotic parrot, with sculpted dark black eyebrows that appeared painted on with a marker pen, thick eye shadow trowelled on and glossy lipstick. It was hard to know if they looked exactly how they wanted to look or if somehow, prolonged exposure to heavy-duty make-up increased your tolerance to it, the way drinking booze every day means you have to consume more to get drunk, so that when they looked in the mirror, they didn't see they were wearing a thick mask, but thought it was quite understated.

Nick patrolled the counters. He always felt out of his depth in these situations. The women were very intimidating - the female equivalent of the macho alpha male - almost aggressively female and keen to thrust it down your throat with piles of coiffured hair, acres of tanned cleavage, red lips, big hips, and tight dresses.

But despite the proliferation of make-up masks, it was obvious which woman was Jim George's girlfriend. She stood in one corner with a French perfume display, a squirter in hand ready to hose down any interested woman with the odoriferous napalm.

'Hi, there,' he said, 'I'm Nick Guymer.'

She smiled. Her skin even under a lot of make-up was really, really odd. Around her eyes looked swollen and around her lips the skin was tight, in the way that lips look tight after you've been hit in the face. It had to be Botox, same as Jim George. Underneath the strange, slightly plastic appearance, she was a good-looking woman with soft brown eyes, a better-looking woman than you might imagine Jim would have attracted, but she'd ended up looking like someone who had suffered some third-degree burns.

'Hello, there, can I interest you in our special 2 for 1 offer?'

'No, thanks.' He cut to the chase. 'I knew Jim George. I was so sorry to hear of this death and I understand you and he were close. I saw you at Big Fish's party.'

'Oh, hello. He was very nice about Jim, wasn't he? He said about you and his brother being there, actually. I'm still dead upset, to be honest. I just came into work to take my mind off things.'

There was no easy way to say what he wanted to say.

'Look...I don't know your name...sorry.'

'Yvonne Wright.'

'Look, Yvonne, I'm afraid to have to tell you this, but Jim may have been killed.' He kept his voice down. A distressed, confused look spread over her face.

'What? I don't understand. I thought it was a car crash.'

'It's complicated. I'm trying to get to the bottom of it for the police...' well, it was only a small lie. 'Why did he go to BioResearch in Hartlepool? Do you know?'

She looked around her. 'Who told you about that?'

'The police. They think he was behaving suspiciously.'

She was obviously puzzled but didn't seem to want to hide anything. 'That's where he got the stuff from...the botulism bacteria stuff.' She spoke in a whisper now, then gestured for him to follow her outside. 'I'm just going to the loo, Tammy,' she called out, presumably to her supervisor.

They went out a side door.

'He had this scheme to make a lot of money,' she said, lighting a cigarette after offering him one.

'Using botulism to make Botox?'

She shook her head. 'No; well, sort of. He's been feeding the bees with it all winter, mixed in with glucose. That's what bees feed off. Y'see.'

Nick could hardly believe what he was hearing.

'He's making Botox honey? Is that what you're telling me?'

She nodded. 'Yeah. It's brilliant. It works. We've been testing it out.'

Whether it worked aesthetically was open to question, but that wasn't his call to make.

'So the hives, Graceland, they're full of what are effectively Botoxed bees?'

'Sort of, yeah.'

Maybe that's why they were so aggressive.

'All you have to do is smear the honey on instead of having to get injections. It's all under your own control. Much better and totally natural. He'd just perfected it, really. He was going to launch it later this year. I think it'd have made a fortune.'

'But why bees? Why honey?'

'Honey has botulism in it naturally, and it can't ever go off - it's brilliant stuff, is honey. And, like I say, it's natural. Is that why he was killed? Has a business rival done that to the poor lad? I didn't know him that long but he was a funny man and I liked him a lot.'

'Have the police interviewed you about him?'

She shook her head again.

'Well, I'm sure it'll all come out eventually, Yvonne. Just one other thing. Do you know if he could hypnotise people?'

She nodded right away. 'Oh, yeah. He did it in one of his old stage acts, he said. He hypnotised me to stop eating chocolate.'

'Really? Did it work?'

'Yeah, I don't fancy it any more and I was a right pig for it before.'

Nick looked up the street. 'Look, I have to go. Give me your number and I'll call you when I have more information.'

She wrote down her mobile number, and he squeezed her hand and thanked her for her help.

CHAPTER 13

As he parked the car back in Green Dragon Yard, the air felt warm and he took the short walk up to the shop in just his black t-shirt and jeans. It was always easy to mistrust the weather in the northeast. You got caught out by it so often. Just when you thought it was warm, it would start hailing or a bitter wind would get up. Other times you went out in a coat and ended up carrying it everywhere because it was so warm. If you got the amount of clothes right, it was all by pure chance.

'Hello, gorgeous,' said Emily, as he walked into the shop. There was a smell of bacon cooking from the cafe. 'Oh, you look nice in that tight t-shirt. Showing your tan and your muscles off, are you? Sssssexxxy!' She wiggled a shape with her hips and giggled her slightly annoying childish giggle.

'Hello, pixie features. Isn't it a lovely morning?'

'It is indeed. Jeff said you had a bit of an adventure last night when he came by to pick up Argie.'

'You can say that again.'

He squeezed behind her and went through into the stock room to use the toilet, a feat he managed without any effort, even though he could hear Emily moving boxes around. That would normally have totally put him off, but not any more. God bless hypnotism.

'Nice wee?' she said, turning to him as he came out after washing his hands.

'Very satisfying.'

'Do you want to see my new tattoo?'

'Go on then. Where is it?'

She lifted up her Racer X t-shirt and pointed to her small, bare left breast on which was a heart entwined with barbed wire.

'That must have been painful, Em. On the old mammary, like.'

She giggled again. 'It's still a bit sore. Do you want to rub it better?' She took his hand and put it on her breast.

He laughed. She often did this sort of thing during the few times they were alone together. He always enjoyed it. 'I don't know, Em, you'd get a shock if I actually took you up on one of your flirtations and removed your doubtless very tiny pants.'

'Oooh, promises, promises. The fact you never would is what's nice about it, though.' She pushed at him in the belly, pulling at his jeans waistband, making as though to unbutton them, laughing all the while.

He lightly tweaked her nipple between his thumb and forefinger, pulled her t-shirt down, kissed the top of her head and gave her backside a quick rub and a pat. 'Come on then, that's enough sexy for now.'

She gave him a little hug and grinned up at him. 'Well, if we can't give each other a little feel from time to time then we'd all be the poorer, wouldn't we?'

'Yeah, 'course we would. Come on, I'll give you a hand with this box.'

Her flirting with him was something he doubted he'd ever stop enjoying and was somehow made all the more enjoyable by the fact that it would never lead to anything. In fact, if it had, it would have ruined the whole thing. It was a classic example of restraint providing more long-term pleasure than indulgence - as important a life lesson to learn as any.

Jeff walked in with Tommo.

'Look who I met, all got up in his best clobber,' said Jeff, pointing to the normally dishevelled Tommo, who today was wearing a pair of blue trousers that were actually clean and another brightly patterned shirt.

"Tommo - you look ace in that shirt I got you,' said Emily, skipping around and patting him on the back. Tommo was very pleased with this attention.

'Just thought I'd make an effort as it's a nice day, like. It's a bit Hawaiian, this one, eh?'

'Matty will get your coffee,' she said, linking his arm and taking him through to the cafe area. 'And we've got pineapple upside down cake. That'll go with your tropical shirt.'

Jeff grinned at Nick. 'She's a saint, that lass,' he said, quietly in his ear.

'A saint who now has a tattooed left breast. She just showed me.'

Jeff rolled his eyes. 'You jammy get. I don't know how you do it, it's like being back at college again. I pull them in, you get the physicals. It must be your animal magnetism. Mind you do look ripped and hunky in your fitted t-shirt, darlin'. He picked at the t-shirt contemptuously. 'You're a bloody fashion model, you...what happened to the scruffy tramp?'

'Jules likes me in it.'

'Aye, I bet she does. Owee, let's grill Mr Thompson.'

Nick sat down opposite the old fella and sipped at some coffee.

'Now then, Tommo, you know we asked you about Jim George the other day and you said he was born in Russia.'

'Aye, in Kiev, what about it?'

'Do you know anything else about him? What did he do before he did the Elvis act?'

'He used to do impressions, didn't he? I told you before, didn't I? I saw him at the Mallable Club on Norton Road a few years ago. I think the Elvis gig came out of that. His impressions weren't very good. Then I never saw him for a while. Next time I saw him he was doing a comedy turn - always fancied himself as a bit of comedian. He'd added in that bit I told you about where he was supposed to hypnotise people but he pretended he was rubbish at it.'

'Did he ever hypnotise you, by any chance?' asked Nick.

'As a matter of fact, he did. I wanted to give up the ciggies, but I couldn't manage it - so he said he'd get me to stop by hypnotising me. I don't know what he did, but it worked. I've never wanted a fag again. So like I say, he could do it.'

'I actually just met his girlfriend. She was hypnotised by him as well - to stop eating chocolate.'

'Well, I never. Aye, he could deffo do it. No problem. He just didn't have the patter to make it into an act.' Tommo finished his cake.

Nick looked up at Jeff and made a gesture with his head to meet him outside. Standing out in the bright sunshine, Jeff followed him out of the shop and slapped Nick on the back.

'It's exactly as you said yesterday. Elvis had gone up there with Big Fish and one way or another he put his spell on him and Brian.'

'I know. I must be brilliant, eh?'

'I wouldn't go that far. It was my idea, remember, albeit one I made up for a laugh. But I'll tell you what I'm going to do. Just to make sure.' He took out his phone and called his brother. 'BF? It's just me. It's about Jim George again. This might sound weird but did he ever hypnotise you and Brian?' As he listened to what was being said, he raised an eyebrow at Nick and then made a satisfied nod and put a thumb up. 'Yeah, I see. OK, well, he did something...I'll explain when I see you next. No, it's nowt to worry about.' He rang off.

'So he did hypnotise them?' said Nick.

'BF says he didn't, but he did show them how it was done. Did a demonstration. He says it didn't work, that they just sat there, eyes closed and it was all bollocks.'

'That is sort of what happens. You don't know how long you've been under. He's done them alright, the crafty sod and it's exactly like you said, he's stolen the cup and replaced it with a fake one, which in turn was stolen, probably by Macca, the dead jockey. I mean, when he was fighting Mickey, Mickey was saying, "I know you're a thieving twat".'

Jeff twizzled a strand of his beard. 'Hmm, so it looked like one crime when it was really two. And it's actually nothing to do with Regency Stables or Chekov or Cameron Baxter-Smythe?'

Nick shook his head. 'No. It's not. Macca was working alone and stole it as revenge because he thinks Blakeston cheated, and didn't know he'd stolen a fake trophy. In fact, it was probably a private battle between him and Mickey. They're rivals. When I was hiding in that cupboard, I heard Mickey say, "Macca is furious because I've won more races than him". Hey, you know what - maybe he then found out it was a fake, and came back to get the real one when we were on the phone to Brian. He broke in through the window, just as he had before, only he went in the living room by mistake...'

'...and Shadow is there as protection for Brian, chases Macca through the house, hence the debris around, does his neck snappy on him because he assumes he's after Brian or after something in the house.'

Nick was excited now. 'I need a drink. Owee in the Royal Oak for a swifty.'

They went next door and ordered a double vodka each and took a table in the corner.

'There's a lot more to this. Now, Tommo said Jim was born in Kiev, didn't he?' said Nick, taking a sip.

'Yeah, he did.'

'OK, Kiev *was* under Russian control back in the days of the old USSR.'

'I miss the USSR. I always liked it as an acronym,' said Jeff, a finger raised.

'CCCP is better. Triple letters rule. But, no matter, Kiev is actually in the Ukraine and has long had a history of being independent. When the USSR fell apart, they were quick to become independent again but now Mother Russia wants Ukraine back, don't they? There's all sorts kicking off over there.'

'Oh yeah, I've heard about that. Tanks on the border and everything.' Jeff looked on his phone for news about Ukraine. 'Yeah, basically, Ukraine wants to remain as its own state, but Putin or whoever it is in charge, wants it back. You've got two sets of nationalists going head to head. Now if that isn't a recipe for a big boom of some sort, I don't know what is. That's why Colin was shitting it about the Ukrainians you saw on the moors. They're the dirty bombers. Bloody hell.'

Jeff's was thinking quickly now. He tapped on the table. 'OK, Shadow Man is a hit man for the British government, just as Kev always said but obviously they only know some of the pieces of the jigsaw. They don't know exactly who is involved or maybe who is organising it all. There's some rogue element and that's what has put the wind up Colin and everyone else. If they knew who they were looking for, they'd probably have nipped this in the bud already.'

Nick pulled at his stubble, deep in thought. His phone buzzed. 'Yeah?'

'Nick Guymer?'

'Yeah.'

'Nick. Cameron Baxter-Smythe. I thought we had an appointment, old boy.'

Shit. He'd meant to cancel. He couldn't risk going over there. This called for a good lie.

'Oh, I'm so sorry. I'm afraid I've been tied up in A & E all morning. My friend had an accident. I should've called, Cameron. Sorry.'

'Ah, nothing serious, I hope.'

'No. It's fine.'

'Shall we reschedule?'

'Yes. I'll check the diary and get back to you.'

As Nick spoke there was a clicking on the line and some noise - the sort of noise you hear when there is someone talking in the ear of the person on the other end of the phone. Removed but indecipherable voices.

'Cameron, can I ask you something?'

'Certainly, old boy.'

'A man err...stopped me and my partner and said I should stay away from you and the Regency Stables...just the morning after I'd seen you in the hotel...do you have any idea at all why?'

There was more background noise. CBS cleared his throat.

'How odd. I have no idea. What did he look like?'

There was a lot more distant chatter then the line went dead.

Nick looked at the phone and banged it on the palm of his hand - his preferred high-tech solution to anything that went wrong with anything. Then he tried CBS's number again but got a phone company message saying no such number existed. A shiver went down his spine.

'Jeff...listen to what just happened.' He explained about the noises on the line.

'What was it like?'

'Distant chatter - nothing you could make out.'

Jeff pulled on his beard, his eyes flicking to and fro as he worked out what it all meant. 'They're tapping his phone. Security services. They cut the line before you could tell them who had stopped you. That can mean only one thing, CBS is a suspect. They're listening in on him.'

'Shit, you mean he's funding terrorism? The car that was at his house was watching the terrorists on the moor. Oh, my god.'

'Come on, sup up, I need to use the big computer.'

They went back to the shop and Jeff sat behind his big screen. 'Right, let's find out who all these people are.' He typed 'Yuri Chekov' into Google. 'Yeah, Chekov is a Muscovite, as Russki as you come, that. Let's have a look now. Made his money in the sell-off of oil companies under Yeltsin. Yup, we knew that, didn't we?'

'Same as Roman Abramovitch.'

'Aye. Interesting stuff here. His company is called Moscow Industrial and they've got a controlling share in an oil refining business that have sites out by Wilton and up the coast as well. He's also bought land in the northeast as well at the Regency Stables. So he's invested a lot in the area.'

'I bet he fancies himself as a country gent.'

'Maybe. He sounds quite cool, actually.' He read out from a newspaper article from earlier in the year. "Yuri Chekov has a globally renowned collection of Russian Art Nouveau paintings and will be loaning some of it to Middlesbrough Institute of Modern Art in May for a special exhibition". I heard about that actually, there was something on the local news the other night. I think it's just opened. I didn't twig it was anything to do with him.'

'Makes me think he'd bloody love that Fabergé cup, wouldn't he? Primo Art Nouveau artefact, that. You know what? I bet Elvis sold it to him and got enough money to buy his new house in Thornaby.' Nick tapped Jeff on the arm. 'That's a good idea, that. He wasn't working but he had enough money to buy a house. He was up at the Stables, he hypnotised Brian and the Fish, nicked the cup and went up to Regency to see Chekov, who was only too happy to have a rare Russian artefact and paid him a stupid amount of money for it.'

Jeff muttered something. 'Hmm, money is like piss to these blokes. Yeah, maybe, hold on, I'm just going to look up BioResearch. Shadow wouldn't have gone there for no reason. It's not like they've got a cafe or gift shop selling tea towels or something, is it? So let's have a look at them.'

He typed some more and sat looking at the screen, then yelled out, 'Shit!'

'What? What's up?'

'BioResearch in Hartlepool...'

'What about it?'

'It's actually owned by UGC - *Ukraine* Global Chemicals and its head office is in, surprise, surprise, Kiev. It's the UK arm of a Ukrainian company!'

Nick walked around the counter and looked at the computer. 'You're jokin' me...the Ukraine again?'

'Aye, I've translated it.' Jeff clicked on company details. A list of executives, each name with a small picture beside it, showed eight men, the last of which was very familiar indeed. Nick exclaimed, and turned his back and briefly put his head in his hands. 'Whoa! I don't believe it!'

Tommo looked over at him from the cafe. 'Have you found out who killed Jim, Nick?' he said.

'Maybe we have, Tommo. Maybe.'

He turned back to the screen. Jeff was pointing at it with a Biro. 'The British CEO of UGC is none other than Cameron Baxter-Smythe, Lord sodding Thirsk. Head like a beef tomato. His great grandfather was Sir Walter Francis who the trophy that Jim George stole was named after...' he did some more typing into Google '...and I'll wager my best pair of underpants that Walter Francis was something to do with...ah ha...yes, get in! I *knew* it. Walter Francis was Minister for Overseas Trade in the Whig government of 1837, he married Olga Rurikovich in Kiev. She was from a high-ranking family, practically royalty by the look of it. That's where this all dates back to. One side of his family are all Ukrainians.'

Emily came across. 'What are you boys so excited about?'

'It's complex, Em,' said Jeff. 'My brain is about to burst.'

Nick leaned against the counter. 'No, this is easy, man. It's all falling into place. Listen, there are two or three things going on here.' He held up one finger at a time. 'First, Elvis, Jim George, he was Ukrainian but that was irrelevant here - just a coincidence. He bought botulism from UGC to use in his honey. He needed money to do that so a few months ago, he hypnotised Brian and Big Fish, stole the Fabergé trophy, sold it to Yuri Checkov - like I said, that's why he could move to the new house in Thornaby when he's not got a job. The rest of it, the fake cup he replaced it with, Macca's theft and subsequent killing when he returned to the house to steal the real trophy, we know about.'

Emily squealed. 'Brilliant.'

Nick held up another finger and looked from her to Jeff. 'Secondly, right, Regency was sold to Chekov by CBS. Chekov is a rich Russian dude. Ukrainians of CBS's heritage don't like Russians. They're their oppressors, aren't they? So CBS must have had to sell the stables to him for some very good or desperate reason. So he'll want his own back for that. He'll want revenge.'

'Because they're enemies?' said Emily.

'Yeah, I reckon so. Family and history is everything to these aristocratic nobs. Chekov is new Russian money, CBS is old Ukrainian royalty. That's how he'll see it. Now, third, the car that is at his house was watching the men who Colin thinks are Ukrainian terrorists. He has the money to fund something like that and he is CEO of a company that does research into bacteria and disease - which would be very bloody useful if you wanted to commit some hellish biological terrorist act.'

It was all forming into a picture now.

'I wonder who brokered the sale of Regency?' said Jeff. 'If we knew that, we might find out how the whole thing was handled and why.'

Nick took out his phone. 'I might be able to help on that.' He found his lawyer, Leslie West's, number.

'Hi, there, can I speak to Leslie, please. It's Nick Guymer.'

Leslie West's voice came booming down the line like an aural version of an oak barrel.

'Nick! How are you, sir?'

'I'm very well, thank you, Leslie. And how are you?'

'As good as I can expect to be, aged 72 and a half. To what do I owe this call? Nothing untoward, I hope. Is Julie well?'

'She's in fine form, thanks. Well, it's a bit of a journalistic call, actually. You know the Regency Stables in Middleton?'

'Indeed, I do.' He wheezed like a pair of malfunctioning bellows into the phone receiver. He was almost permanently out of breath. How his body kept going was surely a miracle medical science would never explain.

'I understand they were sold to a Russian last year...is that right?'

'Yes, yes...a great surprise to us all. The Baxter-Smythes had owned that place since Victorian times.'

'So how come he sold it? Any idea?'

Leslie did his imitation of a harmonica, his breath noisily leaking out of him and then being sucked back in again, almost in desperation. 'Can I ask why you'd like to know, Nick? Is it for an article?'

Nick thought about it for a moment. He'd fully intended to lie to Leslie West and say that's exactly what it was, but with the big man on the end of the phone, a man who had helped him so much over his dad's estate and who had been the first person to visit him in jail a year ago, it wasn't right to be anything other than honest. Instead, he explained the situation as best he could, about what had happened to he and Julie and what they'd since discovered.

As ever, the old country lawyer took it all in with a calm, firm assurance, breathing low and slow as Nick spent a few minutes on the synopsis.

'This is quite a tale, Nick. And I wish you'd come to me with this information earlier.'

'You're the second man to tell me that today. Why's that, Leslie?'

'Because there have been rumours about Cameron Baxter-Smythe within certain, shall we say, elevated circles for some time, maybe for as long as 20 years.'

'Rumours about what?'

'His involvement in funding the Malina - an especially vicious Mafia based around Odessa. All of his family on his mother's side are from that region, you know.'

'Bloody hell. He funds a Ukraninian Mafia? Yeah, that makes sense. I think I've seen some of them.'

Jeff and Emily stared at him with open mouths.

'I've been told that by two men in authority who have a good reason to know. Of course, he owns the job agency in Darlington and it has been pointed out that an awful lot of East European are on its books. Nothing illegal ever proven, of course, but there are those that say that it is a front for importing illegal labour into the country. Cameron is a powerful and rich man, it would be wise to deal with him, if indeed you are going to deal with him, with a lot of caution.'

'Job Agency?' said Nick. 'Is it called The Jobs Worth, by any chance?'

'You've heard of it?' said Leslie.

'Yeah. Yeah, I have. Why did he sell the stables to Yuri Chekov, though?'

Leslie cleared his throat of what sounded like a half a pint of catarrh.

'A connection of mine at the North Yorkshire Chamber of Commerce suggested to me in confidence but with some degree of inside knowledge that it was as part of a settlement in a dispute between the Malina and a Russian Mafia group.'

'Really? My god. Colin Harcombe would love to know all of this.'

'...ah, Colin...if you see him, send him my good wishes...'

'...he said there was an international incident being played out on Teesside.'

'Really? And you accidentally walked into it. It goes without saying that these Malina people are absolute swine. Ruthless people who will stop at nothing. I would suggest your Shadow Man was so harsh with you in order to impress upon you the need to stay away from anything to do with it.'

As ever, Leslie's firm mind and straight thinking told a simple, powerful truth. 'Yeah. I think you're right.'

'Well, well, who'd have thought we'd have this on our doorstep? I do hope it all comes to nothing. We don't want that sort in our midsts,' he said with typical restraint and understatement.

'Thanks for your help, Leslie. It's helped make everything much clearer. Hopefully, it'll all blow over soon.'

'Indeed. Give my regards to Julie.'

Nick put the phone down. 'I love Leslie West. If the world was run by men like him, we'd not go far wrong.' He outlined to Jeff and Emily what he'd said.

'So that explains why you saw so many Ukrainians up at Middleham, including our two doormen from the Ballroom,' said Jeff. 'He's bringing them all over through the job agency. What if they're all Mafia, though? I mean, the way we've seen some of them work - like the bouncers at the Ballroom. They looked pretty ruthless. And you saw them training on the moors. What the hell are they doing that for?'

'Sounds like a private army, to me,' said Emily.

'It does to me as well. You'd better call Colin and tell him all of this in case some of it isn't known to him. Then you should call Kev and tell him to keep out of the way. We don't want them beating up Shadow Man while he's hunting down proper terrorists.'

'Are Julie's brothers really that bad?' said Emily.

Jeff made a throat cutting gesture at her. 'Ricky and Kev are fucked up beyond belief. They're not normal...trust me, Em...even they think it's their destiny to die in a hail of bullets whilst running out of a building towards certain death. They'd rather go out like Butch and Sundance than sit at home and watch TV in their dotage.'

'Excuse me, but that's mad,' she said.

'Don't try and apply logic or humanity to those two,' said Nick. 'It isn't appropriate.'

He found Kev's number on his phone. It rang twice.

'Now then, Nick.'

'Kev. Me and Jeff were at the house last night and we saw what you did to the Range Rover...'

'...eh? You were...'

'...shuttup and listen to me. There's some serious shit going down between MI-5 and the Russian and Ukrainian Mafia, right? They're terrorists. They've got a dirty bomb somewhere on Teesside. We don't know for sure but there's a good chance some one from MI-5 saw you last night...'

'...you're tripping off your tits...that's bullshit...no-one followed us, we made sure we left enough time after spotting him...'

'Kev man, this isn't dumb plod you're dealing with. This is the forces of the state. That house is almost certainly under permanent watch. There had been a fight there before you arrived and a man was upstairs dead with his neck snapped. This is way out of your league. The fact you couldn't see them makes no odds. You're not meant to see them.'

That seemed to speak some truth to Kev.

'Shit. So are they coming for us, like?'

'I don't know. They might have sussed who you are by now, but these lot aren't local, they don't know you like Harcombe's mob do. Where are you?'

'I'm in Saltburn with Ricky having a drink up.'

'Has Jules been in touch with you today?'

'No. Why, like?'

'No reason. Well, stay out there or just disappear for a week. Go off the map. Right? I'll ring you when it looks like things have settled down. There's talk of a terrorist act on Teesside and Shadow Man is part of the team fighting it. You can't take it out on him. He's got bigger fish to fry.'

'OK, Nick. Ta. We'll lie doggo somewhere.'

Nick rang off, shaking his head.

'Do you think he'll do what you said?' asked Jeff.

'Your guess is as good as mine. They're hardly famous for making good decisions, so I'll put my money on the answer being no.'

'They'd have been pulled in by now if they were going to be,' said Jeff.

Nick called Colin's phone and left a three-minute message to cover everything Jeff had found out. Then he called Julie and brought her up to date as best as he could.

'Bloody hell. This is terrible. What do they hope to achieve with a dirty bomb?'

'I'm not sure it yields to logic, Jules. It's a sort of power struggle. It might be a battle between Chekov and CBS, I think. Listen, have you spoken to your mam yet?'

'I was just about to go 'round there.'

'Well, don't call the lads. Tell your mam first. Don't even mention it to them. We want them away from the area.'

'That's what I was going to do, anyway. I thought it'd be best, if she'll agree to meet him, to meet up on neutral territory.'

'Yeah, good idea. Treat it like it's a cup semi-final.'

'Aye, that way it's likely to reduce the chance of trouble.'

'Where have you got in mind?'

'I thought the cafe in MIMA.'

'In the Boro? You're not showing your mam the Art Nouveau collection, are you?'

'She wouldn't know Art Nouveau from Ant and Dec. It's just that it's quiet in there and as it's a civic building, she'll keep her voice down and not start swearing...or at least that's what I'm hoping. I may be hopelessly wrong. I'll text you if I get it set up. I still can't help feeling it's a big "if", though.'

As she spoke, a horrible thought flashed into Nick's brain. A thought he didn't want to actually think. He was probably wrong, but a major exhibition of Russian art – that would be a great symbolic and literal target for an attack by the Ukrainians. 'Do you need me there?'

'Yeah. I'd like you to come. Bring Jeff, too, if you like. It'll reduce the chances of a big showdown and a fight. We might need Jeff's big presence to separate the warring factions, especially if mam tells Ricky and Kev without my knowledge, which she might.'

'OK. I'll put the armour on. Good luck. Stay strong.'

'I'm going to need it, I reckon, luv.'

Nick put his worries to the back of his mind. He had to stop thinking negatively about things. Stop looking for the bad in situations. It was crazy. He turned to Jeff. 'Do you fancy a trip to the Boro to act as peacemaker?'

'Does it involve wielding a gun and wearing a cowboy hat?'

'It could do. Have you got a gun and a cowboy hat?'

'Ah. No. This is where my plan falls apart. OK, I'll ride shotgun for you, sans actual gun and actual riding. Where are we going and why?'

Nick explained the situation.

'If she arranges the meeting, we'll head straight over there. I'll hear from Jules in a bit.'

'I reckon her dad is quite a cool bloke, from what I could tell last night, anyway. Seemed to have had an interesting life Down Under. I know what he did was wrong back in '77...but it might well have been for the best in the long run.'

Emily nodded. 'She should forgive him. There's no point in not forgiving him. Holding onto all that angst and pain won't help.'

Nick shook his head. 'Maybe, but what he did was a really bad thing. Not so much the leaving, but the not getting in touch - that was the really terrible aspect to it. Any way you cut that, it's cowardly and cold. Even if he was mentally ill, there have been a lot of years for him to write a letter or pick up the phone.'

, 'Yeah. But I still understand why that'd happen,' said Jeff.

'Oh, aye, I do, too...but that doesn't make it right or excusable,' said Nick. 'You can't just throw that to one side like it's nothing.'

'He's not looking for excuses though, is he? Not from what I heard in the Royal Oak. He wants to make it right. He's not trying to look for sympathy or anything. I thought that was decent.'

'I wonder if he will move back here?' said Emily.

'He didn't seem insane enough to do that. Why leave sunny Oz for smelly Teesside? It might seem like a nice idea in your head but once he's spent a few days here, the reality will probably put him off,' said Jeff.

'Jules seemed to have got on with him, right away. So if he does stay, I think it might be good for her, psychologically, like. It fills in a big hole she's had in her life. She's always been the high achiever, the sensible one...relatively, anyway...but her dad seems to have done well over there and he isn't a knuckle-dragger.'

'Aye, she obvious got all of her brains and good looks from him, didn't she?' said Jeff.

'Totally, yeah, and she got her fight and grit from Jackie. Thing is, I think, if things work out, having her dad in her life might help her get over the miscarriage, properly. It could be another emotional prop for her...'

'...she seems fine to me,' said Jeff.

'She's OK on one level. Her dad would be an outsider but also a sort of insider and she's not got anyone like that. I'm caught up in it with her, Jackie just isn't empathetic enough and the rest of them are too wrapped up in themselves to care about how she feels.'

'What about her mates? Surely they're supportive. Some women are good at that sort of stuff, unlike most men, who would rather pretend they have no emotions, at least until they're almost comatose from drinking,' said Emily, collecting dirty cups.

'Yeah, she does talk to a couple of close friends, obviously, but even so, it doesn't seem to have helped massively, mostly because what she's been through is something you need to sort out in your own head. The fact is, you've only got one dad. It's not like he's a mate...he's your dad...I dunno, I just think it might be a really positive thing in her life to have him around, even if he doesn't live here.'

Jeff drummed his fingers on the desk. 'I feel proper sorry for Jules. Us blokes have it so easy. The ups and downs her body must have been through in the last year or so, twice being pregnant, it's a tough gig.'

'Yeah, well, it's the last time. We're taking precautions now,' said Nick.

'Pre-bloody-cautions. It sounds so 1950s, that word, doesn't it? One of those terrible euphemisms that somehow sounds worse than the thing you're using it to describe. Belongs to the world of plain brown envelopes under the counter,' said Jeff.

'Like prophylactic,' said Emily, grinning and putting her tongue against the gap in her front teeth. 'Why do we call them johnnys? Any idea?'

'I think it's a hangover from yonks ago when the only people to use them were prostitutes and their clients were called johns,' said Nick.

'Huh. Funny how these things survive. So you're back on the sheath, are you? Or in the sheath, to be more accurate,' said Emily, with a cheeky little grin.

'That's a worse word, if anything,' said Jeff. He rubbed his neck. 'I've paid little thought to this in my life, but Julie's situation has really made me think how that side of things is so quintessentially female. Along with breast feeding, it's something we can never ever really understand as blokes. So when it all stops, it must be weird. Imagine if we stop producing sperm aged 51 or whatever. We'd feel weird about it, wouldn't we?'

Nick went on. 'I was thinking the other day that I've always thought us blokes had it easy, from the first moment I learned about periods. I was so shocked when they told us about it in biology. I remember thinking it was vaguely barbaric...like, surely we must have evolved some more efficient fertility system than this? All the responsibility and physical pressure was on the woman and all we had to worry about was...well...nothing, really. It's piss easy being a bloke compared to being a woman. I've *always* thought that. The only upside seemed to be the fact that you could more easily have more sex - but even that fails you, because if you put it around a lot, you just end up having terrible sex with unsuitable people.'

Emily made a noise in agreement. 'Been reading my diary, have you, Nick?'

'I suppose all we blokes have to do is avoid the random acts of physical violence and the general inclination of the northern male to glass someone after 10 pints, when the Boro have lost,' said Jeff.

'Even that impacts on women more - domestic violence, I mean. Jules has got all the stats on it. Like when Celtic play Rangers, the incidence of domestic violence - of women getting assaulted by men - goes up 70 percent,' said Nick.

'Disgusting,' said Emily, bringing the tea.

'Eh?! Why? Because your team lost?' said Jeff, incredulously. 'I was joking when I said that, by the way. Men hit their wives because their football team has lost? My god.' He shook his head in disbelief.

'Yeah. They're pissed off, often full of drink and go home and beat the crap out of their missus.'

'They all think they're the big man, but only a small, pathetic man would do that,' said Jeff.

'That's not the half of it, man...the stories Julie tells me about domestic abuse. They beggar belief. It's not just one slap dished out during a row - it's all part of a wider pattern of controlling, abusive behaviour by these fucked-up blokes. They've got away with for so long - since the beginning of time, pretty much. It's only now some inroads are being made into it by places like where Julie works.'

Emily sat down and glanced at Tommo, who was now working his way methodically through two large boxes of old 7-inch singles, plucking out records and looking closely at them.

'It is truly shocking,' said Emily. 'If you've not gone through it - like I haven't - it's almost hard to believe.'

'Aye. She's a brave one, is Jules. Can't be easy work,' said Jeff.

'Nope, but it needs doing and even though she's happy to get a paid job, they're chronically underfunded and she's working for not much more than 20 grand a year,' said Nick.

'Jobs like that which take dedication are always shite pay, for one reason or another. It does seem like your good nature gets abused.'

'Yup. That is the way of the world, which is why I'm always going on about fighting the power and being what you call a left wing nutter. Don't you see, Jeff? That's what it's about - I don't care about what political labels anyone gives it, that's all bollocks - it's just about equality and fairness and not exploiting people.'

Jeff stood up and saluted. 'Aye, aye, Comrade Guymer, Sir!!' He sat down again. 'No, I do get that and I do dig it...as long as you don't start wearing dungarees, eating brown rice and goji berries, I'm cool with it.'

'You'd look nice in dungarees, Jeff. Like a 1930s farm hand from a Steinbeck novel,' said Emily with a giggle.

Nick's phone rang.

'Hey, Jules. How goes it?'

'You won't believe this.'

'What? Has your mam fainted?'

'No. She's agreed to meet him!'

'Was she shocked?'

'A bit. But she just said, "Eee, well, I suppose we'd better meet up for a chat then". No shouting or swearing or anything. She was almost reasonable.'

'Reasonable? Is she stoned on something?'

'No more than usual. She was sort of intrigued, I think.'

'Weird. I expected rage or bitterness.'

'I think being with Con has mellowed her out a bit. As much as I am repulsed by the thought, I think the sex has released a lot of pent-up tension in her.'

'That is too gross to even briefly let pass in front of our imaginations, Jules. But you might be right...there's nothing like a good shagging to ease your worried mind.'

'You're not wrong there, sunshine. Anyway, I'm going down to pick her up in the Porsche. I've just texted dad and arranged to meet him in MIMA at 2.30pm. They've given me the afternoon off, so I'm in no rush.'

'Righto, me and Jeff will come down.'

'Right, I'll see you later. I'm quite excited about this.'

They took Nick's BMW to Middlesbrough. As they drove down Newport Road, it coughed and spluttered, cut out and then started again, all within a three-second period.

'I must get Jules to service this properly.'

'How old is this car, now?'

'21 years. It's done at least 450,000 miles...probably more, because I'm sure it was clocked when I bought it.'

'They go on forever, these Beemers.'

'Not quite. I think 21 years might be this old girl's limit. The Porsche is 35 years old and is in better condition.'

'That's because Jules has greased her tubes properly. Funny how cars lend themselves so well to sexual analogy.'

'There's nothing on the car you can't use like that, except the steering wheel.'

'Let me grip your wheel, baby...no, that doesn't work. Steer me round the bend, honey...no, you're right. There's nothing sexual about a steering wheel.'

'Told you. It's this linguistic understanding that I'm hoping to deploy in my first novel.'

'Ah, you're definitely doing it?'

'I've written a plan for it. I'll knock out a couple of chapters and then send it to a couple of publishers, see if anyone fancies it.'

'What's it going to be about?'

'It's going to be a modern romance, set against the Boro's UEFA cup run in 2006.'

Jeff looked at him in mock horror. 'A romance? A romance!'

'Yeah. What's wrong with that?'

Jeff held up a big hand.

'A. It's unmanly. B. It involves knowing about human emotions and by your own admission, you're terrible at understanding that sort of thing.'

'Well...I thought I was...and I am sometimes, but maybe I'm not quite as shite at being human as I think I am in my darker moments.'

Jeff shook his head and made a mooing noise.

'Why are you mooing?'

'Argie likes it. I've got into the habit of doing it. It's inspired by Dot's dad's honking cow horn, remember?'

'Oh, yeah. That was utterly surreal.'

'Is this novel going to really be the story of how you and Julie got back together? Will it be full of your overactive sex life?'

Nick laughed. 'It'll draw on my experience of life but I'm not writing about me and Jules, no. I might put a woman called Wendy with a huge vagina in it, though...'

'...and a mad thrusty woman in stripy knickers? You've got to use her.'

'Oh, yeah, she'll find a place in it, along with a dirty German woman who nearly chokes during oral sex...'

'Eh? Dagmar?! Did she do that?'

'I've already said too much. You don't want to hear it. It's too gross. Writing about sex is boring, though. The mechanics, I mean. Sex is all about what's in your head.'

'Is it? I must have been doing it wrong. I thought it was mostly in the trouser department. Traditionally, like.'

'Well, yeah, there's some physical...'

'...some? A lot of physical, if you ask me...I don't know how you do it, but I do not have sex with my brain. It'd never reach. I'm not a contortionist like you, remember.'

'Don't go on about *that* again.'

'What? About being able to fellate yourself when you were a teenager?

I think the council should give you a medal or something - use you as a good example to the youth of today. If they could get more lads to do that, they'd probably stop a load of teenage pregnancies. No boy would leave his room for long enough to get a lass up the duff if he could...'

'Alright, man. You don't need to go on about it.' He rubbed his forehead, feeling tired and stressed out. 'You know we're getting married in August at the Riverside?'

'Of course, yeah. I'm already looking forward to having sex with a bridesmaid.'

'There'll not be any bridesmaids, I'm afraid, man.'

'Well, the registrar better get ready for a shock then!'

Nick cleared his throat and yawned. 'Afterwards, I thought we'd have a holiday...we could bloody use one, what with everything we've been through.'

'...a honeymoon, it's traditionally called,' said Jeff, drumming on his lap with the palms of his hands as Nick turned off the A66.

'Yeah. Thought we'd go up to the Edinburgh Fringe Festival. We've never been and it's supposed to be really great.'

'Nice idea. Very arty. You can see some comedy performed by lesbians wrapped in cling film, an improvised play about 13th-century hats acted out by naked dwarves and an exhibition of pencils in jars of horse piss. Ideal.'

'Ha ha, yeah, I think so. Who doesn't love a good cling-filmed lesbian?'

They drove into Middlesbrough city centre.

'Where shall we park? It's bloody terrible parking in the Boro,' said Nick. 'Cleveland Centre?'

'Nah. I hate multi-storey car parks. They give me claustrophobia.'

He drove down Albert Road. 'These are all permit parking,' said Jeff, pointing at parking bays. Nick slung the BMW over into one anyway.

'Bollocks. Let's risk it. We'll be driving around all day otherwise.'

Jeff pointed across the road at an old blue Porsche.

'Looks like your missus has had the same idea. That's hers, isn't it?'

'Oh, yeah. Only one 1975 blue Porsche like that on Teesside.'

'You'll both get tickets, man.'

'If we do, I'll get DI Harcombe to have a word.'

'Nice. I love a bit of favoritism.'

Nick hoisted up his jeans and took a look around. It was a lovely, sunny, warm afternoon.

They walked across the square, past the attractive Victorian central

241

library building and right down to the newly built Middlesbrough Institute of Modern Art.

Essentially a glass cube with a brick and glass, wonky rectangle stuck onto it, it was a quality modernist building very much in sympathy with the sort of art it was created to house. People who called themselves 'traditionalists' didn't like it, but then, traditionalists never like anything new, seemingly oblivious to the fact that the traditions they're so fond of were also, once upon a time, new and modern, too. The fact that a post-industrial town like Middlesbrough had a primo modern art facility had to be seen as a brilliant bit of progress and Nick wasn't about to give an inch to any contrary viewpoint.

'Still amazes me that they put this place here,' said Jeff. 'And I'm glad they did.'

'Yeah. It's cool. I bet it seems weird to Robbie Wells.'

'Aye, when he left, the idea of modern art in Middlesbrough wasn't exactly on anyone's cultural agenda. Basically, if it didn't involve football, the massive consumption of Cameron's Strong Arm and smoking Capstan Full Strength, then it was irrelevant.'

The whole of the cafe end of the building was glass from floor to second-storey roof. Even at a distance, they could see Jackie, Julie and Robbie sitting around a table.

As they approached, Nick looked over towards the Town Hall, which sat in Gothic splendour across the pedestrianised square. As he did so, a large black Range Rover pulled in beside it. He stopped. That was weird. Firstly, it was pedestrianised on that side so no car should have even been there. And second, it looked very familiar.

'Jeff...see that car...' Jeff stopped, too, and followed his gaze.

'Yeah. What about it?'

'That was the car with bull bars outside of Regency Towers and on the moors, as well. It must be Cameron Baxter-Smythe. It's his car. He's here. Why is he here?' Something stirred in Nick's sixth sense and, suddenly, he felt a nameless fear. 'He's funding them, according to Leslie. Fucking hell, Jeff...' realisation after realisation flooded into his synapses all at once. 'Shit.'

'What? What's wrong?'

'The Ukrainian Mafia are here to do something and do it now. And CBS is here to watch it go down. This is what they've been training for. He was watching them on the moors. He's brought them in to explode the dirty bomb. He's behind it all. There's going to be an attack,' Nick looked around him, turning 360 degrees. 'I don't like this at all. Something bad is going to happen, Jeff.' He grabbed his old friend's arm, feeling a real terror now.

Jeff shook him off. 'Get out of it. He's probably just come to do some shopping,' said Jeff, walking on, taking a laid-back attitude. 'There's no Ukrainians here. See, there you go again...it's like I was saying the other day, you're always looking for the worst in any situation. You've got to break that habit, man.'

'You reckon? Maybe,' said Nick, taking deep breaths and wanting comfort to soothe his shredded nerves. 'But blokes like him don't come to Middlesbrough to do anything. If it's not made out of tweed or you can't strap it to a horse, his type don't buy it. And who parks there? That's a weird place to leave your car.'

'He's probably just buying some new pink trousers. Relax, man.' Jeff pointed to the cafe. 'The three of them are already in there. Doesn't look like any cups have been thrown yet.'

Nick breathed out and made a low groan in his throat. Maybe his imagination *was* running away with him. 'Yeah, that's a good sign, anyway.'

Jeff pulled open the door to the building and went in. Nick stopped, lingered at the door and looked around again, his whole psychic existence flooded with an overwhelming sense of danger. There are times in life when you know, you just know, something is going to happen. Little things or big things, it doesn't matter. There are moments when we are connected to a knowledge that is not part of our regular linear existence, times when, in microseconds, we leap ahead of where we are, see the future and return with at least some crumbs of knowledge about what that future might look like.

That's when he saw them. Oh, shit.

CHAPTER 14

Coming from the opposite direction was a tall man dressed in an army flak jacket, accompanied by a shorter, stocky man in a black leather jacket, both carrying long, flat cases. Nick knew he'd seen them on the moors and later on Jeff's phone.

He looked back the way he and Jeff had come. Two more men, tall, one in a flak jacket, the other in a green fleece and army pants, also carrying canvas cases, were walking towards the seats that lined up outside of the library, facing the cafe side of MIMA.

Nick look at them as they passed by. The realisation almost hurt.

Oh, god.

It really was the two bouncers from the door at the Ballroom who had dealt with the fight, and two of the Malina who'd been training on the moors. He'd said to Julie he had thought it was them at the time. And now here they were, once again, under the gaze of CBS.

Nick knew he wasn't wrong.

He let the door close behind him and walked past the reception desk, his mouth dry. He followed Jeff and turned right to walk down to the cafe area. Julie, Jackie and Robbie were sitting around a table in the far corner, each with a coffee in front of them.

'Hello again, Robbie, and you too, Jackie,' said Jeff, pulling up a seat. 'How are you? I've not seen you for a while.'

'Well apart from just having had the shock of my life, I'm alright, thanks, big Jeff,' she said, with an expression that passed across her down-turned mouth as at least an imitation of a smile. She seemed in a good mood. Julie grinned up at Nick as he sat down.

'We were just saying how new all of this is,' said Julie, gesturing at the building '...and how different it is to the old Boro.'

'Oh yeah, it is that, like,' said Nick, feeling totally distracted, looking beyond her and out into the square. The four men had now sat down on the line of park benches that faced the museum. They clearly knew each other. One was pointing to his right, another to his left. The men from the ballroom each had a phone to their ear.

Julie turned around and looked out of the glass wall to see what had caught his attention. She knew right away he was concerned about something, able to read his expression and body language in an instant.

'What's up?' she said, her eyebrows knitted into a frown.

'Err...nothing...I just thought I saw someone I knew.' He couldn't calm down at all. Something about all this was wrong. The feeling of imminent danger increased. 'Why don't we go somewhere else?' he suggested nervously.

'Eh? No, we've just got here,' said Jackie. Julie looked at him, concerned.

Nick turned to Jackie, trying to rid the bad thoughts from his brain. After all, what could they be going to do? It didn't bear thinking about. He didn't want to let himself think about it. 'So this must be a bit of a shock then, Jackie. Would you have recognised him?'

'Of course I would, we knew each other for nigh on 15 years before he buggered off.'

'Like I was saying when I came in, the main reason I wanted to come back was to say sorry to you, Jackie. I know that's just a small word and it doesn't make up for all the...well...you know...no point in raking that over...I know what I did was wrong and I needed to say sorry. So...I am sorry.'

Jackie looked at him with a face as wrinkled and saggy as a wet paper bag.

'You'll never know the hurt I felt...never...you left us with four kids and I didn't know if you were alive or dead.' She didn't seem angry, though. She was just stating the facts.

'I know. I wish I could explain it easily but I can't. I jumped ship. I couldn't cope and leaving seemed to be the only way to stay alive.'

Jackie just nodded. 'Aye, well...if you'd turned up any time before the last year I'd have probably ripped your balls off. I carried a lot of bitterness for a long time. But you live and learn, don't you? The things this lad has gone through recently...' she pointed at Nick '...it teaches you that sometimes people do things because they're not right in the head and I'm fed up with being angry at people for what they've done to us...so I've let it all go...Con told me that's what I should do and he's right. He reckons that stuff only hurts you if you choose to let it hurt you...'

'He sounds like a wise man,' said Robbie with a half smile, 'and we always did fight like cat and dog.'

'We didn't used to before you started drinking like a fish.'

Robbie nodded and held his hand up and, tentatively, put it on top of Jackie's and squeezed. 'Sorry, darlin'.'

Julie smiled at her mam and dad. It was a lovely thing to see. Her with her parents. Both of them. And Jackie slipped her small, old, gnarled hand out from under his and intertwined it with Robbie's fingers.

'You were a good man, Robbie Wells. I'd not have married you if you weren't. I won't pretend I didn't hate you for decades but I'll be damned if I go to my grave full of all that. So I forgive you.' She smiled and then added. 'You big sodding twat.'

It was a nice pay-off line that Big Fish would have been proud of. Everyone laughed.

'Thanks, Jax.'

'Eee, no-one has called us that since you left. Jax.' She tutted, almost nostalgically.

For a moment they looked at each other and it was possible to see the young people they had been. Young people who loved each other and who had enjoyed being with each other. It was sad but it was also some flavour of beautiful.

Nick stood up to go and get a coffee. He put his hand into his jeans pocket and was just about to ask Jeff if he wanted one when he glanced up and out of the glass wall. What he saw now was beyond comprehension. All the nameless fears that had clouded his brain for the last few minutes still hadn't prepared him for this. He could see it but he couldn't really believe it. People were already running away and someone, somewhere out there, screamed.

The four men on the benches had taken AK-47's out of the bags they'd been carrying and were putting them together like a short line of infantry about to charge the enemy.

It all came together in Nick's head. It all finally coalesced. It was an attack on MIMA. Home of the Russian art exhibition donated by Chekov, a Russian, the man CBS had to sell the stables to. It was an attack by Ukraine on Russia. It was CBS's revenge, but it was also a bigger political statement of defiance by Ukraine against Russia.

And it was already too late. The first man, the man who had stopped Jeff at the door of the ballroom, raised the rifle to his shoulder and pointed it directly at Nick.

He dropped to the ground as fast as gravity could work, yelling, 'Get down! Get down on the ground! Get down now!! All of you!!'

Jeff looked over and saw what was happening. 'Shooters!!!' he yelled, diving to the floor. Julie rolled off her seat and lay flat on the ground.

'Mam, dad! Get on the floor!' she yelled it twice, gesturing frantically at them.

But the old couple's reactions were slower and they both just looked confused at the commotion. Now there were screams from the two women working in the cafe. They ran for their lives through the reception area after seeing the gunmen outside.

Jackie got onto her hands and knees.

'Robbie!!!' screamed Nick. 'Down on the floor! Get down, man!!'

The old lad looked at him with wild blue eyes and fell heavily onto the floor as a hail of bullets flew into the glass, shattering it into a storm of shards.

'Daaaad!!! Daaaad!!' screamed Julie. Nick held his hands over his head to protect himself from the glass. As he did so, he saw Robbie Wells fall. He'd been hit. He'd been too slow to react and had surely taken a bullet somewhere.

All was chaos.

More bullets now, pinging and ringing around the building. Sod this for a game of soldiers. Nick's skin prickled with an overload of adrenalin. They had no defence, no way out of this, but they had to put up a fight somehow. This was the terrorism that Colin had feared. He'd been right, and he had also said they had a dirty bomb. Jesus. That might kill thousands of Teessiders. No way. They had to fight back. This had to be stopped. Surely the cops and the army and whoever would be here soon. They just had to keep alive until then. If only they had some weapons.

'Daaaad!' shouted Julie again. 'Are you alright?' But he didn't move on the floor. He was lying there, covered in fragments of glass, hands over his head. Christ almighty. Just when he'd come back into their lives, he'd been taken from them.

Julie scuttled over to him and put her hand on his neck. 'Dad! Dad!' she shouted the three-letter word in fear. Suddenly, he twitched and moved. He was alive.

'Yes! I'm...I'm alright...I hit my head...what the hell is happening?' he said, not sure whether to move or just to stay as still as possible to save his life.

The warm air from outside was now blowing through the space the glass had occupied. Nick looked the full length of the building. Right, c'mon, let's get this sorted. At the far end, a set of stairs went up to the other floors. That had to be safer than here because it was stone and wood.

'Julie! Get them up there,' he pointed to the stairs. She responded without hesitation.

'C'mon, mam, do as he says. Run low. Keep low. You too, dad,' she said.

'What the bloody hell? Is it a bomb?' said Jackie, as they scuttled past Nick and Jeff. There was no time to answer her.

Another round of bullets flew in, breaking more glass and causing puffs of plaster to burst out of the walls.

'Fucking hell, we're dead meat in here, Jeff. We've got to get after these bastards,' said Nick. 'We're not going down like a bunch of fucking pussies. No fucking way!'

'You're not bloody kidding,' said Jeff. They rolled over and down behind a wall of over-turned tables so the bullets would go over their heads.

'They're going to storm this place - they're after the Russian art,' said Nick. 'It's a big "fuck off" to the Russians. They'll have this place surrounded, man. We're just collateral damage. And they've got a dirty bomb, remember?'

'Aren't they just lovely?' said Jeff, bitterly.

Nick turned. Julie and her parents had made it to the stairs. They'd be safer up there for a few minutes. Sirens and alarms blared out.

'There's going to be a hell of a firefight here in a minute,' said Jeff. 'Brits v Ukrainians. We'll be better off up those stairs, as well. We just need to live long enough for our lads to take these bastards out.'

Nick peered out from behind the tables. 'Shit. One of them is running this way.'

'Oh, fuck.'

Nick laid low, squinting at the man. 'It's the big lad off the door of the Ballroom who wouldn't let you in. Got a gun over his shoulder. A rifle. He's a hard twat.'

'Is he on his own?'

'No, his mate's with him...the other bouncer. They're going to the entrance. Owee, let's 'ave them.'

'Right. Fucker didn't even know who I was.'

They sprinted across the crunching glass gravel and stood either side of the glass entrance door that they'd have to come through, Jeff hidden to the side of a metal shelf unit, Nick with his back against a plaster wall.

Heart pounding, Nick got ready to hit the man with his best right hander. He needed to drop him in one. Really damage him.

The glass door opened slowly. Come on, a bit further, a bit further, you twat. The big man stepped into the room with his gun in advance of him. As soon as its black barrel became visible to Nick, he took one step forward, yanked the gun backwards and out of the hands of the man. The Ukrainian was so shocked that he stood there for a split second just looking. In that moment, Nick saw his chance, held the gun by the barrel and swung the wooden butt into the man's face, using it like a baseball bat. The hard angle of the hard wood broke his face right open with a thrilling tear of skin. Yeah, you want some son?! Eh?! This is fucking Teesside and we die fucking hard.

He collapsed to the ground with a groan. A voice shouted out. It was the second man, also holding a rifle. He'd been a few steps behind his mate. 'Don't move, any of you!' he yelled, jabbing the gun at them.

'Whoo hoo! Hello, darlin', remember me?!' screamed Jeff in an unearthly high-pitched voice, as though he was a 12-year-old girl. It shocked the second man just enough for Jeff to swing a big left hook into the man's face. It was the only punch Nick had ever seen him throw and with his 15 stone and 6 feet 3 inches behind it, it delivered a lot of power, lifting the stocky short man off his feet and sending him staggering back and over onto his backside.

'I'll have that,' said a familiar voice. A man dressed in a short-sleeve checked shirt appeared, seemingly out of nowhere.

Kev Wells plucked the rifle out of the second man's hands as he fell to the floor and looked at it. 'AK-47. Sweet. And what the holy shite is going on here? Everyone is going fucking mental out there. There's some cunts with shooters!' He looked at the glass-strewn devastation but somehow without as much shock as a normal sentient human being should have had.

'Is there a ruck in here, Kev?' It was Ricky, right behind him, clearly hoping there was.

Nick pulled them inside. 'What the fuck are you two doing here?'

Kev looked around. 'Fuck me, it's a war zone. What the...' he looked at the guns. 'These are both AK-47s.' He pulled an impressed face at Ricky and then looked around. 'Ukrainians, is it? Right. Let's fucking sort these cunts out.' He threw one AK-47 at Ricky, who caught it like he was in a movie and not some fat dumb fuck off the Hardwick estate.

In an insane situation in life, you bloody well need a nutter. And now they had two. Somehow, it was comforting. 'Keep an eye on these two, shoot them if they look like getting up. They're terrorists. So you've every right. OK?' said Nick.

'Right,' said Ricky. He immediately began bossing the two men. 'Right, cunt faces. You by the door, get up and sit next to him down there by that counter. Eh? Comprende?'

They did as they were told, as you would when confronted with a tooled-up pair of heed-the-balls.

Kev looked at the gun. He seemed very familiar with the workings of an AK-47. 'We came from the opposite side. Never saw anything over there. We thought the shooting was a car backfiring. Mam texted us. Said our dad is here. Is that right?'

'Yeah, they're up the stairs,' said Nick. 'But there's bigger shit going down now. The Ukrainians want to burn this place down or blow it up...it's full of Russian art, they hate the Russians. It's probably at least a 12-man Mafia team, right? They're well-trained and tooled up and they've got a dirty bomb. If they explode it, we'll all die.'

Kev nodded, like this was just normal life. This was his home territory. A ruck, confrontation, aggression, violence. It had been his life and his life had, in effect, trained him for just this moment. 'Right, right. Gotcha. Standard terrorist outfit. We'll fucking have them, no bother.' His confidence was absolute and extraordinary.

'Yeah, fuck it, we can 'ave them,' said Ricky. The two Ukrainians sneered up at him.

'You don't understand what you're involved in here,' said the tall one. 'This will end badly for all of you!'

Ricky looked down and then hit him in the face with the butt of the gun. Just smashed him without compunction. It broke his nose and poured blood instantly. The man screamed in pain.

'You were saying?' he said with a sneer formed in a life of such violence. But this was no time for sensitivities.

There was a boom and an explosion, like an earthquake. Was it a bomb? There was a shattering noise from the top floor of the building and a waterfall of glass rain.

'What was that?' said Nick, grabbing the non-bleeding Ukrainian by his collar.

'Grenade.' He gave him a look of contempt. 'You will all die here.'

'You don't know Teessiders very well, do you, son?' said Nick and sank his fist into the man's face, knocking him spark out for a moment.

Julie and her parents came running down the stairs covered in brick dust or plaster, followed by four terrified members of the MIMA staff.

'Something exploded up there,' she screamed down at them. 'We've got to get out!'

'Aye, aye, dad. Fuck me, you look old,' said Kev. 'What happened to you? Hang on, tell us later. I've got to butcher some Ivans.'

Jeff ran back over to the overturned tables and looked out at the benches. 'They've set up a machine gun! They'll mow us down if we go out there.'

'Screw this. If we're going down, I'm taking a shit load of them with me,' said Kev. 'This is my bastard town. No bastard Ukrainian is fucking with it.'

He was about to storm out of the door in a fatal rage when a man stormed in. Bullets pinged off the pavement as he dived in through the door and rolled to a halt at their feet. He'd only just avoided getting shot by inches. Nick recognised him immediately. Ricky had his gun raised to shoot him. Nick held up a hand.

'He's on our side!!!'

It was Shadow Man, in army pants, black t-shirt and an incongruously smart and expensive pair of Adidas trainers. He got to his feet and looked at Ricky and Kev.

'Oh, for god's sake, it's Abbott and fucking Costello,' he said. He stood and in a commanding voice began shouting. 'Right. I'm in charge! This is a terrorist attack by the Malina, Ukraine's elite Mafia soldiers. They want to blow this place sky high. They also have a dirty bomb. We have one task and one task only: to stop them. Do what I say and some of us might walk out of here alive.' He had the sort of cold, rational eyes you needed in a frantic, scary situation like this, so everyone trusted him. There was no choice. Out of a leather shoulder bag he produced three pistols.

'What the fuck is this?' said Nick, looking at it as Shadow Man passed one each to him, Julie and Jeff.

'Oh, my god,' said Julie, hand over her mouth, taking it from him.

'Don't wet yourself, darlin', you know how to shoot. You took a target shooting course in 2001, remember?' said Shadow. 'These are Baretta M9s. You've got 15 shots in them. Remember that.'

'Do we get them 'an all?' said Ricky, like a kid looking at sweets. You couldn't faze him. He didn't care enough about being alive to be scared of dying.

There was no time to lose. Another rapid burst of bullets from the machine gun was discharged seemingly at random as the Ukranians set about destroying the building.

'You're already sufficiently tooled up. Right. You two. You want to serve your country? Eh? Well, do you?'

'Yeah, of course I do. I was in the Territorial Army,' said Ricky.

'Me, too,' said Kev.

'Right. Stand to attention, soldier!' Shadow Man barked out the order. They did what he said, like they'd been programmed. Maybe it was a chip the army put in them. They stood, chest out, shoulders back.

Jesus Christ. This really was war.

'They've got a machine gun set up outside of the library. We need to take that. Are you with me?!'

'Yes, sir!!' They said in unison.

'Right. This is what happens. Ricky, Kev, there's a unit on the south side of the building. Four men. Two submachine guns. You have to kill them and get those guns. Nick and Jeff, you've got to get behind that low wall so you can get the shooters on the benches.' He pointed out of the window to part of the pedestrianised landscaping. 'Julie, you cover them upstairs. There must be a huge hole in the glass where that grenade exploded. Use that.'

'What if they throw another one?' she said.

'Then you'll die. But if you don't do it, we'll all die anyway. The rest of you six...' he pointed at Robbie and Jackie and the four MIMA staff that had been working in the cafe and gift shop '...as soon as you hear Ricky and Kev giving them hell, run for your lives. You're on your own out there - look for cover at all times. That's as much hope and advice as I can give you.'

It was all utterly terrifying. But you couldn't give in. You had to respond. There was no hiding.

'Right, let's do this,' said Nick, 'Let's get behind that wall, Jeff,' said Nick pointing to the low landscaped area outside.

'Wait for me to get to that concrete waste bin,' said Shadow Man, pointing at a large round container, inside which was a metal bin. 'If they kill me...just give it everything you've got.'

'But won't the army be here soon?' said Julie.

'Yeah. They're not far away, but these bastards have that dirty fucking bomb. They're going blow this place sky high and release god knows what into the air. We have to stop them doing that; if we don't, thousands will die...it's down to us. If we die, but we stop them, then that's what we do have to do? Right? Right?!! This is our land, right?! No-one takes our land. Right?! We are Teesside and we live and die as Teessiders. Right?!!'

'Right!' said Julie and Nick and Jeff together, swept up in the emotion of it. It was too much to take in. All you could do was obey the man in authority. You surrendered to it totally. There was no room for individuality, nor even for thinking. This was trench warfare, brutal and fatal, and there was no escape. You had to fight or die, or, more likely, fight and still die. But this attack had to be stopped, it could not and would not stand.

'Right, I'm going upstairs. I'll see youse boys later,' said Julie, turning to climb the stairs.

'Jules. I love you,' called out Nick.

'It'll all be fine...the Boro always win at home against East European teams - remember Steaua Bucharest,' she said, with a more relaxed smile than the situation demanded.

'Be careful, Julie,' said Robbie.

'Dad, I've not seen you for 33 years. I'm not about to say goodbye now.'

She screamed at the top of her voice to release the tension, 'C'mon, Boro!!!' and ran upstairs.

'Let's fucking do this, Jeff,' said Nick. They hi-fived and followed Shadow Man out of the door. It sounded like a war zone outside. Sirens, alarms and gun fire. It was hard to even conceive that the crack-crack noises were bullets that could kill you. The grenade boom you could understand, it was big and powerful; the bullet more like a high-speed fly in comparison. Shadow held them back with his arm, looking to the right and the left. All the firepower was on the left.

'Good luck, kids. Let's fucking rock the shit out of this.' Shadow Man sprinted for his very life across the paved area. Nick pointed the pistol around the door and began shooting, pulling the trigger once, twice, three times and more. If that was giving someone cover, it worked, because Shadow Man got to the concrete bin alive, rolled behind it and gave them the thumbs up.

'One, two, three...c'mon, Boro!!!' Jeff and Nick both screamed it - maybe for luck, maybe as a last act of defiance, maybe to just let the psychic angst out of their souls.

It was perhaps 50 feet to the low wall that would give them protection and open out the battle scene to them. As they ran, they both fired shots towards the machine gun position that had been set up behind the wooden seats that the Malina men had arranged as a primitive defence barrier. Shadow did likewise to give them cover.

Nick saw the man on the machine gun turn to them and move the gun on its pivot. His legs wouldn't go fast enough. In football, when you're running onto a ball to volley it, you instinctively know how many strides you'll need before you connect with it and you always know if the defender will get to the ball first. Your brain does the maths and Nick's brain did the maths and it was obvious, even as they sprinted, that they were about 10 feet short. The gun was turned on them and the wall was still too far away. As soon as the Ukrainian squeezed the trigger, a hail of bullets would rip them both apart. There was nothing to be done. All you could do was keep running and prepare to meet your maker. Side by side they ran like they'd never run before, Jeff's long hair streaming out behind him like a greying cape. Nick looked away from the shooter, he didn't want to see the man that would be his killer. He tensed for the feeling of hot metal in his body and the searing pain. Ten feet to the wall, eight feet, six feet, four...then they heard two single shots in quick succession. They both leaped for the wall and rolled behind it, hearts at maximum BPM. Nick rolled over and turned to look at the machine gun man. He was lying on his back. He'd been shot.

Yes. Get in.

'Strange time for him to take a nap,' said Jeff, peering behind the wall, spitting out congealed saliva, his face contorted with the breathless effort they'd made. 'I have never moved like that in my life. Sports days would have been a bit different if they'd only set up a machine gun on the roof of Ian Ramsey School.'

Nick looked at his elbow, which was badly grazed from his leap over the wall. But his body was so full of adrenalin it wouldn't allow him to feel pain.

They watched as one of the man's buddies dragged him away, firing upwards with a small handgun as he did so. He got two shots off before a bullet hit him in the neck and he fell to the ground.

'It's Jules! It must be!' said Nick, pride and fear and absolute joy at being still being alive flooding through his body.

'Bloody Ukrainians never bargained for a Hardwick lass with a gun. Fucking lethal!' said Jeff. 'How many of these terrorists are there? Twelve, you said?'

'Yeah, at least. There were 12 on the moors. This is them. Ten left, then.'

Nick pointed at Shadow Man. Whilst Julie had shot at the machine gunner, he'd moved further around and was now holed up behind a flower bed and was shooting at someone who was out of their view, but as they watched, two people got out of the back of the Range Rover, both in army green t-shirts and trousers, both loading pistols as they walked.

'Fucking hell...they're going for Shadow. He can't see them. They're over his back. In his blind spot. How far do these fucking things fire?' said Jeff, looking at the pistol.

'I don't know, but I'm going to find out,' said Nick. Nick he held the gun out at arm's length, one hand wrapped around the other. 'You take the left, I'll take the right. On three. One, two, three.' The two old friends squeezed triggers in unison, the bullets discharging in the same satisfying mid-range octave.

The amazing thing about firing a gun is how little movement is needed to affect such profound change. Their index fingers released bullets that flew the distance to the two Ukrainian assassins in microseconds. Both were hit in the torso and fell. That small movement of their fingers had potentially ended two lives.

'That was almost too easy,' said Jeff, looking at the gun, impressed. 'I make that Bad Guys nil, Good Guys four. There's eight of them left now.' There was no time to contemplate what it meant to be taking people's lives from them in this way. All you could do was try to survive.

Shadow turned to them, thumbs up. But it was a short-lived victory. Things were about to get worse. An army Jeep came roaring around the far side of the town hall heading right towards Nick and Jeff's position, its raw engine coughing out revs. Someone was standing up in the back just shooting at random, knocking chunks out of pavements and walls. Nick squinted, aimed and squeezed the gun again, striking the shooter in the shoulder and making him fall backwards off the vehicle, hitting his head on the concrete. He looked unconscious.

Seven left.

The Jeep swerved and headed towards the machine gun position, which had now been taken up by another man, taking protection from Julie's line of fire behind a stack of wooden benches. But then, from the opposite side, came another unit of Ukrainians.

'Shit. There's more than a dozen here...look, there's five more of them...what the fuck are they doing?' said Jeff, crouching low behind the wall.

Nick licked his dry lips. 'They're the bombers, they're going to put the dirty bomb in MIMA. See, look, the one with the shaven head - he's got a black rucksack on his back. It'll be in there.'

'How do you know?'

Nick just pointed at the terrorists. All of them were putting on gas masks.

'Oh, fucking lovely,' said Jeff. 'As if we don't have enough bloody pollution.'

The shit had really hit the fan. This was the unit that had to be stopped. The others had been tasked with destruction, these were the ones tasked with death.

Shadow Man stood up and waved at them. 'Get him!!' he yelled at the approaching unit, firing his pistol. He hit one right in the head, bursting him like a ripe plum.

Six left now.

A rapid hail of shots from the reoccupied machine gun made Shadow dive for cover. Nick and Jeff had to lie flat on the ground behind the low wall to avoid getting hit.

Sirens and a loud hailer barking out instructions meant the army and the police were around but they were too late. These bastards were going in. They didn't care if they were killed or not. This was their mission.

From behind the wall, Nick and Jeff fired shots at the bombers but missed.

Still six left.

The machine gunner unleashed another round. They all hit the ground flat again and just prayed a stray bullet didn't hit them. Eventually, it went quiet; he must have discharged everything he had and needed to reload.

The bomb team were nearly at the MIMA entrance. Fuck this, Julie was in there. Nick stood up and fired a shot at the four men, but missed. He squeezed again, but nothing happened. He was out of ammunition. He'd forgot to count to 15. He must have fired most of it when they'd first come out of the building.

Jeff discharged his last bullets, two of the Ukrainians fired back, bullets whizzed over their heads as they dived to the ground again. They were done. No way to defend themselves now. There was nothing to stop the bomb team.

'We can't let them do this, Jeff. We can't...Julie is in there.' Body or mind, whatever he had, he had to give it to her. He'd promised. Nick got up, intent on running at them and just fighting even though it was hopeless. The bomb unit had reached the entrance to the building, but just as they did, from the far side of the gallery building, two figures stood for a moment, took the scene in and then began running, shooting as they went. The firepower from their weapons was simply incredible.

It was Ricky and Kev.

And they'd got hold of the two large submachine guns from the other Ukrainian unit on the far side of MIMA.

The bomb team turned and raised their weapons but Ricky and Kev had the element of surprise in their favour as they ran around the side of the building. In seconds they had mowed down the bomb team like ducks in a fairground shoot. Each brother with an AK-47 rifle over their back, they looked like Teesside bloody Rambos. The overwhelming rapid fire totally caught the remaining Ukrainians by surprise. Most were dead before they'd even turned to face Ricky and Kev. Together the brothers advanced from around the building just firing and firing and firing at everyone and everything.

The machine gunner, still reloading, took a hit in the face as their bullets shredded the wooden benches. All it took was the courage or stupidity to walk out there and fire, and stupid Hardwick hard man courage had won. The element of surprise and the superior firepower meant the bodies just piled up as Ricky and Kev annihilated all before them, including the man with the black rucksack. Those who weren't dead were too hurt to fight.

As they advanced, screaming obscenities, even Nick and Jeff hid low and hoped to avoid getting killed. These boys were out of control...and they bloody loved it.

It didn't take long, maybe 30 seconds. Ricky and Kev owned the place, only stopping firing when there was simply no-one left to fire at. Then they threw the guns to the ground and started giving it the full on your toes football hooligan, adrenalin-fuelled yelling - 'C'mon then, let's fuckin' 'ave you...come on you fuckin' Ivans, you want a piece of Teesside? Eh! I don't fuckin' think so, do you? Eh?! You fuckin' no-marks!' As some soldiers approached them from across the square, they leapt into each other, bumping chests together, just as they probably had after a fight in jail, outside a pub or at school.

Somehow, it was never in doubt. Both brothers were bleeding from wounds acquired in obtaining the guns from the back of the MIMA building where another unit must have been set up. But as soon as they had made their appearance, not one terrorist was left standing.

Nick peered out from behind the wall, now pitted from gunfire and saw Shadow Man running from the scene. His work here was done.

'Fuck me. Those lads were born to be soldiers of fortune,' said Jeff, closing his eyes and blowing out air. 'Do you think now is the time to tell them that the enemy are not actually Ivans?'

'I don't think they're sensitive to the accuracy of their national stereotypes, do you?' said Nick, spitting out foamy saliva.

Suddenly, soldiers were everywhere, closing the whole pace down. Those not dead or dying were held at gun point by uniformed army men. All around was mayhem but Ricky and Kev were laughing like it had been a paintballing session, even with the dead at their feet bleeding obscenely. It didn't bother them at all. Maybe they had been born to do this. Years as the hard men of the estate, of fighting in and out of jail, of not really giving a shit, had made both brothers ideal lunatics for just this situation. They were being patriotically violent and they knew that they had a free pass to unleash as much mayhem as possible and in doing so, they had saved the MIMA building from total destruction, though one side of it was nonetheless devastated; but more importantly, they'd saved the unleashing of some nameless biological agent - no doubt manufactured at BioResearch in Hartlepool - into the skies of Teesside, to god knows what consequence.

'Nick! Nick!'

He swung around. Julie came running out of the MIMA building, past the soldiers and up to him and Jeff, panting.

'Did you see what my brothers did? They took them down, man. All of them!' She screamed and whooped. 'I was watching from up there on the stairs. I hit two. Don't think I killed them, the recoil on the gun caught me by surprise so I wasn't that accurate.'

'Accurate enough to save our lives, Jules,' he said, an arm around her shoulder.

'Is it over, do you reckon?' said Jeff, still rolling his now-empty gun in his hand, looking around at the chaos.

'Yeah, I think they've got them all,' said Julie. 'Mam and dad ran out of the back with the staff once Ricky and Kev had taken out that unit and got their guns. Totally caught them by surprise. Shot them both in the head just like that. Then it was clear over there. They took those big bloody machine guns and just fucked everybody up. It was the most amazing sodding thing I've ever seen!' She whooped again.

Army soldiers started moving across the square with loud hailers demanding that people give themselves up or risk being killed.

'They've not got all of them,' said Nick, pointing at the black Range Rover parked by the town hall. 'That's CBS's car. He's somewhere around here. He's behind this and now he's got to get out without the army and police jumping on him.'

She squinted into the distance. 'He'd want a good view, wouldn't he? He thought they were going to blow this sky high, so he'd need protection. There's only one place he could see it and that's the town hall.'

Jeff turned around. 'One of those small top-floor windows is my guess. Best view of everything would be from up there.'

'Right, let's flush him out,' said Nick. 'You up for it, Jules?'

'Yeah, let's get the posh sod.'

'Be careful, eh,' said Jeff, a hand on each of their shoulders.

They sprinted towards the town hall, the main entrance of which was on Corporation Road. They ran around to Albert Road, knowing that CBS would have to walk down there to get back to the car. He was hardly likely to run away, being about 18 stone, and there was no point in chasing him through the building.

'Let's wait across the road,' said Julie, getting her breath and checking on her gun, jammed into her back pocket.

They crossed over and stood underneath some scaffolding in the shadows. Police cars were blocking traffic off at the turning from Corporation Road and people were being held back. They were the only ones around and would soon attract police attention as they swept through the whole area. Sure enough, two officers soon began to walk down towards them, having seen them cross the road, clearly suspicious of their movements, and that was when the large form of Cameron Baxter-Smythe emerged from a Gothic wooden door on the south side of the town hall. He looked quickly from side to side before making the three steps into the Range Rover driver's seat, and within seconds he had turned the engine and moved off. 'He's away. Come on, Jules, we've got to follow him.'

They ran down Albert Road towards Julie's Porsche as CBS's car passed them, only to be stopped by a police car 30 yards down the road at the junction with Borough Road where a roadblock was being set up. As they ran towards her car, they saw CBS wind the window down, lean out and speak to a policeman, make a hand gesture, nod and then move off.

'Typical. Posh twat has just lied to that copper - nothing to do with me, officer. I'm Cameron Baxter bloody Smythe,' said Nick as they reached the car. 'The fucking rich and the aristocracy always have a get out of jail free card in this country. Well, not any more. C'mon, Jules.'

'Remember his family motto, "he who owns the land has the power". Well, sod him. We'll let him have a bit of Teesside power, see how he likes that!' She spat the words out in a rising fury.

She turned the engine, revved it and pulled out, taking a right up Baker Street, before the roadblock. There was no time to explain to the police who they were and why they had to be allowed through. It was a one-way street, but no traffic was coming down. She gunned the Porsche to the junction with Linthorpe Road, emerging to head towards the A66 dual carriageway, seeing the black Range Rover up ahead in the distance.

'I'll try and keep right back a bit. What are we going to do?' said Julie, winding down the window and wiping sweat from her forehead.

'I don't know...my mind is in a blur. I can't grasp what we've just been doing. That was the most terrifying 20 minutes of my life.'

'I quite enjoyed it, after a weird fashion. Once you accepted it was insane, it was easier to deal with.'

'He'll be going back to Middleton, won't he?'

She shook her head. 'No. It's all gone tits up. He's got to get away. How can he do that? A66 and then the A1 north or south? We could be chasing him down to London, pity I've only got a half a tank of fuel.'

Nick thought for a moment as they joined the A66 and took off west.

'Got it! The airport. He'll have a plane or a chopper waiting. Probably to take him to Kiev.'

He was right. In the distance, the Range Rover took the Long Newton exit off the A66 which led down to the airport. Julie put her foot down and accelerated. 'Ah, you prick! This is a quiet road - right, let's bloody have him.'

She took the Baretta out of her waistband and gave it to Nick. 'I've still got eight shots in there.'

The car was a few hundred yards in front on a long, straight empty rural road with low hedges on either side.

'I'm going get alongside him, as soon as I do, shoot his tyres out...'

'What? Shoot his tyres?'

'Yeah. That's make him stop and he's not exactly going run away from us, once the car is dead. We'll take him off the road and then get Colin here. He's not getting away. We've bloody got him!'

She took the Porsche up to 110mph in a few seconds, which quickly brought them right up the backside of the big black car. She looked at the road ahead. It was straight and clear, so she swung out and alongside CBS. Nick rolled the window down, gave him the sort of silly wave that Jeff would have done - all teeth and flappy hands - then he raised the gun, held it in both hands and fired a shot into the right front tyre and another into the back. He was too close to miss.

'Got him!' yelled Nick.

'Right, call Colin!' she shouted, as she accelerated in front of the Range Rover, to keep out of its way in case CBS lost control. Nick turned and looked at it slow and then drift to the right before scudding around as he tried to keep control of it. It veered off onto the verge and bucked into a halt.

'It's his answer phone. Colin, it's Nick.' He told him where they were and what they were doing and why, while Julie brought the car to halt on the grassy verge, 30 yards in front of the stricken Range Rover.

She took the gun from him, got out and stuck it in back in her waistband.

'Be careful, Jules,' said Nick, running alongside her, scared the big man might lean out of the car and shoot them. 'He might be armed. Cover me.'

She stood to his left as he pulled open the Range Rover door, pointing her gun, prepared to shoot immediately.

Cameron Baxter-Smythe sat imperious behind the wheel. The car was so big and the driver's seat so lofty that it made him look like a king sitting on a throne. He wasn't armed. Perhaps that would have been too incriminating.

'Out of the car!' Nick yelled.

'Mister Guymer. What *do* you think you are doing?' said CBS, indignant and pompous.

'I'm stopping a terrorist from escaping.'

'Are you now? Really? How ridiculous. You have no idea who you're talking to or what you're doing.'

'Get out of the car,' said Julie, holding the gun at him with both hands.

'Ah, Miss Wells. She of the lunatic brothers. Pleasure, I'm sure.'

He was red in the face, his thin hair revealing a glowing, sweaty head.

'Yeah, and they kicked your Ukrainian mob's arses, single-handedly. Now raise your hands in the air and get out of the car,' she said.

'Oh, really. Who do you think you are?'

'Just do it and don't be a smart arse,' said Nick.

The big man stepped down from the vehicle, hands up. 'You're making a terrible mistake and had you bothered to turn up to our little meeting, Mr Guymer, I could have told you that. I expect you think the chap whose car your brothers so helpfully destroyed is working for the British government or some such. Is that what he's told you? Yes, I thought so. Absolute rubbish, of course. That man is a traitor to his country. A double agent working to his own agenda.'

'Frankly, mate, I don't give a toss. You can tell this to the police. They'll be here soon enough,' said Nick.

'No, they won't, dear boy. And even if they did perchance to turn up, one sight of me and they'd turn and leave immediately.'

'Why would they do that?'

'Because I am a very important person and I play an important role in keeping this country safe.'

'A load of old rubbish,' said Julie. 'Why would Shadow Man...'

CBS raised his thick eyebrows.

'...is that what you call him? Shadow Man? How imaginative, but inaccurate. He is anything but a shadow. He is all too real. He works for the British government and for the Russian government. He thinks we don't know he works for Putin, but we know he does.'

'We? Who's we?'

'MI-6, dear boy. That's one better than MI-5.' It was clearly a quip he made regularly and one which he thought very clever.

'Bollocks,' said Nick, convinced he was lying.

'Absolutely true. Which is why I know all about you two. I know you drink in the Royal Oak, that you work at the Teesside Women Centre, that your father has just returned home after over 30 years abroad, and I even know you have recently had a miscarriage, Ms Wells. Please accept my condolence in that regard.' He gave her the sort of patronising smile that a teacher might give a slow student.

'What?! How dare you! Shut your filthy mouth! I don't want your condolences!' She looked at him with furious indignation.

'It is our business to find out about people like you when you get mixed up in our affairs.'

'People like us? We're just normal people.' said Nick, wondering where Colin's men were. This fat idiot wasn't telling them the truth, was he? Surely Colin *was* going to come.

'Normal people who have become entangled with very dirty business.' He leaned against the Range Rover, arms crossed. 'I hope you have noted the distinct lack of police presence, Nicholas Guymer. Hmm? Let me tell you, you are a brave man and a good man, I'm sure, and you have many good qualities - the depression aside...' there was the patronising smile again. 'But you are hardly an intellectual. Too many feelings and not enough brains.'

'Maybe you're right and maybe right now my feelings are saying that I should hit you in the face until you stop twitching,' said Nick.

Calm under pressure, CBS smiled in a patronising manner. 'That would be a very silly thing to do. A far better thing to do would be to take me to the airport and we shall forget this little meeting ever took place because, believe me, if I were to choose to, I could make life unbearable for you. A life so unbearable, suicide would be a blessed relief for you and I know that you know what that might feel like, dear boy.'

'Leave him alone. You're a lying twat!' spat Julie. 'This is all bullshit. You're a terrorist. We know all about you and your family and your Ukrainian past.'

CBS put his hands down and leaned on the Range Rover, nodding.

'Ah, Julie Wells. You are too emotional for your own good. A woman with two fine degrees should be a little more advanced in her thinking; a little more clever, I would speculate. But then you have always thought more from below the waist than above, haven't you, my dear? Always a touch of slut about you. Perhaps it's as well you lost that baby. Does the planet really need another Wells to pollute it? No, I think not.'

She could have just shot him and, anticipating that, Nick was about to grab the gun off her. But that wasn't in her mind. That would have been too easy and not have exorcised her pain properly. Instead, she carefully put the gun into her waistband and, unleashing her rage, flew at him, grabbing him by his large ears and head-butting him in the face all in one movement, not just once, but twice in quick succession, kneeing him the groin as she did so. But that wasn't enough, as he doubled over in pain, she stepped back and began kicking him in the face with her leather boot, big swinging kicks until he fell to the ground. Then she leaped on him with a screech so unearthly that it could have come from the bowels of hell. Not just primal in its intensity, it was uncontrolled and wild. She tore into him. He hadn't seen that coming. Where he was from, this didn't happen to people like him. Where Julie was from, it bloody did.

It was the breaking of her emotional dam. Every single negative feeling that she had suppressed and swallowed down and held back about the miscarriage. All the years of upset and hurt at her missing father. All the loveless years of loneliness and isolation. All the disconnect from herself and from her true soul. All that pain burst through the veneer she had laid over it, in the same way blood always soaks through the bandage tied over a deep wound.

As she thrashed at the corpulent man, she screamed tearful rage, wildly beating him on his head and back with her fists and finally, as he keeled over, head buried in his hands, curled up to defend himself against the onslaught, she stamped between his legs.

He let out a bellow of anguished pain and promptly vomited.

Nick could have stopped her. He could have interrupted this puking out of her inner torment but he didn't want to, this was some kind of exorcism. The end game. And anyway, he had it coming. So he stood back and admired the beating she dished out to the big man. One way or another, the Wells family had kicked, quite literally, CBS's arse. He might have owned the land, but lying here on the side of the road, he no longer had any power...nor, quite possibly, any testicles.

Spitting a final big gob of saliva onto the prone figure, she withdrew, wiping her mouth, her eyes streaming tears of emotion, whilst not actually crying. And that was going to have to be her defence when this came to court. She had been provoked and she had, temporarily at least, lost her mind. Because if he was an agent of the British state, she surely wasn't going to get away with this. You can't go around making a mess of MI-6's finest fat dude.

Nick pulled her back from him, an arm around her shoulder. A car drove past, the driver staring at them, the third to do so during the assault. Surely it wouldn't be long before the police were called now. Still Colin hadn't replied.

She looked at him as he pulled her into him, with all the hurt and upset of recent weeks in her eyes; with a look that was both lost little girl and distraught woman.

'I'm so sorry...I'm so fucking sorry,' she said.

He rubbed the tears from under her eyes. 'Don't worry, Jules. Everything is going to be alright.'

He said the words but he didn't believe them. This man had known so much about them, right down to her medical records, things only someone in MI-6 or the security services could have access to.

CBS groaned and fell onto his back, lying supine, arms out wide, his nose pouring blood, his white shirt spattered with it.

Nick got out his phone and called Colin again. 'Colin. Where are you? If you can't come for some reason, at least bloody well tell me, for god's sake. We've kicked the crap out of CBS...what would you like me to do with him now? If I don't hear from you within five minutes we're taking his car keys and leaving him here.'

Julie had walked away and was leaning against the back of the Porsche, wiping her mouth and eyes with a tissue, composing herself. She spat as he came over.

'I totally lost it,' she said.

'Best head-butt I've seen since 1980s football. Good use of the ears to get leverage, I thought. Very professional.'

'Is he actually telling the truth? Is Colin not coming? Are we in the shit?'

'Well, he's not here yet, is he?'

She closed her eyes and shook her head. 'Fuck. What have I done?' She put her hand over her mouth.

'You may well have kicked the crap out of an important person.'

'He was disgusting. So disgusting that I don't regret it. Whatever happens, he fucking deserved it. That's the only way us common people can get our own back against his sort. Why should we be polite? People like him have been fucking us all over for centuries. He might own the land and the power but now he owns a lot of pain as well and that's *exactly* as it should be. Him and his sort have got it coming. We've had enough of them.'

'I'll ring Jeff and see what's going on back at the war zone.'

'Yo, crazy dude!' Jeff seemed back to his usual self, remarkably enough.

'Are you OK? How's things going down there?'

'All cool. The place looks like the Battle of the Bulge. Full of army and coppers and media. The Brothers Wells have been taken off to make statements about the mass slaughter they inflicted upon evil and I'm just about to do likewise. Shadow Man has gone. Do you realise he never even told us his name? Did he even really exist? He melted away like, well...a shadow.'

'How many did we kill?'

'Ah, well, as it turns out, me and you and Julie killed no-one, as far as I can tell. We maimed a few but we are no Kev and Ricky, are we? They did the proper butchering, but I think you're allowed to kill terrorists in Middlesbrough between the hours of two and five. There's a bylaw allowing it, I'm sure.'

'So Shadow Man isn't there?'

'No. He's totally gone.'

'I think he might have been setting us up, Jeff.'

'Eh? Did CBS tell you that? Have you caught him?'

'Yeah. Jules has...she's sort of incapacitated him. He reckons he's MI-6 and Shadow Man is a double agent.'

Jeff dismissed that with contempt. 'Nah, that's rubbish. Whoever Shadow was, he stopped that bombing happening. He was a British Agent all along. I'm certain of it. He was bloody brilliant, actually. Made me feel like fighting was a duty for my country and I never thought I'd ever feel like that.'

'Yeah, well, we may need your creative thinking in court, soon enough, I reckon.'

'Bollocks. We did a good thing. And we were under massive pressure. I nearly deployed *brown* as a verb on more than one occasion.'

'Ha, yeah, me too. Have you seen Colin?'

'Nope, though his mob are all here.'

'I've called him but CBS reckoned he'll not come. He's still saying he's immune from police attention.'

'Crappola. He's just trying to con you.'

'I think I believe him. If the police don't turn up soon, we'll come back into Middlesbrough and I'll walk into the police station and then we'll see what's what.'

'OK, brother. I'll call you if I find out anything or if I see Harcombe. It'll all be OK. Trust me.'

Nick walked over to Baxter-Smythe, who had now propped himself up against the tyre of the Range Rover.

'You're in deep shit over this, old boy,' he said to Nick with a bitter, quiet aggression. 'Take me to the bloody airport or I'll have you fucking shot as a traitor, you and your dirty bitch.'

Nick looked at Julie. She narrowed her eyes and slowly shook her head.

'Is she the boss of you, man?' said CBS looking up at Nick again. 'Hypnotised by the tits and the arse, are we? Pathetic. A grown man being led around by his dick.'

Nick got down onto his hunkers. 'For a man who clearly thinks he's clever, you're being very stupid, because were I to choose to hurt you, you would not easily recover, right? It would make all of this damage so far look like a mere scratch. Old. Fucking. Boy. Right? So shut up. One more word out of you and without further warning I will unleash unimaginable pain on you. And if you've done your research, you will surely know that I can fucking hurt someone...'

His anger was rising now as he said the words, the one feeding the other in an unvirtuous circle. He pushed him in the shoulder to finish his sentence.

But CBS wasn't about to keep quiet. 'You're a dead man. If you don't take me to the airport, you are dead. The people waiting for me there will hunt you down and kill you. Both of you. You and little miss hoity toity here.' CBS was getting more and more angry and more indignant. Maybe he was too desperate to be MI-6. Far too desperate.

'Can't you just stop being a vile, sexist pig for a moment?' said Julie, arms folded.

CBS looked up at her with a dark hatred.

'Oh, do go and get fucked, my darling, and I'm sure that's just what my army will do to you, three at a time, on my behalf, shortly before putting a bullet in your bitch brain.'

That was it. No waiting. No hesitation. CBS owned the land but it was time he felt a bit of proper Teesside power. Nick sank a crunching right hander in CBS's face. The soft jowls yielded under the force of the punch as it came to rest against his cheekbone. As the energy surge drained from his shoulder and into the flesh, in the distance a siren came into hearing.

CBS slumped sideways, unconscious. Nick hit him hard again, just for good measure. And a third time.

Nick stood up and wiped his knuckle on his jeans. It hadn't even hurt.

Julie applauded slowly.

'Quality right handers. Hopefully, they'll let us share a cell.'

'I don't think I could stand that much sex, Jules. In jail and nothing else to do, we'd die of dehydration.'

He pointed at the sky as if to catch the siren noise on his finger.

A police car came screaming along the A66 and turned down their road.

'This is either very good news or very bad news,' said Nick as they rested together against the Porsche, arms around each other.

'If Colin gets out, we're OK. If it's anyone else, it's bad,' she said as a black Merc approached at speed and braked to a screeching halt on seeing them.

One second passed. Two seconds. Three.

Then the passenger door opened and the tall figure of Colin Harcombe emerged.

He cast a glance at the unconscious, bloody body of CBS.

'Taking a nap, is he? Well, he's had a busy day.' He stood ram-rod straight and saluted them both, finger tips to his forehead, gave a frosty smile and nodded.

'Good work, you two. He was on his way out of the country. There's a chopper at the airport for him. We've just got a man over there. That's why I was late getting here.' He came over and shook Nick's hand with a hard, dry grip. 'Are you alright, Julie?'

'Fine Colin. Absolutely bloody delighted to see you.' She leaned forward and flung her arms around him.

Colin Harcombe did what he was very good at. He took control. He organised. More police arrived. He told his men what to do. It was a relief to be in his hands after the chaos of the last hour. He told them they should drive home and he'd drop by later that day to personally take statements. CBS was taken under police guard to Darlington hospital.

As Nick drove the Porsche back into Stockton, Julie burst out half-laughing, half-crying. 'All we did was go for a dirty weekend in Middleton-in-Teesdale and as a result of that, all of this has happened. Christ, I've had dirty weekends go wrong, but never turn into a terrorist attack.'

'Well, we did have some vigorous sex in that hotel. MI-6 can't let that sort of thing get out into the public domain. Everyone will be wanting it and soon enough the country will go to wrack and ruin. We're a threat to decent society, me and you. That's what this was really all about.'

'Ha ha...yeah, that's true. Nothing would ever get done. We're a public menace.'

Nick gripped himself. 'Warning: This erection can overthrow the state!'

Julie put her hand between her legs. 'Do not touch this clitoris: It may explode and kill you!'

He drummed on the wheel and looked over at her. She looked back. Her eyes were clear now.

'How are you, then?' he asked.

'I'm alright. Yeah.'

'Sure?'

'Yeah.'

'You really lost it back there, you know.'

'I know. I let it all go.'

'Yeah, I spotted that. You did go wild,' he said, with considerable understatement.

She sat and twirled a long curl of hair around her finger as he drove down Bishopton Lane. 'I think I know, maybe for the first time in my life, what being unhinged really means.'

'That's a good word for it. That's what it looked like.'

'You hear about women who have been abused for years and one day, they murder the man who is responsible. Maybe that's what it's like. You lose it and you just want to make it all stop.'

'...and we had just been in an intensely stressful situation.'

'You can say that again. When I was shooting that pistol out of the top-floor window of the MIMA building, I was barely able to comprehend it. I just lived in the moment and tried to do what Shadow Man had told me to do.'

'You and me both. I thought I was dead on more than one occasion.'

'We can be proud of ourselves, and of my brothers, for once in their sorry lives.'

'Where did you learn to head butt someone like that? Have you done it before?'

'Of course I haven't, but somehow, it just seemed a quite natural thing to do. Must be watching Kev and Ricky sticking the nut on lads when I was a kid. It's in the Wells DNA. Didn't even hurt. Caught him right on the bridge of the nose. Seems almost like a dream now...I was in such a weird state of mind. I feel like I've been purged.'

'I like a good purge. Leaves you feeling cleaned out and empty. Like when you throw up. Afterwards, when you no longer feel sick, there's a sense of elation, isn't there? The contrast between how you felt pre-puke and how you feel post-puke is so big. I'm sure the act of being sick releases some hormones that make you feel good once the nausea passes.'

'Well, I feel like I've emotionally or psychologically or mentally puked my guts up right down to the bile and I have to say, it feels bloody good. I feel a weight has been lifted from me and a light shone on all the shadows that were cast over me. It all just goes to prove, you can't beat kicking the crap out of the landed aristocracy.'

'Yeah, right on, sister. You showed him. As Big Fish might say, "Don't Cross the Tees"!'

CHAPTER 15

A week later, Jeff knocked on Nick and Julie's door.

'Look who I found hanging around outside, looking shifty,' said Jeff, as Nick pulled open the door. He was pointing at Don Preston, who waved. 'He's converted me already,' added Jeff. 'I am now a believer.'

'Everyone is a believer, Jeff. It's just that some believe that the lizard people are behind it all and some think it's Jesus.'

'Ah, I am a believer in the Lizard King, though. He can do anything.'

'Owee in you two,' said Nick. 'I've got the dinner nearly ready.'

They stepped in and kicked off their shoes.

'I hear you're opening a rock club, Jeff,' said Don. 'Is that right?'

'Aye. It's that old church hall building on Castle Street. I just put in a low, speculative bid for it - and they accepted it right away. Just heard yesterday. Well chuffed.'

'It's owned by the church?'

'It is, yeah, at least until this heathen gets his sweaty mitts upon its holy bricks and mortar. It'll be a great place for some righteous rock 'n' roll - or it will be when I've had it totally renovated and brought into the 21st century. It's going to be a bit of challenge, but that's what I like about it.'

'I think it's a great idea...I shall come and shake my booty - is that the modern expression?'

Jeff pushed open the kitchen door. 'It's *an* expression Don, but forgive me for not wanting to picture you or your booty and the shaking thereof. Not without a drink in me, at least.'

Julie was opening bottles of wine in the kitchen as they went in.

'Now then, boys, you must have heard me pull the corks. Red or white?'

'Half and half for me,' said Jeff, wafting his beard. 'And make sure you get a head on it.'

'Blood of Christ for me, Julie,' said Don, 'or if you don't have that, some

269

of that Merlot will do fine.'

Jeff grinned and pointed to the vicar. 'He's your go-to man for Christianity-based japes, isn't he? I suppose doing sermons is a bit like a stand-up routine.'

'Oh, yeah, only without the swearing and references to genitals, bodily functions and paedophiles,' said Don, 'Unless I'm reading from...' he dropped his voice down to an American movie trailer-style deep growl '...the Bible Black.'

Jeff patted him on the arm. 'I dig it, Don. Religion *and* references to *Heaven and Hell* songs.'

'I always liked Ronnie James Dio,' said Don. 'That's your fault, Julie.'

She looked up with a smile and pulled at a bra strap under her loose black shirt. 'Me? Why me?'

'Because you played me that Black Sabbath record almost every day for a whole term when we were students.'

She grinned at the recollection. 'Oh, yeah, their first with Dio. I bloody loved that record.'

'Many a head has been banged to that. Many a brain cell dislodged,' said Jeff. 'Magnificent production on that record. I remember me and you, Nick, sitting in the Percy Arms in Newcastle listening to the first single off it - "Neon Knights".'

'Aye. We both expected to hate it, because it wasn't Ozzy singing, but we both bloody loved it from the first few bars.'

Julie poured the drinks while Nick took the leg of lamb out of the oven, wrapped it in foil and let it rest as he finished off the vegetables.

'That smells wonderful,' said Don, eyeing the meat. 'Thanks for inviting us over. I'm sorry Gail couldn't come - she's a big cheese at the WI and just couldn't put it off.'

'No worries,' said Nick. 'We thought it'd be nice to get you over. After last week's stress, we all deserve a decent feed and a drink up, I reckon. Robbie will be over later for drinks.'

'Ah, is this your long-lost dad I've been hearing about?' said Don, sipping at his wine.

'Yeah.'

'What a blessing for you.'

'Well, we've got a lot of catching up to do, that's for sure.' She took a big drink of white wine.

'I'm just glad we're all here. There were moments when I was shooting that Baretta when I thought it'd be the last thing I was going to do,' said

Nick, draining some broccoli.

'I had Colin Harcombe and his number two, Amanda Beale, round my gaff last night,' said Jeff. 'Still doing a bit of debriefing.'

'Yeah, they were here this morning,' said Julie. 'They've got it all sorted out now, it seems. Cameron Baxter-Smythe actually wanted to press charges against me for assault.'

'What? You're kidding. But he was funding terrorists,' said Jeff.

'At the risk of sounding un-Christian, doesn't that, in lieu of the Lord's vengeance, remove your rights not to be beaten up?' said Don.

'No, it doesn't. He was well within his rights to sue me for GBH. I broke his nose and a rib and badly bruised a testicle.'

She held out her arms wide and took a bow while they applauded.

'I take it Colin dissuaded him from this ludicrous course of action,' said Jeff.

Nick began to carve the meat. 'It was pointed out to him that, while he was entitled to take legal recourse, as he was attempting to flee the country at the time, following organising a terrorist act, it would play badly for him in his own trial. So he's decided to give them some names instead, to try and mitigate what is likely to be a life sentence. Right...come on...let's eat.'

'Excellent. So, you're actually above the law, Jules,' said Jeff, sitting down at the kitchen table.

'About time, too,' she said with a short laugh.

'I don't understand what on earth he thought he was doing,' said Don. 'This looks fantastic, Nick.'

Nick smiled, pleased to have got it all ready together at the same time.

'He's a good cook, Don. Better than me,' said Julie, topping up their wine.

'Why do chefs wear those tall hats?' said Jeff, apropos of nothing. 'I've always wondered that. They're hardly practical.'

'Good question. I have no idea,' said Nick, pouring gravy onto their plates. 'A kitchen is no place for a hat of any sort.'

'Wearing a bowler hat whilst cooking, would give the chef a certain eccentric quality,' said Don, to everyone's amusement. 'Shall I say grace or will it just embarrass the grubby Pagans amongst us?'

'I've not said grace since I was little,' said Julie. 'Go on, Don.'

'Aye, my digestive system can do with any divine help it can get,' said Jeff, putting his hands together in supplication.

'Thank you Lord for the gift of food, of friendship, of wine, of gravy, and of Ronnie James Dio, for which we are all truly thankful. Amen.'

Jeff laughed and hi-fived Don. 'Good work, vicar.'

'So tell me about this Elvis character,' said Don as they ate. 'He sounds extraordinary.'

'He was,' said Nick, 'and he was very unlucky. He was caught in the centre of the security services' hunt for the Ukrainian Mafia cell.'

'But he *was* actually Ukrainian?' said Don.

Jeff nodded. 'Yup. Coincidentally, he was. More unfortunate still, he was buying botulism bacteria, quite legally, if bizarrely, from the same place that was covertly manufacturing a biological agent for the Mafia to use in their bomb.'

'...and that place, BioResearch, was Ukrainian owned and, in effect run by Cameron Baxter-Smythe,' said Nick.

'So it was a legitimate company, but with an evil element to it?' said Don.

'CBS was the evil, yeah. He hated Yuri Chekov after having to sell the stables to him to settle a debt between the Moscow Mafia and the Malina. So when it was decided that a big terrorist incident was needed to strike a blow against the Russians - it all coalesced around the region that Chekov had bought into and in which CBS owned so much land. It was a literal blow and a symbolic one too for the Ukraine against Russia,' said Nick.

Julie intervened. 'It was also a personal revenge thing. Colin Harcombe was telling me about it all this morning. They're still trying to find out exactly what kind of biological agent was in that dirty bomb,' she said, sitting back to drink wine. 'God only knows what would have happened if it had been released in an explosion.'

'Lord help us all,' said Don, shaking his head. 'And how was this Elvis chap using the botulism?'

'He was, in effect, getting bees to manufacture facelift honey,' said Jeff. 'There's two words you never thought you'd hear together - facelift honey. The bees were fed on the botulism-laced glucose, so they made honey with increased levels of botulism in it. It's always in honey anyway. Botulism is used in Botox injections, so it worked in the same way but you used it like a lotion. But judging by how they both looked, controlling its effects was a bit difficult. My guess is they couldn't regulate how powerful it was and that it just varied.'

Don laughed. 'That is simply extraordinary. Why would anyone want to do that to themselves?'

'Botox is a massive business. It's not the daftest idea to create a non-invasive way of applying it. OK, it does make you look like you've been hit in the face with a cricket bat, but it does iron out the wrinkles,' said Nick.

'At this point I am contractually obliged to say something about how we should all be happy with how God made us,' said Don. 'However, when you're fat and bald, like me, I'm aware that is always a hard argument to make!'

'Ah, but, if you think about it...' said Jeff, finger aloft '...God must have made us to be unhappy about how God made us, didn't he?'

'...or she,' said Julie with a mouthful of lamb.

'That depends on your view of free will,' said Don.

'You can choose from phantom fears and kindness that can kill, I will choose a path that's clear, I will choose free will,' said Jeff, strumming an imaginary guitar.

'I should know what song that comes from,' said Don. 'Did you use to play it to me at college, Jules?'

'Aye. "Freewill", from Rush's *Permanent Waves*. Brilliant record, one of my three fave Rush albums, in fact. You remember "The Spirit of Radio", don't you? That's the first track on it.'

Jeff pointed at her and put his thumb up. 'Chicks who dig Rush, you gotta love 'em, Don.'

'I do remember that, actually. You still hear that song on the radio. Chap singing sounds like he's got some skin caught in his zipper. Accidental circumcision - always a nasty one, that.'

'*Zipper Catches Skin* - Alice Cooper's 14th studio album - 1982, if I remember right.' said Jeff.

Nick hi-fived him. They laughed. Don went on. 'So let me get this story right about Elvis...how did he die?'

'That's the tragic thing. Because British security services thought he was working for the Ukrainian Mafia, and because they suspected they were putting together a dirty bomb, they put two and two together and made nine. The agent we called Shadow Man murdered him, thinking he had the bomb bacteria with him, and he did have something, but it was...'

'...the botulism?'

'Exactly,' said Nick. 'It was terrible mistake to make. He was murdered by the state. He had the botulism in the attaché case. Shadow Man got hold of it...initially they thought they'd foiled a terrorist attack but obviously, they hadn't.'

'Poor man. God bless him,' said Don, almost under his breath.

'Mind, he was not without sin,' added Jeff. 'He'd hypnotised my dad and brother so they'd not notice when he stole and then sold the valuable Walter Francis Cup to Chekov, the Regency Stables owner, and replaced it with a cheap plain cup of the same shape and size...'

'...which Macca the jockey then stole, as an act of revenge for some perceived grievance with Mickey and the Blakeston Stables,' said Nick.

'But that was a sort of sideshow as well, right?' said Don.

'Totally. The stupid thing was, these Malina types were already here - working as bouncers and bar people for people like Big Fish and at the hotel we stayed at. CBS brought them in through his own job agency. Then we saw them training on the moors, practising the manoeuvres that they used to attack the MIMA building, under the watchful eye of CBS,' said Julie. 'But we couldn't have guessed any of that...I mean...you don't imagine East European Mafia types are on your doorstep, do you? Not in Teesside.'

'So why were you attacked on your way home from Middleton?' said Don, mopping up gravy with his mashed sweet potato.

'By Shadow Man?' said Nick. 'That was just to scare us away. They were struggling to find the terrorist cell, didn't know what was going to happen or when. Everything he said to us, and the fact he was so violent, was designed to keep us from getting any more involved and if he hadn't done that, we probably would actually have got a lot more involved. But in the end, we walked right into the middle of it anyway, just being in the wrong place at the wrong time at MIMA.'

'What I'd like to know is how Baxter-Smythe knew so much about both of us,' said Julie. 'He even knew I'd had a miscarriage.'

'Information isn't secure in this day and age,' said Jeff. 'My guess is he had a mole in MI-5 who found out everything about you. He was so highly connected, what with being in the House of Lords and everything.'

'But why?' said Don. 'You're just two innocent people.'

Jeff pushed his empty plate away. 'That was delicious, Nick. You'll make someone a lovely housewife, especially in those tight jeans and t-shirt. Yeah, but, y'see Don, CBS didn't know that for sure. I think he thought we all might be agents for the British government because we were with Elvis before he died, my dad already being a known agent, Nick and Julie hanging around Regency Stables and the house that weekend. Then me and Nick were at the house when they went there to kill Brian. They got there too late, Shadow had already got Brian away after Macca had broken in and then been killed by Shadow who, naturally enough, thought he was working for CBS; but he wasn't. It was just a thing between him and Mickey. The Ukranians shot at us as they arrived, coming cross country so as not to be seen by MI-5. MI-5 knew they were around, but didn't know where - that's why Colin warned us. We were just leaving when they fired, but we got lucky. CBS was paranoid because he knew the big day was approaching, so he looked into who we all were. I'll just be glad if the only Shadow Man I hear of in the future is Hank bloody Marvin.'

Nick cleared their plates away.

'Anyway, it's all done with,' said Julie.

'Indeed, now you can look forward to getting married in August,' said Don.

'Can you actually marry people at the Boro, Don, what with it not being consecrated or whatever the word is? Do you have a licence to roam? Have dog collar, will travel, stylie?' said Jeff, filling glasses from another bottle of wine.

'The registrar has to do the legal stuff, but I can do the vows and such. Give it the full God, like. I'm really looking forward to it. Here's to you both.' He raised his glass. Jeff did likewise.

'Yeah, what could possibly go wrong?' said Nick, grinning at Julie.

'Knowing us, almost anything,' she said and made a wide smile back at him. All the shadows were finally gone, for now, anyway. And let's face it, now is all any of us has ever got.

THE END

Books in the Nick Guymer Series
Published by HEAD PUBLISHING

1. Teesside Steal (2013)
2. Queen of the Tees (2013)
3. Teesside Missed (2013)
4. DJ Tees (2014)
5. Teesside Blues (2014)
6. Tyne Tees (2014)
7. High Tees (2015)
8. Teesside Meat (2015)
9. Teesside Shadows (2015)
10. King Tees (2016)
11. Teesside Dreams (2016)
12. Blood on the Tees (2016)

A Nick Guymer Comic Short Novel
Published by HEAD PUBLISHING

Knickers Always Go Down Well (2016)

Kindle/Paperback

http://www.johnnicholsonwriter.co.uk

About John Nicholson

John is a well-known football writer whose work is read by tens of thousands of people every week. He's a columnist for Football365.com and has worked for the Daily Record, The Mirror, Sky and many other publications over the last 14 years.

Books in the Archie Taylor Series
Published by HEAD PUBLISHING

1. The Girl Can't Help It (2014)
2. Sugar Mama (2016)

Kindle/Paperback

http://www.johnnicholsonwriter.co.uk

Other John Nicholson Books
published by Biteback Publishing

We Ate All The Pies -
How Football Swallowed Britain Whole (2010)

The Meat Fix -
How 26 Years of Healthy Eating Nearly Killed Me (2012)